THE GENIUS PLAGUE

Also by David Walton

Superposition

Supersymmetry

THE GENIUS PLAGUE

DAVID WALTON

an imprint of Prometheus Books
Amherst, NY

Published 2017 by Pyr®, an imprint of Prometheus Books

Cover illustration © Eric Nyquist
Cover design by Nicole Sommer-Lecht
Cover design © Prometheus Books

Inquiries should be addressed to
Pyr
59 John Glenn Drive
Amherst, New York 14228
VOICE: 716-691-0133
FAX: 716-691-0137
WWW.PYRSF.COM

21 20 19 18 17   5 4 3 2 1

Library of Congress Cataloging-in-Publication Data

Names: Walton, David, 1975- author.
Title: The genius plague / by David Walton.
Description: Amherst, NY : Pyr, an imprint of Prometheus Books, 2017.
Identifiers: LCCN 2017011549 (print) I LCCN 2017016357 (ebook) I
    ISBN 9781633883444 (ebook) I ISBN 9781633883437 (paperback)
Subjects: I BISAC: FICTION / Science Fiction / High Tech. I FICTION / Science
    Fiction / Adventure. I GSAFD: Science fiction.
Classification: LCC PS3623.A454 (ebook) I LCC PS3623.A454 G46 2017 (print) I
    DDC 813/.6—dc23
LC record available at https://lccn.loc.gov/2017011549

Printed in the United States of America

For Ruth
WIKYS HBFFV RDHFF BUUYE PLVKR HWPQC MVSHB

Life did not take over the globe by combat, but by networking.
—Lynn Margulis, symbiotic evolutionist

In the Amazon rainforest, more kinds of plants and animals thrive than in the rest of the world combined. A single square kilometer can host over a million different species, each relying on its relationship with the others to survive. But the Amazon covers an area nearly the size of the contiguous United States, and much of it is still unexplored.

A single creature dominates this ecosystem, a creature neither plant nor animal. It is new-grown, and yet it is old. Extending across thousands of acres of rainforest, it stretches through the soil, wrapping around the roots of trees. It has no central organ by which it can be killed. It branches and divides, its millions of microscopic tendrils transmitting information about moisture, nutrients, and genetic diversity through the network of its body. It exudes enzymes in response to this information, culling and shaping. Changing the rainforest to meet its needs.

It grows rapidly, yet it is not satisfied. Its fruiting bodies swell and burst, ejecting spores into the wind. The spores find the stalks of plants, are inhaled into the lungs of animals. There they implant and grow, sending filaments through soft flesh. They sift, taste, adapt, and ultimately, control. The animals continue on their way, unaware of the thing inside them, but their behaviors are subtly influenced in ways advantageous to the creature. It grows in reach and strength.

Eventually, toward the edge of the great forest, the creature encounters something new, a species more sophisticated than any it has yet encountered. A potential threat. But also an opportunity.

PROLOGUE

Paul Johns hadn't seen another human being in six days.

He emerged from the Amazon rainforest, tired and sore, but exhilarated, the sudden brightness bringing a smile to his face. The river sparkled, a vast body of water several kilometers across, even this far from its mouth.

Ahead stood a riverboat station, little more than a few rotting benches and a sign propped against an ancient wooden dock. The sign listed the boat pickup schedule in Portuguese, Spanish, and English, the words faded and water stained. A dozen or more tourists sat on the benches or milled around nearby, waiting for the boat. Seeing them felt like spotting a rare animal in the brush. Paul's first instinct was to approach quietly, lest he startle them away.

He had taken at least two wrong turnings before finally finding this path, adding several kilometers to what had already been a long hike. His pack felt like a boulder on his back, his muscles ached, and the skin along his shoulders felt rubbed raw.

The pack was heavier than when he'd first come to the Amazon. Then, he'd been weighed down with freeze-dried food packets, energy bars, a water purifier, his sleeping bag, and hundreds of sample containers. The weight eliminated by eating the food, however, was more than taken up with the fungi samples he'd collected, many of them species never before cataloged or studied. He had even dumped his waterproof blanket and some extra clothing to make room for as many samples as he could carry.

He approached the gaggle of tourists. These were a hardier breed than those you would find at Disney World or the Eiffel Tower, mostly young singles searching for adventure far from home. The shorter, more accessible tours started from Santarém, closer to the coast and civilization. The longer tours made it down as far as Manaus to see the Meeting of the

Waters, where the Rio Negro emptied into the Amazon in great swirling spirals of silt. But very few tourists ventured this far past Manaus, and those who did tended to be serious hikers and campers, looking to get beyond the veneer of wilderness and experience the reality.

Judging from their bedrolls, this group had probably been dropped off the day before and spent a night out here, pitting their bravery against the darkness. They might not have slept much, but they talked animatedly, with the charged energy of people who had stared danger in the face and come out the other side.

Paul joined them, knowing that he looked the part. He was young and fitted out with the latest gear, though his beard was perhaps a little longer and his pack larger than the others. He doubted any of them had twenty pounds of mushrooms on their backs. He eased the pack to the ground and stretched luxuriously. This was his third scientific foray into the Amazon, and it had been by far the most productive.

"Hey, where did you come from?" a voice said. He turned to see an attractive young woman studying his face with a half-smile on her own. She was blond and fit, with a restless energy that kept her bouncing on the balls of her feet, like a runner keeping limber before the start of a race. "Don't tell me you've been here all along and we haven't met."

He stuck out his hand. "I'm Paul."

She took it and grinned. "Maisie."

"How long have you been waiting for the boat?" he asked.

"An hour," she said. "Seriously, though, you just appeared out of nowhere. Where did you come from? Were you camping on your own?"

"I've been moving around. Collecting samples for my research," he said, giving his pack a kick.

"What are you, some kind of scientist?"

"A mycologist. I study fungi."

"Well, *that* must be exciting," she said, with a laugh that was both pleasant and meant she didn't think it sounded exciting at all.

"It can be," he said. "There are so many species out here. People are always finding new kinds with amazing properties. A few years ago, somebody came back with a mushroom that can grow on oil spills and chemical dumps, literally soak up the waste and turn it into a thriving ecology."

That got her interested, and Paul thought she was sincere, not just humoring him. Her questions were insightful, and he found himself talking freely. It would be good to have somebody to help pass the monotony of the ride home. Riverboat schedules on the Amazon were notoriously variable, and Paul knew the boat's planned arrival time was little more than a vague concept. They might wait an hour or two before it showed up, and then the trip back to Manaus would take a good six hours after that.

Maisie struck Paul as the bored type, a rich girl who had never had to work in her life, and who had turned to extreme fitness and activism as a way to give herself purpose. She would try anything and apparently had, from fried piranha to base jumping, and never turned down a dare.

What Paul liked best about her was that she seemed to understand these things about herself and accept them. She could tell you that her fearlessness gave her a sense of power over her life, and that the fund drives she ran for poor inner-city kids were at least partly driven by a sense of guilt about her privileged lifestyle. She thought the fact that her boyfriends never lasted very long was due to an expectation of betrayal from men that she had learned from her father.

"Ever consider a career in psychology?" Paul asked her.

She laughed, a musical outburst that threw her head back and showed off her slim throat. "I'd sooner be a mycologist," she said.

"Not everyone can be so lucky."

The rainforest towered on both sides of the river, giant trees choked with vines. Humidity rose thickly from the water, and thousands of insects darted and skated along the surface. They could hear the screech of distant monkeys and the sharp cries of birds. Sweat streaked Paul's face and clothing, but despite the heat and insects he was sorry to be leaving.

"So, seriously," Maisie said. "Fungus? That's your thing? You're going to spend your whole life studying mushrooms?"

"If I can keep getting my grants funded."

"What, you have a PhD already? How old are you?"

"Twenty-four," Paul lied. In truth, he was only twenty-one, but he didn't want to deal with the inevitable questions about how young he'd been when he graduated, or what he'd scored on his SATs. Once he did, that was all anybody wanted to talk about, and he'd learned that although women were impressed with such things, it wasn't the kind of impressed that led to any kind of relationship. More like being a circus monkey in a cage. "Besides," he said, "it's not all about mushrooms."

"No?"

"Mushrooms are only a small part of fungal anatomy. A mushroom is just how a fungus has sex."

Maisie's slim eyebrows arched high. "Oh, really," she said.

"It's true. A single fungus in a forest like this can go on for miles, underground, wrapping itself around tree roots. The mushrooms are just its reproductive parts. Fungi are some of the largest living things on Earth. Each tendril is nearly microscopic, but put together they can weigh far more than any California redwood or blue whale."

"So you're saying yours is bigger than all the other biologists'?"

Paul grinned. "Absolutely. See, a mushroom thrusts its way up out of the ground or out of the side of a tree," he said, demonstrating with his hands. "When it grows big enough, it sends millions of spores flying through the air or floating through water. When one of the spores finds an acceptable environment, it germinates, which lets it combine with another germinating spore to produce a new fungus."

"So fungi have sex from miles away."

"Sure, you could say that. Sometimes even across continents."

"That doesn't sound very intimate."

"Well, you do have to give mammals some credit. They've made some improvements over three hundred million years, especially where sex is concerned."

The riverboat finally appeared, a two-story affair with weathered blue paint and a flimsy white roof erected on the top deck to keep off the sun. The pilot cut the engine, and the boat drifted ponderously through the water until it bounced against the dock, the collision cushioned by tires strapped along its hull. The pilot jumped lightly down and tossed a rope around a piling. He was dark skinned and weather beaten, his face so lined by sun and wind that it was impossible for Paul to tell his age. The tourists pressed forward, and the dock creaked and sagged. Green water sluiced between the boards.

Paul hoisted his pack onto his shoulders and joined the line. He felt a pleasant pressure at his side and discovered Maisie's hand on his arm, ostensibly for balance on the shifting dock. He wondered if she was planning to stay the night in Manaus. The pilot urged them in broken, accented English to board carefully, and they shuffled onto the boat.

The larger tourist riverboats were designed for multiday cruises. They had rows of hammocks, a kitchen that provided meals, and a wet bar open around the clock. On the more traveled routes, you could hear their music pounding away before you even saw them, the top deck a continuous nightclub of carousing foreigners. Paul couldn't understand why anyone would come to the Amazon and then make such a racket that no animals would come within miles.

This boat was much more subdued, designed for day trips, and fitted with little more than deck chairs and railings. A cooler near the pilot's seat held water bottles and cans of Skol beer. A meal was supposed to be served halfway through the trip, but Paul couldn't see where it was hidden. He hoped there would be something, as he had run a bit low on food packets by his last day.

There was only one other woman in the group, and Maisie joined her, looking over pictures the other had taken with what looked like an expensive camera. Paul found a chair on the top deck and settled in, facing south, where he could see more of the river. He was looking forward to a hot shower and a good meal in Manaus, maybe even a massage.

Below, an argument broke out between the pilot and one of the men over the price the pilot was asking for the beer. The passenger thought it should be included in the cost of the trip, for which he had apparently paid much more than Paul had. In this part of the world, everything had a price, but everything was negotiable, too. It helped if you knew the language. Eventually, they settled on a lower figure, and the passenger irritably handed over his money.

With an exhausted sigh, Maisie threw herself into the chair next to Paul. "I am so looking forward to getting back to civilization," she said.

"Are you staying in Manaus?" he asked.

She nodded. "One more night."

"Where at?"

"The Tropical."

Paul whistled. "Nice. That one's not in my budget."

She flashed him a grin. "Maybe I could give you a tour."

A large splash rippled the water, but Paul couldn't tell what had made it. Some large creature briefly cresting the surface and then returning to the deep. Fish here could grow huge, some as big as a man. Even a pink river dolphin was possible, though those were endangered enough now to be a rare sight.

They chatted about her home in northern California, about the sights they had seen in the rainforest, about how Americans were perceived by the native Brazilians. She was fascinated by his stories of growing up in Brasília, his father a diplomat/spy for the US embassy. It had been a fairly ordinary childhood, as far as he was concerned, but he embellished the tales to make them sound more romantic. He loved to make her laugh. Looking out over the miles of empty water, they could almost have been the last people on Earth. Almost.

A few hours into their journey, the relative quiet of their own small boat motor was pierced by the rattling roar of a powerful engine. Paul rolled his eyes, expecting a large pleasure cruise, though they weren't a common sight this far upriver. Instead, it was a Brazilian Navy patrol craft, its high prow cutting through the water much faster than the sluggish riverboat, throwing a spray of water behind it on both sides.

Paul expected it to cruise on past, but instead it converged on them in a wide arc, slowing and coming alongside. After a few shouts back and forth between the pilot and a uniformed man on the deck of the patrol boat, they threw ropes and tied the two boats together.

"What's going on?" Maisie asked. They had to shield their eyes from the bright sun to see what was happening.

"I don't know. Drug inspection, maybe?"

The two crafts killed their engines, leaving an eerie, throbbing silence in their absence. The river lapped against the hulls, causing them to rock gently. A hawk high above them screamed. In the patrol boat, men in fatigue pants and olive drab shirts moved about, tying ropes and talking to each other.

"Something's wrong," Paul said softly. Suddenly it seemed like he should whisper.

"What do you mean?"

The soldiers in the patrol boat seemed oddly coordinated, their activity synchronized without any apparent communication. It looked more like choreography than ordinary movement. At a glance from an officer, they stopped as one and came to attention.

The officer stepped down from the patrol craft onto the riverboat. He wore aviator sunglasses, which he took off, folded, and slid into his shirt pocket. The pilot said something to him that Paul couldn't hear.

"We should hide," Paul said.

Maisie looked around, her face worried. There was nowhere to go. "What is this? Are you in trouble?"

"I think we're all in trouble."

The officer smiled at the riverboat passengers and nodded. He was clean-shaven, with a wide face and laugh lines at the corners of his mouth. From the upper deck, Paul could see that he had a small, sunburned bald spot. The man gave the pilot a broad shrug, as if sorry for the inconvenience. He seemed like a reasonable man, a man you'd like to get to know. Until he drew a pistol and shot the pilot in the face.

It was so sudden, so unexpected, that for a beat nobody moved. A bloody spray erupted from the back of the pilot's head, and he collapsed to the deck. The shot echoed across the water, startling a flock of birds out of the trees. Then chaos broke out.

The passengers screamed and scrambled away. On the patrol craft, three men lifted automatic weapons in tandem and began to fire into the riverboat. Paul didn't think; he just reacted. Maisie was still staring at the patrol craft, frozen in shock. He took her by the shoulders and pushed her over the railing. "Swim for shore," he shouted after her.

On the deck below, the other tourists were dying. There was nowhere for them to run. A few of them managed to jump into the water as well, but Paul couldn't tell if they had been hit or not. It didn't matter. There was nothing he could do for them. He dove into the water after Maisie. With the riverboat between them and their attackers, they struck out for shore as fast as they could swim.

It turned out she was the better swimmer. The northern shore didn't look that far away, but he swam to the point of exhaustion, and it didn't seem to be getting any closer. They had kicked their shoes off, but their clothes were heavy and soaked through. Maisie stayed with him and helped him, encouraging him to float on his back when he needed to rest. He was young and in good shape, but he never would have made it if not for her.

When they finally reached the shore, he heaved himself up on the swampy bank, shuddering and coughing, his arms and legs shaking with exhaustion. Still, she urged him forward. "Come on, into the forest," she said. "We want to be out of sight, in case they come looking." He dragged himself to his feet and leaned on her as they stumbled in among the trees.

The light dimmed as they pushed their way through the vine-choked undergrowth. Once they were inside, the foliage thinned out, no longer fueled by the sunlight into riotous growth. The air was moist and the sounds from the outside deadened. They sat on a fallen branch and just breathed for a time, recovering their strength.

"What are you, some kind of Olympic swimmer?" Paul finally said.

"I do triathlons," she said woodenly. They were both shivering from the damp, despite the warm air. Paul felt like his clothes were constricting and trying to smother him. He pulled his phone from his pocket, but it was wet through, and when he pushed the button, nothing happened. "Mine, too," Maisie said. She produced her phone and shook it, and he could hear the water sloshing around inside the case.

They were silent again, until Maisie said, "What happened out there?"

"I don't know. They weren't Brazilian Navy, I can tell you that."

"How did you know what was going to happen?"

"I didn't. But the men in the boat weren't speaking Portuguese. It wasn't any language I recognized."

"There are indigenous languages spoken around here," Maisie said. "Couldn't it have been one of those?"

Paul shook his head. "Not in the military. Doesn't make any sense."

"Do you think the others . . ." she started, but she couldn't finish the question.

"I don't know," he said. "There were some who made it into the water, so they might have escaped." He tried to sound positive, but privately he thought Maisie's friends were probably all dead. "How well did you know them?"

She shrugged. "Hardly at all. We put a group together over the internet, to get a package rate on the trip. I met them all a week ago, when we arrived in Manaus."

He touched her arm briefly. "I'm sorry."

All the electricity of their flirtation on the boat was gone now, and he felt the gulf between them of strangers stranded together. He didn't know this woman, didn't know her background, how she handled things emotionally, or how she would react to this situation.

Paul stared at his hands, not at all sure how he was handling things himself. His muscles still twitched from the adrenaline of the unexpected attack and the grueling swim. People who just a little while ago had been laughing over photographs and arguing about the price of beer were now dead. His mind raced and spun, unable to think about anything clearly.

Finally, Maisie broke the silence. "What are we going to do?"

The question focused him. "We're going to survive," he said. "We're going to make it back to Manaus, tell the police what happened, and go home."

She raised her hands, indicating the jungle around them. "We must be fifty miles from Manaus. That's a long way in the rainforest. We have no food, no packs." Her voice had an edge of panic.

"Relax," he said, trying to sound more confident than he really was. "There are plenty of things in the rainforest to eat, if you know what you're looking for. And we have the river to navigate by, so we can't possibly get lost. We'll be fine."

He was wrong about getting lost. The land near the riverbank was a swampy marshland, almost impossible to walk through, forcing them deeper into the interior where they could no longer see it. The higher the ground, the easier it was to negotiate, but the tendency to steer toward drier ground led them farther from the river. The thick canopy blocked the sun, and there were no paths. Paul had left his compass behind with the rest of his pack. They were forced to navigate by dead reckoning, which he knew full well was a good way to get thoroughly lost.

If they could just keep heading east, they would hug the river and eventually get close enough to Manaus to find a road or other people. The problem was, it would be all too easy to veer north instead, where there was nothing but rainforest for hundreds of miles.

"Maybe we should just go back to the river and wait for a boat," he said.

"No." She was adamant. "No more boats. If those men were thieves, that means they're lying in wait for any tourist boat that comes through these waters. I don't want to give them a second chance at me."

Paul didn't argue. He didn't think the patrol boat would still be out there, but he also thought it unlikely there would be boats of any other kind, or that they could get a boat's attention from the shore if there were. It was better to press on, and do what they could.

As they walked, he kept an eye on the ground, occasionally stopping to examine a mushroom or a fungal shelf growing out of the side of a tree. "What are you looking for?" Maisie asked.

"Our supper."

She made a face. "I've never been much of a mushroom fan."

"They'll taste pretty good if you're hungry enough."

"Are they hard to find?"

"Not very. There's fungus all over this forest. All through the soil, growing up around or even inside the trees. It's like a huge network, keeping the forest alive, culling some plants and allowing others to survive."

"You make it sound like the fungi are in charge."

"Well, they sort of are. Organisms aren't self-sufficient out here; they need the whole ecosystem. Fungi are like the bloodstream. They transfer the moisture and nutrients to where they're most needed." He settled gratefully into the familiar topic. Talking about mycology made it easier to avoid thinking about the blood exploding from the back of the riverboat pilot's head.

"How can a fungus know what trees most need nutrients?" Maisie asked, sounding skeptical.

"You'd be surprised. A fungus has all sorts of senses. It can determine the health of a tree, even detect animals moving around in the forest. Every time you step down"—Paul took an exaggerated step to demonstrate—"you're stepping on a network of more than eight miles of microscopic mycelia, all intertwined beneath your foot. It can detect the pressure and the weight. When you lift your foot"—again, he demonstrated by lifting his own—"the mycelia immediately move out into the indentation, soaking up the moisture and detritus you left behind. You can't see them, but they're there."

She shuddered. "Sounds creepy."

Eventually, Paul found a nice patch of *Favolus tenuiculus* growing out of a stump. The white polypore mushrooms were lovely specimens of the type, their caps pocked with dozens of holes like a Swiss cheese. Maisie took one warily. "You're sure they're safe?"

"Quite sure," he said, taking a bite. "This is what I do for a living. This variety is pretty common in the area. You could probably find it on restaurant menus back in Manaus."

She smiled wanly. "I had been hoping you might take me out to dinner tonight."

"There," he said. "Wish granted." They smiled at each other, but there was no joy in it.

The mushrooms tasted fine, but they stuck in Paul's throat, and neither of them ate very much. Their main problem was not food, but water. River water, especially the swampy kind around them, was brackish and swarming with protozoa, bacteria, and viruses—not to mention millions of fungal spores—that could give them a wide array of illnesses. Paul had brought an ultraviolet light water purifier as well as chlorine dioxide tablets, but both were, of course, lost with his pack. They had no way to make a fire. Paul found some waxy leaves with rainwater pooled in them, which they dribbled into their mouths. It wasn't much, but he hoped that they would make it back to civilization before it became a problem.

Night came quickly. It was murky under the trees even in the afternoon, but as the sun lowered, the shadows deepened, until they could barely see where they were going. "Let's stop," Paul said. "It's dry here; it's as good a place as any."

The darkness, when it came, was complete. They had both been sleeping outside in the rainforest already, but this was different. Instead of mastering their environment, it felt like they were at its mercy. They leaned their backs together against a large tree, unwilling to put their heads down among the crawling things on the bare ground.

Paul sat awake, uncomfortable in his damp clothing. He had considered taking them off and hanging them to dry, but he knew from experience how bad the insects could be at night, and he wanted as much of his skin covered as possible, especially since they had no mosquito netting or bug spray. Beside him, Maisie shifted in the dark, as sleepless and uncomfortable as he.

"What's that?" she asked.

He listened, thinking she had heard something, but a moment later realized that she was seeing something instead. As his eyes grew accustomed to the darkness, he saw a faint green glow resolve out of the gloom. He knew what it was. Foxfire.

"What's foxfire?" she asked when he told her.

"Bioluminescent fungi. A lot of species excrete an oxidative enzyme that glows at night, attracting insects to help spread their spores. Kind of like bright flowers attracting pollinators. Watch this." Paul clambered to his feet and felt his way carefully toward the glow. It was still extremely dark. He couldn't actually see his feet, and he stumbled a few times before he found it. A dead log, about the size of his leg, emitting a faint green light along the cracked seams of its bark.

He picked it up. "Fungi are the great decomposers of the forest," he said. "Any kind of dead organic material will be riddled through with mycelial strands within a few hours after death. Soil couldn't exist without fungi breaking things down. They were the first organisms to colonize the land, a good hundred million years before plants." He heaved the log into the woods. It struck a tree and exploded apart, sending a shower of green sparks through the air that illuminated them with an eerie green glow. Paul made his way back to her, able to see slightly now in the dim light.

"I can't sleep," she said. "I'm wet, and I'm scared, and I'm so angry I would kill those men right now, every one of them, without a second thought, if I had the chance. What were they doing? We never did anything to them. They just murdered a dozen people, for no reason at all. Why? Who would do something like that?"

Paul sat down next to her again. "There's been a lot of nationalist sentiment in Pará and some of the other northern states," he said. "People saying that Americans are ruining their country, wanting them to stay out, that sort of thing."

"That's stupid," Maisie said. "Their whole economy is based on tourism."

"Maybe a few of them took the sentiment too far."

"No. That doesn't make sense. These people were *organized*. If they weren't Navy, then they stole a Navy boat and military uniforms. They had automatic weapons. This wasn't a few guys with too much to drink taking their emotions out on a few Americans. They were too well outfitted for that."

"You're right. I don't know who would want to do such a thing."

"I just want to be home," she said. "I want to be back in California, where things make sense."

Paul couldn't help it. He laughed, though he immediately regretted it. "I'm sorry," he said. "I just never thought of California as making sense."

She didn't take offense. "More sense than they do here, anyway."

The green glow hadn't diminished. If anything, it had grown brighter, though maybe that was his eyes still adjusting. He could make out the expression on her face now, and see the basic lines of her body next to him. He stood, wanting to see what was left of the rotten log, but instead he saw something strange. Luminescent spots, more of them, stretching out into the distance. He squinted, trying to make sense of them in the darkness. It was hard to get a good idea of how far away they were, but they seemed to be forming two glowing lines. Straight, parallel lines. He shook his head, afraid he was hallucinating, but when he looked again, they were still there.

"Check this out," he said.

Maisie joined him on her feet. The green splotches glowed brightly, and the lines were unmistakable. "It's a path," she said.

It certainly looked like one. But what kind of path would be illuminated by fungi? Paul stepped forward, then bent down and examined the first of the spots, which was on the side of a tree. The tree itself was covered in fungal patches, and a few conks grew from one side, but only this single patch was glowing. He walked to the next patch, this one on the ground, and found the same thing—an area full of fungi, but only this one small patch glowing. What was going on?

"We should follow it," Maisie said.

"What?"

"It's got to be man-made, right? Nothing organic goes in straight lines like that. If it's a human path, then it has to lead somewhere."

Paul couldn't argue with her reasoning, but neither did he know of any way a human could make a path out of selectively triggered bioluminescent fungi. "It is leading in the direction we want to go," he said, shrugging.

"And it's not like we're getting any sleep. I don't want to sit here all night feeling sorry for myself and getting sick. I want to get home."

"I guess we don't have anything to lose," Paul said. He wanted to get up and move just as much as she did. And besides, as a mycologist, he found it hard to leave a mystery like this unexamined.

They walked side by side, the foxfire providing just enough light to see the path ahead of them, but not enough to see much beyond it. The going was relatively easy, and the double lines curved to avoid swampy areas and other pitfalls. They made better time than they had walking during the day.

From time to time, Paul stopped to examine the glowing spots, but he learned nothing new. The fungus all appeared to be the same species, one that he didn't recognize. He wanted to take a sample, but he knew it would be useless to do so. All of his sample bags were still in his abandoned pack, and putting samples in his damp pocket would just mean a pocketful of decaying slime by the time he could retrieve them.

The path continued on for miles, leading them unerringly across easy terrain and around obstacles. They followed it, its twin glowing lines stretching deeper into the dark forest, until the light vanished. Without warning, the luminescence shut off as suddenly as if someone had thrown a switch, plunging them into complete darkness.

He felt Maisie's hand groping for his, and he grasped it, holding on tightly.

"Paul?" she said, her voice tight with fear. "What's going on?"

CHAPTER 1

The day I heard what happened to Paul, I spent the afternoon at my father's house, listening to the rain patter on the roof of the enclosed porch, and wondering if my dad even knew who I was anymore. Outside, the leaves of the maple tree rustled in the wind, but inside, the house was still, the steady sound of the rain only increasing the sense of quiet. I shuffled the letter tiles in front of me, waiting for him to make his next move. Chill air seeped from the windows, and I thought the rain might turn to snow overnight.

"Whose turn is it?" my father asked.

"Yours, Dad."

He reached out and, one at a time, placed the tiles T-A-P on the board. Four points. I dutifully recorded the score, and placed my own word, *praxis*, taking the double word score and using the S to pluralize another word. Forty points.

My dad chuckled and shook his finger at me. A sudden gust of wind rattled the windows and sent ripples running across Marley Creek. My parents' property didn't actually touch the water, but they shared a tiny wedge of waterfront with two other homeowners. My dad's boat was moored there, though he never used it anymore. The porch smelled faintly of fish.

Time creaked by. "Whose turn is it?"

"Yours, Dad."

He studied his letters again. "When is Neil coming back from Brazil?" he asked.

"I'm Neil," I said. "It's Paul who's in Brazil, and he's supposed to be home the day after tomorrow. I'll pick him up at the airport after my interview at the NSA."

My dad's mouth split into a big smile. "The NSA, eh? Say hi to

Richards. And tell Masterson that ten-dimensional Kalman filter of his is never going to work."

"I will," I said, though I had no idea who those people were. My father had worked for the NSA for three decades before Alzheimer's cut short his career, and people and memories from those days sometimes popped up in his conversation without context. He had been only fifty-six when he was diagnosed, quite young for the disease, but that didn't save him.

The symptoms had come on slowly. At first it seemed like nothing much. He would forget his keys or his jacket, or mix up names. Apparently the change was noticeable enough in his work, however, that the NSA had encouraged him to see a doctor. The diagnosis was like hearing the word *guilty* at a murder trial. There was no way to take it back. And there was no cure.

He lost his skill with higher math first, followed by an inability to make new memories reliably. He forgot words, forgot experiences we'd shared. Each week, it seemed, something new was lost, made all the more painful by the fact that he knew it was happening. In his final months at the NSA, he had endured psychological evaluations, revoked security clearances, and going-away parties, and then he was out the door.

After several disastrous college experiences, I had moved in with my dad, both as a place to stay and to take some of the burden of caring for him off my mom. But there was something terrifying about Alzheimer's that seeing it all the time hadn't taken away. I didn't even drink anymore, because the thought of giving up control of my mind, even slightly, made my chest tighten. Little by little, it robbed him of his identity, turning a brilliant, decisive, passionate man into a hesitant and confused shadow of his former self, like a horror movie played out in slow motion.

My dad studied his letter tiles, his huge gray eyebrows furrowed, and I remembered how intimidating those brows had been when he hoisted them at me as a boy. *Think*, his eyebrows would say. *Dig deeper. There's more to discover.* And he was always right. Now, there seemed to be only struggle behind those lowered brows, as if combining seven letters to form a word was the hardest thing he had ever attempted.

Once, my dad had dominated all comers in this game. He used to say that a cryptologist who couldn't anagram was no cryptologist at all. He regularly produced words like *tersion* and *matzoon*, sending us scrambling for the dictionary, only to find that he was—of course—correct.

Ever since we were small, the letter magnets on our refrigerator were a continuous family challenge. What messages could we leave for each other when we were limited to only one of each letter in the alphabet? My father was king of the game, and triumphs like "PUT BACK MY ENGLISH WORD" had been passed down in family lore. He loved word games and puzzles of every type. The family joke was that he had fallen in love with my mother—whose first name was Hannah—simply because her name was a palindrome.

My dad chose three tiles from his tray and made the word *stix*, using the letter X that I had placed previously. He peered at it, uncertain, but eventually leaned back and left it there. I made no comment and recorded eleven points on the score sheet.

I had grown up knowing that my father was a cryptologist but not much more—the details were classified, and we were always left in the dark. In truth, I doubt he did much actual code breaking himself, but there was no way to know. There were no take-your-family-to-work days at the NSA.

Most of his thirty-four years had been spent at NSA headquarters at Fort Meade, but we had also spent a decade living in Brazil when I was a child. He had been a spy—not the James Bond kind with exploding pens and sexy *femmes fatales*, but the real kind, officially assigned to the diplomatic corps and unofficially an NSA liaison to *Agência Brasileira de Inteligência*, the Brazilian intelligence service.

For most of my growing up years, I had wanted to be just like him. I wanted to work for the NSA, perform mathematical and linguistic magic to break enemy codes, and make the world safe for democracy. It was a dream I had never really left behind.

And now I would get my chance. I had an interview—a real, live interview—with the NSA on Monday morning at nine o'clock. The time couldn't go fast enough. I knew I would get the job. I had to get it. It was like destiny. My only regret was that my dad would never really know.

"Neil!" My mom strode into the room, agitated. She was a small woman, but energetic, always juggling three activities and excelling at all of them. She wasn't actually married to my father anymore—hadn't been for fifteen years—but she had moved back in when he was diagnosed and took care of him even more than I did.

I stood. "What is it?"

She swept the remote off the coffee table and pointed it at the TV, which burst into sound, breaking the tranquility of the quiet room. It was a news channel, and the banner across the bottom of the screen read, "Fourteen Dead and Two Missing in Amazon Massacre."

My stomach clenched into a painful knot. "What happened? Is it Paul?" Mom just shook her head, eyes glued to the screen.

The newscaster described a scene of horror: twelve Americans, two Canadians, and one Brazilian pilot had been gunned down on a river-boat somewhere on the Amazon river. The names of the victims were not being released until the families could be contacted. Two other passengers were missing, possibly kidnapped, or else their bodies were floating down the river and had not yet been found.

We watched, numbed. I didn't know how much my father understood, but he sensed our agitation. *Until the families could be contacted*. I stared at my parents' house phone, willing it not to ring. Surely there were many American travelers in the Amazon basin. There was no reason to think that Paul had been on that particular boat. Then my cell phone rang, startling me so much that I nearly tripped on my chair. I spotted it vibrating on the coffee table and lunged for it, answering on the second ring.

"Hello?"

"Hey, little brother," Paul said. "Is Mom there? She must be worried sick."

"You're . . . alive," I said, my tongue like rubber.

The voice on the other end was serious. "It was a near thing."

"It's Paul," I said to my mom. "He's okay. He's alive." She let out all her breath in a rush. "What happened?" I said into the phone. "Were you on that boat?"

He gave me a brief overview, until my mom snatched the phone and took up the conversation where I'd left off. He had been inches from death, by the sound of it. When I finally got my phone back, I said, "How did you get back to Manaus? I missed that part."

He hesitated. "I don't remember."

"Were you hurt?"

"No . . . I don't think so. I just can't remember. We walked for a long time . . . and that's it. We must have found our way to a road." He coughed violently.

"Have you been to a doctor? You don't sound like yourself."

"I'm fine. Just some infection I'm fighting off."

Paul confirmed that he would be home on American Airlines on Monday evening and would meet me there. The police had interviewed him for hours, but he was a victim, not a suspect, and they couldn't keep him in the country.

He spoke to my father briefly, who seemed more like himself for a time, recognizing Paul's voice and teasing him about a girl he'd apparently met on his trip. When he handed the phone back, however, his smile disappeared, replaced with the increasingly familiar expression of fear and panic as some part of him realized that there were critical things he couldn't remember. It tended to happen whenever his mind made a brief connection to the person he used to be, enough that he could recognize that something was missing. He sat down again and studied his tiles.

"Now I don't know what to do," my mother said. "We were supposed to visit Julia this weekend." Julia was my sister, older than Paul by a year, and she had just given birth to my parents' first grandchild, a girl named

Ash. My parents had driven up to see her the day she was born, but my mom had been anxious to return.

"You should go," I said. "I'll be here to pick up Paul. Julia needs you more than he does."

She sighed. "I'm already packed. We just need to get in the car and go."

"Enjoy," I said. "Give them both a kiss for me. Honestly, it'll probably be easier on Paul not to have a crowd worrying about his well-being."

"All right. But you call if he needs me, okay?"

"I will."

I sat across from my dad again. After a few minutes, I placed the word *perjury* on the board and quietly recorded my points. Dad would get upset if I didn't keep score, so I always did. He would also get upset if he thought I wasn't playing my best.

While Dad and I finished our game, Mom collected the last few things she needed and brought them out to the car. I used the last tile, and then subtracted Dad's remaining letters from his total. "What's the damage?" he said.

I folded the score sheet so he couldn't see it. "It's time for you to go," I said. "Can you believe you're finally a grandfather?"

"What's the score?" he said. "Don't tell me you won."

"It was a good game. Let's go find your coat."

His face changed to confusion, anger. "Don't patronize me, Neil. What's the score?"

I sighed. "Four hundred and twenty-two," I said, pointing to myself, "to seventy-eight."

"What are you talking about, seventy-eight?" His eyes radiated anger. "Are you messing around with me? Tell me my score."

Mom reappeared. "What's wrong?"

"Your son won't tell me my score," Dad said. "Seventy-eight points, what kind of a score is that?"

"He meant four hundred and seventy-eight," Mom said. "It was a close game, but you always come out ahead."

I winced. I didn't like to lie to him. It felt like disrespect to treat him like he was a two-year-old throwing a tantrum about losing in Candyland. Mom could often handle him better than I could, though, and sometimes a lie would turn aside a problem before it made him really upset. I couldn't really fault her.

My dad wore a magnanimous smile. "Well played, Neil," he said. "Sometimes the right letters just aren't there for you."

I nodded and smiled half-heartedly. "Have a good trip to New York," I said.

Dad stood and shook my hand. "Good luck on your interview."

I was surprised he'd remembered. "Thanks," I said. "It'll be a snap."

"Good for you," he said. "I always wanted to work for the NSA."

CHAPTER 2

When I drove my battered Nissan through the NSA gate the next morning, I felt hopeful but nervous. I knew I had a lot to overcome. My school record wasn't exactly stellar, and although I hadn't been convicted of any felonies, or anything else that would directly interfere with a security clearance, there were some things in my history that were hard to explain.

The screening and interview process took place at the Friendship Annex, a surprisingly jolly name for a complex that housed thousands of employees ranging from cyber espionage experts to signals intelligence analysts in the world's largest intelligence agency. The Friendship Annex, or FANX, was a twenty minute drive away from NSA headquarters at Fort Meade. It had been named after the nearby Friendship International Airport, which had since been given a more dignified title. I thought they should have renamed the NSA complex, too. The Crypto Annex, perhaps, or the Annex of Cyber Warfare.

Two armed MPs scrutinized my driver's license and application letter. They took so long checking their list that I started to get nervous, but eventually they waved me on. At the next checkpoint, I was asked to step out of my car while a K-9 agent and his German shepherd checked it for explosives. Nobody smiled. It was a serious place, for a serious purpose. It was a place I wanted to belong.

My upbringing gave me an appreciation for the importance of good operational security. Even 256-bit encryption didn't keep your message safe if the enemy had access to your private key. A password wasn't secure if you told it to someone who said they worked for the data center. In a world more and more governed by computers, people were often the weakest link.

I pulled up to FANX III at 7:00 a.m., two hours early. They let me in, which was fortunate, because it was one of the coldest days of the year, and my Nissan's heater didn't work anymore. The security guard watched as I untangled two scarves, gloves, a hat, and a coat, and put them on the conveyor belt to be X-rayed. My wallet and keys followed them, and I stepped through the metal detector without a hitch. Finally, they gave me a bright red-and-white striped badge with "Visitor—One Day Only" stamped on the front in two-inch high letters.

I sat in a molded plastic chair next to a vending machine. I was hungry, having skipped breakfast to make sure I had time to find where I was supposed to go, but the vending machine ate my dollar bill without relinquishing my chosen candy bar. The metal spiral turned, but the bar clung tenaciously to its position, refusing to fall. The next customer would probably get two for his money, but I was out of cash. I thought about shaking the machine, but I thought that might not give the right impression to my potential employers.

I slouched in the chair, watching a flat-screen television mounted on the wall that was set on endless loop. It showed a two-minute video extolling the virtues of the NSA. It was called *Information Is Power*, and it featured clips of high-tension battle scenes and a deep male voiceover saying things like "Intelligence saves lives on the battlefield," and "We protect our nation's borders through global cryptologic dominance." The first time, I thought it was awesome. By the fifth time, I had it memorized. By the tenth, I had fallen asleep.

I woke up at 9:05 with a stale taste in my mouth and sense of panic, which only intensified when I realized my name was being called. The lobby, which had been empty, was now full of candidates. I thanked the receptionist who was calling my name and rushed down the hallway she indicated. My interview letter said I would be interviewed in room thirty-two by a Ms. Shaunessy Brennan. I pictured a red-haired Irish woman, her fiery locks tied back and a merry twinkle in her eye. When I peeked into the room, however, a young black woman sat there with her arms crossed, wearing a scowl. "Um, hello?" I said.

"Neil Johns?"

I halted. "Yes."

"You're late."

"Oh. My paper said a Ms. Brennan."

"That's me."

"Right. Sorry, I just thought . . ."

"You didn't think there were any black women in Ireland?" Her voice was steel, and I now realized there was a bit of an Irish flavor to her vowels.

"Apologies," I said.

She stood to shake my hand. She was young and fit, dressed in black slacks and a loose green blouse, with long hair twisted into tight braids and pulled back in a silver clasp. Her handshake was businesslike and cold.

I sat down and tried a smile. "Shaunessy, that's a lovely name."

Her look impaled me to the chair.

After that, it only got worse. She asked me nothing about the WWII-era ciphers I'd invented in my spare time, nor did she quiz me on famous cryptologists of history, which I would have knocked out of the park. There's a certain kind of person I can impress with charm and a winning smile, but Shaunessy Brennan was not one of them. Her baleful gaze didn't falter, no matter how many witticisms I attempted, and soon I stopped trying. I sensed that my dream of following in my father's foot-steps was about to die.

Her accent was beautiful, light and musical, and soon I found myself listening to the sound of her voice instead of what she was saying.

"Mr. Johns?"

"Yes, I'm sorry. I was thinking."

"You do realize," she said, "that you applied to the Computer Science division of Signals Intelligence? We do large-scale computing. Practically everyone in this division has advanced degrees in Computer Science. You don't seem to have any formal computing education at all."

"I'm pretty good at math."

"With three failed attempts at a degree to show for it."

I shrugged. "Signals Intelligence seemed like my best shot. I don't know anything about network security, and I haven't really studied any foreign languages."

She frowned. "Your resume says you know Portuguese."

"Well, yeah. I kind of grew up in Brazil, so Portuguese is easy. I know a little Spanish, too. And I can get by in Tupi-Guarani."

"But you don't know any foreign languages," she said, deadpan.

"I wasn't counting those because I learned them as a kid. I haven't learned any recently, as an adult." She raised an eyebrow. "Which, granted, hasn't been very long," I pushed on, rambling now. "I mean, I don't know any of the really important languages, like Arabic or Russian or Chinese. I'm guessing you don't get much signals traffic in Tupi-Guarani."

Her face was impassive. "Let's talk about your school record."

I would have rather not, but it didn't seem helpful to say so.

"It says here that over the course of three years, you managed to be expelled from MIT, Princeton, and Carnegie Mellon." She looked at me over the top of my resume. "An impressive feat, I suppose, but not in a good way."

"I was young then," I said. "It was a long time ago."

She squinted at me. "How old are you now?"

"Twenty-one."

She riffled through the papers in front of her. "You started at MIT when you were sixteen," she said. "You were expelled a year later. Admitted to Princeton at seventeen, and expelled a year after that. Carnegie Mellon at eighteen, and that time you lasted only two months."

Her eyebrows asked the question.

"That last one wasn't my fault," I said. "I thought the university president was embezzling funds. I did a probability analysis, based on the donation profile of similar schools, the number of attending students and the published scholarship numbers, and the report of available capital I happened to see on his secretary's desk. But nobody was going to believe me without evidence. I had to break into his office to prove it."

"I take it you were mistaken."

I shrugged. "Sort of. The embezzler was actually the provost."

She regarded me with an unreadable expression. "Do you have a problem with authority?"

I felt the blood rushing to my face. I was getting tired of her raised eyebrows and barely veiled disdain. How much did a degree and a neat resume really prepare someone for a job? The Alan Turings and Claude Shannons of the world had been eccentric, inventive, forceful people. Rule breakers. The people at Bletchley Park and Room 40 didn't stop to check boxes; they got the job done no matter what the cost. This NSA seemed more interested in writing procedures and creating flashy videos than in saving the world. "I might not be a cookie-cutter candidate," I said. "But I'm more than qualified. I *belong* in the NSA."

She drummed her fingernails on the desk for a moment, thinking. Then she pushed her papers into a stack and rapped them on the tabletop to square the edge. It was a dismissal. "I'm sorry," she said. "You're obviously a pretty smart guy. But we don't hire candidates without at least a bachelor's degree."

"I know that's your policy. I was hoping that you'd make an exception."

She sighed. I guessed that interviewing candidates wasn't her usual job, and she was anxious to get back to whatever it was. "And why is that?" she said.

I squared my shoulders. "Because I care. Because I know that every war, every battle, every skirmish over trade rights and clear waterways is won and lost by intelligence. When I attack a problem, I don't quit until I solve it. Nobody in this building will work as hard at this as I will."

"It takes more than just ambition. You need to finish your education."

"I'm a quick study. Anything I don't know, I'll learn on the job."

"You're too young."

"If you don't mind me asking," I said, "how old are *you*?" It was a cheeky question, and I thought it might get me thrown out of the room, but it actually evoked the first hint of a smile. "I'm twenty-four," she said. "Unlike you, however, I actually graduated, with a degree in Computer Science from the University of Maryland. I've been working here for three years."

"And they have you interviewing unlikely candidates?"

Her expression soured. "It's a temporary thing. It's something my manager usually does, but she was unavailable." She handed a sheet of paper across the table. It was maybe thirty rows of unreadable letters and numbers in five-character groups. Under each row was a blank line. I assumed it was an encrypted text, and the blank lines were to write the plaintext message.

"Now you're talking," I said.

She pressed her mouth into a line. "Look. This is the practical portion of the interview. You can try it if you want." Her tone of voice communicated that I shouldn't bother.

"But you've already made your decision, is that it?"

"I don't make hiring decisions. I'm a software engineer, not a manager. I just report on my impressions of your technical qualifications. I'm pretty sure the only reason you got an interview at all is because my manager saw something interesting about your resume—don't ask me what. If she wants to offer you a position, or call you back for another interview, she will."

"Okay."

She indicated a computer on the table to my right. "There's a file in the home directory with the same encrypted message. When you've got it solved, copy it down onto the sheet of paper." Her slim shoulders gave a slight shrug. "They still like their hardcopy around here."

She stood, gathering her folder and handbag. "I'll leave you to it. Good luck, Mr. Johns."

"Do most people solve it?"

She met my gaze. "Most competent ones, yes."

She left me alone in the room. I pressed the power button on the computer. Nothing happened. It was just as well. I felt more comfortable with a pen and paper in hand than typing numbers into a spreadsheet anyway.

I crossed to a printer on the far side of the room and ripped a sheaf of paper out of the tray. Then I started to work.

The first thing I did was to make a few deductions. First of all, they expected new college graduates to solve this thing. That meant it wasn't encrypted with modern methods. Public key encryption could be cracked, but it required banks of high-powered computers working in tandem for hours or days or, depending on the length of the key, weeks. So this would rely on somewhat simpler methods.

I figured the most likely was a Vigenère cipher or something in the same family. It was the dominant style of cipher used during the World Wars, and although it would take some serious effort to crack, I was confident I could do it. In a Vigenère cipher, the message was encrypted by adding a repeating key phrase to it. So if the message was:

MYFUTUREINTHENSAISDOOMED

and the key was Shaunessy Brennan, then the message would be encrypted by treating each letter as a number and adding them together. 'M' would be added to 'S', 'Y' would be added to 'H', etc. If any sum went higher than Z, it would just wrap around again to A.

```
  M Y F U T U R E I N T H E N S A I S D O O M E D
+ S H A U N E S S Y B R E N N A N S H A U N E S S
  E F F O G Y J W G O K L R A S N A Z D I B Q W V
```

If you knew the key phrase, then deciphering the message was as simple as subtracting it out of the cipher text. If you didn't know the key phrase, then figuring it out could be remarkably difficult. Fortunately, avenues of attack had been worked out for such ciphers over the years, and I knew them. Unfortunately, it eventually became clear to me that the problem in the exercise was not a Vigenère cipher.

By "eventually," I mean that two hours had gone by, and Ms. Brennan had peeked in on me three times, in between her other interviews, to see if I was done yet. I don't think it was concern for my well-being that had her checking in as much as a desire for me to vacate the interview room. There was a lobby full of other candidates. She must have given up on me after that, because she didn't check again.

I was getting pretty worried. I had expected the practical part of the interview to be where I would impress them. I had a working knowledge of cryptological history, and as I told Ms. Brennan, I was pretty good at math. But I was starting to think I had underestimated the competition. The NSA was, after all, the biggest employer of mathematicians in the world, in a country that had dominated world politics for decades. These were the best of the best. Ms. Brennan had obviously expected me to solve it quickly, and the increasingly patronizing expression on her face when she peeked in let me know that I had already failed the test.

But I don't give up. Maybe it was a genetic deficiency, or maybe my big brother had knocked me in the head once too often growing up, but I had a complete inability to let a problem go once I'd sunk my teeth in it, no matter what the consequences. So even though I'd been there for hours, my stomach was growling, and I had to pee, I kept on working.

I tried frequency analysis and the Kasiski examination and the Friedman test. I tried digraph mapping and the shotgun hill climbing method. Finally, out of options, I tried the time-honored approach of every stymied exam taker in the history of exams. I guessed.

An unknown cipher could be cracked much more easily if you knew some portion of the plaintext. It dramatically reduced the number of possibilities to be analyzed, and if you could determine which portion of the cipher text matched the portion you knew, then in most cases, you could crack the rest of the message as well. I didn't know a portion of the plaintext, but I still had the deep tones of the male voice actor from the NSA video running through my head.

I decided to take a gamble. It wasn't much of a risk, really, since I didn't have any other ideas, and time was ticking away. They might let me spend all afternoon here, but I didn't think Ms. Brennan and the NSA were going to let me spend the night working on it. It was now or never.

I wrote "GLOBAL CRYPTOLOGIC DOMINANCE" on a new sheet of paper and got to work. Twenty minutes later, I had it cracked. It was a Playfair cipher, named for the British lord who promoted its use by the British in World War I. The plaintext message wasn't an exact transcript of the video, but it was the same sort of high-minded advertising jargon lauding the mission and vision of the NSA. I was annoyed it hadn't occurred to me sooner.

When I emerged from my cave, the lights were turned low and the hallway was empty. I peeked into rooms until I found Shaunessy Brennan hunched wearily over a terminal, typing. "Long day?" I said.

She looked at me in surprise. "Are you still here?"

I held up the paper. "Solved it," I said.

"The last of the candidates went home hours ago."

My heart sank. "I guess I'm a little rusty. I did get the answer, though."

She sighed. "Fine." She held out a hand for the paper, which I passed over. She glanced at it briefly, then set it on the desk. "I'll add it to your file. Did you certify completion on the web page?"

"Web page?"

"The portal, I mean. When you logged in and accessed the decryption tools, the last step was to certify that you'd successfully completed the test. Some people forget that step."

"I didn't use the computer."

She stared at me, eyes hard. "The computer in the interview room. For the practical exam."

"I never turned it on. I hit the power button and nothing happened, so I just ignored it."

"So how did you decrypt the message?"

I shrugged. "Pen and paper." I felt a glimmer of hope. If she had been expecting me to use the computer, then maybe she wouldn't hold my slowness against me. Not that I type any faster than I write, but there might have been tools, Matlab or Mathematica for instance, or at least a calculator, that would have sped the process a little.

Without changing expression, she stood and walked past me. I followed her back to the interview room. She stopped short when she saw the table, strewn with pages and pages of calculations from my failed attempts. She crossed to the computer and hit the power button, as I had done. Nothing happened. She followed the power cord from the back into a snarl of cables behind the table, and found the plug dangling loose beside an outlet. The outlet was covered with a wide strip of masking tape and a sign that said, "Outlet loose. Maintenance notified. Do not use."

She straightened and looked at me, her expression still suspicious. Feeling foolish that I hadn't thought to check the plug, I shrugged. "Sorry. I like pen and paper. I thought it would be allowed."

"The computer has a web portal that introduces you to several decryption tools," she said. "It assumes a knowledge of Java or C, but it requires no knowledge of cryptography techniques. Most competent programmers can put it together in half an hour and find the answer."

I was feeling really stupid now. "I didn't know. I thought the computer just had the file with the cipher text. And maybe a calculator or something."

She picked up one of my pages of calculations, examined it, and set it down again. She shook her head. "You really decrypted a Playfair cipher . . . *by hand?*"

Now she was laughing at me. It was probably a story she would put in her repertoire, to tell future candidates about the idiot who spent all day solving it on paper instead of checking the plug. "It was a misunderstanding," I said. "And I would have had it done faster if I hadn't started with a Vigenère."

"I've never seen anyone solve a Playfair by hand. Or a Vigenère, for that matter. Either you're the smartest mathematician we've seen in a decade, or you're trying to scam your way into this agency." Her tone of voice made it clear which she thought was the more likely.

I didn't say anything. I assumed that she could verify whether or not I had logged into the computer.

"Does that mean I don't get the job?"

"As I already told you, that's not my decision to make. However, *if* my boss decides to make you an offer, that still doesn't guarantee you a job. All offers are conditional on passing the security check, which is no small hurdle. It requires a full lifestyle polygraph, psych exam, background investigation, the works. It can take at least six months for the paperwork to go through, and usually more like nine."

"It's a pain, too," I said. "I went through it several years ago, when my dad got me an internship with Lockheed Martin."

The look she gave me was almost pleading. "Are you telling me that you *already have* a CSI security clearance?"

"Well, it's lapsed," I said. "But they can usually get those turned around in a week or so."

"And you didn't think that was worth mentioning on your resume?"

I shrugged, feeling stupid again. "I figured it wouldn't matter unless I got the job."

Her gaze tried to dissect me. She seemed to think I was pulling a fast one over on her, but she couldn't quite prove it. "I'll pass on that information, along with my impressions of this interview. I warn you, they will have your claims—*all* of your claims—thoroughly investigated. It will probably take at least a week before you hear back, one way or another."

"Fair enough," I said. I could feel the grin splitting my face, but I couldn't hold it back. I could tell that, although she didn't agree, she thought her superiors would make me an offer. I was going to work for the NSA.

CHAPTER 3

I walked out to my car, as high as a mycologist on his own hand-picked stash of magic mushrooms. I was going to work for the NSA. I was going to break codes like Alan Turing at Bletchley Park. I would be an agent, with access to classified information and insights into world politics. I did a little dance as I walked through the parking lot, and it wasn't just because of the cold.

I took off my gloves long enough to fish out my key and turn it in the lock of my Nissan—the keyless entry system had broken long ago—and climb inside. I hastily pulled my glove back on before my fingers froze. Temperatures had reached record lows this February, and the meteorologists had been gleefully competing with each other for synonyms of "frigid."

I was late to pick up my brother at the airport. Fortunately BWI—the airport formerly known as Friendship International—was only a mile away. I had expected to have some time after the interview, at least enough for some dinner, but he was probably already on the ground wondering where I was. I would have given him a call, but I had left my phone at home, having been warned that I wouldn't be allowed to bring it into any of the NSA buildings. No matter. I would be there in a few minutes.

I turned the key in the ignition. Nothing happened.

I cursed in Portuguese, Spanish, and Tupi-Guarani, and made up a few languages of my own for good measure. The Nissan had been my father's for a decade before he had sold it to me for a dollar. It had almost two hundred thousand miles on it. The check engine light had been on for months. So I couldn't really complain. But I was exhausted from a day of decoding, and I hadn't eaten anything all day, thanks to the NSA's miserly vending machine. All my good feeling from the end of the interview was gone.

I tramped back into the building and headed through the metal detector for the lobby front desk.

"Whoa, sir. Stop right there!" An armed MP blocked my way and put a hand on my shoulder.

"I was just here," I said. "You saw me walk out of here thirty seconds ago."

"Sir, you need to show me your ID."

"My car broke down. I just need to make a phone call."

The MP put his hand on his holstered weapon, and his partner started to circle around me. I raised my hands, surrendering. "Okay," I said. I backed up, pulled off my gloves, and fished my driver's license out of my wallet. "Here. Same as before."

"Sir, we're going to need you to empty your pockets."

"Again? Look, I'm not coming in, not really. I just need . . ."

The MP actually pulled his weapon out of his holster. He kept it pointed at the floor, but it was as serious a move as I had ever seen anyone make. "Right now, sir."

I emptied my pockets. The MP with the gun stood watching me. The other one came around the X-ray machine to pat me down thoroughly. Both were young, muscled, with close-cropped hair and hard, unwavering expressions on their faces. These weren't men with a sense of humor.

A woman's voice caught my attention. "Mr. Johns?" I looked to see Shaunessy Brennan in a dark wool trench coat and a plaid scarf, slipping on some leather gloves. "What's going on? Did you forget something?"

I felt the heat creeping into my face. "My car won't start," I said. "I was just trying to get into the lobby and make a phone call." Though to tell the truth, I wasn't even sure who I was going to call. My parents were in New York, visiting Julia, and Paul was at the airport, waiting for me. I had attended too many colleges and lived in too many places over the last several years to have any friends close enough to call.

One of the MPs found my name on a list. "I'm sorry, sir," he said. "You're not cleared for access to the building."

"What?" I said. "I was just here. I just walked *out* of the building."

"You were cleared for a four-hour temporary interview access, this morning only," the MP said. "That access has expired."

"You've got to be kidding me." I could see the front desk through the glass. It was maybe twenty steps away, through the metal detector. I pressed two fingers into my forehead. "I was supposed to pick up my brother from the airport. He's probably wondering if I'm dead on the road."

Shaunessy came around to join me. "You have a phone right there," she said to the MP. "Can he use it to call someone to pick him up?"

"Sorry, ma'am. That line has to stay free. No personal calls."

She sighed. "Here. You can use my phone." She walked over to a plastic bin at the end of guards' table. I saw that it was filled with electronics, mostly smartphones, but a few other devices as well—mp3 players, pedometers, portable battery chargers. Shaunessy rummaged around in the bin for a while before surfacing with a Nexus in a hot pink skin.

"You just leave your phone in a bin?" I said.

"They're not allowed in the building, and nobody's going to leave them in their car in this weather," she said.

"Aren't you afraid it'll get stolen?"

She raised an eyebrow, and her mouth quirked slightly in an amused smile. She held out the phone.

I took it, noticing that the pink skin had a cute cat design on it. I thumbed it on and dialed the new number my brother had given me. Apparently his phone had ended up in the river, and he'd been forced to buy a temporary replacement. "Paul," I said when he answered. "It's Neil."

"I was wondering," he said. His voice sounded scratchy, like he had a cold. "Where are you calling from? This isn't your number."

"My car broke down," I said. "I'm still at the . . ." I trailed off and glanced at the implacable face of one of the MPs, not sure if I was supposed to say where I was. "I'm going to have to call a tow truck and a taxi, and I'll have the taxi pull around and get you, too. It might just be a little while." Actually, I was pretty sure I didn't have enough money for a taxi, and I wasn't sure they would let one through the gate anyway.

"Look, forget about that," Shaunessy said. "I'll give you a ride."

"What?" I put my hand over the phone. "You don't have to do that. My brother's at the airport, and I have to—"

"He's at BWI? And where are you going after that?"

"My father's house in Glen Burnie."

She waved her hand. "That's a ten minute drive. Tell your brother we'll pick him up, and I'll drop you both off."

"You're sure?"

"Don't worry about it. I can spare half an hour."

Paul had been talking at the same time, but I'd missed most of it. "Stay where you are," I said. "We'll be there in five minutes."

Shaunessy drove a black Infiniti, only a few years old and still looking factory new on the inside. I thought of the landfill of fast food wrappers that was the back of my Nissan, and I was glad it wasn't me giving her a ride.

"So, no family, then?" I said.

She didn't wear a ring, and I assumed her willingness to give a ride to a near stranger meant she wasn't in a hurry to get home to anyone.

"A father, three brothers," she said. "No husband or kids, if that's what you mean."

"My sister just had a baby girl," I said. "They named her Ash."

"Ash?"

"Yeah. Not Ashley or Ashlynn or anything. Just Ash."

"That's pretty," Shaunessy said.

"I think it's a little weird," I said. "But I'm pretty pleased at being an uncle."

She didn't respond. We rode in silence for a bit. A sign read "Baltimore/Washington International Thurgood Marshall Airport" and pointed the way toward Arrivals. Shaunessy turned into the right lane and followed the arrow.

"How about your name?" I said. "I've never heard it before."

She angled her head away from the road long enough to raise an eyebrow at me. I was beginning to recognize that as one of her favorite facial expressions.

"Seriously," I said. "Where's it come from? Your mother's maiden name?"

"The bottle of stout my parents were drinking at the time," she said, her voice flat.

I barked a laugh. "You're kidding."

She shook her head. "Wish I were. That's the whole story. Though the name of the stout is spelled with an extra 'gh' in the middle."

"Well, I think it's really beautiful."

She grunted noncommittally.

"Are you really Irish?"

"Sort of," she said. "Both of my parents were born and raised there, but they moved to Virginia when I was five."

She turned again, following another sign toward Arrivals.

"Thanks for doing this," I said. "My brother had a harrowing time in Brazil, and I'm glad not to keep him waiting."

That caught her attention more than anything else I'd said so far. "He was in Brazil?"

"Yeah. Did you see the news about the group of tourists that were gunned down on a boat? That was my brother. He was there. He was one of the survivors."

"Did he get a good look at his attackers?"

She was oddly engaged now, and her question took me aback. "I don't think so," I said. "He hasn't said a lot, though I know he talked to the police down there."

"I'd like to talk to him."

Her interest seemed strange to me, but I just shrugged. "You'll get your chance."

She pulled into the pick-up zone. "Which airline?"

"American. There he is; I see him."

She stopped the car, and I climbed out and waved until Paul saw me and headed in our direction. Shaunessy got out and opened the trunk for his suitcases.

I thought my brother might look tanned from his Amazon jungle expedition, or at least a bit more rugged, but he looked as pale as if he had spent the month in an office under fluorescent lights. I supposed not all that much light filtered down to the rainforest floor, so maybe it wasn't all that surprising. He studied mushrooms, after all. They weren't known for growing in places with a lot of sunlight.

I gave him a brief embrace. "Back from the wilds of the Amazon," I said. "Welcome to the frigid North."

He started to respond but was prevented by a coughing fit that took him a few moments to clear. "It's good to be back," he finally managed.

"Whoa," I said. "What tropical disease did you pick up?"

"It's nothing. A cold."

I introduced him to Shaunessy. "Shaunessy, this is my brother, Paul. Paul, this is . . ." I hesitated, wondering what to call her. My friend? My interviewer? ". . . Shaunessy," I finished lamely. "She was kind enough to give me a ride."

Paul didn't respond. He seemed frozen in the moment of shaking her hand, holding on for longer than was polite. Did he recognize her? Shaunessy's expression was alarmed. Paul's face was pale, paler even than I had realized at first. "Paul, are you okay?" I asked.

He coughed again, and blood erupted from his mouth, spraying Shaunessy and spattering the pavement. His eyes unfocused, and he started to tip. Shaunessy gave a little shriek as his hand pulled out of her grasp. "Paul!" I shouted. I tried to catch him, but he was too big, and he was sliding away from me. Making no move to protect himself, Paul collapsed, falling backward over his suitcase and knocking his head against the street with an audible crack.

CHAPTER 4

I sat in the waiting room of the Baltimore Washington Medical Center, wondering how long it would take before they would tell me anything. The hospital vending machines accepted my credit card, and I loaded up on peanuts, barbeque-flavored potato chips, and Snickers bars, the first food I'd eaten all day. Outside, it started to snow.

As soon as Paul collapsed, Shaunessy had dialed 911, and an ambulance appeared in an impressive five minutes. Paul had regained consciousness by then, and complained loudly that he was fine while the EMTs strapped him to a stretcher and loaded him into the back of the ambulance. Another EMT asked me questions. I told him everything I knew about where Paul had been and what he might have come into contact with, but it wasn't much.

Shaunessy drove me and followed the ambulance to the hospital. She offered to stay, but I insisted that she leave, after I borrowed her phone again call my parents and sister. I had already milked her kindness far more than seemed reasonable, and I didn't know whether Paul's blood was going to wash out of her blouse. An hour and a half had passed since then, and all my inquiries at the front desk had been met with the patient response that I would be told as soon as they knew anything.

Finally, they called my name, and I was introduced to a Dr. Mei-lin Chu. She looked nearly as young as me, but I assumed she must have graduated from medical school and been through a residency. Her long hair was slipping out of the clip that held it out of her face, and she looked tired.

"Is he conscious?" I asked.

"He is," she said. "He's lucid and responds appropriately to questions, though he seems vague about the details of his trip. I'm concerned he doesn't remember more."

"What happened to him? Do you know?"

"Your brother has fungal pneumonia. At some point while he was in South America, he breathed in some spores, and they lodged in his lung tissue and started to grow. We've taken a biopsy from his lungs to determine just what type of fungus is involved. Do you know what he might have come into contact with while he was down there?"

I laughed, and she looked at me quizzically. "Didn't he tell you?" I said. "He's a mycologist. He probably touched, sniffed, and sampled a thousand of the rarest fungi he could find."

"We'll know more once the labs come back. Fungal infections can be quite serious if untreated, but in most cases, we have good results. I'll tell you more as soon as I know it."

And with that, she was gone, leaving me to wait again. Two hours later, after I'd eaten enough candy and chips to feel pretty sick myself, Dr. Chu returned.

"It's called paracoccidioidomycosis," she said, the word flowing off of her tongue as easily as breathing. "The good news is, it's fairly common in that part of the world, so we know how to treat it. However, this a serious illness, one with some pretty serious side effects if it's not addressed."

Her small hands gestured in quick motions as she spoke. "The fungus takes root in the lung tissue and starts sending out microscopic tendrils, called mycelia, between the cells of the lungs. The immune system attacks it, but this releases fluid and blood from the surrounding vessels, which can inhibit the alveoli—the structures that exchange oxygen for carbon dioxide—from functioning properly."

"But he's going to be okay," I said.

She nodded. "The worst of it is past. We'll have to keep him here for a few more days, though. We're giving him an antifungal drug called amphotericin B intravenously, and we need to monitor him. Even after we release him, he'll need to stay in bed, and he'll continue to have a fever and a nasty cough for at least a week. I'm prescribing him voriconazole, another antifungal drug that he can take orally. But—this is important— he's going to have to keep taking it for at least three years."

"Wait—years?"

"Years. I told him, but I'm telling you, too, because it's important. Fungus is hard to eradicate. It can come back, and if it does, it's usually a lot worse than the first time around. You can end up with a chronic lung infection, or it can spread into joints or into the lining of the brain. You don't want to mess around with it. He needs to take the medication."

She shook my hand and walked away before I could even thank her. She spoke so quickly, the whole exchange had taken less than a minute. Eventually, they told me I could see him. I wandered back through halls that smelled like latex and cleaning agents and found him propped up in bed, as pale as the walls, a gently beeping IV in his arm.

"Hey," I said. "You gave us a scare there. How do you feel?"

He coughed wetly. "I'm fine."

"You're not fine. You dropped like a rock in the middle of the airport pick-up zone and you've got fungus growing out of your lungs. Not to mention almost getting yourself killed down there."

"The hazards of international travel." He shrugged. "Really. I feel fine."

"More like the hazards of extreme mycology," I said. "I told you to stay away from the magic mushrooms."

"Yeah, yeah. So just how are you getting out of here without a car?"

"I'll have to call a taxi."

"That's what I get for trusting my little brother to get me home."

"Oh, so now you're blaming this on me?"

Paul grinned. "You've got to get yourself a real job one of these days, so you can afford a real car."

That reminded me that my Nissan was still in the NSA parking lot, gathering a layer of snow. I was going to have to figure out how to get a tow truck in there to pull it out, and I feared that the cost to fix it would be more than I could afford, and probably more than the car was worth.

"So, what happened down there?" I said.

"What do you mean?"

"Come on, Paul. I know more about your ordeal from watching the news than I do from you. Who attacked you? Why? How did you escape?"

Paul related what little he knew, about military-looking men in a Brazilian Navy patrol boat who had attacked for no obvious reason. How he and a girl had made it to shore and walked for miles through trackless jungle to civilization. He was vague about that part of the journey, saying only that they had survived on mushrooms and gotten lucky.

"To tell you the truth, that part of it is a blur," he said. "I remember getting to shore, but I don't remember a whole lot after that. I guess I must be blocking it out."

It seemed odd to me that he would block out a trek through the jungle, but not the violent murder of a dozen people, but I didn't say anything. "How's the girl you escaped with?" I asked instead.

Paul looked pained. "Maisie!" he said. "She's probably sick, too."

"Did you travel back with her?"

He shook his head. "She left the same day, but she lives in California. Wine-growing country. We took different flights."

I stood at the window. The sun was just starting to rise, reflecting brightly off the snow and giving the room a pinkish hue. "Doctor Chu was concerned that you couldn't remember everything that happened to you in Brazil," I said.

"I remember fine," Paul said. "I just don't want to think about it. She wanted a list of the biological agents I'd come into contact with, and I told her those numbered in the millions. I have no idea what actual species of fungus it is."

"How does a fungus in your lungs mess with your brain badly enough to knock you unconscious?"

He shrugged. "Interfered with my oxygen supply, I guess. The changing air pressures from the flight probably didn't help."

"Breathing isn't exactly optional, you know."

He nodded gravely. "I'll try to keep that in mind."

Paul reached a hand over to his jeans, which were folded beside his bed. He fumbled with them, trying to get his fingers into the pocket.

"What are you looking for?"

"My phone. I want to give Maisie a call, make sure she's all right. Any spores I breathed, she probably did, too."

"They don't want you to use cell phones anyway. Here," I said. I took the handset from the phone on the wall and stretched it over to him, the cord just barely reaching.

"Can you dial it for me?" he asked.

He pulled a torn piece of paper out of his wallet, and I dialed the number that had been written on it in a rounded, feminine hand. I heard the phone ringing on the other end.

"Yes, I was hoping to reach Maisie Berquist," Paul said. I slipped out into the hallway to give him some privacy. With nothing else to do, I visited the bathroom. When I returned, I was surprised to see that he was already off the phone.

"Your girlfriend doesn't want to talk to you anymore?" I said. I was going to add a jab about the challenges of long-distance relationships, but I stopped when I saw his face.

I couldn't really say he had gone pale, since he was already as pale as a living human being could be. But his expression had the kind of shock in it that made me think the blood would have drained from his face even if he hadn't been sick. "Are you okay?" I asked. "Should I call a nurse?"

He opened his mouth and paused, as if his lips and tongue wouldn't obey his instruction to speak. He bit his lip and swallowed. Finally, he said, "She's dead."

I stared at him. "Maisie? What happened?"

"Fungal infection, just like me." Paul's voice was even, but there was a sharp edge to it. "I talked to her sister. Maisie started coughing on the plane, apparently, but she didn't seem as dramatically sick as I did—no blood, no passing out. By the time she started coughing hard enough that they were worried, she was at home. They called 911, but the ambulance didn't get there in time. She was gone"—he took a shaky breath—"before the EMTs even arrived. Her lungs stopped working, and she couldn't breathe. Her sister tried to make it sound more peaceful than that, but I could tell it was pretty horrible."

I put my hand on his arm, too shocked to know how to respond. "I'm so sorry," I said.

"I barely knew her. We met five days ago."

"Still," I said. "You went through an ordeal together."

"She was so strong. She ran triathlons. She was healthier than I was."

I shrugged. "Sometimes that doesn't tell the whole picture. Maybe she had some other medical problem, something that made her susceptible."

"I can't believe it," Paul said. "She lived through a terrorist attack and a fifty-mile trek through thick jungle, only to die at home of a lung infection."

His breathing was faster, more labored. "Take it easy," I said.

"It should have been me. I was the one picking up mushrooms all the time. If somebody was going to die of a fungal infection, it should have been me."

I stood by his bedside, impotent. "Do you know when the funeral will be?" I asked, falling back on practicalities.

"It doesn't matter. Even if I'm out of the hospital by then, I wouldn't go. It's too far, and nobody there knows me. I'm not even a friend, not really."

"Maybe not. But you survived together."

Paul's voice drifted, as if he were somewhere other than the Baltimore Washington Medical Center. "Only she didn't," he said.

CHAPTER 5

I could always tell which of my parents had cooked any dish. My mom was an Iowa farm girl who grew up in a town of five hundred people, most of whom still lived there. She learned to cook from her mother and favored beef and potatoes and everything-in-a-pot casseroles. My father didn't learn to cook until he was stationed in Brazil and had a more adventurous bent. The dishes he made were all Brazilian, a mix of indigenous and Portuguese flavors, which almost always featured rice and beans. There was even a Brazilian expression, *arroz com feijão*—rice and beans—that meant commonplace, everyday. For me, it was comfort food, and eating it felt like home.

Incredibly, the ability to cook was a skill my father still retained, although my mother always watched him carefully while he juggled hot pans over the stove. He had cooked for so many years that making familiar dishes was automatic to him, requiring no recipe or measuring cups. Somehow, those neurons had escaped the strangulating plaques and tangles so far, though I had no doubt they would eventually succumb.

When I finally came home from the hospital, my parents were there, having driven back from New York when they heard about Paul. It was, by then, one o'clock in the morning, but everyone was famished, so Dad heated up some shrimp bobó over rice and we all shoveled it down.

"So Paul's going to be okay?" Mom said.

"Physically, I think so," I said. "The doctor said the worst was past. Emotionally, I don't know. He tried to call Maisie while I was there. Apparently she got the same infection he did, only she died of it."

Mom gasped and put a hand over her mouth.

Dad looked confused. "Who's Maisie?"

"The other survivor," Mom said. "The young woman Paul rescued and brought safely through the wilderness."

She said it patiently, matter-of-fact, with nothing in her voice to suggest that my father should have remembered that detail.

"Paul's taking it pretty hard," I said. "He says it's not a big deal, that she didn't really mean anything to him, but I don't believe him. He's having trouble coming to terms with the fact that she's dead, and he's still alive. Out of all the people on that riverboat, he's the only one who made it."

"We'll go visit him in the morning," Mom said. "There's no worry, then, for Paul? That he might . . . ?"

She meant that he might die, too. "The doctor I talked to didn't seem too concerned. She said we should take it seriously, make sure he took his antifungals. But I don't think his life is in any immediate danger."

"Well, then." Mom slapped her hands on her knees, closing the subject. "Enough talk of death, then. Charles, we should show Neil pictures of his new niece."

Dad looked startled. "Did you take any?"

"No. That was your job."

"I don't have a camera," Dad said.

"You have an iPhone, dear. And you did take pictures; I saw you do it."

I scooped another helping of shrimp. "Julia sent me some pictures of Ash already," I said. "She's a cutie."

"Bald as a ping-pong ball," Dad grumbled. "And what kind of name is Ash? Ash? That's the black stuff you dig out of a fireplace. It's no name for a child."

"It's a perfectly lovely name," Mom said. "Girls named Ashley are called Ash all the time."

"But her name *isn't* Ashley," Dad said. "Ashley wouldn't be strange. There are thousands of good names out there; why does she have to get creative?"

"Be nice," my mother said. "She's your granddaughter."

"It's my daughter I was complaining about."

Mom was beaming. She had a granddaughter, and Paul was safe, and

Dad was actually responding appropriately, bantering with her like he used to do. I finished the last of my shrimp bobó and eyed the serving bowl, wondering if I would regret taking a third helping. I decided to risk it. "I was hoping to visit Julia this weekend," I said. "But my car . . ."

"You can take mine," Mom said.

"Are you sure? You don't need it?"

"Your father and I can make do with one car for one weekend. Take it. Julia will be happy to see you."

My father argued good-naturedly with me about the best route to take from Baltimore to Ithaca. It was about a five-hour trip regardless, but my dad was convinced you could shave a few minutes off if you went up Route 81 through Wilkes-Barre and Binghamton. It was the sort of argument he excelled at—meaningless and impossible to prove—and even before his Alzheimer's, he had loved to debate a subject endlessly without worrying about reaching a resolution. The fact that he could actually remember the names of the roads made me smile. It was always surprising what things he could bring to mind and what things seemed out of reach.

⊕

I drove up to Ithaca and met my new niece. Julia's husband was Japanese, which gave Ash an intriguing blend of genetic features. When I looked into those complex dark eyes, I had to admit that Ash was, for some reason I couldn't explain, the perfect name for her. On my return to my parents' home, I announced as much, leaving my dad as the only remaining malcontent.

The next day, Shaunessy Brennan called.

"How's your brother?" she asked.

"On the road to recovery," I said. "He has pneumonia. Some weird fungal thing he picked up in the Amazon."

"I'm glad to hear he's okay."

"Thanks for helping us out. I really appreciate it."

"You're welcome. Look, I called to tell you that my boss, Melody Muniz, is offering you a job. The formal letter is in the mail, but I thought you'd like to know."

My grin was wide enough to split my face. "That's good news. That's very, very good news. Thank you."

"You're welcome. Though I had nothing to do with it. It wasn't my choice."

"I appreciate the call, anyway. Thanks for thinking of me."

"It's just part of the job."

Her tone was stiff, maybe even a little resentful. "You don't like me much, do you?" I asked.

She didn't respond for so long that I wondered if she'd hung up. Finally, she said, "It's your type I don't like. Young whiz kids with entitlement coming out their ears who think the rules don't apply to them. Fine, you're smart; I get it. But here, everybody's smart. And the rules are there for a reason."

"I can follow the rules," I said. "And I'll be good at the job. You'll see."

"Report to FANX III again next Monday, 9:00 sharp. Don't be late. You'll join a group of new hires in what we call the Tank, where people go to wait for their clearance tickets to come through."

"The Tank?"

"It's officially the Awaiting Clearance Pool. But informally, it's the Tank. We verified your lapsed tickets, so, as you said, they should be able to turn yours around quickly. You won't be there long. In the meantime, you'll take a few orientation courses."

"Good," I said. "Does this mean I'll be on the same team as you? Will we be working together?"

"Don't take this the wrong way," she said. "But I hope not."

Ouch. I winced as I hung up the phone, but I couldn't keep the grin off my face for long. The NSA! After a lifetime kept in the dark, I was finally going to be on the inside. I would know things. I would be allowed to learn all the secrets my father could never tell me. Who cared what Shaunessy Brennan thought? She'd done her worst, but she couldn't keep me out.

After a little dance of triumph, I went to find my dad to tell him the news. I discovered him in the living room, reading from a thick book of collected short fiction. He liked short stories because he could finish them in a single sitting, unlike novels, which he tended to lose track of before he reached the end. He was crying as he read, tears running down his face unchecked.

I looked to see what story he was reading. It was "Flowers for Algernon."

I gave his bony shoulder a squeeze and kept my news to myself.

CHAPTER 6

NSA agent Benjamin Harrison looked nothing like his presidential namesake. He was large and bald, with crimson cheeks that turned an even brighter red when he spoke. He seemed out of place in a suit and tie, and his tight collar left an impression against his wide throat. His normal speaking voice seemed to be a shout as he addressed the newest employees of the National Security Agency.

"This is the largest intelligence agency in the world," he said, his booming voice filling the room. "And most of the country's intelligence comes from right here at FANX or our sister location at Fort Meade. We give our troops a decisive advantage in war. We stop terrorist attacks before they happen. We locate chemical and biological weapon factories, track troop movements and missile programs, and slow the traffic of narcotics into the country. We are the nation's first and last line of defense."

I wondered if Agent Harrison could be the voice actor from the video in the lobby, but I dismissed the idea. His delivery wasn't trained enough, though he seemed to be drawing from the same basic script. Did they have a cadre of professional writers on staff just to produce this stuff? Come to think of it, in an organization the size of the NSA, with the kind of public relations problems they had, they probably did.

I sat in a training classroom with a dozen other new hires, listening to Harrison preach. The room was organized with rows of long tables, each of which had three computer stations. The monitors were recessed into the tabletops, angled upward, and blocked by panels on each side to prevent any student from seeing another student's screen.

"The biggest battle we fight is an invisible one," Harrison said. "We have been fighting it for decades, and it never ends. It's the battle of cyber warfare, in which our enemies try to discover our secrets by infiltrating our computing systems, and we try to return the favor. It's a battle where everything we know is at stake—the designs of our fighters and missiles and carriers, the locations of our defenses, our vulnerabilities. Every war ever fought in the history of the world has been won or lost by information."

Most of the class was listening with rapt attention, though two or three were doodling or using the computers. Harrison didn't seem to notice. At least half of the incoming class were young women, and I entertained myself by guessing their names. The tiny brunette with short hair and a cute face I decided was Maggie. The tall freckled one with red hair like a sunrise was Kathleen. Megan had wide eyes and cracked her fingers, neck, and knees compulsively, and Diane was the one looking around the room like me and missing nothing. Our eyes met for a brief moment, and I winked. She looked away. The men were less interesting to me, but I assigned them names, too: Ronnie and Argento and Goddard and Max.

Then I noticed that everyone else was typing and staring down at their recessed monitors. Agent Harrison had stopped orating and had given the class some kind of instruction, which I hadn't heard at all. I looked up at the front of the class, a flood of adrenaline kicking into my system. I didn't want to make a bad impression on my first day.

"You're all hackers now," Harrison said. "Breaking into this enemy system could mean the difference between life and death for American citizens. Let's see which of you can be the first to crack it."

I looked down at my monitor. It showed a training website, with links to different courses and online resource texts. It was an unclassified network, connected to the internet and presumably with no connection whatsoever to any of the NSA's secure systems. One of the links said "Introduction to the NSA course exercise." I clicked it. A new screen appeared with a username and password. This, presumably, was the "enemy system" that we were supposed to crack.

The other students were intent on their work, fingers moving quickly. They probably all had computer science degrees, maybe with courses in cyberespionage or web security. I hadn't the first clue how to hack into the site. But that didn't mean I was going to give up.

I sat there, staring at the login screen, trying to think. Guessing passwords wasn't likely to get me very far. I didn't have the chops to make any kind of technical assault. I would have to do this my own way. I went back to the original website and pressed a few links until I found the phone number for technical support.

I raised my hand. "Agent Harrison," I said. "I have to use the bathroom."

"This isn't middle school," he said. "Get up and go."

I walked out, moving quickly. In the hall, I turned right—away from the bathrooms. I felt very conspicuous wandering the halls with my bright red visitor's badge, and I was certain that at any moment someone was going to stop me and demand an explanation of where I was headed. In a few minutes, however, I found what I was looking for. Another training classroom, identical to ours, but dark and empty. I stepped inside.

The instructor's desk had a phone on it. I dialed the tech support number. "Yes, this is Agent Benjamin Harrison," I said, doing my best to imitate my instructor's grandiose tones. "I'm teaching a course here, and I need a password reset on the unclassified network."

"Name and badge ID," said the bored voice on the other end of the phone.

"Benjamin Harrison," I repeated. "And . . . hang on, I can never remember it. My badge is in my coat pocket. I'll call you back."

I hung up, denied but not discouraged. I went back to the classroom and put on an embarrassed, confused look. "Mr. Harrison?" I said.

He looked up. So did a few of my classmates.

"Um. Where is the bathroom?"

He was sitting behind the front table, and I still couldn't get a good look at his badge, so I doubled over with a hand on my stomach. I tried not to overplay it. As I hoped, he stood and came around to put a hand on my shoulder. "Are you all right, son?"

I saw his badge. The number was printed small on the top right corner, but I memorized it quickly: 7014603. I straightened and gave him a sickly smile. "A little ill, sir. I'll be okay. I just need the bathroom?"

"Out the door, to the left, then left again toward the lobby."

"Thanks," I said. I went out the door and turned left. I wanted to get back to the empty classroom, however, which was in the other direction. Our classroom had glass walls, and I didn't want to be spotted going the wrong direction. I waited until a man and a woman walked down the hall the way I wanted to go, and then walked next to them, keeping them between me and the classroom with my face turned away.

Back in the empty room, I called tech support again.

"Benjamin Harrison," I said. "Seven oh one four six oh three."

I didn't dare ask for the password to the student exercise to be reset, partly because I didn't know what to call it, and partly because it might seem suspicious. Instead, I just asked for a reset to Harrison's main unclassified account.

I heard typing in the background. "Okay," said the bored voice. "You should be all set. Your new password is the first three letters of your last name, followed by the last four digits of your badge number. Change it within the hour, or the system will lock you out again."

I thanked him and returned to my class. I nodded weakly at Harrison. A few of the women glanced at me as I made my way back to my seat. Maggie gave me a sympathetic look, but Diane eyed me suspiciously. I smiled at them both. None of the men looked up at all.

I sat down at the terminal and logged off, then logged in again using Harrison's account and the temporary password. I held my breath, but no sirens wailed. The account welcomed me, and I was in. I brought up the training web site again, which now contained several new options like "Instructor Resources" and "Course Curricula." I followed the curricula link and found the listing for the Introduction to the NSA course. As I had hoped, the course was given by various instructors, who were provided with a script. I scanned it quickly, until I found the student exercise. And there it was. Username: alanturing. Password: bletchleypark. I smiled.

Five minutes later, Agent Harrison checked his screen and looked up. "It looks like we have a winner," he said. "I'm not sure it's ever been cracked that fast before."

The students all looked at each other, some in surprise, some in annoyance. I smiled at Diane and gave her another wink. She wasn't as cute as Maggie, but I guessed she would be bright and opinionated. I wondered if she would be interested in going out for some Thai food afterward.

"Neil Johns," Harrison said. "Please stand."

I did so, with a flourish and my best winning smile. The expressions on the others' faces ranged from resigned to disgusted. I guessed they were all pretty competitive and didn't like to be beaten.

"Congratulations," Harrison said. "You've got a great career in cyber espionage ahead of you. The rest of you, keep at it! Second place is still up for grabs."

I was still looking around the room, basking in my victory, when three men pushed through the door. Two of them were dressed in very serious-looking uniforms with MP armbands and their hands on their sidearms. The third was in his thirties, bearded, wearing jeans and a striped shirt. The third man took the lead, scanning the computers. He walked down the aisle until he reached my place and tapped on the table next to my terminal. "This is the one," he said.

One of the MPs eyed my temporary visitor's permit. "Neil Johns?"

"Yes," I said. "What is this?"

The first MP took me by the elbow, while the other drew a pair of handcuffs from his belt. "You're under arrest."

CHAPTER 7

FANX was essentially a large group of office buildings, not a military base like Fort Meade. This meant, presumably, that they didn't have any proper cells to lock me in. They stuck me in a small room with a table and chairs—and no computer—with an armed guard to make sure I didn't leave. The guard was shorter than me but looked as though she could rip my arms off and would be glad to do so given the chance.

She had no sense of humor. I couldn't get her to crack a smile. In fact, I couldn't get her to respond to me in any way. Attempts to engage her in conversation, to ask how long I would be kept there or to demand a lawyer all met with the same impassive gaze. I considered just trying to walk out the door, if only to get her to respond. I suspected that if I did, however, I'd regret it. The phrase "shot while trying to escape" had an unpleasant ring to it.

Time can seem incredibly slow when you have absolutely nothing to do and your future is in doubt. It occurred to me that if I were a foreign agent, applying for a job at the NSA would be a great way to get in the doors. They must be vigilant about security for such unvetted visitors. On the other hand, they *had* told us to hack into the account. I was just doing the exercise.

There was no clock in the room, and no windows, so I had no idea how much time had passed before I was joined by a uniformed man with the silver bars of an Army captain. He sat across from me at the table. I thought they might send someone to shout at me, to threaten to bury me in a hole where I would never again see the light of day if I didn't tell them who I was working for. Instead, the captain—Scaggs, by his name patch—was soft-spoken and professional. He asked me for every detail of what I had done and why, which I was eager to provide. He went over it several times, asking the same questions in different ways. He sometimes asked me about technical concepts, using words I didn't understand.

I had plenty of time to study his uniform while answering his questions, since I was afraid of looking him in the eye. I noticed a patch on his sleeve—a blue circle with an eagle carrying a key. Around the circumference of the patch were a series of letters and numbers that looked like a code. I recognized it as the emblem of the United States Cyber Command.

"Wow," I said. "You're with USCYBERCOM, aren't you?"

"Let's stick to talking about you," he said.

"Okay. But wow. I'm a fan. You're the guys who wrote that software worm that destroyed Iran's nuclear centrifuges, aren't you?"

Scaggs gave me a sidelong look. "I can't comment on that."

"Yeah, I know. You had nothing to do with it. But that was some piece of work. You guys are my heroes."

"What connections do you have with members of the Brazilian government?" he asked.

I sighed. He had asked the question already, and I still didn't have any connections with them. I hadn't even been to Brazil in five years, and though my father had kept in touch with some of the movers and shakers until a few years ago, I barely knew their names. The closest thing I had to a government contact was a childhood friend whose father had worked for Brazilian Intelligence, but I hadn't talked to my friend in years either.

We went around and around for what seemed like hours, him trying to trip me up or make me reveal whatever I was hiding, and me trying not to shout at him that I was exactly who I said I was and wasn't hiding anything at all. I wasn't truly afraid—I had heard stories about people disappearing into the labyrinth of the US intelligence agencies, held under clauses allowing detainment of suspected terrorists, but I didn't really believe they could just yank an American citizen off the streets and never let him out again. My real concern was that my hopes of working for the NSA—or any other intelligence agency—seemed to be going up in smoke. They might let me leave, but they were never going to let me back in again.

The sound of raised voices in the corridor snapped me out of my funk. I heard my name, but I couldn't make out what else was being said. Scaggs left me in the room and went out, apparently to join the conversation.

Eventually, somebody new came in. She was small and slight, wearing black slacks and a thin red sweater with three-quarter-length sleeves. Beneath a tasteful layer of makeup and red lipstick, the skin around her eyes and neck was deeply wrinkled, making me wonder if her long black hair was dyed. Her posture was military straight, but she walked carefully, like someone for whom walking is no longer as easy as it once was. Real NSA badges—not the visitor kind—had grids indicating which security compartments the bearer was cleared for, and hers was packed with number and letter signifiers. It also gave her name: Melody Muniz.

"Mr. Johns," she said, and held out an elegant hand. "You're lucky I heard the news." Her voice was clear, commanding, with no hint of age.

"You're Shaunessy's boss," I said.

She gave me a nod. "Melody Muniz. Pleased to meet you. You do know how much trouble you're in?"

I glanced at my armed guard and then back. "I'd gotten an inkling," I said.

"Whatever possessed you to break into your instructor's account?"

"He told us to hack our way in!"

"Into the seminar account. The one being used for the assignment. Not into your instructor's personal login."

"I didn't know hackers were bounded by rules."

Her face was unreadable. "The truth is, you fell afoul of a trap. There are a number of such measures in place to catch foreign spies trying to use the application process to gain access to our systems. You fell for the most basic of these traps, in fact—the call to tech support for a password reset. As you might imagine, there are a number of more sophisticated ones."

"So what happens now?"

"Good question. I'm afraid the fact that I don't personally believe you are a spy holds very little weight with the counterespionage unit. If they turn you over to the FBI on an espionage charge, that is a very serious thing indeed."

I was aghast. "You mean I could go to jail?"

"Not if I can help it. In fact, if I can pull the right strings, you're going to keep the job that you very nearly threw away in your first few hours of employment."

I was relieved, but surprised. "Why do you care?"

She pressed her lips together. "Shaunessy told me you solved a Playfair cipher by hand."

"I wouldn't have thought that was an important skill set in the digital age."

"It's not. Our computers can solve them quickly, in any language. But they do it by brute force, plus a few tricks. You did it through some mix of ingenuity and mathematical intuition, and that's something I'm very interested in indeed."

I thought it would be a bad time to mention that it had been mostly guesswork. "Thank you, ma'am."

"Melody, please. Or Ms. Muniz, if you must. Don't call me ma'am."

"Okay . . . Melody." It was difficult to say. She didn't look like a Melody, for one thing. She looked three times my age, with a hard professionalism that made me feel like a child. "I do appreciate it. And I'd like to come work for you. But I have one condition."

She looked at me like I was mad. "I'm offering to use my influence to get you employment instead of jail time, and you have a *condition*?"

"Yes, ma'am . . . I mean, yes."

"All right, let's hear it."

"I don't want to work with Shaunessy." She looked incredulous, but I pressed on. "She doesn't like me. She doesn't think I can do the job, and she doesn't trust me. I appreciate her helping me out when I needed a ride and telling you about my predicament. And I don't want to repay that by making her uncomfortable."

Melody's eyes narrowed, and she looked angry. "Condition denied," she said. "Shaunessy works for my team, and so will you. We don't have room for any dilettantes. If you can't handle that, I'll serve you up to Counterespionage right now, and believe me, they're eager. I don't care if you don't like her, but you'll treat her with respect and you'll do your job."

"I do like her. That's why—"

She waved a hand. "Enough. This may be a huge mistake, but I'll make this all go away. Just don't make me regret it."

Call me crazy, but I was disappointed when they escorted me out. I was happy not to be arrested, of course, but I was so intent on working at the NSA that I couldn't bear the idea of waiting any longer, now that I was so close. Melody had told me to return to FANX the next day. I would sign various documents to confirm the accuracy of my identity, surrender all pretense of privacy to the US government, and agree to be prosecuted to the fullest extent of the law if I leaked classified information to any uncleared person. Once I did, I could be photographed and issued my badge. My badge! I would have spent the night in the lobby if they would have let me.

After several minutes of wandering, I managed to find my mom's car in the parking garage. Remembering where I park has never been my strong suit, and it was several minutes of searching before I remembered I wasn't looking for my Nissan. I started the engine—relieved when it purred to a start—and pulled out toward the exit.

I drove through the gate at a crawl, uncertain what the process was, or whether I would be searched. The guards at the security hut were facing the other way—toward the entrance—and there didn't seem to be any obstacle or checkpoint. It was only when I had nearly reached the road that I realized I still wore my visitor's badge around my neck.

I panicked. If they had reacted so badly to my little hacking stunt in the exercise, how would they react to me stealing a facility badge? I looked in my rearview mirror, and saw what I had failed to notice on my way through the gate—a metal box with a sign that read "All Visitor Badges Must Be Returned Here." Hoping it wasn't too late, I jammed the gearshift into reverse and pulled back toward the box. I heard the guard shouting at me just before my rear tires slammed into the metal spikes embedded in the road.

The tires burst with a pop like gunfire. The rims screeched, grinding against the spikes before I thought to lift my foot off the gas. Soldiers ran out of the security hut and surrounded the car, shouting at the top of their lungs and pointing automatic weapons at me. Adrenaline flooded my system, but I was frozen in place, too terrified to twitch a finger. Blood pounded in my temples and behind my eyes.

Finally, my overwhelmed mind began to comprehend the words the soldiers were shouting. "Turn off the engine and step out of the car! Come out with your hands in view!"

Hands shaking, I turned the key, killing the engine, and stepped slowly out of the car. One of the soldiers lowered his weapon and pushed me into the side of the car, pinning my arms and patting me down. "I was just trying to return my badge!" I managed to say. They didn't answer.

A line of cars was forming behind me, NSA employees ready to get home to their families. The door opened in a blue sedan three cars back in line. Melody Muniz stepped out. She walked up the line until she could see me clearly. My eyes met hers, and I gave her a shaky, mortified smile. She shook her head. "You have got to be kidding me."

CHAPTER 8

Even with a recent security clearance, it took weeks for me to get my badge. I had to take a polygraph—apparently even current employees were now getting them quarterly, ever since Edward Snowden had disclosed several thousand classified documents to journalists back in 2013. I also had to update and verify my security paperwork, take a drug test, and list in detail any relationships I had with foreign nationals.

While I waited, I visited Paul, sometimes several times a day. He gained strength quickly, much faster than the doctors seemed to expect. Finally, the hospital staff disconnected his IV and pronounced him fit for discharge. My mom and I came to pick him up. Before we could take him, a nurse repeated Dr. Chu's earlier instructions about his prescribed sulfadimethoxime.

"Don't skip any doses," she said. "If you miss one, take it as soon as you realize. It's dormant now, and you'll start feeling fine, but it can come back. If it does, it'll be resistant to the medication, and it will hit you a lot worse.

"Stay in bed for a week, even if you start to feel better. Drink plenty of fluids. Your body needs a lot of energy to fight this off, so take it easy." To Mom, she said, "If his fever goes above 103 degrees, or you notice any other symptoms—any rashes, lesions, discoloration, difficulty breathing, pain in other places in his body—then he needs to see a doctor right away."

We agreed to follow these instructions to the letter, and she brought a wheelchair to cart him out to the lobby. Once there, Paul stood, and though he was still pale and coughed a lot, he seemed his normal self. He walked out to the car, and we all drove back home.

—◦—

The next week was hard. Paul gained strength and looked healthier every day, but he was morose and irritable. I knew it was a kind of survivor's guilt, a struggle against the apparent wrongness of his continued existence when everyone else involved in the incident was dead. It implied something supernatural, that he had been preserved for some higher purpose. It put a pressure on his life, as if he were living it for all of the people who had died. Maisie most of all, whom he had failed to save.

At least, I *thought* that's what he was thinking. He didn't say much, and he resisted any attempts on my part to broach the subject. I even suggested once that he ought to consider seeing a therapist, but he dismissed the idea. "I'm sad," he said. "It'll pass eventually, but for right now, that's how it is. I'm allowed to be sad, aren't I?" I admitted that he was and let it drop.

As he recovered, Paul started to move around a lot more. He tired of sitting still and watching daytime television. He was lucid enough to play chess, which he always won, and Scrabble, which I did.

One evening, he took me aside and showed me an online article from *Folha de S. Paulo*, a Brazilian newspaper. I skimmed the Portuguese, taking in the meaning without processing every detail. It reported a dramatic increase in the number of fungal lung infection cases in the Pará and Amazonas states, including a large number of deaths. "Don't you see what this means?" Paul said.

"What?"

"If there's an epidemic, some new fungus that's getting around, then Maisie wasn't my fault."

I gave him a hard look. "She was never your fault."

"I'm the one that took her through the jungle. I gave her mushrooms. I'm supposed to know about these things."

I wanted to argue with him, but it seemed better to let it go. "You're right," I said. "She could have picked up that infection even if she'd never met you."

"She was a great person," Paul said. "Nothing was ever going to come of it, between us, not living on opposite sides of the country. But she didn't deserve to die."

I couldn't disagree with that. "I'm sure she didn't," I said. "I'm sorry she couldn't have lived as well. But I'm glad you're alive."

Finally, I was given my badge—with surprisingly little pomp for what was to me a momentous occurrence—and told to report on Monday morning to my new job.

FANX was a pretty big place, but it was nothing compared to Fort Meade. The NSA Headquarters was the size of a city, complete with bank, post office, hair salon, movie theater, and medical center. It was home to thousands of people and a daily place of work for thousands more. The fact that so many other people were doing the same thing dulled none of my excitement, however, when I pulled off the Baltimore-Washington Parkway and joined the stream of cars onto Savage Road, my very own badge around my neck.

From a distance, the obsidian glass of the giant headquarters building caught the eye, but the true scope of the place wasn't immediately obvious. The road brought me between two guard towers, beyond which a pair of ten-foot fences topped with razor wire marked the edge of the property. Between the fences, guard dogs patrolled, and the soldiers at the gate wore fatigues and carried the biggest guns I'd ever seen.

I stopped at the checkpoint, holding up my badge, which had my picture and name printed on it. I had spent most of the weekend sneaking looks at it, trying it on, and admiring myself in the mirror. The soldier at the gate scrutinized it and compared it to my face. I donned my most serious secret agent expression and nodded at him smartly when he handed it back. He ignored me, already looking toward the next car.

The misunderstanding at the FANX gate a few weeks earlier had been cleared up without too much difficulty. Apparently I wasn't the first idiot visitor to try to back up in the exit lane, though I was the first to actually shred my tires on the security spikes. Once the car was thoroughly searched, the soldiers had pushed it out of the way—requiring eight of them to actually lift the back of the car off of the spikes—and I had called the same bemused tow truck driver to retrieve yet another car of mine from the NSA facility.

My employee badge allowed me to bypass the K-9 search, and I rolled right into one of several enormous parking garages. I was still driving my mom's car, now with a new set of tires. I had promised to repay her for the tires the moment I got my first paycheck, and to buy a car of my own soon after that.

I walked toward the building, breathing the fresh air and admiring my surroundings. The high fences, the concrete stanchions designed to stop a tank, the towers bristling with antennas and manned with armed soldiers—all of it combined to make me feel like I was special, someone worthy of being trusted with the secrets of the United States government. I was entering the sanctum sanctorum, a place very few people—comparatively—were permitted to go.

If I hadn't already been inclined to approve of everything I saw, I might have been disappointed by the working facilities in Melody Muniz's room. I had envisioned a state-of-the-art mission center, huge wall displays with the political status of the world, intense and busy agents working at high-tech stations. Kind of like Houston's Mission Control, but futuristic and top secret. Instead, her group worked in a basement office with burnt orange cubicles that looked fifty years old. It could have been an office in any aging tech company in the country, probably one whose stock was plummeting. A low hum permeated the space, like the background engine noise in an airplane.

The cubicles were arranged in quads, four seats each, and there were three quads in the room, plus a tiny kitchen area and an office for Melody. That made twelve team members, including Melody, with me as the thirteenth. Not that I was superstitious or anything.

Melody took me on the tour, introducing me to each of the members of the team. They were mostly young, and friendly enough, but I forgot their names almost as soon as I met them. Names had never been my strength.

I did notice that seven of the twelve were women, a higher percentage than I had expected, and what I would later find out was well above the NSA average. I mentioned it to Melody, who shrugged and said, "Women don't posture. There's no room on this team for personal ambition or for trying to appear to be something you're not. If I get even a hint of that, I'm not interested. Your average male intelligence agent, well . . ."

"I'll keep that in mind," I said.

"This will be your quad," Melody said. The other three chairs were taken by an older white man with a fringe of white hair at the back of his head, an Asian woman with a slender face and large glasses, and Shaunessy Brennan.

"You've got to be kidding me," Shaunessy said.

Melody ignored her. "And this will be your seat." The fourth spot had a sagging swivel chair with a broken arm, and no computer.

"You mean you vouched for him? After he pulled that stunt?" Shaunessy said.

"We were *told* to hack into the account," I said, for what seemed like the twentieth time. "I was following instructions."

"He's part of the team, for better or worse," Melody said, and that seemed to end the discussion. To me, she added, "We'll get you a machine and a better chair. Office furniture requisitions take forever around here. You'll need your own account as well."

"Don't worry, he can just hack into somebody else's," Shaunessy said. "Though I don't know why he needs a computer at all. Just give him a pencil and a stack of paper."

"Why don't you come with me for now, and we'll get you set up as best we can," Melody said.

THE GENIUS PLAGUE

I followed her back to her office. It was crowded with knickknacks, mostly geekware of some kind or another. I saw a binary clock, a chess set with a half-finished game, and a plush Cthulhu. Her bulletin board had a photo of a little girl—I was guessing a granddaughter—dressed as Chewbacca, and a hand-lettered sign that read TANSTAAFL.

Melody sat in her swivel chair with the same elegance she might have if it were a throne. "Welcome to the team," she said formally.

I took the chair opposite her desk. "Thank you. Just what team is this?"

"The team of misfits," she said. It seemed to be a joke, but she didn't smile. "I'd like to say we do the jobs nobody else can do. But often we just do the jobs nobody else wants to do."

I didn't answer. My eyes roamed the office and settled on the chess set. White was a knight up, but its pawn structure had been demolished. I liked Black's chances better.

"The vast majority of all traffic these days is encoded with public key encryption," Melody said. "Which, I'm sorry to say, is unbreakable."

I waited. The whirring noise in the background was the only sound. "As far as most people think," I prompted her.

"I'm afraid not," she said. "RSA encryption really is unbreakable, if it's done right. We have more compute power than anyone else in the world, and we can't touch it."

"But this is the NSA," I said.

She sighed. "Then I guess your disillusionment starts here. You're a mathematician. Do I really have to give you a primer on big numbers?"

"But . . . the NSA," I said.

"2048-bit encryption. The kind your phone can manage in a few milliseconds. How many possible keys is that?"

"2^{2048}," I said immediately.

"Which means that to find your key in a brute force attack, I need to make 2^{2048} guesses. Or half of that, on average."

"But you don't brute force it," I said. "Come on, you've got the Sieve of Atkin, at the very least, to narrow the guesswork, and you've probably got a lot better tricks than that."

"We do," she said, the hint of a smile playing around her lips. "But bear with me. Say I have a computer that costs one dollar and can make a billion guesses a second. We're not even in the ballpark there, but let's just imagine such a computer exists. How many computers would I need to guess your key in, say, a million years?"

"Brute force?" I did the math. "A billion is 2^{30}, give or take. A year is maybe 2^{25}, so a million years is 2^{45} . . . altogether, call it 2^{1973}," I said.

"And how much do you think we can knock off with prime sieving?"

"That allows you to skip all the non-prime numbers," I said. "The rule of thumb is an average separation of 2.3 primes per digit, so with numbers of that size, I'm going to guess you have a prime every, what, one or two thousand?"

"Which brings it down to what?"

"2^{1969}," I said. "Ish."

"And do you think we have 2^{1969} computers?"

My faith in the NSA was waning, and I was starting to feel a little foolish. "No."

"Or 2^{1969} dollars to buy them?"

I sighed. "I get the picture. I just thought that there would be, you know, another way. That somebody would have invented something by now to crack it."

Melody smiled beatifically. "Now don't despair. I said *properly* encrypted messages were unbreakable, but, fortunately for us, very few messages are properly encrypted. Even now, less than ten percent of HTTP traffic goes through SSL, and of those that do, the vast majority use the primes hardcoded in their key exchange software. Software packages that do the encryption can have bugs, which we can exploit if we find them or know about them. Also, although the message might be sent encrypted, it has to be decrypted on the other side, and that computer system itself might be vulnerable to attack."

"So . . . that's what this team does?"

"No. The NSA already has thousands of hackers, algorithm experts, and mathematicians who work on those problems. We have experts on every operating system and software package out there, teams that invent ways to identify non-randomness, teams that look for ways to knock an order of magnitude or two off of the time it takes to crunch through a trillion keys."

"But not us."

"No. Nothing so banal. We work on messages that *aren't* public key encrypted. That's a very small percentage of the overall traffic. Usually, that means they use some old tried and true method, and can be cracked by a Raspberry Pi with one hand tied behind its back. Occasionally, though, we get messages that aren't encrypted with any recognized variation of obsolete technique, and we can't read them. I'll be honest with you: most of those are never cracked. But we're the team that gets to try."

I couldn't help grinning. "Sounds like just my kind of team."

"It's not glamorous, and it's not all that valued. I have to constantly fight to keep funding. A lot of the messages we wrestle against probably aren't even meaningful at all—just scrambled signals that were encoded wrong or garbled by atmosphere or bad equipment. But every once in a while, we crack something that nobody else could."

"And that's not valued?" I asked.

She blew out a long breath and rubbed the back of her neck. "You have to understand, the vast majority of the messages the NSA intercepts have no intelligence value whatsoever. We go for quantity, not quality, and then try to pick the needles out of the haystack. That means that even when we triumph and crack an indecipherable message, it's just as likely to be somebody's grocery list as it is to be something important."

She was trying to lower my expectations, but it wasn't working. I had dreamed about doing this for so long that nothing she could say would lessen my excitement. I was going to pit my mind against the enemies of the United States, and I was going to win. The shabby facilities, Shaunessy's disapproval, none of it mattered. I worked for the NSA.

"So, welcome to the team," Melody said. "Sorry about the seat. We'll get that replaced, and get you a machine and an account as soon as possible."

"What's the noise?" I asked.

She looked confused. "What noise?"

"That constant humming sound. It's like we're in a wind tunnel."

"Ah." She nodded in comprehension. "I'm so used to it, I don't hear it anymore. Come with me, and I'll show you."

We walked back through the cubicles to the back of the room, to a large wooden door with a keypad. Melody passed her badge over the keypad, which beeped and turned its indicator light from red to orange. She pressed a series of numbers. The light turned green, and a heavy clunk indicated an electromagnetic locking system unlatching. She opened the door, and the whirring sound grew much louder.

We walked through into a cavernous room. I couldn't have been more surprised if the door had led directly to the White House. The ceiling was probably twenty feet high, and we were near the top of it. A flight of stairs led down to the floor. For as far as I could see, there were rows and rows of rack-mounted servers, probably thousands of them. Despite all the heat the machines must generate, the air was frigid.

"The server room," she said. "And this isn't the end. We have a hundred thousand square feet of it. Not nearly enough to crack a single properly encoded message with a 128-bit RSA key, mind you. But give us enough information, and we can launch quite an attack on a lot of things."

There were a few people among the racks, but the room was mostly empty. One person was riding a bicycle down one of the aisles, which seemed like a good idea, given the amount of distance there was to cover. I noticed that the doorway we had come through was significantly thicker than it needed to be and had grooves on both sides. I asked Melody about it.

"There's a steel cage in the wall above the doorway," she said. "In the case of an attack on the building, it and others like it would crash down, blocking the entrances and making it extremely difficult for anyone outside this room to get in."

"And anyone inside to get out," I said.

"Well, yes. But in the unlikely event that this building is successfully breached by an enemy force, you're probably safer locked in here than anywhere else."

I also commented on what looked like a ridiculously large yellow locker marked Emergency. "What are they storing in there, automatic weapons?" I asked.

"I doubt it," Melody said. "But that's NSA bureaucracy at its best. It probably took a committee three months to decide on what to put in that locker, and I'll bet if you actually had an emergency, you'd find it contained every possible thing you could think of, except for the one thing you need."

We retreated to the office, and Melody closed the door, which latched with an audible clunk. "I have to catch a plane to Germany this afternoon," she said. "I'll make sure I get the ball rolling on getting you a machine and an account, but you'll have to get the team to show you the ropes."

That took the smile off my face. "Wait. You're leaving? For how long?"

"Just a week. You'll be fine. It'll take a while for you to learn the organization, the security procedures. You'll have some more mandatory classes to take. The week will go quickly. Just do me a favor."

"What?"

"No more trouble with security. I don't think I could rescue you a third time."

"I'll do my best," I said.

She held my gaze. "I hope your best is good enough. I want you to be here when I get back."

CHAPTER 9

"I can't tell you anything," I said. "Seriously. Come on, you know that."

Paul and I were playing Scrabble again, and surprisingly, he was up on points. He had used all his letters with the near-miraculous word *zugzwang* (using a blank tile for the second Z), which he placed on a double word score for a total of ninety-five points. It was rattling my sense of the balance of the universe, and I was determined to make up the difference.

"I'm your brother," Paul said. "I'm not going to tell anyone."

"It doesn't matter if you're my wife. Dad didn't tell Mom about the programs he worked with, and I can't tell you what I'm doing at Fort Meade."

"At least tell me if the NSA is listening in on my phone calls."

I gave him a look. "Nobody would want to listen to your phone calls. I doubt even Destiny wants to listen to them, but she doesn't have much choice."

It had been a month since Paul's return to the United States, and he was doing fine. Better than fine, in fact. He seemed full of energy, enjoying life to the fullest, and had even started dating a girl named Destiny that he'd met at a local chess club. I had thought it would take longer for him to recover from his ordeal, but apparently what he had learned from the experience was the ability to appreciate the life that he had. It seemed a healthy reaction, and I was glad he was doing so well.

I used Paul's Z to place the word *blitz* for thirty-two points, which brought me to within ten points of his lead. I gave him a smug smile, which vanished as he used my B to place *babirusa*, using all his letters again.

"What's with you today?" I said. "Have you been studying the dictionary or something?"

He raised his hands in an exaggerated shrug. "Maybe you're just slipping. The NSA is scrambling your brain."

"The NSA's the best thing that ever happened to me," I said, more a statement of faith than of certainty. I still barely knew what I was doing, and half the time I got lost trying to get back to my room from the cafeteria.

"Deciphered any messages yet?" he said.

I hadn't, but as I placed the tiles for my next word, I said, "That's classified."

"At least tell me if there are any hot women secret agents."

"Radioactive," I told him. "They breed them in underground labs with an alien dark-energy generator they retrieved from outer space. The ones that don't explode on contact they use as spies to seduce secrets from our enemies."

"I thought that was the CIA," he said.

"Common misconception. The CIA does it old school, with electrodes and a soldering iron."

Paul suddenly winced and touched his temples.

"You okay?"

"Headache. Just the beginning of spring allergies, I think."

"Do you need to lie down?" I never used to worry when my brother had a simple headache, but ever since his collapse at the airport, I had been quick to fear the worst.

"You wish," he said, and placed the word *quisling*, tile by triumphant tile, across two triple word scores.

My humiliating trouncing at the Scrabble board was repeated the next day. In desperation, I suggested chess, usually Paul's game of choice. That turned out even worse, with Paul chasing my pieces across the board with a series of brilliant moves, each of which gave me little choice but to cede him more control of the center of the board. Eventually, he skewered my queen and king with a combination I didn't see coming, and I acknowledged myself beaten.

Despite losing all of the samples he had taken on his Amazon trek, Paul was apparently making great strides with his research, too. He was full of stories about multilocus genotyping and clonal lineage, largely incomprehensible to me but greatly exciting to him.

My time at work, on the other hand, was making me feel like the greatest moron ever to walk the planet. The NSA used more acronyms than they used actual English words, all of them symbols for this or that program, person, country, technology, or division. I felt like I was learning a new dialect of English, one with no dictionary. When I asked for clarification, the answers were usually cluttered with just as many incomprehensible terms as the original statement. I was left with the impression that there was no reason to bother encrypting the NSA's inter-office communications, since no one outside the NSA would understand what they were talking about anyway.

I spent most of my time working with Andrew Shenk, the other man in my cubicle. He was a Spanish speaker and mathematician, who was the team's specialist on South American indecipherables. There had been a recent rash of such messages from Colombia, all of which had a similar signature, but which no one had been able to crack. The messages had been traded between representatives of Colombia's two major guerrilla armies, the FARC (*Fuerzas Armadas Revolucionarias de Colombia*) and the ELN (*Ejército de Liberación Nacional*). The two groups were historically hostile not only to the government but to each other, yet they had recently been working with some degree of cooperation.

I was getting a crash course in Colombian politics, and while I had known of the existence of these two groups—they had been involved in ongoing rebellions and terrorism against their government for decades—I was surprised to learn that they consisted of thousands of well-armed soldiers and dominated significant portions of the country. The Colombian police and military were more or less powerless in FARC- or ELN-controlled territory, where the guerrillas conducted all kinds of illegal activities, including logging and mining in protected regions of the Amazon jungle and the forcible taxation of local farms. Their primary source of funds, however, was the drug trade, supplying the never-ending appetite of the United States and Europe for cocaine.

"Why are we worrying about drugs anyway?" I asked. "Isn't that the FBI's job?"

Andrew looked at me like I was an idiot. He had a great *surprised-at-the-depths-of-my-ignorance* look, and he used it often. "Drugs are money," he said. "Money is power. Keeping track of the balance of power in South America is all about understanding the flow of drugs. More than troops and weapons, even. The FBI tries to slow the torrent of drugs into this country; that's not our concern, at least not directly. But how it affects the balance of power? That's central to what we do."

I was in too deep to pretend I knew what I was talking about, so I decided to dig a little deeper. "What does it matter who is in control of which part of Colombia? One of them gets assassinated, another one takes his place, the FARC gets the upper hand over the ELN for a few months—why do we care? If it affects how the drugs are getting smuggled, then I get that. But it's not like Colombian revolutionaries are going to threaten the sovereignty of the United States."

I was interrupting his work yet again, but he sighed and waved me to roll my chair over to his. He reminded me a bit of my dad, though they looked nothing alike. My dad was tall and thin, with thick hair, while Andrew was short and heavy and mostly bald. Maybe it was just the intense way that he talked about his favorite subjects.

"So. Why do we monitor the world?" Andrew asked.

The question was so fundamental it took me aback. I tried to think of what answer he might be looking for. Because intelligence won wars. Because it was what the NSA did. "Um . . . I guess I thought we needed to be ready for any threats to our interests. So that if we had to fight, we would know what we were up against." As I said it, I realized how that would apply to the drug lords. If it became necessary to fight them, we would want to do so with as little loss of life as possible, and that required precise intelligence of the enemy's intentions and capabilities.

"That's part of it," Andrew said. "But not the whole part. You think you know where the serious threats are. Iran. Russia. China. But it's not always as easy as just taking out a threat. In fact, it never is."

Andrew stretched and leaned back in his chair. "Any time we inter-fere in a foreign situation, we affect change, and change is complicated. It has consequences that are hard to predict. If we weaken one nation in a region, we give a competing nation more power. If we take out one dictator, we enable other factions to take control. Every change has ten-drils that run deep. In order to create the results we want, we need infor-mation. Thorough information, accurate information, about how power flows, what its sources are, and where it will go if we alter the current."

"So . . . Colombian revolutionaries?"

"Part of the picture. It's not just about collecting intelligence in case we have to fight them directly. It's about keeping track of how they fight one another, and making sure none of those thugs ever gets enough power to take over a country or a real military and make itself a threat to its neighbors. That would upset the balance of power, which would make it more likely that we'd have to step in to maintain it. To maintain the balance, however, we need to know who the players are, how much power they have, and where they get it."

"Okay," I said. "So what do you want me to work on first?"

"Doesn't much matter. The best thing is probably to pick a message, crunch on it for a day or two using any method you can think of, and then come back and show me what you've tried. We're all about originality in this group, and these are messages everyone else has given up on. So you can't do any harm."

I chose at random a group of messages from the stack. There were twenty-four in the group, probable text emails traded over the course of three days between members of the FARC in La Uribe and members of the ELN in Quibdó. The messages were thought to be encrypted with the same method due to various mathematical similarities, but there was no way to be sure.

The shortest message was less than a kilobyte; the largest was over twenty. Reasonable sizes for text, but too small for much in the way of images or data. Using tools that Andrew had shown me on my new computer, I set about compiling some basic information about them. Frequency tables, showing how often each letter, number, or other symbol appeared. Bit patterns that repeated with statistically improbable frequency. One tool allowed me to enter guesses at words that might appear in the unciphered message, which it then used to look for matching patterns, much as I had done with my entrance exam. It came with a huge list of significant words—in English, Spanish, Portuguese, and several local languages—that had been previously used in communications by these two groups.

All of this work had been done before, with the results bundled with the files, but I did them again, both to familiarize myself with the tools, and to start to get a sense for the messages themselves. It was tempting to concentrate on the shortest message only, which was small enough that I could print it out on a single sheet of paper and stare at it. I knew, however, that the more text I had, the more likely I would be to find patterns that would help me crack it.

I stayed until almost midnight that night, long after everyone else had gone home. When I finally left, my eyes blurring and my stomach growling for the dinner I had missed, I was not one step closer to finding a solution. It wasn't that I had found no patterns. There were too many patterns, most of them either coincidental or not consistent enough to be helpful.

That night in bed, my restless brain concocted endless arrangements of symbols, their meanings slipping aside every time I tried to look at them. I woke twice, convinced that I had solved the puzzle, only to realize that my brain was playing tricks on me. It was like playing hours of Tetris and then seeing the pieces still spinning endlessly behind my sleeping eyes.

The next day, I thought about pulling a different set of messages, but there seemed little point. A new set was unlikely to be any easier to crack—these were the indecipherables, after all. The trick was to think of ways to approach the problem that I hadn't tried before. Half of my team were software specialists of one type or another, mobilizing banks of servers from the room next door to crunch through tremendous quantities of data. That wasn't my skill set, and never would be, and besides, those avenues were already being explored. I had to get original.

Originality meant thinking out of the box, considering approaches no one had thought of before. I decided to list my most basic assumptions.

- The message is text in a written language.
- The text was written in a standard computing symbol set.
- The message makes sense.

There wasn't much I could do about the last assumption. If the message was random atmospheric noise or a bad transistor, then I was wasting my time. The first one, also, seemed pretty basic. The second assumption was interesting, though—if the message encryption was based on some unusual character encoding, then considering the bytes as message elements might be a mistake.

I spent a few hours with this idea. Any message that came through a computer system was, of course, a series of zeros and ones, but that data was generally turned back into letters and numbers through a standard 8-bit encoding set such as UTF-8. There was no reason a creative person might not use a 5-bit system, for instance, or an 11-bit system. It would be unusual, but it could be done.

By the end of the morning, however, I had discarded this notion.

There were portions of the message that, when ASCII-encoded, had distinct patterns, such as:

5 5 5 6 6 7 7 7 8 8 8 9 9 0 0 : : ; ; = > ? @ B C D C B A ? > = < ;

The sequences ran straight through the ASCII "alphabet" in order, sometimes repeating, sometimes skipping a symbol, but always rising and then falling again. This pretty much clinched that it was an 8-bit encoding scheme, because that pattern couldn't be coincidental. It raised a serious question, however, about the likelihood that this was a message at all. What possible communication could contain steadily rising and falling letters through the alphabet? It just seemed like noise.

One of my goals for the day was to actually eat a meal at the right time, so I took a break and wandered down to the cafeteria. The NSA cafeterias were enormous, serving thousands of people, all of them strangers to me. I went through the line and bought a chicken salad wrap and a lemonade. Looking for a place to sit, I was surprised to see a face I recognized. An Army captain with a USCYBERCOM sleeve patch. It was Scaggs, who had debriefed me after I was arrested for hacking, and he was eating alone.

I put my tray down across from him and sat. "Captain," I said. "Mind if I join you?"

He looked startled to see me, but I couldn't tell if that was surprise at having someone join his table, or surprise at seeing me with an NSA badge. He recovered quickly, though, and offered me his hand. "Mike Scaggs," he said. "Glad to see that was all just a misunderstanding."

"Me, too," I said. "You had me worried."

"Come on, now. I'm not exactly intimidating as an interrogator."

I admitted he wasn't, and we laughed. I took a bite of my wrap, which was surprisingly good for cafeteria food. I had been expecting something closer to what they served at my high school.

"So what's it like working for the Major?" Scaggs asked.

"For who?" I thought he must have me confused with someone else.

"Major Muniz," he said. "The one who rescued you from counterespionage. I thought you must be working for her."

"Oh. I am. She's a major? She's always dressed casually; I thought she was a civilian."

"Ah, no." Scaggs looked embarrassed. "She's a civilian. 'The Major' is just what everyone calls her. It's kind of a nickname. She's pretty well-known around here, has a lot of clout, even with the muckety-mucks up on Mahogany Row."

"I see." I had never heard anyone on her team call her Major. "Why do they call her that?"

Scaggs chuckled. "Uh . . . I'm pretty sure it's short for 'Major Pain in the Ass.' She has a reputation for being tough and stubborn and getting her way most of the time. I guess it's not exactly a compliment, but I think people have called her that for a long time. I've even heard her refer to herself that way."

I nodded, taking all this in. "She's always been pretty nice to me," I said. "Though she's often not around, either off meeting with other people or out of the country."

"I didn't mean to insult her," Scaggs said. "I know some people hate her, but I don't have anything against her."

"No worries."

"I mean, she's been here since forever. She would have been an agent here back during the Cold War. Can you imagine? I'm sure she's hit some serious chauvinism over the years and had to develop a forceful personality to overcome it. They say she once briefed President Nixon."

"Not possible," I said. "Nixon resigned in, what, 1974? That would make her seventy years old, minimum."

Scaggs shrugged. "I know she's turned down retirement. She must be getting up there."

"Besides, people don't brief the president when they're new hires. I barely know my way to the cafeteria."

"Yeah, she was probably a lot smarter than you, though."

I grinned. "I don't know. I bet she didn't hack her way into someone else's account on her first day."

The lemonade was too sour for my tastes. I tore open four sugar packets from the holder on the table and poured them in, ignoring Scaggs's raised eyebrow while I stirred. "How long have you been here?" I asked him.

"Going on ten years, now. Which is unusual—normally us military types get yanked around to a new assignment every two years or so. Just so happens my assignments have all been in this building."

"You like it here?"

"Yeah, pretty well. I remember my first month, though. Turned around every which way, not understanding half of what anybody says to you."

"I've mostly just been staring at messages from South America that are impossible to decipher and failing to decipher them," I said. "Doesn't take much skill, really."

"Those messages from the *Ligados*, then?" Scaggs said.

I frowned. I recognized the word as Portuguese for "connected" or "plugged in" or as a slang expression for "in the know." I wasn't aware of any group of people called the *Ligados*, though. "Who's that?"

"Don't follow the news? It's the terrorist group that took credit for that tourist boat massacre back in February. They apparently hit a nature preserve last night. Left no one alive."

I hadn't heard about that at all. "I've been working a lot. I haven't been watching much of the news."

"I just saw it on CNN last night."

"My brother was on that tourist boat," I said. "He was one of the survivors."

Scaggs gave a long whistle. "Wow," he said. "I'm glad he's okay."

But I wasn't listening to him. The sound of Scaggs's whistle was still playing through my mind. A long, even sound, rising and then falling.

I jumped out of my seat, banging my leg against the table and almost spilling my lemonade. "That's it!" I said.

Scaggs was gaping at me. "Sorry," I said. "Gotta go."

I took off toward the hallway at a jog, leaving my tray and an astonished Scaggs behind me. I reached my desk and crashed into my seat. I mistyped my password twice in my haste, finally taking a deep breath and getting it right the third time.

I brought up the indecipherable. It had to be. I selected several of the phrases with rising and falling letters and graphed them as numbers. They were 8-bit words, but they weren't ASCII-encoded at all. They were musical notes.

I was certain I was right, but even so, it took a lot of time to prove it. An hour later, I was in the NSA library, hunting through their vast linguistics section. It was my first time there, and it was overwhelming, an incredible collection of books on anything an NSA analyst might possibly need to research, including perhaps every book, doctoral thesis, and academic paper written on the study of languages in the world. After a long hunt, and with the help of one of the library staff, I made it back to my desk with a book called *Aspectos da Fonologia do Johurá*, written in Portuguese by an American linguist with an organization called the Summer Institute of Linguistics.

An hour later, I had it. I leaned back in my chair and shouted "Eureka!" as loud as I could. I'd like to say I was just caught up in the moment, but really, I've just always wanted to say that. Watching Shaunessy Brennan jump two inches out of her seat made it all worthwhile.

"What?" she practically snarled.

"I cracked it," I said.

Andrew and Shaunessy and a few of the others gathered around my computer, and I showed them what I'd found. "The message isn't encrypted at all," I said. "Not really. It's an encoding of the sound of a whistle."

"A whistle," Shaunessy said.

"There's a tiny people group living along a tributary of the Amazon called the Johurá," I said. "Maybe three, four hundred people tops, who speak this language that's so weird and difficult to learn that it was decades after they were first discovered before anyone cracked it. It only has three vowels and eight consonants—the fewest phonemes of any language in the world. It's tonal, like Chinese, only more so. The meaning in the language is communicated through tones more than the phonemes themselves. The word for 'one' and the word for 'two' are the same word, only with a different tone. It's all like that."

"And there's a written form of this language?" Andrew said. "You're saying somebody's using it to pass messages like the Navajo Code Talkers?"

"Not quite," I said. "One implication of such a tonal language is that it can be whistled. You can actually communicate effectively without the phonemes at all, just by whistling the tones. A native speaker can infer what the phonemes should be by context. That's what this message is. Johurá whistle talk."

"So?" Shaunessy said. "What does it say?"

"I have no idea," I said. "I don't have enough information. I picked out a few words, enough to be sure I was on the right track, but there's no dictionary."

"Does anybody at the NSA speak the language?"

I chuckled. "*Nobody* speaks this language. A few hundred Johurá along the Maici River, a missionary family that lives with them, and two linguists. Two. In the world."

Andrew shook his head and grinned. "Then I guess we're going to need to find one of them."

CHAPTER 10

Later that evening, when most of the team had gone home for the night, Melody found me and dropped a carton of Kung Pao chicken on my desk. "Brains need food," she said.

The hot chicken smelled delicious, and my stomach growled, reminding me that I hadn't eaten since my abandoned lunch with Captain Scaggs. She handed me a plastic fork, and I dug in, while she sat in Shaunessy's chair and ate from a carton of her own.

"Andrew tells me you cracked one of the Ligados messages," she said.

There was that word again. "Is that who it was from?" I asked. "The Ligados?"

She nodded. "We've been inundated with indecipherables from them. It's starting to be a big deal. They're growing in influence, taking hostages in Colombia and Brazil and demanding responses from their governments. They seem to have a lot of connections to existing groups— FARC, ELN—but we can't pin down who they are. We're intercepting all their messages, but we can't read them. The DIRNSA wants to know what they're saying." The DIRNSA was the Director of the NSA, which she pronounced like a single word, *dernza*. "So do we know what the message says yet?"

"No. I did manage to turn it into sound, though."

I hit play on my computer, and a series of whistles played out over the speakers. "I had to guess at the actual pitches," I said. "I figured a 2000 hertz midpoint and a 100 hertz step between each unique value. It might not be accurate, but it seemed reasonable . . . ish."

"Nice," she said. "If we can find someone who speaks the language, that might be enough for them."

"The problem is, almost nobody speaks this language. It's not taught in any school; there's no alphabet or grammar for it that I've been able to track down. Though my resources are pretty much the library and Google, so if you've got any better ideas, let me know."

"One step ahead of you," Melody said. She lobbed a thick manila envelope at me, which I caught. The label on the front read *Summer Institute of Linguistics*.

"What's this?" I said.

"Research on the Johurá from SIL International. They're stationed in Dallas, so I had an agent from our San Antonio office drive there and fax me everything they had."

I was astonished. San Antonio to Dallas was a five-hour drive. Some poor junior agent had spent all day on the road just to acquire this document and secure fax it to us. Deciphering these messages was apparently more important than I realized. I was also starting to see how "the Major" might have earned her nickname.

"I skimmed what they sent," she said. "There are acoustical graphs of Johurá whistle language covering a range of their vocabulary. Maybe not enough to understand everything, but hopefully something. Have you sorted through any of the other South American indecipherables to see if they use the same code?"

I was embarrassed that it hadn't occurred to me.

"Well," she said. "We've got our work cut out for us tonight."

—⊚—

After an hour of working with her, I thought Melody Muniz was possibly the most brilliant person I had ever met. Her field of expertise was in cognitive computing, which, from what I could gather, meant using insights from the way the human brain was organized to invent new ways of processing data with computers. It was a cross between neurology and computer science, and her explanations of the methods she was using left my mind spinning. It occurred to me that her group might retain its funding not just because of the occasional message it managed to decipher, but because of the groundbreaking research being done by some of its team members.

She put together a program to recognize the basic pattern of the whistle message and set it churning through the thousands of indecipherables to find the ones that matched.

"The problem with computers," she said, "is that they can't forget things. They can't generalize. You recognize my face, not because you have an exact mapping of it in three-dimensions, but because you unconsciously forget all the parts that don't matter and hang on to those tiny bits that do. You couldn't articulate what it is about my face that makes it unique, but your brain knows."

"So forgetting things is good," I said, thinking about my father.

"It's one of the human brain's chief strengths," she said. "There was a man, a research subject, years ago, who couldn't forget anything. Literally anything. He could memorize pages and pages of random numbers, just by reading them once, and then years later—years!—recall them perfectly. He remembered every word that was ever spoken to him in his entire life, along with the date and place and situation. And it was a terrible handicap."

"How is that a handicap?" I asked, amazed.

"He couldn't generalize. You could show him a page with an easy pattern—numbers increasing by threes, for instance. And he couldn't see it. He could recite every number of the page in order, but he couldn't recognize the pattern.

"He had a terrible time with faces, because they were never exactly the same. Seen from a different angle, or with a different expression, or in shadow, they looked different to him. His brain couldn't boil it down to those few, essential, defining characteristics that would allow him to distinguish your face from mine, regardless of the circumstance."

"Still," I said. "Forgetting too much can be a handicap, too."

She sighed and nodded. "I'm sorry about your father. We lost him too early. He had a lot to contribute."

"You knew my father?" I was surprised. Of course, they would have been at the NSA for a lot of the same years, but Fort Meade was a gigantic place. I had assumed that no one I was working with would remember him.

"Yes, I knew him," she said wistfully, in a tone of voice that implied more.

"I never met you, though," I said. "Did you ever visit the house?"

She looked sad. "No. I didn't know him all that well. Just by reputation, as a colleague. A talented one."

A thought struck me. "That's not why you offered me a job, is it? Because of my father?"

She shrugged. "It was what I first noticed about your resume. But that wouldn't have been enough, by itself. I need people who can think outside of the box, and you seemed to be that sort of person. Like him."

It made sense, then. Her willingness to make me an offer, despite my lack of a degree, and then sticking out her neck to defend me when I was arrested. It was because of my father.

While her search program was running, we worked on deciphering the whistle message. With the data from SIL, we could match graphs of the frequency distribution of certain whistled "words" with their meanings. It was tedious and far from comprehensive, but it worked. Sort of. A little past eleven o'clock, we had a rough English translation.

MANY BOW SHOT [indecipherable]
THE CROOKED HEADS UPRIVER COME

"Hmm," Melody said.

I sighed. "Doesn't make much sense, does it?"

"We're probably missing some nuances. We're going to need linguistic help before this is over, if we can get it. In the meantime, we'll do the best we can."

"What I don't understand," I said, "is how this language is being used as a code at all. This is a primitive group of people. They hunt and fish and canoe on the river. They don't have computers or cell phones, or even electricity or running water. The concepts that can even be expressed in their language are very limited. They can't do math; they don't even have words for numbers higher than two! So who is using this code to communicate? Not the Johurá, that's for sure."

"Surely there are tribespeople who leave the tribe," she said. "Sail down the river, learn Portuguese, join a different community."

"I guess there must be. But how many? Five? We're talking about a people group of four hundred members here. All of the characteristics that make this difficult for us to translate—its difficulty, its rareness— would make any kind of widespread use as a code impossible. I suppose the Ligados could have two wandering Johurá, and are using them to communicate between two locations."

Before going home, we checked the results of Melody's program. Thousands of indecipherables, most of them recent, had been flagged as probable whistle messages. "Incredible," Melody said. "You may have found the motherlode. We'll have to get Shaunessy in on this tomorrow."

"Why Shaunessy?" I asked.

"Programming skills," she said. "I've got the cognitive theory, and I can muddle about, but for any serious Java work, we need somebody with the right experience. This is far too much to translate by hand, and we're going to need a specially written program to do most of the translation for us, preferably one that can distribute the work over hundreds of servers to get it done fast. Shaunessy's the master at that kind of thing."

"Okay," I said. "I'll see you in the morning."

—⌀—

But I didn't see her in the morning. Her office was empty, and when I finally asked, Andrew said she was taking a personal day. "But I saw her late last night, and she didn't say anything about that," I said.

Andrew just shrugged. "She called this morning. Personal day. She'll be back in tomorrow."

I did my best to explain to Shaunessy what Melody and I had discovered the night before, and what Melody wanted her to do. We worked on it together, me showing her how to match up the frequency distributions in the SIL material to the whistled words in the messages, and her whipping up some software to automate the translation.

"I'm amazed by you guys," I said. "You, Andrew, everybody. Knocking out sophisticated software like it's as easy as breathing. It's awesome to be here."

Shaunessy gave me a lopsided smile. "As long as you pay proper homage, we may deign to grant you the occasional boon."

I grinned. I liked her better without the chip on her shoulder. "I live to sit in the dust at your feet," I said. "But seriously. This team kicks ass."

"Seriously back at you. Nice job on this one." She shook her head. "Whistle language. That's something else."

—⊘—

Despite the supposed personal day, Melody did show up in the office just after lunch. I peeked into her office and found her rummaging through papers in her safe.

"Not now, Neil," she said. "I'm not really here."

"Is everything okay?"

"It's nothing. A personal crisis. There's just one thing I need to do, and then I'm leaving again."

"If there's anything I can do to help . . ."

"There's nothing, but thank you."

"Will you be in tomorrow?"

"Yes. I hope so. I think I will."

I backed out of her office, troubled, but knowing it was none of my concern. She wasn't a friend, not really, and I had no business pushing my nose into her life.

I went back to my cubicle. "Melody seems out of sorts," I said. "Did something happen?"

Shaunessy shrugged. "Don't know. Probably something we're not cleared for."

"Seemed more like a personal thing," I said.

"In which case, none of our business. She'll tell us if she wants us to know."

I knew Shaunessy was right. But I had trouble letting it go. A genetic deficiency, as I said. So I logged on to the unclassified network and searched for her name on Google. It wasn't hard to piece together her personal information: husband, deceased, of a stroke two years before. Two children: one son in the Navy and one daughter married with three kids of her own. Member of Women in Technology International. And then I saw it. A news article from that day's *Washington Post* that referenced Emily Muniz, Melody's oldest granddaughter.

The article was titled "Steroids for School. Why Smart Kids Are Turning to Drugs." It described a brand-new drug flooding the illegal market called Neuritol, which was supposed to enhance brain function and memory. It apparently went a step beyond classic nootropic supplements like Piracetam or Aniracetam, both in terms of the clarity of the enhancement experience and the potentially harmful side effects. Emily Muniz had bought the drug from another high schooler, packaged in a repurposed albuterol inhaler, and then had been admitted to Baltimore Washington Medical Center when she lost consciousness during a math test. As of the writing of the article—early that morning—her survival was still uncertain.

I checked Melody's office, but she was gone. Back at my desk, I stared at the screen, the words drifting out of focus. Shaunessy had been right. Now I knew what was going on, but there was nothing I could do about it. Annoyed at myself and feeling guilty for my nosiness, I threw myself back into my work. Shaunessy's software was running well now, leaving me plenty of semi-translated messages to sift through.

VILLAGE WITH STRONG DAUGHTER HOUSES FOR
MANY GUNS IN TWO DAYS GIVES [indecipherable]
WHEN RAIN BEGINS

[indecipherable] COMING TO HUNT WITH [indecipherable]
AFTER THE CHILDREN DOGS ANTS COCKROACHES
PALM STICKS LEAVE RIVER TO TRADE NAMES WITH
JUNGLE SPIRIT AND DRINK MUCH WHISKEY

They still weren't making much sense, but I hoped that with more volume, we would start to get enough context that some kind of meaning would become clear. If not, we would have to find one of the few linguists who understood the language and work out some kind of temporary security clearance to allow them to translate the messages.

Around dinnertime, Shaunessy opened up a container and the sharp smell of Thai food wafted through the office. "Smells delicious," I said. "Where did you get that?"

"I ordered it from the cafeteria. They deliver."

"Wow. You can do that?"

"Sure. They can't really have you ordering pizza or whatever from outside the complex. There are thousands of people living here, though, and thousands more working late. The solution is in-house takeout." She held up the container. "The guy who makes it was a CIA informant in Thailand for a decade before they pulled him out."

Twenty minutes later, I was digging into my own container of Chicken Kao Phad.

"So what's it like to be following in your father's footsteps?" Shaunessy asked. "All those years, he couldn't tell you the secret things he did at his job, and now you work here, too."

"It's bittersweet, actually," I said. "I always wanted to be like my dad. But he has Alzheimer's. He'll never really know."

"Wow, that's rough. I'm sorry."

"He was my hero, especially after my mom left. Paul always took Mom's side. He went the academic route, got a doctorate—he even works at the University of Maryland, just like Mom did."

"She was a professor, then? Your mom?"

"Astrophysicist. She still teaches some classes at UMD, though she cut her hours way back to help take care of Dad."

Shaunessy used a napkin to wipe a stray piece of noodle off her chin. "I thought you said they were separated."

"Yeah." I waved a hand vaguely. "It's complicated."

"Sorry. I shouldn't pry."

"No, it doesn't matter. It's old news. My dad was stationed in Brazil when I was five and Paul was six. Mom had her career, teaching high-energy astrophysics, doing research into neutron stars and black holes. She didn't want to leave the US."

"And your dad just went without her?"

"That's what Paul would say, but it wasn't like that. Originally, she was going to come along. They made all the plans for relocating together. When it came to handing in her notice, though, she couldn't do it. She said she just had some things to finish up for the summer, and then she'd join us. Only she never did." I shrugged. "She might tell the story differently, though. I don't know."

"How much do you remember?"

"Oh, I remember it all, at least what I could see and understand at the time. Five years old is old enough to hold onto something like that. I hated her for a while. And I hated Paul for defending her."

"How long were you in Brazil?"

I stirred my rice. "You saw my resume. Ten years, near enough. Only, about three years in, suddenly Mom showed up in Brazil. She had worked out some kind of co-research arrangement with Pico dos Dias, a big observatory in Minas Gerais, more than a twelve-hour drive from Brasília. She visited every other weekend for three years, and then she was gone again, back to the States."

"Sounds pretty rough," Shaunessy said.

I looked for a trashcan to toss my empty food container. Some kind of green initiative in the NSA had swapped all the normal office trashcans for divided ones with a large compartment for recyclables and a tiny one for other trash. The foam carton didn't fit, so I broke it up into tiny pieces and inserted them one by one.

"So your mom takes care of your dad now?" Shaunessy asked.

"She does a lot of it. We all pitch in, though I've been helping a lot less since I started working here." I felt a twinge of guilt at that. Before I started at the NSA, I had spent more time with him than anyone. "Have you ever known someone with Alzheimer's?" I asked.

She shook her head.

"It's like going through early childhood again, but backward," I said. "I don't just mean losing mental function. Alzheimer's actually follows the same myelinization paths in reverse, eroding your brain centers in the reverse order that they develop in early childhood. You lose the ability to form long-term memory first—one of the last things you develop as a child. Then you start losing vocabulary and sentence structure. You can't handle finances or pick appropriate clothes to wear. You lose the ability to use the bathroom or walk or speak at all. By the end, you can't even smile or hold up your head. It's like reverting back to infancy." I found there were tears standing in my eyes. "And there's nothing that anybody can do to stop it."

—⟳—

I was the only one still at work late that evening when Melody returned to the office. "How's the whistle translation going?" she asked. She looked tired and worn.

"Fine," I said. "Lots of translated words, not much understanding."

"I found a linguist," Melody said. "Katherine Wyatt, a retired Christian missionary. She and her husband were the first outsiders to crack the

Johurá language, almost forty years ago. I'm flying her in from Massachusetts tomorrow."

I was amazed. Her granddaughter might be dying, and she still found the time to track down a linguist who was probably the only person in the United States who could translate our messages. And made travel arrangements.

I hesitated before speaking. "I'm sorry about Emily," I said.

Melody seemed to physically collapse in on herself. Her professional demeanor crumpled, and she sank into Shaunessy's chair. "I don't know what she was thinking," she said.

"It's tough sometimes, being a kid. Trying to measure up."

"It's my fault, really," Melody said.

"Yours?" It seemed unlikely. I didn't think Melody was out buying her granddaughter illegal drugs.

"I pushed her mother too hard into science and math. She dropped out of college instead and did her own thing. But now she's pushing her own kids the same way. Emily's bright, gets top grades, and her mom wants her to go to an Ivy League school. It's a lot of pressure."

"Is she going to be okay?" I asked.

Melody nodded once. "I think so. I was just at the hospital, and they say she's going to pull through."

"Good news," I said.

Melody shook her head and didn't answer.

"You should get some sleep," I said.

I made it home before eight o'clock—the earliest that week—and joined my dad and Paul for a game of Scrabble. Halfway through the game, my dad fell asleep in his chair, and Paul and I finished up without him. As usual since his return from Brazil, Paul trounced me. I would have said I was losing my touch, but the truth was, I thought I was playing as well as I ever had. It didn't stop Paul from beating me every time.

"You wouldn't believe the breakthroughs I'm making at the lab," Paul said. "We're talking Nobel Prize–level discoveries."

I laughed, not sure how seriously to take him. "Has there ever been a Nobel Prize awarded for fungus?"

"Sure. 1945. Sir Alexander Fleming. For penicillin."

"Penicillin is a fungus?"

"Of course. It's a mold. Molds are fungi."

"I see. So you're working on the next penicillin."

He grinned, and his eyes sparkled. "That would be telling."

"Come on! I'm your brother."

He shook his head. "Nope."

"Have you told *anyone*?"

"Not yet. Not until I publish."

"When will that be?"

"These things take time. A year, maybe."

"Fine," I said. "I'm not telling you what I'm working on either. It's Top Secret. So there."

He did tell me about Destiny, at greater length than I really wanted to know. I told him about my coworkers, relating stories about their personal quirks or funny things that had been said. I also told him about Melody's granddaughter and the Neuritol she had overdosed on.

"I actually think those drugs should be legalized," Paul said. "If a drug can make you think more clearly or remember things better, then why not? It just makes sense. If she was taking it with her parents' knowledge, and with a doctor's prescription, she'd be much less likely to overdose."

"There's a reason it's illegal," I said. "Any drug that can seriously alter your brain chemistry is pretty scary stuff. It's not the same as blocking pain or lowering blood pressure. Drugs like that can change your personality, your state of mind, your sense of ethics. I wouldn't want my daughter using it."

"What if there was a drug that could cure Alzheimer's? Would you want Dad to take it?"

I rolled my eyes, annoyed. "Of course."

"That would be brain altering. So why not a drug to make you smarter?"

"It's not the same thing. Dad has nothing to lose, for one thing. Brain drugs can have serious side effects. As Emily found out."

Paul shrugged. "All drugs have potential side effects. It's a matter of weighing the risk against the potential gain."

"And Emily doesn't need to be smarter. She's a bright kid, top of her class. She shouldn't be pressured into altering herself chemically to reach some idealized standard."

"Alter herself chemically? You make it sound like a science experiment gone wrong. Every time you drink a Coke, you alter yourself chemically."

I folded my arms. "Taking Neuritol is not like drinking a Coke."

"Nope. It's a whole lot more helpful, and for a lot longer. Don't be so timid. It's a survival-of-the-fittest kind of world out there, and it's not like humanity has reached the apex of possible evolution. If we can improve ourselves, we should do it."

CHAPTER 11

The next morning, Katherine Wyatt landed at Baltimore/Washington International airport and rode in an NSA security SUV the two miles to FANX III, where we met her in a secure conference room. She was seventy-five years old, a bit stooped, with thinning white hair and a mottled face that sagged with loose skin. Her eyes, however, regarded me with a bright intelligence.

From my research, I knew that she had spent thirty years among the Johurá with her husband and three children. Her husband had died ten years earlier, and, of her children, two were now foreign missionaries themselves and one was a pastor somewhere in New England. Mrs. Wyatt agreed to keep confidential anything she might learn from the messages she helped us translate and signed a document to that effect. I'm not sure what we would have done if she had refused.

"Mrs. Wyatt," Melody said. "Thank you for coming to help us."

"Please, call me Katherine."

"Katherine, then. Welcome."

"Never seen the inside of the NSA," Katherine said. "It's a bit of an adventure."

It still seemed like an adventure to me, too, though I was surprised to hear that opinion from a woman who had spent decades living in the Amazon without the most basic of modern amenities.

Melody and I sat across the table from her. "We have some messages that we intercepted from the Johurá," Melody said. "Naturally, we've had some difficulty in translating them. Are you ready to start? Do you need a drink of water, or some coffee?"

"I'm fine," she said. "But I haven't decided yet if I will be translating any messages for you."

Melody's eyebrows rose.

I gaped. "We flew you all the way down here!" I said. "What did you think that was for, to give you a tour? This is a matter of national security!"

I stopped my rant when Melody put a hand on my arm. "You are under no obligation," she said. "But can I ask, what makes you hesitate?"

And why did you agree to come if you weren't going to help? I wanted to say, but didn't.

"The Johurá are a complex people, in their own way," Katherine said. "But they have no understanding of the world outside their villages. They are no threat to the United States. They can barely conceive of it as a place. It's about as real to them as heaven, and considerably less real than the spirit world. I can only assume that the NSA's interest in them is misplaced, or else exploitative." She smiled apologetically.

"I gave the best part of my life to the Johurá. Though I only visit them once a year now, they are probably the closest friends I have. I doubt the language you are intercepting is Johurá at all, since they don't transmit messages or use phones or computers of any kind, and if they did, they would have no one to talk to. And even then, I wouldn't translate them for you, since I can see no value in making the private messages of my friends—messages that could have nothing to do with you—available for scrutiny by Americans who would have no context by which to understand them."

Her diction was precise, her speech carefully structured. Melody smiled warmly. "The language is Johurá," she said. "There's little doubt of that. And I agree that the Johurá are unlikely to transmit any messages of their own free will."

She let the implications of that hang in the quiet room. Katherine's expression grew fierce. "So you think . . ."

Melody nodded. "The most likely explanation is that several Johurá are being coerced into using their unique language to pass messages for another group, probably a drug cartel."

"It's not so easy as that," Katherine said. "Their language isn't easy to translate, and the Johurá don't know or care about things outside of their experience. Ask a Johurá to pass a message for you, and you might not recognize what came out the other side."

"There's one way to find out," I said, but shut up again when Melody glared at me.

Katherine Wyatt was silent a long time, considering. I was actually starting to wonder if she had fallen asleep or was having some kind of medical crisis, when she said, "All right. Play the messages, and I'll see what I can do. But if I get the first inkling that you're playing me, or using this information to harm the tribe, then we're done."

Melody showed no expression. She gestured to me to play the first of the intercepted communications. She listened, and I showed her my attempt at a translation.

MANY BOW SHOT [indecipherable]
THE CROOKED HEADS UPRIVER COME

Katherine laughed. "Harder than it looks, isn't it?"

I felt a little insulted. I had done pretty well, I thought, given the circumstances.

"Can you help us?" Melody asked.

"Play the message again."

I played it, and Katherine cocked her head, listening intently. It was a short passage, and when it was done, she whistled it softly to herself in a lower register. "Not bad," she said. "You had most of the words, just not the sense of it. The first part is a measure of distance. The speaker is saying that the event he's telling about happened several miles away. It's a loose term, which can mean all sorts of distances, but they would use it for distances they can't communicate over—and a Johurá whistle can be heard clearly up to a mile away. It would also be a distance small enough for them to travel during a hunt, since any distance farther than that is just 'far away' to them.

"The part you couldn't decipher is their word for a type of boat. Then the 'crooked heads'"—here she grinned in amusement again—"is actually the term for foreigner. The word they use for themselves comes from the word for a straight line. They're the people who have their heads on straight. The other people—the rare people from outside their culture that they sometimes encounter—are a bit crazy, crooked in the head. That's the root of their word for foreigner."

"So the real message is something like, 'Several miles away, some foreigners are coming up the river in a particular kind of boat,'" I said.

"That's it," Katherine said.

"Is there any indication of where exactly the foreigners are?" Melody asked. "Which river? What location? Which direction they're moving? Or even what kind of foreigners?"

"There's none of that," Katherine said. "Johurá don't talk in those kinds of particulars, and their language can't really carry that information. It's part of why this doesn't make any sense."

"Can you tell anything from the message about the Johurá who sent it?"

Katherine leaned back in her seat. "No Johurá sent this message."

"What do you mean?" Melody asked.

"The concepts it expresses . . . no Johurá would speak that way. For instance, the speaker used the phrase '*xaoói piiboó xaaboópaitahásibiga.*'" Here an incredible sound came out of Katherine's mouth that didn't sound like a language to me at all. It was the first time I had heard the language spoken instead of whistled, and it sounded like a cross between a cough and bird song. "That's the second half of the message, about foreigners coming up the river. But the verb construction indicates that the speaker witnessed it happening. Johurá verbs are very complicated, with different forms indicating complex shades of meaning. In this case, however, it's the *wrong* verb form, since in the previous portion, the speaker stated that this was happening many miles away. So he couldn't have witnessed it."

"Could there be a camera involved?" Melody asked. "If the Johurá was looking at a feed from a camera showing this movement on the river, then he could have witnessed . . ."

Katherine shook her head before Melody finished speaking. "He wouldn't see it that way. A camera, if he even recognized what it was, wouldn't count as witnessing an event. He would say *xaaboópatíixísa*, witnessed through a spirit, or maybe *xaaboópai*, stating the coming of foreigners as a fact, without indicating how the knowledge was come by at all."

"So what are you implying?" I asked. "That a non-native speaker has learned Johurá well enough to whistle it, but not well enough to use the right verb construction?"

She shrugged. "I'm not implying anything. There are maybe twenty non-native people who speak this language at all, and most of them speak only a few words, so they can trade metal tools or whiskey to them. The only people outside of the tribe with this level of facility are myself and my children, and we would not make this mistake any more than a native would. Besides, I would recognize my children's voices."

I couldn't help myself. "But it's just whistling. How could you recognize their voices?"

Her aging face creased, and she gave me a devastating look, probably the same look of disapproval that had kept her children in line while she was raising them in a jungle village. I recalled that telegraph operators could often recognize each other from the way they tapped out Morse code, and let the matter drop.

"Katherine, this is great information," Melody said. "If you're willing, we'd like to go through as many of these as possible and have you translate them. And any insights you can add about unusual usage or shades of meaning would be very welcome."

Katherine's face was intent. "I'm trusting you," she said. "I don't know if I should, but there's something wrong here. Something is happening to these people that I don't understand. Something that shouldn't be possible. If they're being used or manipulated, and you can do something about it, then you have my full support."

—⊙—

With Katherine Wyatt's help over the following days, we started to put together a picture, though that picture did little to shed light on the mystery of the Johurá. The FARC and the ELN were mixing to an unprecedented degree, sharing resources and jointly occupying territory previously disputed between them. They were also in communication—using the same Johurá whistle code—with *Sendero Luminoso*, or "Shining Path," an old Maoist guerrilla faction in Peru deeply involved with the cocaine trade.

This level of collaboration was unprecedented, but not inconceivable. All three groups had decades of revolutionary activity tied originally to communism, and all funded their operations through a stranglehold on local drug trafficking. That they might be working together was a concern, but it made some sense, in the same way the American Mafia might forge a working relationship with Mexican drug cartels.

The mystifying part of it was how the Johurá fit in. These groups all operated on the edges of the Amazon jungle, but that was like saying Los Angeles and Hong Kong both shared an ocean. The sparsely populated Maici River basin, where the Johurá lived, had roughly the land area of France, and it was located in the state of Rondônia in Brazil, nowhere near Colombia or Peru. The guerrilla groups weren't exactly close to each other either, but they were separated from the Johurá by what would be a two-hour plane flight over a thousand kilometers of the most trackless and unexplored jungle in the world. How was it possible that these terrorist organizations were using such an obscure language to communicate?

Melody's superiors didn't care much about how the messages were encoded; they just cared about the political implications of the information we were deciphering. The operation grew bigger than just our little group, as whole divisions of the NSA concerned with South America—

not to mention their counterparts in the CIA—added their opinions and analyses to the growing pile of intelligence. We were rapidly sidelined, since the messages were no longer indecipherables. Two linguists began studying Johurá with Katherine Wyatt, and I didn't see her anymore.

But I couldn't let the question go. Even as I moved on to other indecipherable messages, my mind worried at it. What set of circumstances could possibly explain how three groups of guerrillas in Colombia and Peru started communicating with a language from one of the most isolated tribes in Brazil? The messages also shared the characteristic of a lack of precision. Distances and places were vague, groups of people unidentified, numbers of any kind almost non-existent. It was driving the analysts crazy. It also implied that the guerrillas had some other means of communicating that type of information, since without it, the messages appeared almost worthless.

Even so, I was feeling pretty proud of myself for kicking off such a furor. We had a front row seat to unfolding world events because of my work. I had complete confidence that the NSA machine would uncover the secret agendas of the guerrillas and know what to do in response. This was the NSA, after all. The largest and most well-funded intelligence agency in the world.

A week later, on the same day, and with no warning despite all our efforts, the presidents of both Colombia and Peru were assassinated.

CHAPTER 12

Multiple terrorist organizations claimed responsibility for the attacks, including the Ligados, the group associated with the attack on Paul's boat in Brazil. It was starting to seem like everything was connected—the presence of armed guerrillas raiding tourist boats on a previously peaceful stretch of the Amazon, the increased activity of FARC and ELN and their communications with Shining Path, and now the assassinations of two South American leaders. Something big was happening, and we were only scratching the surface.

"Listen to this," Shaunessy said. She pressed play on a video on her unclassified computer, and the president of Venezuela appeared on an outdoor stage surrounded by serious-looking military types and Venezuelan flags. He was a large, intimidating figure, and he shook a meaty finger as he spoke.

"Venezuela applauds the brave actions of these freedom fighters," he said. He spoke in Spanish, but I could understand well enough. "It is never easy for the poor to throw off the rule of their Fascist overlords. We call for the people of Colombia and Peru to insist on fair elections and resist the right-wing extremists who have controlled them for so long. Heroes like the soldiers of Fuerzas Armadas Revolucionarias de Colombia light the path for free people everywhere."

"Wow," I said.

"That's a first," Andrew said from over my shoulder. "Colombia has been accusing Venezuela of supporting FARC for decades, but they've always denied it before."

"What does this mean?" I asked. "War?"

Andrew dropped back into his swivel chair, which creaked in protest. "Hard to say. For us, it means we'd better figure out what's actually going on down there before someone up on Mahogany Row—or heaven forbid, the White House—starts demanding answers."

Melody appeared around the corner. The wrinkles around her eyes were pinched, and her normally neat hair flew out behind her. "Follow me, right now," she said. "The DIRNSA wants us in his office."

Andrew and Shaunessy and I looked at each other. "Who does he want?" I asked.

"Me, actually. But I want the rest of you there with me."

—⟨∞⟩—

NSA director Mark Kilpatrick was an Air Force four-star general who had made his career in the intelligence services. He was only fifty years old and looked younger, tall and athletic enough to play basketball in his immaculate and heavily decorated uniform. His expression was grave. He addressed Melody without waiting for introductions to the rest of us.

"Harvin says you know something."

"That may be overstating it."

"Well? Don't make me beg."

Melody summed up our knowledge in short, declarative sentences, sticking only to the facts. Kilpatrick cut her off regularly to ask new questions, which she took in stride without a hint of annoyance. I watched them like it was a tennis match, words bouncing rapidly between them, and then it was over. We were out the door before I realized we were leaving.

"Whew," Shaunessy said. "Another first."

"You've never been in his office before?"

"I've never even been on this floor."

We regrouped back in our room. "This is serious stuff," Melody said. "The government of Colombia is asking where the United States will stand if Venezuela invades them. FARC demonstrations have tripled around the country, and several major highways have been shut down with landmines. FARC is apparently seeing this as their chance to seize control."

DAVID WALTON

"What are their chances, realistically?" I asked. "The Colombian military hasn't been able to shut them down, but the government still has the far superior force, right?"

"You'll have to ask the CIA for the over-under on that one," Melody said. "Our job is to figure out who's pulling the strings and what their end game is. That was an incredibly coordinated attack. From now on, the term Ligados is our official umbrella name for these people, whoever they turn out to be. My money says the messages in Johurá we've been cracking are directly related. But there are an awful lot of questions we can't answer."

"How were the assassinations accomplished?" Shaunessy asked. "Do we know?"

"The investigation is ongoing by the national police in both countries, but in both cases, it looks like top, trusted staffers strapped bombs underneath their clothing and suicided. Complicit security personnel who enabled them to avoid electronic detection have since disappeared. The plots were carefully planned and remarkably similar. The real mystery is how the Ligados managed to compromise high-ranking, carefully vetted people in *both* governments. It's not like they haven't dealt with threats like this before."

We worked late into the night again. Around eight o'clock, team members started to leave, and by ten Melody and I were once again the only people left in the room. She stopped by my desk and dropped a clipped stack of paper next to my keyboard. For an organization with so many computers, the NSA sure killed a lot of trees, and Melody was one of the worst offenders. "Take a look when you get a chance," she said. "It's a media analysis one of the data mining teams put together."

I picked up the bundle and paged through it. It was a collection of news stories from multiple countries, mostly in Spanish or Portuguese, many of them from small city newspapers located in the Amazon basin. I picked one out at random.

"Genius of the Amazon," the title read in Portuguese. It went on to describe a Sateré-Mawé tribesman who had walked out of the jungle and

121

showed genius-level aptitude in mathematics and, after learning Portuguese in a matter of days, tested with an IQ of 180. He appeared to be in his forties (he didn't know his precise age) and had spent his life until then hunting in bare feet and growing guarana.

The article was sensationalistic, and I doubted a number of its claims. I paged through the others, and found that they were similar, differing wildly in location and details but with the same basic concept: native with no formal education demonstrates astonishing intellect. Individually, they could be dismissed. As a group, they held some weight.

"What's the relevance to our assassinations?" I asked.

Melody shrugged, a tired, barely noticeable movement. "Maybe none. But given our impossible Johurá code talkers, I'm inclined to keep it in mind."

I waved the stack of papers. "Has anyone mapped these?"

"Not yet."

"You go ahead and get some sleep. I'll map them, and we can talk about it in the morning."

She shook her head and sank into the seat next to me. "It'll go twice as fast with two. I'll sleep next year."

We used an in-house version of Google Earth, one that was hosted somewhere in the vast server farm that adjoined our basement room. The surface of the globe was covered not just with the imagery Google acquired from commercial satellites, but with classified imagery as well. The National Geospatial-Intelligence Agency kept it current, and anyone in the NSA could link their own time- and date-stamped intelligence to it as well. As a result, you could zoom in on any part of the world and find images and links to practically everything the NSA knew about what was going on in that part of the world.

It wasn't perfect. Some groups didn't bother to link their data to it, while other groups inundated it with irrelevant or inaccurate information. On the whole, though, it was the coolest piece of software I had ever played with. The top-secret world at my fingertips.

For the next hour, we tagged the stories in the packet to the locations on the globe where they had happened, along with the date and time, when it was available. If the nationality or origin of the indigenous person was known, then we tracked them back to the village they had come from. By the time we worked through the whole stack, a picture had emerged.

On the globe, oriented to show the whole Amazon region, a pattern of dots and lines radiated outward. The earliest stories came from logging camps or other towns embedded in the rainforest. The natives who would later show dramatic signs of intelligence were, at that point, still living in their villages as members of the Ocaina, the Ticuna, the Culina, the Sharanahua, the Nukuini, the Poyanawa, and the Asheninca-Kampa. All of these were deep jungle tribes, far from civilization, near the border of Brazil and Peru.

As time passed, members of those tribes started appearing in towns and cities, and the progression of the stories proceeded outward toward the outskirts of the Amazon. The first stories of the Ligados killings and abductions came after that, followed by increased guerrilla activity in Colombia and Peru and the Johurá communications between FARC, ELN, and Shining Path.

"It's spreading," I said. "Moving outward from a central location."

That central location was hard to pin down with very much accuracy, but it seemed to be coming from the Maici River basin, home of the Johurá and one of the most unexplored and hard to reach territories in the world. The globe just turned green in those areas, thick jungle into which the cameras of satellites and drones could shed no light.

It was midnight. I yawned, and Melody did, too. "Good work," she said. "We'll pick it up tomorrow."

We walked out together, my mind still spinning with the implications of the data. Something had apparently happened to drive all those indigenous people out of their villages and into towns and cities, where they displayed sudden and unexpected intellectual prowess. Had that genius been there all along, waiting for an opportunity to show itself? Or had something happened to alter them?

We stepped through the metal detector and out into the parking lot. The night was cool and crisp, and stars spread across the sky. I spotted Venus just over the horizon to the west. Another line of lights stretching into the distance came from the planes queued up to land at Baltimore/ Washington International.

"How's your granddaughter?" I asked.

"She seems to be doing okay." Melody shook her head. "I wish I had more time to talk with her. To tell her she doesn't need drugs to succeed. Though she probably wouldn't listen to me anyway."

"No lasting side effects from the overdose?"

She shook her head. "In fact, she took her Advanced Placement exams this week. Six of them."

I drove home to my father's house, thinking of Paul's ordeal in the Amazon. The spot where his boat had been hijacked was nine hundred kilometers away from the Maici River valley, which fit with the timeline of the spread of intelligent-tribesman stories. An image popped into my head of Paul triumphantly laying down the letters for *zugzwang* on the Scrabble board, followed by all of the games he had won handily since he had come home from the hospital.

Gravel crunched as I pulled into the driveway. My parents would both be asleep by now, so I was surprised to see a light coming from the first floor. Paul had long since moved back to his apartment near the University of Maryland, and I hadn't seen him for a week.

I swung the door open and closed it quietly behind me, then followed the dim lights toward the back porch. Paul sat in a wicker chair with a laptop perched on his knees, typing rapidly. A table lamp shone dimly through a yellow shade, but the white glare of the screen on Paul's face was the brightest thing in the room. I sank into an upholstered chair and watched him.

"Working late, or playing chess online?"

Paul startled, nearly dropping the laptop.

I laughed. "Didn't you see me come in?"

"I was concentrating." He continued to peer at the laptop and pecked at a few keys.

"Why are you here?" I asked.

"I wanted to visit Dad. Make sure he was doing okay. Mom says you're never here anymore."

"I've been working pretty late. There's a lot to do."

Paul didn't answer, just kept typing.

"How are you feeling, Paul?"

He closed the laptop and studied me suspiciously. "What do you mean?"

"Breathing okay? Sleeping well? Experiencing anything odd?"

"I'm fine."

"Have you been taking your antifungals?"

"No, as a matter of fact, I haven't."

I made a frustrated noise. "You're supposed to keep taking them. For three years, they said. The infection could come back."

"Do I seem sick to you?"

"It's not a matter of feeling sick. You don't want to mess around with this stuff. If it comes back, it'll be a lot harder to treat."

"I'm fine. Why the third degree?"

"Well, there were all those fungal infection cases in Pará."

"You've known about that for weeks. There's something else." He studied me. "Something at work. You discovered something that made you concerned about me."

His perceptiveness gave me a chill. Was this just normal intuition? Or something else? "There have been news cases of indigenous people, uneducated people, doing brilliantly in math all of a sudden, or learning new languages in a week. A few of them are involved in some pretty bad stuff, willingly or not, I can't tell. The people who attacked you are probably part of it."

"And you think, what? That I'm involved with . . . ah." He smiled and nodded to himself. "The Scrabble games."

I felt some heat rise to my face. "Not to be arrogant or anything," I said, "but I always used to crush you at that game."

"So you think that if I get the better of you at Scrabble, I must be involved in some international conspiracy?"

I paused. "Paul? What are you working on in your lab?"

CHAPTER 13

Paul's mycology lab operated as part of the University of Maryland, located inside the notoriously traffic-heavy Washington, DC, beltway. We took the train to the College Park station, which dropped us only a few minutes' walk from his building.

"You have to promise not to tell anyone what I show you," he said, for what seemed like the tenth time.

"I've got it," I said. "I told you I wouldn't, and I won't. I don't want to tell your secrets. I just want to know you're okay."

He laughed, though it sounded a little forced to me. "I'm better than okay," he said.

The lab was in the Plant Sciences building, a newly built red-brick facility with white trim. I smirked at the "Plant Sciences" sign, remembering various times Paul had complained that Fungi was a kingdom in its own right, with over a hundred thousand distinct species, and deserved a building of its own.

Paul let us in with his ID card, a security check that seemed ludicrously minimal now that I was accustomed to daily trips in and out of Fort Meade. The painted cinderblock halls echoed like my memories of high school. He unlocked a door labeled Chaverri Mycology Lab, and I followed him in.

It was antiseptically neat. Microscopes stood aligned on the table with laser precision, at right angles to the computers, which were as white and clean as everything else in the lab. Rows of small plastic drawers decorated the counters, each meticulously labeled, behind Bunsen burners and Erlenmeyer flasks and other items I vaguely remembered from chemistry class. Under one counter was a large device I didn't recognize that looked like a washing machine. On a central table sat rows of petri dishes, also labeled, but with less careful handwriting. I leaned over and peered at them, making out phrases like "Brain Heart Infusion Agar (BHIA), 5% sheep's blood" and "Cornmeal Glucose Sucrose Yeast Extract Agar."

Paul grinned. "The sheep's blood is for primary isolation and cultivation," he said. "I move it to the cornmeal to encourage sporulation."

I peered at the dish. A white splotch in the center bloomed outward, like mold on a piece of bread. A pattern of what looked like millions of tiny filaments spread toward the edges of the dish, shifting in color from white to a greenish brown.

"So this is it?"

Paul nodded. "At the hospital, Dr. Chu said it was paracoccidioidomycosis. That would mean an infection with the *Paracoccidioides brasiliensis* fungus. And while this lovely specimen certainly shares some similarities, I can now state with confidence that that's not what it is."

"No? What is it, then?"

"Something new. Not that 'new' is all that unusual. You could send a five-year-old into the Amazon with a bucket, and he'd come back with a dozen unclassified species. But as far as fungal species thriving in human hosts, there's nothing in the literature about this little guy."

I ran my eyes along the rows of petri dishes, all of which seemed to be versions of the same specimen cultivated in different agar solutions. Some of them had multiple dark-colored stains, while others seemed hardly to have grown at all.

"It's trimorphic," he said, excitement evident in his voice. "Depending on the temperature and nature of its host, it can transition among three different forms: a single-celled yeast that buds to reproduce, or two different multicellular filamentous forms."

"Is that rare?"

"No, not all that unusual, actually. There's a common blood infection that's trimorphic. *Paracoccidioides brasiliensis* is dimorphic, as are a number of other pathogenic species. The ability to transform morphologies is what makes them so hard to kill and so potentially life-threatening. I suspect this species could survive in just about any host, plant or animal."

"So . . . is this where you explain why you haven't been taking your medication?"

"Let me show you something else first."

He logged into one of the computers, which was fitted with a pair of large flat-screen monitors. After a few moments of poking through the filesystem, he brought up a collection of grainy black-and-white images that reminded me of prenatal sonograms.

"These are my lungs two days after I came home from the hospital," he said. I didn't really know what I was looking at, but he pointed out the major features. "These wheel shapes are lesions in the lung wall. That's the yeast form. Then it transitions to a filamentous morphology, sending out mycelia between the cells."

"Preventing you from breathing."

"Well, indirectly. My immune system attacks the fungus, causing all sorts of fluid buildup, and *that* prevents me from breathing."

"I'm not seeing how this makes not taking your medicine an attractive option."

"Patience." He flipped to the next image. "This is my lungs two weeks later."

"No more wheels," I said.

"Right. The yeast form is gone. No more immune attacks, no more fluid."

"Because of the medicine?"

He shrugged. "That probably sped the process along. But the other form, the filamentous morphology, is still there. Look." He flipped to the next image, which showed the lung tissue at a closer magnification. "See all the mycelia?"

"You mean all those little lines? That's the fungus?"

"It's thriving. Insinuating itself into all the spaces between the cells, sometimes tapping them for nutrients."

"It's a parasite, then. It's living inside you. Eating you."

Paul rolled his eyes. "You have more cells of gut bacteria inside you than you have cells of *you*. Don't get queasy about a little foreign life."

"The bacteria is supposed to be there. It's helpful. Necessary, even. This is an infection. Are you intentionally letting it grow inside you just to study it? Isn't there some kind of, I don't know, code of ethics that frowns on that sort of thing?"

Paul leaned back and interlaced his fingers behind his head. "On the contrary. Self-experimentation has a long and storied history that has led to some important discoveries. Werner Forssmann won a Nobel Prize for threading the first cardiac catheter into his own heart. Barry Marshall earned a Nobel for proving—through self-experimentation—that *Helicobacter pylori* was the cause of gastric ulcers."

I gave him my best skeptical look. "And wasn't there a guy who drank cholera?"

"There was! Max von Pettenkofer. He wanted to prove his theory that cholera spread through the air, not through fluid contact. He was . . . um . . . wrong."

I let that hang in the air for a few moments without answering.

"Let's skip to the finale, then," he said, and cycled through a series of images until he found the one he was looking for. The last image was a rotating, three-dimensional color map of something I couldn't identify.

"This is the frontal lobe of my cerebellum," Paul said.

"Wait. Your brain? How are you getting these images?"

"It's from a PET scan."

"Isn't that expensive? When Dad gets one, they cost a thousand dollars a pop."

"A guy on the third floor is doing research on new tomography techniques. I told him I'd be a test subject in exchange for the results."

"Okay. And you found what? That the fungus is in your brain, too?"

"Yup. But in a good way."

I stared at him, expecting him to break out laughing and gloat about how far he'd strung me along. He looked back at me, totally serious. Finally, I said, "How can fungus possibly be in your brain *in a good way?*"

He manipulated the image with a mouse, diving in and rotating to focus on particular features. "You can see how the mycelia have grown up through everything." His face was alight with excitement. "They follow the paths of the neurons, tangling themselves through the whole structure."

I was horrified. "Isn't that how you get meningitis?"

He gestured, indicating his head. "No inflammation. No pain, no confusion. In fact, I've scored top marks on every intelligence test I've taken. The mycelia actually increase the efficiency of the neurotransmitters. Not only that, but there are certain portions of my brain they've remapped, keeping the same functionality with increased efficiency."

"Remapped," I said.

"Yes. The brain, amazing as it is, forms neural pathways organically, so they can be inefficient. Think of it like defragmenting your hard drive. You can fit a lot more in there if you reorder a bit."

"How do you know it's keeping the same functionality?"

He laughed. "You were always the cautious one. I guess I don't know, when it comes down to it, but that's why I'm studying myself so carefully. You'll notice that I haven't published my findings yet. I'm not going to claim success until I'm pretty sure it's not going to hurt anyone."

"Except yourself."

"Except myself. But that's a risk I'm allowed to take. And so far it's nothing short of miraculous. I can hold reams of complex data in my head, even graph it without a computer. I just think about it, and I can see it in my mind. Connections just *come* to me. I'm having eureka moments twice a day. Yes, the long-term effects are unknown. There's going to be a firestorm of controversy once I publish—calls for government regulations, studies galore, and more controversy on the internet than for child vaccinations. But it *works*, Neil."

Despite my misgivings, I found myself catching his excitement. He certainly knew a lot more about the subject than I did, and if he thought it was safe . . . though, how could he know? It wasn't like anyone had studied this before. I didn't want my brother to be another footnote in the history of ill-advised self-experimentation.

"What about Maisie?" As soon as the words were out of my mouth, I regretted them.

His face fell. "What about her? She died of the initial infection. Drowned, essentially, in the blood and fluids caused by her body's immune response." His voice was neutral, but the rigidness in his jaw told me he was angry.

"I'm sorry," I said. "I just meant, if you want other people to benefit from this parasite—"

"There are risks. I admit that. But they can be minimized. Instead of inhaling spores, a cultivated form could be injected or taken orally. Perhaps along with a dose of antifungals to slow the initial growth."

"Does this have anything to do with Neuritol?" I asked.

He frowned. "You mean that smart drug your friend's granddaughter overdosed on?"

I nodded.

"That's interesting," he said. "I don't know much about it. Does it have a fungal component?"

I made a mental note to find out. "And what about all these indigenous Einsteins popping up out of the rainforest?"

Paul stood up from the computer chair and stretched. "Hard to say. It seems unlikely that Maisie and I would be the only people in all of Brazil to be infected. On the other hand, there's no mention of such a case anywhere in the literature. So either it's very rare, and we happened to stumble on it, or it's a very new strain, in which case we could see a lot more cases."

"Thanks for showing me all this," I said.

He narrowed his eyes at me. "You're not going to tell anyone, are you? I'm trusting you with this. Not a word to anyone until I publish."

I held two fingers up, scout's honor. "I won't tell anyone. But there are a few people I want *you* to tell."

"I'm not going to report myself to any ethics board, if that's what you're thinking."

"Not at all. I want to introduce you to my friends at the NSA."

CHAPTER 14

"This is so awesome," Paul said.

He sat next to me in the car as we waited our turn to pass through the security gate at Fort Meade. Like Katherine Wyatt, he was gaining entrance as a consultant, escort-only, with a single-day badge. It normally took weeks to process something like that for someone not already in the system, but Melody had ways of making things happen fast.

Watching Paul's amazement, I marveled at how normal the attack dogs, razor wire, and heavily armed guards now seemed to me, after such a short time. It gave me a surge of pride to be showing it all to Paul as an insider.

"Doesn't it make you nervous?" he asked. "I keep expecting them to peg me as an imposter and drag me out of the car."

"You get used to it," I said.

We parked and went through the metal detectors, where Paul took it all in with the same serious expression as the MPs with guns. On the far side, he accepted his red-striped badge as if it were a Medal of Honor. As I now knew, the badges were electronically tracked in the building, registering silent alarms if any badge entered an area for which it was not cleared, or if an escort-only badge was not in close proximity to a valid permanent badge. Which meant that my little exploit in Agent Benjamin Harrison's introductory class had been doomed from the moment I walked the wrong way down the hall. I'd been lucky not to end up in jail.

I escorted him down to our basement room and into our little conference room, where Melody, Shaunessy, Andrew, and several other members of the team sat waiting. Flashing red lights indicated to anyone entering the room that an uncleared contractor was present, which meant that all classified documents had to be locked away, all classified computers powered off, and all classified discussions held in another room. It was the same arrangement used when specialized outside contractors were needed to repair large-scale plumbing leaks or install new elevators. I made the introductions and gave Paul the floor.

A set of charts with his images had already been processed through security and loaded onto the unclassified computer system. He used them to explain to the team what he had explained to me already. Everyone there had signed non-disclosure agreements at Paul's insistence, legal documents that would prevent them from sharing or benefitting financially from what he told them.

"What does this have to do with all the Colombian guerrilla activity?" Andrew said. "Do we think their members—"

Melody stood up before he could finish. "Thank you, Dr. Johns, for providing this information. Does anyone have any questions about the science involved?"

Andrew stopped talking, reddening slightly. Paul was visibly disappointed that he wasn't going to be privy to any NSA shop talk, but he smiled and looked around expectantly.

"How does the infection spread?" Shaunessy asked.

"Spore inhalation," Paul said. "The mature fungus in the wild produces spores, which the wind blows through the air. If you inhale a spore, it can take root in the lining of your lungs and grow."

"Can it be passed from person to person?"

"No. Not yet, anyway. There's no indication that the fungus will sporulate inside a human host. The mycelial strands are haploid, which means they have only one copy of each chromosome. They can't reproduce unless they encounter another, sexually compatible mycelium of the same species. My guess is that reproduction takes place only in the rainforest, where such encounters are common."

"Why does it increase intelligence?"

"It's a classic symbiotic relationship. The more intelligent the affected animal, the better its survival rate. The more value the fungus brings to the animal, the more the animal will protect or even cultivate the fungus. Each benefits the other."

When the questions were exhausted, Melody thanked him again for his time and looked at me.

"Come on," I said. "I'll give you a peek at the server room before I escort you out."

"What, no secrets?" he whispered as we left the conference room. The red lights were still flashing like silent sirens.

"Did you expect any?"

"I thought somebody might let something slip. You know, like who really assassinated Kennedy or where the alien technology is kept."

I shrugged. "No such luck. One more treat before you go, though." I waved my badge over the keypad and then pressed the correct sequence of numbers. The electromagnetic bolt clanked free, and I pushed open the door.

A blast of cool air ruffled our hair as the air pressure equalized, and the whir of thousands of rack-mounted servers filled our ears. Paul's expression was priceless. He stepped into the cavernous space, eyes bright, gaping at the endless racks of machinery that seemed to dwindle into the horizon.

We descended a flight of stairs to the floor. I had only been in here once or twice since Melody showed it to me, since my job didn't require it. Paul spun, taking it all in. "All the information in the whole world is in here," he said.

"You may be exaggerating," I said. "But, yeah. It's a lot of bytes."

Paul dropped to the floor—at first, I thought he had tripped—and stared down through one of the grates at the bundles of wires and cables that snaked under the floor, carrying information from the servers to the rest of the building. "It's incredible."

"Don't drool on the wiring," I said.

He climbed back to his feet, dusting off his hands. "And you're part of all this. You can access this data, spy on the world, read everybody's email."

"Part of it, yeah. Read everybody's email, no."

"Just the bad guys."

"Something like that."

He grinned. "Thanks for getting me in here. It was pretty cool, even if you didn't show me the telepathic ray gun."

"No problem."

On our way out, we ran into Melody.

"Thanks again, Dr. Johns," she said.

"How's your granddaughter?" Paul said. "Neil told me what happened to her."

I winced inwardly, hoping Paul wasn't about to voice his opinions on how teenagers should be allowed to take drugs to improve their test scores.

"She's doing well," Melody said. "Thanks for asking."

"Out of curiosity, do you know what drugs they used to treat her?"

"I really have no idea."

"Is there any medication she has to keep taking? Now that the crisis is past?"

Melody gave him an odd look. "I think there was, now that you mention it. Her mom said something about a pill she was supposed to take for a long time. A few years, she might have said. I'd never heard of anything like that."

I felt a chill creep up my shoulders. Paul nodded, leaning forward. "This drug, this Neuritol. Do you know where it comes from?"

"Another student . . ."

"No, I mean originally. Who's making it? Where does the supply come from?"

Melody crossed her arms. "Why are you asking all this? Is there something you know?"

"I'm sorry," Paul said. "One more question. Does her intelligence seem greater since her recovery? Has she displayed any feats of intellect, such as remarkable memory or surprising bursts of intuition? Maybe performed exceptionally well on tests above her level?"

I could see the understanding dawn in Melody's eyes. "You're saying this is the same. That Neuritol introduces the same infection that is spreading in South America."

"I don't know. But it seems like a possibility. Someone could be isolating the spores and packaging it as an oral drug."

"Would that be hard?"

Paul shrugged. "Not very. I could do it."

I wanted to say, *But you wouldn't, right?* I settled for saying, "If this is making its way into the United States, we need to know about it."

"Agreed," Melody said, her tone brusque. "Thank you for bringing it to our attention, Dr. Johns. If we have more questions for you on the details, may we contact you through Neil?"

"Of course."

I walked Paul all the way out to the entrance and past the metal detectors. A uniformed MP took his badge, and he was free to take the car and drive through the gate on his own. I had already arranged with Shaunessy to drop me off on her way home at the end of the day. The phone in the guard booth rang and the MP answered it.

"Neil Johns?" he asked.

"That's me."

"Ms. Muniz wants you back in the office as soon as possible."

I rushed back through the halls and back down to our basement room. "What's going on?" I asked Melody.

"The DIRNSA called."

"He wants to see us again?"

"Nope. He wants to see you."

—⚙—

Kilpatrick had his phone to his ear when I eased into his office. "Well, find out," he said. "We can't hold off much longer."

He hung up the phone and looked at me, his eyes active. "Who are you?"

"Neil Johns, sir."

"Of course. Listen, Johns. Muniz tells me you're a rising star."

"If she says so." I was pleased at the compliment, but terrified as to what it might mean. I doubted very much that the director of the world's most powerful intelligence agency had called me into his office to pat me on the head and give me a gold star.

I didn't have to wait long. "You're coming with me to Brazil in the morning," he said. "Our flight leaves at nine thirty."

I felt panic rising. "Sir?"

"I know your history, and your father's service, Johns. During the years he was posted in Brazil, you maintained a close friendship with the son of Júlio Eduardo de Almeida, who is now the Deputy Commander of the Agência Brasileira de Inteligência."

His Portuguese pronunciation was terrible, but I didn't point that out. Neither did I pretend to be surprised that the NSA knew who my childhood friends were. "I haven't seen Celso in five years," I said. "Besides, it's his father who's head of intelligence. Celso's an engineering student. He doesn't even have a security clearance."

"All I want you to do is catch up with an old friend while you're in town on business. Can you do that for me?"

I swallowed. Seeing Celso again would be nice, probably. I hadn't been back to Brazil since I was sixteen. But Kilpatrick was obviously angling for some kind of information or access, which meant I would be using him, not just reconnecting. Then again, Kilpatrick wasn't really asking.

"Yes, sir," I said.

"Good. BWI, nine-thirty."

"How long will we be there?"

Kilpatrick shrugged. "A few days. See Courtney for your tickets."

Courtney was his administrative assistant, and she printed my boarding pass without a word. I was going to Brazil.

—❦—

I left early. I had to pack a bag and prepare for my trip, though I didn't really know what I would need. I remembered Kilpatrick's shrug and mentally revised his "few days" into a week. My phone rang. Talking on the phone while driving was against Maryland law, but I answered it anyway, thinking it might be Melody, or even Kilpatrick.

It was Mom. "I just got the message," she said. "Is he okay?"

"What? Is who okay?"

"Your father. Paul called to say he was taking him to the hospital."

"When was this? Did he say why?" I saw then that my phone showed eight missed calls.

"This afternoon. I had to teach a class, so Paul offered to spend the rest of the day with him after he finished with you. The message just said he was heading to the ER, no details. Didn't he call you?"

"It looks like he tried. Did they go to Baltimore Washington Medical Center?"

"I assume."

"I'll be there in ten minutes."

"I'm still a half-hour away, even if I push it."

"Okay. I'll call you when I know anything."

I threw the phone onto the passenger seat and pressed the accelerator. My mind raced through scenarios, picturing a heart attack, a stroke, a sudden worsening of his Alzheimer's symptoms. I imagined an accident with the stove, or Dad just walking out of the house when Paul wasn't watching and trying to take the car or the boat, with disastrous results. Five minutes later, I veered into the ER parking lot and stopped in the first spot without worrying about the signs. I called Paul as I ran into the building.

"I'll meet you in the ER waiting room," he said.

I asked at the front desk for Dad's room number anyway, but Paul met me there in less than a minute. "Hey, brother," he said. "Not much for answering your calls, are you?"

"You know I can't take a cell phone inside. You should have called my work number."

"I did. No answer there, either."

"Mom's on her way," I said.

"Okay. Come on, I'll show you his room." We walked through the double doors and down a series of hallways. "He's just down here on the left."

There was something in Paul's face. Fear and worry, but something else, too. Guilt. And just the hint of defiance. In an instant, I knew what had happened.

"You've got to be kidding me. You gave it to him. You did, didn't you?"

"What?" His guilty look was all the confirmation I needed.

"That parasite! You intentionally infected him with it, gave him an injection, or else put it in his food or something. What did you think would happen? Did you expect you could cure Alzheimer's with a fungus? The world's leading neurodegenerative disease, and you were going to fix it with a home remedy?"

His expression turned to belligerence. "Just listen for a minute."

"Listen? To your excuses and rationalizations? You performed human testing on our *father*. I don't want to hear it."

"Neil. Neil, wait . . ."

I pushed past him and walked into my father's room. He lay on his back, his head lifted and straining, one arm tied to the side rail with a Velcro restraint. Two oxygen tubes looped around his ears and snaked into his nostrils, held in place with white tape. A nurse stood beside him, speaking calmly to him and trying to restrain his other arm.

"Get away from me!" He batted at her with his free hand, then tried to reach his IV and rip it out of his arm.

"What's going on?" I asked.

"He keeps pulling out his IV," she said. "Are you his family? Can you help?"

"It's okay, Dad," I said. "She's here to help you. Calm down." I caught his wrist and held it so she could fasten the strap around it.

"Who are you? What do you want with me?" he shouted.

"It's me. It's Neil, Dad. Your son. You're sick. You need medicine."

He rattled his hands against the side rails and strained against the straps. He wore a vest with strings that had been tied to the rails, preventing him from getting out of the bed.

"I don't need medicine! What I need is to go to work. I'm late for work, and you're keeping me here against my will."

Paul stood in the doorway, not coming any closer. The IV beeped, but the nurse made no move to check it.

"You don't need to go to work," I said to my father. "You called in sick."

That stopped him for a moment. "I did?"

"You did. They're not expecting you. They've got it covered for today."

I thought I had calmed him, but he gave a huge jerk, yanking his whole body to one side. The rails rattled, and the bed itself squeaked against the floor and shifted slightly to the right.

"We might have to sedate him if we can't keep him calmer," the nurse said. "Ten minutes ago, he managed to pull out his nasal cannula by rubbing his face against the side of the bed."

"You can't break me," Dad growled. "I won't tell you a thing. It doesn't matter what you do to me. You can tell your boss that I'll die first."

I sat on a stool next to the bed and stroked his head, speaking softly. "You're home now," I said. "You made it. You didn't tell. We're going to take care of you."

He calmed slightly, though his eyes still swung wildly back and forth. "Who are you?" he asked.

I whispered in his ear. "Neil Johns. I'm an NSA agent. I'm here to take care of you."

"I didn't tell," Dad said. "I was strong."

I stroked his hair, remembering times as a boy when I had been scared at night, and he had stroked my head until I fell asleep. "I know you were, Dad," I said. "I know."

The nurse left. Paul came into the room, then, but I glared at him. "No," I said. "Get out."

He ignored me. "I was trying to help him. Who are you to send me away? You've barely seen him since you started your job."

"At least I didn't try to kill him."

"He's been worse. A lot worse. He doesn't even know who I am most of the time. Do you think that's what he would want?"

I felt the muscles in my neck tighten painfully. I wanted to punch Paul, or else grab him by the hair and make him look, really look, at what he'd done. "Of course it's not what he wanted. Nobody wants dementia. Then again, nobody wants a fungal infection, either. You could have killed him."

"But if there was a chance! Even a small chance, that he might get better. Don't you think he would want us to try? What does he have to lose?"

The IV pole kept beeping. "Did you even ask him first?"

Paul threw up his hands. "What good would that do? He wouldn't understand."

"You could have tried. You could have asked Mom. You could have asked *me*. We could have decided together."

"Decided what? The choices were between a slow and horrible death, and a chance at something better. It wasn't like he had a lot to lose."

I stood up right into Paul's face, the stool crashing to the floor behind me. My fist clenched, and only the awareness of our father lying next to me held me back from swinging it. "He had plenty to lose," I said. "He had his life. He might have been sick, but his life was still worth something. It wasn't yours to gamble away."

Mom came into the room and saw us like that, facing each other down. "What are you doing?" she said. "Is he okay? You said you would call me!"

I stepped back. "I'm sorry, Mom."

DAVID WALTON

She saw Dad on the bed, restrained, oxygen tubes in his nose and a wild look in his eyes. She rushed to his side. "What happened?"

"He has a fungal infection," I said flatly, with a dark look at Paul. "Looks like it's the same one that Paul picked up in the Amazon."

"How is he? Is he responding to the medication?"

I realized that with all of Dad's agitated behavior and my anger at Paul, I hadn't thought to ask. "They think his chances are good," Paul said. "But he doesn't know where he is or what's happening to him. He keeps trying to get away."

"You told them what it is?" I asked. "So they know how to treat it?"

Paul looked hurt. "Of course, I did."

I righted the stool, and Mom sat down. She took his hand. "I'm here, Charles. It's going to be all right."

His violence seemed to have calmed, but he was still breathing hard, confused. "That's not my name," he said. "You've got the wrong person. I don't know who you are."

Mom's eyes were wet, and she stroked his hair as I had done. "That's okay," she said. "I know who you are."

—⊙—

As darkness fell, he became combative again, jerking at his straps and shouting at us. It was typical for Alzheimer's patients to get worse when it grew dark outside. They called it sundowning, but no one really knew why it happened. At the end of visiting hours, the nurse told us that one of us could stay the night, if we wanted, to help keep him calm, but the others would have to return in the morning. Both Paul and I wanted to do it, but Mom insisted that she wouldn't leave him.

I drove back to my parents' empty house. Paul, despite the late hour, decided to drive home to his College Park apartment. I didn't try to change his mind. When I got home, I realized I still had to pack for Brazil. I hadn't even told Mom or Paul that I was going.

I put some clothes in a suitcase, wondering what I would need. If I was just meant to hang out with Celso, then casual clothes would be sufficient. If I was going to be invited to meetings with foreign diplomats or intelligence officers, then I would need something more formal. I packed some of everything.

I slept fitfully and woke early, wanting to check in on Dad before my flight. I hauled my suitcase out to the car and made it to the hospital by seven o'clock.

"I'm here to see Charles Johns," I said at the front desk.

The receptionist looked back at me like I was a bug. "Visiting hours start at eight."

"I have to be at the airport at eight," I said. "I just want to see my father, make sure he's all right before I go."

Her lips thinned, and her eyes said she'd heard it all before. "Visiting hours start at eight."

"Look, I know you don't make the rules," I said. I gave her my best smile. "But my flight leaves for Brazil in a little more than two hours. I don't know when I'll be back. All I want to do is see him before I go."

Her facial expression didn't change. "Visiting hours start at eight."

I eyed the entrance, wondering if I could just make a break for it. A metal detector stood between me and the hallway beyond, but I didn't think I was wearing any metal that would set it off. I remembered the way to my father's room. I could just run through the door and be there before anyone could stop me.

The receptionist would call security, though, and I'd already given my father's name, so they would know exactly where I was going. If they called the police, I'd have a hard time getting out of there to the airport on time. I needed a better way.

Back outside, I started to circle the building, which was enormous, with so many new wings tacked on over the years that no sense of the original shape remained. There were many smaller entrances, which I assumed required a card for access, as well as loading bays and garages, all of which were shut.

Finally, I saw a truck backed up to an open bay, with three men walking back and forth, unloading boxes. The truck was white and read Gulph Medical Supply on the side. A security guard stood at the gate, watching them. I put my NSA badge around my neck on its lanyard—I had brought it in case I needed ID in Brazil—and kept the badge in my hand where it couldn't be seen easily.

I walked up to the truck. "Finally," I said loudly. "We're running so low on specimen containers I was going to have to have my patients pee in my coffee mug."

I rolled my eyes at the security guard and waved my badge at the guard, fast enough that he couldn't read it. Then I rounded on one of the workers. "Make sure a box of those gets up to the third floor, will you?"

"We only drop them off here," the man said. His accent was Australian. "And I'm pretty sure this lot is all sterile gloves and pads."

I made a sound of frustration. "I'm surrounded by incompetents," I said, and started to walk through the loading bay doors.

"Where are you going?" the security guard asked.

"I'm going to my office," I said, "and if there's not a pot of coffee ready when I get there, and I mean a *full* one, then I assure you, my staff is going to be looking for new employment."

I marched past him, holding my breath, waiting for him to call after me. Nothing happened. I walked through the far door, and I was in.

Not that I was out of the woods yet. From there, I had to actually *find* the room. The hospital was a maze. I couldn't ask for directions, or even appear to be lost, so I strode confidently from hallway to hallway, trying to study the signs when no one else was looking. Once I barreled into what might have been a surgery prep room, causing five men and women in surgery gowns and gloves to look up at me in surprise. "Has anybody seen Harry?" I asked.

One woman shook her head. I stalked away, muttering imprecations against Harry under my breath.

Finally, I found a recognizable sign and a familiar-looking hallway. I walked by the nurses' station with the same air of confidence and marched into my father's room.

The bed was empty. The sheet was neatly pulled up under the pillow. The restraining vest was neatly folded and the Velcro strap removed from the side rails. I gaped at the bed, a rush of adrenaline setting my heart racing. He was dead. He had died during the night. But if that had happened, wouldn't Mom have called? Finally, I noticed the figure sitting in a guest chair in the corner.

"Dad?" I said. "What's going on? Are you all right?"

He didn't stir, and I realized he was asleep. I crossed over and stood next to him, watching his chest rise and fall with his gentle breathing. On the table next to him was a newspaper section folded to the crossword puzzle, which was completed. My father held a pen in one hand and a piece of hospital note paper in the other. The paper had the Brazilian Portuguese alphabet written on it—the older alphabet, before they had officially changed it for orthographic consistency with Portugal—with each letter crossed out. Under the alphabet was a sentence in Portuguese: *"Um pequeno jabuti xereta viu dez cegonhas felizes,"* meaning "A nosy little tortoise saw ten happy storks." It wasn't the meaning of the sentence that caught my attention, however. It was the fact that it contained every letter of the alphabet at least once. It was a pangram, the sort of wordplay that my father used to love to do in both English and Portuguese when I was young.

I realized someone was standing behind me. I turned to see Mom, a brilliant smile lighting her face.

"Is he okay?" I asked.

"Okay? Neil, he's more than okay. It's unbelievable."

I turned back to Dad and found that his eyes were open. He met my gaze, clear intelligence evident in his look.

"Hello, Neil," he said.

CHAPTER 15

I nearly missed my flight. My father was back. He was awake and alert and knew who I was and remembered everything he was supposed to know. He charmed the nurses with jokes and good humor and smiled at my mom so much I thought they would both burst from pleasure. It was as if the Alzheimer's had never happened.

"So you're working for the agency?" he said.

My chest felt warm with pride. "I'm cracking indecipherables," I said.

"Any good at it?"

"I'm doing okay so far. I wish I could tell you about the one code I solved . . ."

"What department are you with?"

"It's kind of a side group, out of the main organizational structure. I don't know where Melody gets the funding, but—"

"Melody? Don't tell me you're working with Melody Muniz."

"Yeah," I said. "You remember her? She said she only knew you by reputation. As a talented colleague."

He pursed his lips and shot Mom a furtive glance. "It was a bit more than that."

"She's great," I said. "Really sharp, and she cuts through bureaucratic red tape like it's soft butter."

"Is she impressed with you?"

I gave an embarrassed smile. "I think. She told the director I was a rising star."

"Watch it." Dad shook his head. "You don't want to be calling attention to yourself. Do good work, but keep your head down. If the brass starts to learn your name, you're in trouble. They'll never give you a moment's peace."

I smiled wryly. "It may be too late for that. I'm flying to Brazil with the director this morning at his personal request." I listened to what I had just said and jumped up in panic. It was eight o'clock. The airport wasn't far, but I was going to have a tough time getting through security before the plane left if I didn't get moving.

I said goodbye and headed for the door just as Paul was walking in. His eyes were bloodshot and his clothes and hair disheveled, as if he'd been sleeping in his car. He stopped cold, staring over my shoulder at Dad, his mouth literally hanging open. I pushed past him. "You still shouldn't have done it," I said. I walked down the hall without another word. After a glance at my watch, I broke into a run.

I didn't want to leave my mom's car in airport parking, so I took a cab from the hospital. By the time it dropped me off at the gate, it was almost eight forty-five. The plane was scheduled to start boarding at nine and take off at nine thirty. I impatiently shuffled my way through the line to check my suitcase. The desk employee glanced at my boarding pass and shook his head. "You'd better hurry," he said.

I pelted up the stairs and down the hallway to security, where I waited again, checking my watch every thirty seconds. I practically threw my shoes through the bag scanner and stepped through the metal detector before the official was ready, causing him to shoo me back and lecture me about waiting my turn.

"My flight is leaving!" I said.

He cocked his head at me. "Baltimore/Washington International recommends you arrive at the airport at least ninety minutes before departure."

"Please?" I said.

He beckoned me through. On the other side, I grabbed my shoes and took off down the hall without bothering to put them on. The gate was, of course, at the far end. By the time I got there, I was gasping for breath and my watch said 9:27. A woman in a blue uniform shirt was just closing the door.

"Wait!" I called.

She stopped and looked at me. "Delta to Brasília?" she asked.

I nodded, out of breath, and waved my boarding pass at her. She shook her head. "You almost missed us," she said. "Head down and take your seat."

I rushed down the deserted ramp and climbed into the plane. Kilpatrick was seated in first class, looking comfortable in his uniform, a laptop on the table in front of him. "Thought you were going to stand me up," he said. He glanced at the shoes still clutched in my hand, but didn't say anything. I made my way back to coach and collapsed into my seat.

—⊙—

The flight was twelve hours long, with one stop in Atlanta. Long before we arrived, I was stiff and sore and exhausted. In my haste to pack, I hadn't brought any books along, and the thriller I bought from a bookstand in Atlanta didn't hold my interest. The in-flight movies were ones I'd seen before, and I hadn't liked them all that much the first time around. It was hard to concentrate on anything for very long.

I didn't want to be on this plane. It felt like such a detour. My life was back in Maryland, where I was just starting to figure out how to do my job, and where my father could fully remember who and where he was for the first time in years. Now, here I was, flying to my childhood home on the front line of some intelligence game that I didn't begin to understand. It was all happening too fast.

I didn't even know what to think about my dad's recovery. On the one hand, I was ecstatic. It was miraculous, like bringing someone back from the dead. The dad I knew had been gone, and now he was back. I knew it wouldn't all be roses and rainbows, of course. He would have to come to terms with the years he had lost, grow accustomed to the person he could be now. But the thinking, reasoning, remembering father I had known was there to interact with me again.

On the other hand, I was still furious with Paul for doing it behind my back. Not only could it have gone terribly wrong, but it might still end in disaster. There was no telling how long the recovery would last, or what would happen if it wore off. What would the long-term effects be? Would Paul have to continue to give him injections? Would the new injections continue to work as well as the first? I thought again of "Flowers for Algernon." Had Paul given my father a cure, or just a temporary reprieve? Would Dad thank him if the drug meant experiencing a second slow decline into dementia?

It was the not-telling part that aggravated me the most. Paul was supposed to be a scientist. There were review boards and publications and animal trials and federal regulations for a reason. You didn't just try a new drug on a human being to see what it would do. The fact that the human was our father and that it seemed to turn out okay didn't make it right.

It was also baffling, the more I thought about it. Paul was the scientist in our family *because* he was the one who didn't take any risks. He had called me the cautious one, but it wasn't true. I was the one who sneaked into the hospital through the loading docks by lying to the security guard; he was the one who waited until eight o'clock like the rules said he should. I was the younger brother, the troublemaker, the kind of person who got arrested on his first day on the job for stealing his instructor's badge ID. Paul always played it by the book. So why was he acting like a cowboy now?

I found myself wishing that Melody or Shaunessy was on the plane with me, someone to whom I could talk and explain my concerns. I had never been very good at thinking through things silently, at least where emotional issues were concerned. I could work out math problems in my head no problem, but when it came to making a decision or coming to terms with a relationship crisis, I just chewed on the same thoughts over and over without coming to any conclusions. I couldn't tell what I really thought until I explained it aloud to someone and heard what I said.

—⊙—

The northern part of the South American continent was nothing but endless green jungle. Hours and hours of it, passing under the plane with only the occasional serpentine river to cut the monotony. We passed over Suriname first, and then into Brazil. There was no way to communicate the vastness of the Amazon rainforest until you tried to fly across it. It was like a speckled green carpet, dark green with swirls of lime. Sometimes, when no rivers were visible, my mind transformed the flat landscape into water, interpreting the patterns of treetops as ripples in a vast sea.

The forest finally gave way to a patchwork of cultivated fields with a gradually thickening network of roads. Buildings sprouted up here and there, and then clusters of buildings in small towns. The elevation rose to a vast, dry plain dotted with villages. By this time, the sun was setting on the right side of the plane, casting long shadows across the landscape.

Suddenly, there was Brasília, lit up like a carnival in the middle of a desert, the edges of the city stretching out like the wings of a bird. It was a ridiculous location for a capital city, hundreds of miles from the population centers on the coast, a place with no history and no significance. But that was part of why it had been built, planned, and constructed from nothing in the late 1950s, as a way to rewrite history and start from scratch. A new city for a new Brazil.

The plane landed with a screech of tires and a rush of air. When I finally made my way down the aisle and out into the terminal, Kilpatrick was waiting for me, flanked by his security detail. He looked refreshed and energetic, as if he had taken a long nap and enjoyed a good meal. His uniform wasn't even wrinkled.

He seemed surprised when I told him I had a suitcase to retrieve from baggage claim. When he saw the size of it, he raised an eyebrow but made no comment. He carried only a slim carry-on bag. "I didn't know what I would need, so I packed everything," I said, sounding whiny even to myself. He watched me wrestle it down from the conveyor belt, but when he turned aside, I saw him smirk.

We caught a taxi to our hotel. I tried to ask him for more details on what I was meant to do here, what meetings there might be, or what information he hoped to get out of Celso. Kilpatrick shook his head. He pointed at the taxi driver with his eyes and placed a finger against his lips.

Under other circumstances, the secrecy might have been thrilling. I was, after all, in the field, doing spy stuff with the director of the NSA. Instead, it was just irritating. I was tired and stressed and worried about my father. I was starting to think it would have been better if I'd missed my flight, or else called Kilpatrick and cited my father's hospitalization as a family emergency. Then I would be home, talking with my dad and making sure Paul didn't do anything stupid, instead of sitting in a taxi next to a powerful man with no idea how to act or what was expected of me.

CHAPTER 16

The next morning, I woke to a steady rain outside my window. It was still the rainy season here, so it would rain most days, though rarely for very long at a time. It was also a good thirty degrees warmer than it was in Maryland, which would make for a nice change.

I found Kilpatrick at the breakfast bar, digging into a plate piled high with eggs, ham, couscous, tapioca crepes filled with *requeijão*, and fresh fruit. I sat across from him. "So," I said. "What am I supposed to be doing today?"

"I think you know."

"But what am I supposed to find out? What do you want me to ask him?"

"You're a smart kid. I'll leave that up to your judgment." He produced a pen from a hidden pocket in his uniform and scribbled something on a napkin. He slid it over to me. It said, *We can be heard.*

I frowned. He hadn't bothered to explain my mission to me ahead of time, and now, apparently, we couldn't speak freely. "And what will you be doing?"

He munched on his eggs and didn't answer, just looked at me over his fork. I gave up. Outside, the rain had stopped, and mist steamed from the wet streets. I could see the twin towers of the National Congress, and beyond them, the sparkling blue of Paranoá Lake. Somewhere over there, too far to see, was the *Palácio da Alvorada*, where the president of Brazil lived.

Brasília could be difficult to navigate on foot, since the city was pretty much designed for cars. The roads were almost all throughways, with no traffic lights or places for pedestrians to cross. Pedestrians had their own paths, often circuitous routes that looped around shopping malls or passed through long tunnels underneath the highways. For a tourist, it would have been nearly impossible, but I had grown up there.

Half an hour later, I was strolling through the tree-lined greenery of the *Campus Universitário Darcy Ribeiro*. It could almost have been any university in the United States, though I saw a lot more mixed-race faces and a lot more bright yellow soccer jerseys.

Celso didn't know I was coming. I had thought of texting him several times, first from the US, then once I was in Brazil, but it never seemed like a good time, and I kept putting it off. I found his dormitory address from the campus office. As I walked toward it, I realized I was half hoping not to find him. That he would be in class, or soccer practice, or better yet, on travel for the week to some other location. I didn't want to meet a friend under false pretenses or try to manipulate him into giving me information the government of his country was unwilling to share.

Five years had passed since I last saw him, but I recognized him immediately. He was kicking around a soccer ball on the grass in front of his dormitory, only the ball was five times the size it was supposed to be. A half-dozen other young men and women fought for the ball, laughing and shouting in Portuguese and occasionally tumbling over one another in their attempts to maneuver the oversized ball with their feet.

Celso saw me before I said anything. He shouted and left the game to half-tackle me with an embrace. "Hey, *parceiro*! What are you doing here?"

I clapped him on the shoulders. "Look at you," I said. "You never change." He was shorter than me, athletic, and smelled of sweat and fresh grass. He wore a red and black striped shirt and a Yankees baseball cap turned backward on his head, and his smile was the same easy, devil-may-care grin I remembered from our youth.

He introduced me to some of his friends. I couldn't help noticing, however, that although some of them smiled and shook my hand, others gave me openly hostile looks, especially when he told them I was from the United States.

"What's their problem?" I asked Celso. "Did I interrupt your game?"

Celso shrugged, dismissing them. "They've got a thing about Americans."

"Seriously? Why?"

"It's suddenly the popular thing on campus. It's all about protecting the Amazon. Americans come here, they talk like the rainforest belongs to them, or at least like it belongs to the world. They want to tell us how we should run things in our own country."

I didn't remember there being such fervor about the rainforest in the urban centers of Brazil when I had lived here. It reminded me of the anti-tourism sentiment that was apparently gaining traction in Brazil's northern states. "What about you?" I asked.

He gave another expressive shrug. "Seems a stupid reason to hate three hundred million people," he said.

"Will your friends give you a rough time, just because you hang out with an American?"

"Not any of my real friends."

Fifteen minutes later, we were sitting on the ground on one of Brasília's many park-like plots of grass, eating skewers of hot roasted beef from a street vendor. I had forgotten how much I loved the food here. The sun burned through the haze enough to warm our faces. We talked about old memories, about teasing Celso's white pit bull puppy and climbing onto the roof of his house to drop water balloons on his sisters and paddle surfing in the lake to check out the *gatinhas* in their bikinis and stealing all the soccer balls from the school's equipment closet to pile them up inside the athletic director's Fiat. He asked me about my parents and my brother and sister, and I said they were well. I told him about Julia's new baby daughter.

We spoke English, mostly, with a Portuguese word or phrase thrown in where no English one would do. All the time we were talking, a knot of anxiety twisted in my stomach, even though none of our conversation had anything to do with his father or the Ligados or Brazilian national secrets. Finally, I couldn't stand it anymore. I had to come clean.

"Here's the deal," I said. "I'm working for the NSA now. I flew down here with the director, and the only reason he brought me was because you and I used to be friends."

Celso raised an eyebrow, but his relaxed smile didn't waver. "So he wants you to grill me. Find out what I know."

"I guess."

"He thinks my father tells me secrets."

"He must. But what information he's looking for, or why he thinks you would tell me, is beyond my ability to guess. So let's just agree that I'm not going to press you for secrets and you're not going to tell me any, and then I can just relax and enjoy my *churrasco* and reminisce about the old days."

I looked at his face, the cheerful expression just as unconcerned and amiable as ever. And I realized that, despite the fact that I had showed up practically on his doorstep unannounced, he had never asked me what brought me to Brasília.

"You knew," I said.

"Knew?"

"You already knew I worked for the NSA. You knew I was here before I showed up."

He nodded, his grin broadening, and spread his arms wide in surrender. "Of course I did. What did you think? You flew in with the *director of the NSA*. You think nobody was watching?" He laughed. "Director Mark Kilpatrick shows up in Brasília accompanied by Neil Johns, who just joined the NSA a few months ago. So why is a brand new employee hanging out in Brasília with the director? Ah, maybe because he used to be an *amigo* of the son of the deputy commander of the Agência Brasileira de Inteligência. And so no one is surprised when you show up on campus."

"Your father warned you I might be calling."

"He did."

I looked around. "Are there agents watching us?"

"Almost certainly."

There were plenty of university students, but I didn't see anyone in dark suits or sunglasses. In fact, nobody seemed to be paying any attention to us at all. The idea that I had probably been followed from the hotel creeped me out, though I had to admit that it gave me a thrill at the same time. I felt like a spy, even though I was just relaxing on the grass with a friend and eating *churrascos*.

"Sorry," I said. "Pretty lousy of me, I guess."

His smile was like a flashlight. "Forget about it. My dad's an ass most of the time, and it sounds like your director is, too."

We walked the campus and bought coffees and talked about his engineering degree and campus life and why neither of us had a girlfriend. I told him about my three failed attempts to get a college degree, and he told me all the reasons his dad was an ass, especially in how he treated Celso's mother. The five years I hadn't seen him seemed to melt away, and we were best friends again, simple and easy and comfortable together.

Celso asked me again about my family. Hadn't my father been sick? And suddenly I was spilling the whole story, about Paul's infection in the Amazon, his friend's death and his recovery, his sudden and unexplained powers of intelligence and memory, his work in the mycology lab. Finally, I told him about my father's Alzheimer's, about Paul infecting him with the fungus without asking anyone, and about my dad's miraculous recovery. All the anger and frustration came bubbling to the surface, and I spoke freely, though I kept the NSA and the Ligados and Melody's granddaughter out of it.

It felt good to talk. "How can he be so smart all of a sudden, and yet so stupid!" I said. "What kind of person gives an experimental drug to his own father? Wouldn't being smarter make you more careful? More aware of the risks? He's acting like a teenager, like nothing can possibly go wrong."

"Or like someone who cares more about his research than about the risks," Celso said.

"Yes. That's it exactly. But it's not like him. He cares about the science, sure, but he's always been a take-it-slow, don't-publish-till-you're-ready kind of guy."

"Has he been acting strange in other ways?"

I shrugged. "He never seems to sleep. He trounces me at games I used to win easily."

Celso grew quiet. He seemed to be brooding on his own troubles, but when I asked him what was wrong, he just flashed me his brilliant smile.

That evening, we ended up at Pôr do Sol, a nearby bar packed with university students. We sat at one of the square red tables and ordered Heinekens and Brasília's staple bar snack, chicken croquettes. By the time the beer arrived, two girls had joined our table, friends of Celso, whom he introduced as Gabriela and Talita. Talita was dark-skinned, with her hair in thin braids, and reminded me of Shaunessy.

The girls were fun and laughed a lot, but other students gave us dirty looks. One guy went so far as to push roughly past, knocking into me and almost spilling my drink. I let it go, not wanting to get into a bar fight in my first field assignment for the agency. But the animosity worried me. It was completely counter to anything I'd experienced during my decade growing up in the city. A passion for Amazon conservation didn't seem sufficient to explain it.

We tried to keep things light, but I could tell Celso wasn't in the mood. Finally, we left the girls and slipped out into the street, which was nearly as crowded, with students drinking and laughing and dancing to the *sertanejo universitário* music piped through speakers from another bar farther down the street. Celso walked through the crowd like he didn't see them. At the end of the road, he turned left, then climbed up a steep embankment.

When I reached him, he was standing at the rail of one of the thoroughfares that cut the city into straight lines. Cars thundered past, buffeting us with displaced air. From this vantage, we could just see the administrative region of the city, where the major government buildings stood. Celso looked out across six lanes of traffic like he might just make a run for it.

I put a hand on his shoulder. "What's wrong?"

He didn't look at me. "I'm not supposed to tell you. He doesn't want me to tell anyone anything, least of all an American agent."

"Then don't tell me," I said.

He turned to face me, and the easy smile was gone. His eyes looked haunted. "My father has changed. He was never a nice man. You remember that. He was strict and had a temper. But now . . ." He looked back at the traffic, and his muscles bunched. "I think he's been using his power to control who takes office. Putting surveillance on congressmen, blackmailing. Maybe even killing."

"You know this?"

"I suspect. And it's crazy nonsense. Suddenly he's concerned about the environment, wants more protections in place for the Amazon, revoke logging rights, that kind of thing. He's trying to ban all foreign tourism to the Amazon, can you believe that?"

"He's killing people for this?"

"He never gave two reais for the environment until this year. And that's not all." Celso's skin looked drained of life, the passing cars' headlights casting strange, moving shadows across his face. "My mother has been missing for two months."

"She disappeared?" I tried to say it gently. "Have you called the police?"

"The police are afraid of him, I think. He just tells them it's nothing to worry about, that she went to visit her sister Rafaela in Salvador. But she's not there. And she wouldn't have left my father, not without a word to me." He let the alternative hang in the air.

I stared at him, shocked, with no clue what to say. "Isn't there a higher authority you can go to? Anyone who will listen?"

"I've tried. Anyone with enough power is too busy to care, or else needs his support. And what can I say? I have no evidence. I can't even prove she's dead."

"Celso, I'm so sorry," I said. Suddenly all my concerns about my father seemed trivial. I was embarrassed for sharing them, when Celso had a burden like this weighing on his soul.

"Another thing," Celso said. "He's too smart. My dad. Just like you were saying with your brother. He remembers everything he reads, does math in his head. He doesn't sleep. And he figures out what I'm thinking before I say it."

"Has anyone else noticed? Your sisters?"

"I don't know. My sisters are in São Paulo, and they should stay right where they are." Celso slapped the guard rail with his palms. "He scares me, *mano*. I think he killed my mom, and I'm afraid I might be next."

"What about all your mom's family? They must know she hasn't been visiting her sister."

"Most of them live around here, and they don't talk to Rafaela, not since she married a Candomblé priest. They just believe my dad. That or they're afraid of him, too."

A muted thump sounded in the air, like thunder, but with deep enough tones to rattle my chest. "What was that?" I scanned the freeway, thinking there might have been a collision, but Celso grabbed my sleeve and pointed. Toward the southeast, in the direction of the capitol buildings, a column of black smoke rose into the sky.

"What is it?" I asked. "A fire?"

"More like an explosion."

"Is it the congress building?" We were too far away to see clearly, but it was the right direction. A second boom vibrated through my bones, and this time the windows in all the nearby buildings rattled as well. A second column of smoke appeared, this one more directly east, at the edge of the lake.

"*Minha nossa*," Celso swore. "It's the *Palácio da Alvorada*." The residence of the president of Brazil.

The cars on the freeway were pulling over now, and motorists joined us to stare at the rising pillars of smoke. The sound of a third explosion washed over us, this one distant and only noticeable because of the other two. A moment later, over the horizon to the south, a third column twisted into the sky.

"I can't tell," Celso said. He sounded shaken. "What is that one? The cathedral?"

I shook my head. "It's farther away than that."

"What then?"

"Hard to be sure. But my guess? It's the Agência Brasileira de Inteligência."

"My father's there," Celso said.

I flattened my lips into a straight line. "True," I said. "And so is the director of the NSA."

CHAPTER 17

My first instinct was to run toward the explosions. Celso followed me as I navigated the maze of pedestrian pathways. The sites were, however, several kilometers away, and before I made it very far, it became clear from the crowds and the police that I wasn't going to get anywhere near them. Celso coaxed me back to his dormitory, where we watched the unfolding story on the news, and I tried to reach the office back home.

After several tries, I reached Shaunessy on the phone, but she knew less than I did. There hadn't been enough time before I left to buy a SIM card that would work in Brazil, so I gave her Celso's number as a way to reach me. Ten minutes later, Deputy Director Michelle Clarke called me on Celso's phone.

Clarke was a civilian who had risen through the agency ranks. I had never met her. Her voice on the line had the professional calm of a 911 operator or a NASA flight controller. "What's our status there, Johns?"

I explained everything I had seen and heard.

"You're certain Kilpatrick is dead?"

"I don't know that at all," I said. "I was a few miles away when it happened, but I don't have any direct information. I'm just here watching the news."

"You're safe, that's the important thing," she said. "Hold tight. The cavalry is on its way."

The news stations at first showed only chaos: the columns of smoke and the distant wreckage of buildings, the crowds of people and police holding them back. Finally, information started to roll in. The president of Brazil, most of her cabinet, and a large number of senators were dead. In one coordinated move, the country had been cut off at the head. Brazil was reeling, its future uncertain. Even the Brazilian newscasters showed a subtle anti-American sentiment, citing American interference as the reason for the rise of certain terrorist groups inside Brazil.

The news also showed rioting, to a degree that surprised me. Looters broke into stores, destroyed public property, and attacked Americans on the street. Not just in Brasília, but in Brazil's other major cities, too: São Paulo, Salvador, Rio de Janeiro. The vice president of Brazil had been in São Paulo when the bombs went off, but no one on the news had been able to confirm that he was alive or get a clear statement from his staff.

"If he was safe, he would make a statement, don't you think?" I said. "To show the country that he's in control and there's a clear line of succession?"

"Maybe he's afraid that he'll be next," Celso said.

A pounding knock on the door startled me. Celso opened it a crack but kept his foot positioned to block it from opening any farther. "What do you want, Emílio?" he asked in Portuguese.

"What's up with that *gringo* in your room?" The voice on the other side of the door sounded drunk.

"What *gringo?*"

Another pound on the door. "Your American friend."

"Hey, take it easy, *mano*. He's not here."

"Tell him to stay away. We don't want him around."

I wondered how many of Emílio's pals were behind him in the hallway. "Don't worry," Celso told him. "He ran like a rabbit as soon as the bombs went off. He went back home to America."

"Good. Don't be bringing any more *gringos* around, you hear?"

"I hear you, Emílio."

"We don't want them here telling us what to do."

"Couldn't agree more," Celso said, closing the door. He locked it and then leaned his back against it.

"I can't stay here, can I?" I said.

"Of course you can stay. Stay as long as you need to."

"You're a good friend," I said. "But I need to get back to the States. I'll get a flight out tomorrow." As I said it, however, I wondered just how easy that would be.

The talking heads on the news stations kept talking all through the night. When they had something new to say, they delivered it with breathless intensity. When they didn't, they repeated the same news in different words. Gradually, as the hours passed, it became clear that the three synchronized bombs were only a small part of the attack. The colonel in command of Manaus Air Force Base, several kilometers from the city of Manaus in the Amazon, had refused orders from central command and declared the base to be "free from imperialist control." At the same time, the Val-de-Cães Naval Base in Belém had deployed boats on the Pará and Amazon Rivers, apparently turning away tourist boats and denying them passage. Just which parts of the military were under whose control seemed to be an open question.

Finally, César Nazif, the chief justice of the Supreme Federal Court and fourth in succession to the presidency, staged a press conference in front of the national cathedral and proclaimed himself acting president of the nation, assuring everyone that the country was under his control, at least until the vice president's whereabouts could be ascertained. At his shoulder stood the imposing form of Júlio Eduardo de Almeida. Celso's father.

—⟳—

In the morning, I called the airport, but I was told that all commercial and non-essential flights had been grounded, by order of acting President Nazif.

"I'll just head back to my hotel and wait it out," I told Celso. "I can communicate with my bosses from there, and I can stay there without inconveniencing or endangering you."

Celso assured me I was welcome where I was, but he saw the sense in my plan.

"I'll walk over with you," he said.

"You might not want to do that."

"I want to make sure you get there safely."

I could already see the change in the city as we walked the streets of the Federal District. Children were nowhere to be seen, nor were family groups, nor the usual games of soccer or sunbathers on the grass. I saw plenty of men, however, especially young men. One had a bulge under his shirt that I suspected concealed a gun. Whatever was happening, it hadn't started overnight. There were forces here that had been growing for some time. The explosions were just the spark, a kind of promise that life in Brazil was about to change. With the balance of power shifting, those who wanted change needed only to step out of their doors and take it.

When we reached the hotel, the man at the front desk assured me with clipped formality that my room reservation had been canceled for non-occupancy, and the room had been rented to another party. I asked for a new reservation, but he told me all their rooms were full. From the number of cars in the lot, I suspected this was a lie, but I had no way to prove it. When I asked him for my suitcase and belongings, he told me that they had been placed in storage for my safety, and that if I would provide my passport for identification purposes, he would send an employee to retrieve them. Without thinking, I handed over my passport and waited while he took it into a back office to make a photocopy for their records.

I leaned against the desk, my eyes roaming over the chandeliers and plush seating. A half-finished chess game sat on a coffee table, and I wondered if it had been abandoned the night before when the blasts went off. A balding man in glasses who looked like a Brazilian businessman sat in one of the plush chairs. He saw me and stood, and for a moment our eyes met. It suddenly occurred to me how stupid I was being.

"Time to go," I said.

"What about your passport?" Celso asked.

"I don't think I'm getting that back. In fact, I think if we don't get out of here in the next thirty seconds, we're going to be guests of the Agência Brasileira de Inteligência."

Avoiding the front door, I turned in the opposite direction from the businessman and ran down a random hallway, expecting that any hall in a hotel would eventually lead to an exit. I wasn't disappointed. We came out by the swimming pool and made our way around to the back of the hotel. I realized I was keeping an eye out for black sedans, as if I were in a movie. In truth, I had no idea what a Brazilian intelligence agent would drive. It seemed unlikely that the guy in the lobby had actually been an intelligence agent. I didn't know if Director Kilpatrick was alive or dead. One thing I was pretty sure of, though: they had raided our rooms and confiscated our luggage, leaving the desk staff with a number to call if I should turn up. I was an idiot not to have realized it before.

"Where to?" Celso asked. "Back to my place?"

I shook my head. "The American embassy."

⎯⎯⎯⎯✺⎯⎯⎯⎯

The embassy was on Naçoes Avenue, not far in a straight line, but situated on the other side of the capital's most important buildings. A direct route would have taken us right past the cathedral where Nazif had announced his presidency. Instead, we took over an hour circling around, trying to avoid major streets and government buildings—a difficult endeavor in the heart of the capital. When we finally arrived, we found a crowd of demonstrators surrounding the building, shouting slogans about American imperialism. The front gates, usually kept open during the day, were tightly shut. I'd seen the movie *Argo*, and I remembered other accounts I'd read of the storming of the American embassy in Iran by hundreds of Iranian militants. This was looking as bad as that.

There was no way to get past the crowd. I considered making a run for the gates and pounding on the door, hoping that the Marines that had to be stationed on the other side would let me in before the crowd could grab me. Then a youth in the crowd flung a bottle that hit the top of the wall and burst into flame. I walked in the other direction, trying not to draw any attention, Celso trailing right behind me.

Brazil was ethnically diverse, and many Brazilians were as light-skinned as me. I was wearing Celso's clothes, I could speak Portuguese fluently, and I knew the city. I thought I should be able to pass for a native, as long as I stayed clear of anyone who knew where I came from.

"This is insane," I said. "Why does everyone hate Americans all of a sudden?"

Celso took off his Yankees cap and stuffed it under his shirt. "It's not so sudden," he said. "You haven't been here for a while."

We headed south and west, away from the city center, trying to look nonchalant. "There were always stereotypes," I said. "Americans are fat; Americans only care about money; Americans don't care about their families. And everyone thinks America wants to rule the world."

"Don't you?" Celso asked.

I glanced at him to see if he was joking. "We don't want to rule," I said. "We just vigorously advance our own interests."

"Seriously," he said. "The United States is powerful. You control all the oceans and all the shipping lanes. You tell other countries where they can sail their navies, when they're allowed to trade, and when they're allowed to fight with their neighbors. Of course people hate you."

"I get that," I said. "And the whole Amazon thing's not exactly new, either. Remember Miss Palmeira in fourth grade? She taught us that children's textbooks in the US say that the Amazon is part of the United States. She was pretty insistent about it, as I recall, even though I told her it wasn't true. But it was never a big deal before, not to most people. Nobody was rioting in the streets about it."

Celso nodded. "That part's pretty new."

We were several blocks away from the embassy by that time. I stopped. "Where are we going?"

"I don't know." He rubbed at his face, thinking. "My mom's family would probably take you in."

"Too obvious," I said. A low stone wall separated a grassy area from the surrounding streets, and I sat down on it. "What about the Lacerdas? Do they still live in this *quadra?*" Carlos Lacerda had been a school friend, and his mother had often stuffed us with baked treats at her house after school.

Celso joined me on the wall, shaking his head. "Carlos is just like the others now."

"You mean he hates Americans?"

"I mean environment-crazy. Talks about protecting the Amazon, keeping out the tourists. All that."

"*Carlos* cares about the Amazon? Last time I saw Carlos, the only things he cared about were watching soccer and kissing Gabriela Garcia. Both at the same time, if he could manage it."

Celso didn't laugh. "It's all anybody talks about anymore," he said. "It's like a virus."

"A virus," I repeated. My mind was racing. I turned to Celso. "Was it really a virus?"

"What are you talking about?"

"Was Carlos sick? Did he have a fever, a bad cough, any kind of lung infection?"

"I don't know. There's been a lot of that going around this year. Some kind of flu epidemic or something." He considered. "You know, he did get sick a few months ago. Knocked him out for a few days."

"Was it about the same time that he got passionate about environmentalism?"

Celso considered. "Could be. What difference does it make?"

"What about your dad? Did he get sick?"

"I don't know. I guess." He thought about it. "A few months ago, he had some kind of bad cold. Couldn't stop coughing. I told him to go the hospital, but he wouldn't, and after a while it just cleared up on its own."

Goosebumps prickled my arms. A fungal infection, acquired in the Amazon, that increased intelligence. An increasing number of Amazon villagers showing signs of enhanced brain function. And now several highly coordinated attacks on South American leaders with the cooperation of their own security. Were they connected? Could the increase in pro-Amazon sentiment really be traced to the influence of a fungal host? Just how many people had been infected?

"Give me your phone," said a voice in Portuguese.

I whirled to see a man standing by the wall behind us. He had dark hair that receded far back on his head, glasses, skin that was neither pale nor dark, and wore dull-colored clothing. He was so forgettable, I almost didn't recognize him as the "businessman" from the hotel lobby.

"Your phone," he said again. "Quickly."

I froze. "Who are you?"

"A friend. And though I doubt the Agência has the resources of the NSA, cell phones can be tracked. If they're looking for you, your phone will lead them straight to us."

"I don't have a phone," I said. "It was in my luggage, and it didn't have a SIM card that could work here anyway."

The man took a step closer, holding out his hand. "Your friend's, then. The one you used to call home."

Celso looked back and forth between us. I nodded. Celso handed over his phone, and the man snapped the battery out in one smooth motion and threw both pieces into a bush. "Come on," he said. He started walking south, not even looking to see if we were following him. I didn't move.

"Who are you?" I said.

He turned back, annoyance evident on his face. "You don't have much time. We need to get you out of here."

"I'm not going anywhere with you until I know who you are and how you know me," I said.

The annoyance disappeared from his face as if it had never been, and the man grinned. "Good show," he said. "You're not entirely stupid after all. They told me your tradecraft was nonexistent—the phone a case in point—and I wanted to see what I could expect from you."

I crossed my arms. "Well?"

"The Major said to tell you that the next time you plan to back your car over a set of security spikes, please wait until after she leaves."

I nodded and let my arms fall. "Good enough for me," I said. "Let's go."

As we walked, he chatted in Portuguese about the weather, about that year's World Cup, apparently about anything that came into his head. After a few blocks, we came upon a gray car with the yellow-and-green stripes of a taxi idling at the curb. "This is our ride," he said, and opened the door for me to climb in.

I looked at Celso. "Are you coming?"

He shook his head. "This is my city. My family is here."

"They might figure out that you helped me."

"I'm not leaving."

I threw my arms around him and squeezed hard. He smelled like Brasília, like my childhood. "Thank you," I said. "Good luck." I ducked into the back seat. The balding man slid in next to me, and the car drove away. I watched Celso's form dwindle in the back window, and wondered if I would ever see him again.

CHAPTER 18

The taxi drove cross-country to São Paulo, an eleven-hour drive. Along the way, the two agents told me that Osvaldo Gonzaga, the Brazilian vice president—now president, at least according to the constitution—had made an official request for assistance from the United States to help him retain legal control over the country. He claimed that several attempts had been made on his life, and that César Nazif's authority grab was nothing less than a coup. While I slept in the back seat on an endless drive through the Brazilian countryside, the United States mobilized a force to invade.

As we approached São Paulo, the traffic on the other side of the road turned ugly. It seemed everyone but us was trying to get out of the city. I didn't know if there had been some kind of attack here already, or if everyone just assumed that this was where the fight was coming, since this was where Gonzaga had set up his provisional government. I spotted several Comanche helicopters in the distance, and once an F-22 roared overhead.

One thing about the United States military: they didn't do anything small. By the time we reached the command center, it was clear this was a major operation. The first wave, still in the process of arriving from the United States, consisted of a battalion of Marines, a recon platoon, light armored units, combat engineers, a Marine aircraft squadron, air defense battery, an anti-terrorism team, a logistical task force, and what seemed like an army's worth of diplomats and intelligence agents. That was just the São Paulo contingent. A larger group was headed for São Luis in the north, as a staging area to attack Belém, at the mouth of the Amazon, which was apparently in the hands of the Ligados. The second wave, which would begin arriving in several days, included two carrier battle groups, led by aircraft carriers USS *Harry S. Truman* and USS *Abraham*

Lincoln, each of which could project enough power all by itself to conquer most countries. There was no question of the United States winning this fight. It was just a question of how much of Brazil would be flattened in the process.

The diplomats and agents and military staff swarmed the *Palácio do Anhangabaú*—São Paulo's city hall—communicating an air of frantic busyness and importance. I wondered how many of them actually knew what was going on. To my surprise, Shaunessy Brennan was there too, waiting in the lobby to claim me. Her long braids were held back in a functional clip, and she wore jeans and a khaki shirt.

"What are you doing here?" I asked.

She shrugged. "Melody has a thing about being on site. She says intelligence is crap if you don't have the right context for it."

She started walking, and I followed. "What actually happened?" I asked. "Do we know?"

"Complete chaos. Rumors on the street have the bombs placed by the Venezuelans, by the FARC, even by the United States. Nobody in the Brazilian government seems to know any better. We have eighty-five Americans trapped in the embassy in Brasília, at least five reports of American tourists under threat in the Amazonian states, a shifting political balance of power, and a major friendly government under threat of collapse. New crises are popping up faster than we can mobilize teams to address them."

"What about Director Kilpatrick?"

She made a sour face. "Confirmed dead. It's pretty certain. An agent actually saw the body herself. The bomb at the Agência seems to have been timed to take him out along with several of their high-ranking people. That or it was a coincidence, but given the precise coordination of all of these attacks, I have to assume it was intentional."

"But why? Terrorist attacks on major leaders in three different countries? What's the ideology? I don't understand what they're trying to accomplish."

"If they're going for destabilization, they're succeeding," Shaunessy said. "Every group with a grudge is coming out of the woodwork and shaking their assault rifles. Central authority is eroding. We have some military bases, mostly in the south, declaring for Gonzaga, and others in the north declaring for Nazif and the Ligados. It's looking like a civil war."

"Wait," I said. "Nazif and the Ligados? Since when are they connected?"

"Nazif declared the Ligados national heroes. He said they've been fighting for the independent sovereignty of a supreme Brazil and protecting their national treasure—meaning the Amazon—from 'foreign despoilment.' So there's your ideology, if there is one—whenever one of these guys talks, it's always about control over the Amazon."

"'Despoilment?' That's Nazif's word?"

"I certainly didn't make it up."

We entered a grand room with granite floors and an arched ceiling, filled with desks and computers and phones, that had been given over to serve as coalition headquarters. Sunlight slanted in through windows on two sides.

"It's a complete intelligence failure," Shaunessy said. "A guerrilla group gaining that kind of influence and power, and we barely knew about them more than six months ago. Thanks to you, we're starting to crack their communications, but only just. We have no idea how they're organized or who's in charge. Their motivating ideal seems to be an environmental one, which is pretty unique as far as large terrorist organizations go. Not that we even know how many members they have. And now that Colombia and Venezuela are invading, we won't have enough time to—"

"Wait. You're kidding me. Invading?"

"I forgot. You've been out of contact."

"Not that long. Less than forty-eight hours."

"The way this is going, you could step out to use the bathroom and be behind the intelligence curve by the time you got back. But yes, Colombia and Venezuela have declared war and are sending troops into

the Amazon—including the Brazilian states—to clear out foreign contamination. We've already had unconfirmed reports of massacres, both of
foreigners and natives, though our intelligence is spotty."

"But, Colombia and Venezuela?" I said. It didn't make any sense at
all. "They've been at each other's throats for years. Venezuela supports
Colombia's rebel factions. Their governments are totally, philosophically
opposed to each other."

"You're preaching to the choir. Nothing we think we know is holding
true anymore. But this is what's happening."

We turned a corner and saw Melody facing down a Marine colonel
who stood a head taller and out-massed her by probably sixty pounds.
"We're done here," Melody said. "Don't talk to me about 'interface challenges,' as if that means anything. Either get me the information I need,
or tell me you don't have the balls to cross agency lines to get it."

"It's not that simple," the man said. "The exploitation goes through
two different stovepipe systems, built by two different contractors for
two different agencies. They just don't talk to each other."

"All I'm hearing is 'I can't' when I needed that data yesterday. Go
bore someone else with your excuses."

The colonel stormed out, while Shaunessy and I watched in awe.
Melody was not technically in his chain of command, and so couldn't
give him orders, much less dress him down for failing to fulfill them. But
everyone knew she had the ear and trust of those who did give the orders,
which amounted to almost the same thing.

Melody smiled at me. "I hate it when one of my own has to be rescued
by the CIA. They never let you live it down. Welcome to São Paulo."

"Having trouble with the help?" I asked.

"Trying to weed out those who kiss other asses to cover their own,"
she said. "There are people who get things done, and people who just get
in the way."

"What's the problem?"

"All our connection models are falling to pieces," she said. "Half of how we do business is by building up these huge graphs of known connections. X is a known associate of Y who is part of organization A who hired company B, which funds the sale of arms to country Q, like that. We use them to track terrorist networks, shifting alliances, potential defectors, all sorts of things. Only we're finding that our connection models here in South America are completely wrong. People who previously had no known connection are suddenly bosom friends. Organizations with opposing goals are suddenly working together. Old alliances are crumbling and new ones are taking their place, as if someone ran them through a random number generator. I'm trying to verify our models against data from other agencies, but it's apparently impossible for the CIA and NRO and NSA to, you know, share critical information with each other."

"So, about that," I said.

"About what? The intelligence community's cripplingly dysfunctional bureaucracy?"

"No. The failing connection models. I might have an idea why."

"Do tell."

"You're going to think I'm crazy."

She rolled her eyes. "You're arrogant and headstrong and you have no sense of self-restraint, but you're not crazy. If you have an idea, spit it out."

"Nobody's acting like they should, right? We have sworn enemies becoming allies, security agents killing the people they protect, indigenous tribesmen working with high-tech encryption. And suddenly everyone wants to protect the Amazon so bad they're willing to kill for it."

"I thought you were going to tell me something I don't know."

"What if it's the fungus?"

The statement hung in the air, stark and ridiculous, and I waited for her to laugh or fire me or throw me out of the room. When she did none of those things, I said, "What if all the people acting out of character are hosts for the fungus—the same one that infected Paul and your granddaughter and, presumably, all of those uneducated people suddenly doing mental gymnastics for reporters? What if, instead of just making them smarter, it was influencing them? Making them care about things they otherwise wouldn't, like protecting the Amazon? Which, by the way, is where the fungus lives." She was still looking at me without expression, so I rolled on, hoping to convince her. "Apparently fungi do this kind of thing all the time. They influence other species, manipulating them in whatever way improves their own survival. Paul's told me about single organisms stretching for acres underground, infecting trees and controlling where and how they grow, manipulating whole ecosystems to be perfect for fungal habitation."

"Controlling trees is a long way from influencing world politics."

"They control animals, too. Sometimes just subtly, pushing them to prefer certain food or habitat choices that improve the survival opportunities for the host. There's a fungus that can completely take control of the brains of ants, forcing them to climb up high and hang onto a leaf, until the fruiting bodies grow out of their heads and burst, dispersing spores over the rainforest. During the time it's taking root inside the ant, however, it benefits it, fighting off diseases or other infections that might threaten it."

"So you think this fungus is intelligent. That it's intentionally controlling thousands of humans to improve its own survival." I had to give her credit; she said it with a straight face.

"It wouldn't have to be aware of what it's doing," I said. "It could just be following its evolutionary programming. Say it alters serotonin levels in response to intentions that could help or harm it, which makes people feel good about one option and not about another. It could influence people that way without any higher-level brain function of its own. But I'm just guessing here."

I realized I hadn't told Melody about my father's miraculous reversal. There had been no chance to do so, since my plane had left just after I found out myself. It reminded me, too, that I hadn't yet called home. My parents had to be worried sick about me. Not just my mom, but my dad, too.

Had I been too hard on Paul? Dad's healing was something extraordinary. If Dad had known such a thing was possible a few years earlier, he would have paid any price for it, taken any risk. Maybe I should have congratulated Paul instead of scolding him. On the other hand, what if the fungus really was the key to all this? Was my father's mind now infected by a creature that could bend whole nations to its purposes?

"I need to call home," I said. "No one there knows I'm safe, and I'm worried about my father."

Melody let out a long breath, and I realized she was tired. "By all means," she said. "And keep thinking about your idea. Think how we could verify it, one way or another. Ask your brother, too—it would be nice to have a mycologist's opinion on whether such a thing is possible."

I remembered my brother in his lab, giddy about the mycelia entwined through his neural pathways, saying, "There are certain portions of my brain they've remapped . . ."

"If such a thing is possible," I said, "I'm not sure we could rely on my brother to tell us the truth about it."

I finally found a phone in a municipal office that someone said I could use. I dialed and reached my mother's cell phone number. "Hello?" she said. She sounded anxious and breathless, as if she had run for the phone.

"It's me, Mom," I said.

"Sorry, I was just parking the car." I heard an engine turn off in the background, then the sound of a door opening.

"It's Neil," I said. "I'm okay. I'm safe."

"Safe? Were you in danger?"

"I was in Brasília, Mom. Haven't you seen the news? The bombs and riots?"

"I haven't had a chance to watch the news. Neil, your father . . . he . . ."

I felt a flood of worry. "What is it? Is he forgetting again?"

"No, but he's. . . . I don't know how to describe it. He's not the way I remember him."

"In what way?" Her comment sparked some old hurts for me. The man my father had been was the man she'd left behind. Now that he was back, did she already find him unsatisfactory? Did she like him better sick and needy? It probably wasn't fair, but I had never entirely come to terms with my mom's on-again, off-again involvement with our family.

"He's more aggressive, more direct. He flirts with the nursing staff. He's, I don't know, just not the person I remember. Rougher. He scares me a little."

I didn't know what to make of that. It seemed natural to me that he would have changed somewhat. You don't just pop back into your right mind after years of dementia without it affecting you. The lost years, the dependence on family, maybe even remembering doing or saying things that made sense at the time but were completely inappropriate. I could see how getting a second chance at life would make you want to live a little larger, take charge of situations, even flirt a little. It had to be a traumatic experience, a little like Rip Van Winkle, waking up from a dream to see how the world had changed around you.

I heard her car door slam, the sound of her footsteps on pavement, other traffic in the distance. "Where are you?" I asked.

"I'm just heading into the hospital." As she said it, I heard the squeak and buffeting air as she passed through the hospital's large revolving door.

"Is Dad still there?" I asked.

"Yes. They're still keeping him for observation. Dr. Chu is concerned with the numbers she's seeing and doesn't think it's safe for him to be on his own yet."

"Dr. Chu? Isn't that the same doctor who treated Paul?"

"The same one. She's a little paranoid, if you ask me. She always wears a surgery mask when she checks on him, and she was pushing to get him moved to an isolation ward. I mean, I'm worried for him, too, but that seems a bit extreme, don't you think?"

"Did she say why?"

"He still has traces of the infection in his body, and she's concerned about it. Paul still does, too, of course, and he says he feels fine. In fact, it was Dr. Chu who originally told Paul it could stick around for years, wasn't it? She seemed to think it was no big deal then."

"It was. And if she's concerned, I would be, too," I said. "Mom, I'm afraid this fungus Paul picked up might be more serious than just a respiratory illness."

"Oh, I know it's serious. That poor girl Paul traveled with. But look at what it's done for your father—he might stress me out, but I can't deny the Alzheimer's has taken a serious step back. Pretty much disappeared, from what I can see."

"So he's still pretty lucid? How much does he remember?"

"He's here," she said. "You can ask him yourself."

I heard the sound of distant conversation and my mom saying, "It's Neil." Then my dad's voice came on, clear and strong. "Neil! Son! Where are you?"

A warmth spread through me, and I let out a breath I didn't know I was holding. It was real. My father, remembering me. It was almost like he had come back from the dead. "I'm in São Paulo, Dad."

"You disappeared so quickly, I hardly got to talk to you. What's happening down there? They had a coup? It's all over the news here. Fortunately, they left my TV on a news channel. If it was daytime soaps, the Alzheimer's might have been better." He laughed, an easy, happy sound, and I was back in our home in Brasília, telling my father some dumb knock-knock joke I heard at school or delighting him with a Portuguese/English pun.

"Looks like a coup, yeah." I didn't know what was public knowledge, so I didn't say anything more about the political situation or mention Venezuela and Colombia. "Looks like I might be down here a little while yet. I don't know how easy it'll be to get a flight home. I miss you."

"I wish they would let me leave this stupid hospital," he said. "I'm healthy. My mind is working again, as well as it ever did, if not better. There's no reason for me to be here anymore."

"Listen to your doctor," I said. "And be careful how much you listen to Paul. Despite what a mycologist might think, it's not a good thing to have fungal mycelia growing through your body. If Dr. Chu tells you to take medication, take it."

"All right, all right," he said. "Look, you get home as soon as you can, you hear? We have a few years of catching up to do."

—⊙—

My next order of business was to submit to a debriefing by the CIA, a grueling five-hour session that felt more like an interrogation than an interview. I told them everything I knew, including my theories about Paul's fungus. They were, to put it mildly, skeptical. I didn't press the point. I would have doubted me, too.

When they finally let me go, I was ready for bed. Command staff and agency personnel had requisitioned nearby hotels, but before I could find out whether they had a room for me, Melody found me. "I have someone I want you to talk to," she said.

I sighed, expecting another debriefing. "Who's that?"

"Her name is Mariana Fernanda de Andrade," Melody said. "She was until recently, a member of *Dragões da Independência*, the Presidential Guard Battalion, assigned to protect the vice president. We caught her planting a bomb in the Palácio's parking garage, in the spot reserved for the presidential vehicle."

"Is she—"

"Infected? Yes. I insisted on a full battery of imaging tests at the local hospital. A doctor there confirmed the presence of a fungal infection with deep incursion into brain tissue."

"And you want *me* to talk to her? I'm no interrogator."

"Believe me, the professionals have had their chance at her. I want to know what you see."

I rubbed at my eyes. So far, working for the NSA seemed to involve a great deal of operating on insufficient sleep. "I'll do it," I said.

The prison stood on the other side of the city, a twenty-minute drive. It was old, like the neighborhood around it, and made of concrete and steel. The guards wore riot gear and combat boots and carried shotguns and automatic weapons. Two guards brought Mariana de Andrade out with manacles chained to her hands and feet and sat her roughly in the chair across the table from me. They stood behind her, their faces as grim as their black clothing, and their shotguns held diagonally across their chests. She stared at the floor instead of at me, but her expression was belligerent.

"Are they treating you well?" I asked.

She held up the thick chains and spoke English with a heavy accent. "Would you be treat well, you have these?"

I switched to Portuguese. "I'm not a cop," I said. "I have no authority here. I just want to understand why a career soldier on protective detail for the acting president suddenly decides to betray her country."

She made eye contact for the first time and responded in Portuguese. "Is that what you think? That I betrayed my country?"

"What would you call it? You swore to protect the president, and you just tried to kill him."

"*Vice* president Gonzaga gave up his right to the presidency the moment he called for you."

"For me?"

She made an all-encompassing motion, to the extent her chains permitted. "All of you. *Gringos*. Imperialists. You have three-quarters of the world in your pocket, but it's not enough. You want to control Brazil, too."

I watched her face, looking for anything unusual, any distinction between the real Mariana de Andrade and the influence of the fungus. "So, you think it's appropriate to murder a leader who makes a decision you disagree with?" I asked. "I'm surprised you lasted in the service this long."

THE GENIUS PLAGUE

"Not just any decision. *This* decision."

"Why?"

"It's our country. Not yours. When he gave it away, he lost his right to govern it."

"Did anyone suggest to you that you should do this? Were you in any way prompted by César Nazif or his provisional government?"

"We're all connected," she said. The Portuguese word she used was *ligados*.

"Who are? You and Nazif?"

"Everyone who wants to protect this land and its resources is connected."

"So you were under orders? Compelled in some way?"

"You intentionally twist my meaning." Her eyes, which had drifted away to stare at the floor, found my face again. "It was necessary. It was right. It was the only thing I could do."

I decided to try a different approach. "Do you know you have a fungal organism growing in your brain?"

She narrowed her eyes. "A what?"

"A fungal organism. You picked up a lung infection, which would have given you a bad cough for a while, maybe even put you in the hospital. Do you remember that?"

"I was in the hospital three or four weeks ago. I was coughing up blood."

"The organism that caused that infection is still in your body. It's been growing up into your brain."

She shrugged. "I know. The doctor recommended a sugar-rich diet to help it grow."

I gaped at her. "A *doctor* told you it was a good thing to have a fungus living in your brain?"

"Of course. He said his had been growing for weeks, and that he'd found that a diet high in carbohydrates and sugars helped increase its health and size."

I didn't know what to say. I knew my brother welcomed the idea of a fungal parasite, but he was a mycologist. He was weird. "Didn't that strike you as odd? I mean, it's not exactly a common thing."

She smiled. "More common than you think."

A Marine helicopter passed nearby, rattling windows with its chop. "Who is your doctor?" I asked, raising my voice to be heard over the noise.

"It doesn't matter," she said, standing. "There are too many of us for you to stop."

One of the black-clad soldiers behind her said, "The prisoner will sit down." I realized the helicopter wasn't passing by. The sound of its rotors was louder and directly overhead, as if it were landing on the roof.

The soldier took a step toward her, his hand on his weapon. "Sit down. Right now."

"I'm sorry," she said. "I have to go."

The second soldier raised his shotgun without warning and shot the first soldier point blank in the back of the head. The noise was deafening in the small, concrete room. The man's face and neck exploded, showering the far wall with blood. I stumbled backward, falling onto the floor against the wall, adrenaline flooding my system. Mariana seemed completely unsurprised. She didn't even turn around to see what had happened.

I heard nothing but a high buzzing sound and the pounding of my own blood in my ears. In slow-motion, like we were underwater, I watched the soldier turn his shotgun toward me.

"Stay where you are," his lips said, though I couldn't hear the sound. I didn't move while he unlocked her chains and the two walked out of the interview room, or for long minutes after. By the time my hearing returned, the room was quiet but for the faraway sound of shouting prisoners and the beat of a helicopter's rotors receding into the distance.

CHAPTER 19

Melody was furious. She showed it with a kind of quiet energy that did nothing to mask the inferno behind her eyes, a furnace I expected to explode on the first person not in her inner circle who did something she thought was stupid. She had been a kind of queen of intelligence, bullying the bureaucracy into effectiveness and solving the unsolvable. Now, her agency was utterly failing to anticipate the enemy, and none of the tactics she relied on were working.

"We need to test everybody," she said. "All the agents, all the soldiers, the general staff, everybody. We need to know they're on our side."

Melody and Shaunessy and I were crammed into the closet-sized room they'd allocated her for an office. "Is that practical?" I asked.

"Not if we have to do PET scans or MRIs. We need a blood test, preferably one that doesn't take a week of analysis in a lab to reach a conclusion. That's your task for tomorrow. Check with the Brazilian docs who examined Ms. Andrade and see what they can tell you. Then find the Army docs and tell them we've got a potential epidemic on our hands. You said your brother has cultures of this thing?"

I yawned. I couldn't help it. It was two o'clock in the morning, and the last time I'd slept had been in the back seat of a taxi. "He does, in his lab at UMD. I'm not sure if he'll be willing to give them up, though."

"He'll have to. This is an infectious disease issue, so we need to get USAMRIID involved, and the FBI as well. This is a threat we can't ignore."

"Does Deputy Director Clarke know?" Shaunessy asked. "And General Cardiff?" Cardiff was the commander of the US forces in Brazil.

"They know," Melody said, "but they don't really believe me. The evidence is pretty thin, and it's not something they've been trained to expect. If people were dying, and I said 'pandemic,' they'd have docs in HAZMAT suits swarming the place like flies. But people betraying their country because of an infection? It doesn't compute. They don't have a category to put it in."

One thing they had in Brazil was good coffee. I refilled my disposable cup from the pot Melody kept going day and night.

"What was she like when you talked to her?" Melody asked, meaning Mariana de Andrade. "Could you tell? Did she seem drugged, or high, or like anything was wrong?"

"No," I said. "She didn't, and it was pretty creepy. She seemed perfectly lucid and rational. On the other hand, she considered it perfectly normal to have a fungal parasite sending tendrils through her brain, to the extent that she seemed surprised I would question it."

"She knew?"

"Yeah. And get this—she said her doctor was infected, too. That he was giving her tips for how to help it grow."

"We need to find that doctor. Shaunessy, contact the local police tomorrow. They should know how to pull her medical records."

"My brother didn't mind the idea of a fungal parasite either, but I didn't think it was weird coming from him. I mean, it was *weird*, but fungi is his thing. It's like a herpetologist kissing snakes. It wasn't out of character. From Andrade, though . . ."

"To be fair, we don't know what her character was to begin with," Melody said. "But I agree. Weird."

"I'll call home first thing in the morning," I said. "If Paul won't give up his cultures, maybe my dad will allow a blood sample to be sent to USAMRIID."

"I know a guy there," Melody said. "You get your father to give his consent, and I'll take care of the rest."

I followed Shaunessy to the hotel where they were housing American staff, and the cheerful desk clerk informed me that all the rooms were full. "Come on," Shaunessy said. "My room has a pull-out couch. Not much more than a foam cushion, from what I can tell, but it'll be better than nothing."

I felt awkward. "That's okay," I said. "I'll call another hotel. There's got to be some place that—"

"There won't be. They'll be booked for miles around, and by the time you find a place, it'll be morning. Come on. I promise I won't take advantage of you."

I smiled. "Well. In that case."

By the time we reached the elevator, my yawns were coming so fast I could hardly close my mouth. I walked into her room, lay down on the couch without pulling out the bed, and shut my eyes.

After what seemed like only moments, the gray light of morning filtered through the curtain, and the phone was ringing with a jarring tone loud enough to split rock. Shaunessy answered it. She made a few one-syllable replies, then set the phone in its cradle.

"We're at war," she said.

—⊙—

We made it back to the Palácio do Anhangabaú in time for the general staff's daily briefing, which was held in one of the largest rooms and packed with people, both American and Brazilian. An Air Force colonel stood at the front, illustrating his summary with a series of pictures taken from satellite and drone imagery. I recognized the format as the same one used by the intelligence agencies to produce the president's daily briefing. It was the end of the analysis chain, a carefully selected meal of easily digested tidbits linked to maps and statistics.

I also knew how biased it could be.

"Ligados forces initiated hostilities twenty miles west of São Luis at 0300," the colonel said. "The attack was a coordinated land and air assault including a combination of Brazilian and Venezuelan forces. US casualties were light, and the attacking forces were almost completely neutralized. Our fighters followed retreating air units back to Val de Cans airfield in Belém. At 0450, B-52s from the 11th Bomb Squadron com-

menced a retaliatory strike. Bomb assessment confirms complete neutral-
ization of Val de Cans as a future staging area for air assault."

Melody watched the briefing with heavy lids and unfocused eyes. She
wore the same clothes as the day before, and I wondered if she had slept at
all. The colonel switched to a summary of drone coverage of the Amazon
states, noting that the vast area and thick ground cover made thorough
enemy identification problematic.

"He means we have no idea what we're up against," Melody said. She
didn't really lower her voice, so half the room heard her.

The colonel wrapped up his briefing with a series of "happy snaps,"
imagery selected more for its wow factor than its intelligence value.
We saw an F-22 ripping past the explosion of an enemy aircraft it had
just destroyed, the ravaged remains of a Val de Cans airstrip, a ragged
line of enemy troops running into the trees away from an unbroken US
emplacement.

"Stop!" Melody stood, her eyes suddenly sharp. "Whose are those?"
She indicated the bottom right corner of the most recent image, where I
could just make out two blurry aircraft.

The colonel's smile was patronizing. "Commercial craft, ma'am.
Single-pilot turboprops, from the look of them, maybe agricultural
planes. Non-military."

"And what possible reason would a pair of crop dusters have to be
flying through a war zone in the middle of a dogfight?"

"I assume they just found themselves at the wrong place at the wrong
time."

Melody rolled her eyes and turned on her heel, not waiting to hear
General Cardiff's closing remarks. Shaunessy and I traded glances and
then jumped up to follow her.

"What's up with the crop dusters?" I said when we caught up with her.

"Isn't it obvious?"

I considered. "They're requisitioning civilian planes for military
purposes?"

She stopped and faced me so suddenly I almost collided with her. "What do crop dusters do?" she asked.

I opened my mouth, then shut it again, feeling foolish. "You think they're using them to spread fungal spores," Shaunessy said. "They're trying to infect more people."

"I think," Melody said, biting off each word, "that this whole suicidal attack might have been engineered for the sole purpose of getting those crop dusters close to our troops."

—⊙—

The radar data confirmed Melody's suspicions. It was obvious, once you were looking for it. Ten crop dusters in total, flying in pairs from different angles, their approach timed to coincide with attacks by military aircraft. They stayed low and never approached directly, but their course always brought them upwind of the US base of operations or São Luis. In the darkness, the clouds of particles they released wouldn't have been visible.

"I'm talking about biological warfare," Melody said. She stood in General Cardiff's office, which she had entered without knocking, completely ignoring the fact that he was in conference with his top commanders. She had thrown the data on the desk in front of him and insisted that he treat every soldier in São Luis as a potential hostile until they could be tested.

The general was lean and tough-looking at sixty years old. His hair was still dark, with only a touch of gray at the temples, and the deep lines of his face cut sharply, giving him an intense, hardened look. I doubted he could have slept much either, but he seemed energetic and ready to take on the world. "We have a process for this, Ms. Muniz. I have a Theater Army Medical Laboratory on site staffed with doctors trained to recognize biological agents in the field. There has been a significant sickness rate, I'll admit, and they're testing regularly. But the chief doc out there tells me he's not seeing any of the warning signs. Just a bad respiratory infection making the rounds, not uncommon with troops on a different continent."

"This is something different," Melody said. "Mr. Johns here has seen it at work." I was already nervous, standing behind her surrounded by the top brass. Now I wanted to sink into the floor. It was a theory, one that seemed to fit the facts, but hardly backed up with any significant scientific research. If they challenged me on it, I had nothing to back Melody's claims but my uneasiness with my brother and father, and a lot of unconfirmed pattern matching. "It's not designed to kill," Melody continued, when I didn't speak up. "At least not many. It's more subtle than that. It's going to affect their minds, erode their patriotism, influence their choices. It's like Ms. Andrade. Until they're tested, you can't trust them."

"Andrade was a traitor, pure and simple," the general said. "I don't need any viral voodoo to explain that one. And what do you expect me to do? Give brain scans to three thousand servicemen? We don't have the equipment, and we don't have the time. If you want me to take this more seriously, you'll need to provide more concrete intelligence than the appearance of a few turboprops on the outskirts of an air battle. I'm not discounting what you're saying, but it's not enough."

"At least let me speak with the ranking corps officer," Melody said.

"Be my guest. You're welcome to convince him with whatever data you have available. In the meantime"—and here an ironic note slipped into his voice—"may I have your permission to continue meeting with my senior staff?"

Melody didn't even blush. "Of course, General," she said.

As they shut the door behind us, I heard Cardiff say, "So that's why they call her the Major." His senior officers laughed.

If Melody heard them, she gave no sign.

—⊙—

Melody delegated to me the task of contacting Captain Suharto, the ranking medical corps officer at São Luis. I called him and explained my suspicions over the phone as convincingly as I could. He was polite, but unimpressed. He asked what medical background I had, what laboratory tests had been performed, what field studies with substantial statistical findings. The longer I talked to him, the more I started to doubt my own theory.

"General Cardiff said you've seen a lot of respiratory illness," I said. "Has that been fungal in nature?"

"I expect so, but it's mostly a presumptive diagnosis," Suharto said. "Fungal etiology is hard to prove and generally unnecessary to treat in less serious cases. But as you probably know, fungal infections are endemic in this region. The rainforest, the humidity, combined with a large pool of previously unexposed subjects, and a high incidence of minor infection is inevitable."

"Did the number of cases go up this morning?"

I heard him typing on a computer, presumably checking the data. "They did, as a matter of fact, by a good margin. Not epidemic proportions or anything, but a definite increase. What do you know that I don't?"

I explained to him about the crop dusters and our suspicion that they were raining spores down on the camp.

Next to me, Shaunessy typed rapidly at a computer, nested lines of software code that I didn't comprehend spidering across her screen. On two other screens beside her, she monitored the feeds from a dozen drones. The live video tracked military movements, zoomed in on specific buildings or out to view square miles at a time. Shaunessy wasn't controlling them; she had just accessed the streaming data. Before I called Suharto, she had muttered something about training a deep learning network to recognize anomalous activity, but I barely understood what she meant.

"If it's biological warfare, they're not doing a terribly good job of it," Suharto said. "I appreciate the call, and we'll keep our eye out. A little respiratory infection isn't going to destroy our will to fight, though. I had an infection myself a few days ago. Unpleasant at the time, but I felt better after forty-eight hours. That's what it'll be for most of these soldiers."

I paused. "You were infected, sir?"

"Nasty cough, bloody nose, high fever. Knocked me off my feet for a day and a half, and I felt miserable, let me tell you. It's the price you pay when you enter a new microbial ecosystem. Lots of opportunistic organisms happy to find a new home. Life-threatening for immunocompromised hosts, but not a serious danger for the rest of us."

He was so confident, so articulate, that I found it hard to doubt him. But what if he, too, was under the influence of the fungus? Would he even know it himself?

An idea occurred to me. "I suppose it won't matter once Cardiff's plan to raze the rainforest goes into effect," I said. Shaunessy looked up from her typing long enough to give me an odd look.

"What did you say? Raze the forest? As in, burn it?" Suharto said.

"Yeah. I don't think it's classified or anything. He's planning to take out as many acres of rainforest as he can. Use accelerants to make it burn faster, get some real forest fires going. Of course, the Amazon basin is as big as the United States. Obviously he's not going to burn *all* of it. He'll concentrate on those areas where there's suspected enemy activity, burn as much as he can. Part of the whole 'shock and awe' strategy, right?"

When Suharto replied, his voice was shaking. "He wouldn't do that. He couldn't."

"I'm pretty sure he could."

"The Amazon is priceless. It's the only place like it in the world. The number of unique species, the ecological complexity, the carbon and oxygen contribution to the planet. He can't burn it. I'd rather lose this war than see it won through such means."

The strength of emotion behind Suharto's speech chilled me. I didn't even disagree with anything he said—it *would* be a crime to burn acres of rainforest, and the Amazon was valuable for all the reasons he mentioned and more. Furthermore, I had no way of knowing if Suharto had been passionate about ecological preservation before his infection. But the fact that my little test had been so dramatically passed frightened me more than I wanted to admit.

"I apologize," I said. "A staffer here just corrected me. That strategy was apparently suggested but ultimately rejected by the general."

"I should hope so," Suharto said.

"I'm not really privy to policy. Sorry if I upset you. I guess that'll teach me to listen to gossip."

"No harm done." The emotion vanished from the captain's voice. "I'll keep a watch on those infection rates, but really, I think there's nothing to worry about."

Shaunessy waved to get my attention. She looked alarmed. She clicked on one of the Reaper drone's camera feeds so that it filled one of the screens.

"I'm sorry, I have to go now," I said into the phone. "Sorry to trouble you, Captain."

"No trouble," Suharto said. "Good day."

I ended the call and gave Shaunessy my attention. "What is it?"

She pointed to the feed. The way the Reaper's camera was angled, I could see one of the wings, its underside loaded with Hellfire missiles, black with yellow stripes. I could also spot the edge of its 150-kilowatt laser—a new addition to the Reaper weapons catalog that enabled it to attack other aircraft, not just ground targets. The rest of the camera's field of view showed a small city, studded with office block towers and surrounded on three sides by water. The ocean was turquoise and the wide bay beyond the city's bridges a sparkling blue.

"Is that São Luis?" I asked.

"Yes," she said, "but this drone is assigned to monitor Belém, three hundred miles away. Why is it here?"

I shrugged. "Coming back to refuel?"

Shaunessy tapped on the screen, where a column of numbers and abbreviations overlaid the edge of the image. "It's still got three-quarters of a tank."

"Maybe it's malfunctioning, and they're bringing it in for repairs?"

The drone slid over the city and crossed the bay. The precisely ordered tent city of the US Marine camp came into view, the rows of dark green canvas surrounded by sandbag walls. The camera swiveled to locate the vehicle area, where tanks, trucks, armored earth movers, and tactical vehicles of all kinds sat parked in neat lines.

"I'm sure they have it on radar," I said. "Nothing gets within a hundred miles of that camp without them knowing it. The guy flying it is probably *in* that camp."

"That's what I'm afraid of."

"You don't think . . ." I started to say, but I trailed off when a white box appeared in the center of the screen and a red light started flashing in the lower left corner.

"No," Shaunessy said. "No no no no no no."

I snatched the phone and redialed Suharto's number. Reaching the field commander or some other combat officer would probably have been better, but I didn't know how to reach them, and I didn't have time to find out.

"Hello?" The voice that answered was female, stressed, and not Suharto. "This is HQ in São Paulo," I said. "Be advised that a friendly drone is targeting your position. Repeat, a friendly armed drone is about to fire on your camp."

The voice on the other end laughed, high and panicked. "Is that all?" she said. "We've got bigger problems here right now."

With a jet of white contrail, one of the Reaper's Hellfires rocketed off the rails and dropped toward the ground. Seconds later, it hit the side of an Abrams tank and tore it open in a silent explosion. On screen, it seemed tiny, just a distant flash with no color or sound to give it power.

The woman on the line started swearing. "What's happening there?" I demanded.

"Traitors," she said, her voice an anguished growl. "Soldiers all over the camp just opened fire, without warning, killing their commanding officers, their friends, anyone. It was coordinated, sir. They planned it. I don't know why. I barricaded myself in medical, but I don't know how long that's going to last." I could hear the staccato bursts of automatic weapons in the background. "What should I do, sir?"

"I'm not an officer," I said, weakly.

"You said you were HQ!"

"I'm just an analyst." I stared at the screen, numb, as another Hellfire turned the camp's command building into burning rubble. I could see the blurry forms of men running from the blast. The woman on the phone with me disconnected the call, but I kept it to my ear, imagining I could hear the screams. Shaunessy shouted into a headset, telling the brass on the floor above us what was happening. "I don't know what you should do," I said into the dead phone. "I just don't know."

The drone's wide-angle lens gave us a clear view of the camp as five-hundred-pound bombs fell from the sky by the dozens. We found out later that a single B-52H from the 11th Bomb Squadron had failed to release any ordnance on the attack on Val de Cans. Instead, it returned to São Luis and dropped its entire load of eighty-one bombs and twenty cruise missiles on the US camp before flying straight into the ocean.

Of the three thousand soldiers stationed at São Luis, less than two hundred survived.

The combination of shock and exhaustion made my head spin. I felt like a fog was creeping around the edge of my vision. I kept seeing the bombs fall, the military tents erupt into gray clouds of smoke. When I stumbled upstairs to find Melody, she grabbed me by both arms and stared me down until my vision cleared and I looked her in the eye. "Get your brother on the phone. Talk to your father, to the doctors who treated him, anyone you can find. We need to be able to test for this thing. Something simple we can do for thousands of soldiers in the field. That or we need a cure."

"My brother and father are infected," I said. "They'll be just like the traitors in São Luis. We can't tell them anything, or trust anything they tell us."

"Your brother has answers we need. If not him, then maybe his university. Somebody. We need to know how this thing works, how it spreads, and how to know who's infected and who isn't."

"Okay. I'm on it," I said.

I found a free phone out in the big room and made the call. My mother picked up halfway through the first ring. "Neil?" Her voice sounded tinny, and there was a faint echo on the line.

"I need to talk to Paul," I said. "Is he there?"

She said something I couldn't make out.

I cupped my hand over my other ear, trying to block out the bustle and conversation of the office around me. "What?"

"I said he's missing!"

"Who is? Paul?"

"Both of them." Her voice shook with emotion. "They walked out of here together, shortly after you called. When I got back, his room was empty. Neil, you have to come home. Your father's gone."

CHAPTER 20

▌I had no way to call you," my mom said, her voice shaking, verging on tears. "The doctors didn't discharge him. Nobody even saw them go. I have no idea where they went."

My mind raced. I was still reeling from the attack on São Luis, and the world of Glen Burnie, Maryland, seemed impossibly distant. "Did you call the police?"

"They left a note, Neil. A tiny scribbled note on a hospital pad saying that they had important things to do and hoped I would understand." Mom started crying, her tears making her stammer. "The police say there's nothing they can do. That two adult men are free to make their own choices."

"But Dad's sick. He needs care. That's like kidnapping."

I could almost hear her helpless shrug. "He's not sick anymore. And he doesn't owe me anything. Apparently he doesn't need me anymore."

"That's nonsense. He had a few hours of lucidity. We don't know if it will last. We don't know how complete it was. He's out there somewhere with Paul, and what does he remember of the last few years? Is he forming new memories now? We don't know, and I don't think we can just assume he's safe. Certainly not because *Paul* is with him."

"I'm so worried for them," she said. "For both of them. Where could they have gone?"

South America might be coming apart at the seams, but my responsibility to my family came first. Somebody else would have to save the world. "I'm coming home, Mom," I said. "I'll be on the first plane out of here."

—⊙—

The first plane turned out to be one of a fleet of C-130Js making daily runs to and from Eglin Air Force Base in Florida. Melody made no objection to me leaving; in fact, she encouraged it, with the idea that Paul's research and knowledge might be the key to everything. Most of the military planes were coming in, not going out, and São Paulo's three commercial airports had been shut down except for critical travel. The Brazilian air force had taken complete control of Guarulhos International for military purposes. That left the C-130s.

They strapped me to a paratrooper jump seat on the wall of the aircraft's forty-one-foot cargo bay. The Super Hercules, as the plane was called, was known for its incredible carrying capacity and range, but it was not designed for creature comforts. It was loud and cold and vibrated violently enough that my teeth hurt. My seat was made of metal framing and canvas webbing, not much more than a camping chair that pulled down from the side of the aircraft.

By an hour in, I felt battered and sore. After two hours, I was starting to talk to myself over the din, which was loud enough to give me a headache, even though the pilot had given me a pair of earplugs. And it wasn't until we hit the three hour mark that I worked up enough courage to visit what passed for a toilet, which the pilot had referred to as the "honeypot" when showing me my seat. When we finally landed at Eglin eight hours later, I thought that if someone threatened me at gunpoint to get back in the plane, I just might choose the bullet.

When I boarded the commercial flight to Maryland, the cramped economy class seat felt like luxury. It even provided an in-flight phone, which I wasted no time putting to use. I called the University of Maryland first, where the provost told me Paul had failed to show up for his classes that week. I called his apartment building and spoke to the landlord, who informed me that he didn't keep track of his tenants' comings and goings, and he wouldn't give out information to anyone but the police even if he did. I thought about telling him I was NSA and threatening him a bit, but I didn't think that would change his mind. And it was probably illegal.

I tried the police instead but got a similar runaround. Their policy, the duty officer informed me, was to consider each missing person report on a case-by-case basis and determine the duration and intensity of the search accordingly. In the case of my father, there was every indication that he had left willingly and without coercion, and he had left behind a record of his intention to leave in the form of a note.

"But he has Alzheimer's," I said. "He can't just leave. It's not safe."

"According to the file, he left with a legal caregiver."

"He wasn't even discharged from the hospital. My brother just took him, and nobody knows where they are."

"Sir, I'll tell you what I can do. I can put you in touch with the officer who made the report. I can also recommend that you contact the hospital or Mr. Johns's physician. If they can confirm that he is at medical risk, that will raise the priority of his case."

I called the number for the reporting officer, but it went to voicemail. I left a message, expecting that I would have to keep calling until I finally reached him. I dialed the hospital next, and, after several transfers, spoke with the head nurse on the floor where my father had been treated. She confirmed that my father had walked out without a doctor's discharge or anyone noticing.

"How does that happen?" I asked, pretty frustrated by that point. "Don't you have security?"

Her voice was brittle. "We do have security, sir. But we're not jailors. We can't keep people against their or their caregivers' will."

"He had Alzheimer's! He was on a twenty-four-hour patient watch."

"Not on the morning he left. That watch had been canceled."

"By whom?"

"I can't share those details with you."

I was incredulous. "My mentally handicapped father is missing, and you can't share the details of his disappearance?"

"Sir, I'm sorry you can't locate your father, but under patient privacy laws I'm not permitted to reveal any information from his medical records, including the timing and reasons he was removed from medical watch."

"Did my brother cancel it? Paul Johns?" I didn't remember for certain, but it was quite possible that, as the oldest son, Paul had been given power of attorney for my father's care decisions. He was clever and manipulative, though, so maybe he wouldn't even have needed it.

"I'm not at liberty to reveal—"

"Yeah, I heard you," I said. "What if I told you I was going to sue your hospital for letting a mentally ill Alzheimer's patient wander off the grounds?" It wasn't exactly fair—my father had, after all, shown every sign of being cured of his Alzheimer's before I left. But she didn't know that, and I was angry that she didn't seem to care. The point was, he was missing. For all that I knew, his Alzheimer's had returned as quickly as it had gone, and he was wandering the streets with no memory of who he was or how to find his way home.

The phone went quiet. I thought she might have hung up on me until a different woman's voice spoke. "Mr. Johns?"

"Yes."

"My name is Indira Sengupta. I'm legal counsel here at the medical center. I understand you are trying to acquire information about your father."

"My father is missing. He's been missing ever since he walked out of your hospital. I'm not trying to 'acquire information.' I'm trying to determine if he's even still alive." I realized my voice was getting louder and the passengers sitting around me on the plane were staring, but I didn't care. "When he turns up dead, hit by a car or drowned in the river, I'm going to tell the story to every news media this side of the Mississippi. Is that the kind of publicity you want? Not to mention the millions I'll pull in from the lawsuit."

"According to his file, we acted according to the express wishes of the family."

"Yeah? And, in your professional legal opinion, do you think that's going to make any difference in court?"

"Mr. Johns, please. I—"

"What I want is to find out what state of mind and health my father was in when he left, as well as any indication anyone has of where he might have gone. I want this to be treated like an emergency, because as far as I'm concerned, it is an emergency. You don't just let an Alzheimer's patient wander away."

"He didn't wander away," Sengupta said, and there was some steel in her voice now. "He left under the supervision of a family member with legal responsibility for his care."

"How do you know? Were you there?"

"The records—"

"You mean the ones you won't let me see?"

"I'm not saying that you can't see them. Over the phone, however, without any identification, I can't share anything with you. For your father's own safety—"

"Let me tell you what you're going to do," I said. "My mother will come to the front desk of the hospital in one hour. You will meet her there, personally, with a complete copy of my father's medical record, which as his spouse she is perfectly within her rights to demand."

"Legally, the hospital has fifteen days to comply with any request for—"

"Do you have a photocopier?"

"What? Yes."

"And you have access to my father's patient record?"

"Yes, I do, but . . ."

"Then walk over to the machine, press the big green button, and make some copies. Say the words 'fifteen days' again, and my next call is to the *Washington Post*."

I heard a deep sigh from the other end of the phone. "All right, Mr. Johns. If your mother can demonstrate her legal right to the information, I will give her a copy of the record in question at the front desk in one hour's time."

"Don't be late," I said, and slammed the phone into its cradle hard enough that the person sitting in the seat in front of me probably felt the jolt. To my surprise, the passengers nearby broke into light, spontaneous applause.

I collapsed back into my seat and caught my breath before calling my mother and asking her to meet Ms. Sengupta at the hospital. Then I closed my eyes and thought. Where might Paul have taken him? Why did they leave? Could they have gone to see my sister? It seemed like a longshot, but I called Julia anyway. I found that Mom had already talked to her, but Julia hadn't seen or heard from either my father or Paul.

It seemed likely that their disappearance had to do with the influence of the fungus infiltrating their brains. But it wasn't clear to me yet just how that influence worked. My brother had talked about it remapping his brain for greater efficiency. But whatever control it wielded, it worked so subtly that its victims seemed unaware of it. Perhaps the genius of the fungus was not in its ability to implant specific thoughts, but in steering the host into using his or her own sophisticated problem-solving ability in its favor.

Humans are driven by emotion. Much of our so-called logic is merely the rationalization of choices that make us feel good. For one person, a fast car might create feelings of power and control that drove away fears of not measuring up. For another, a sports jersey or a telescope or a scale model of the Star Trek *Enterprise* might evoke associations of acceptance by a group of friends. Walking into a church could prompt feelings of safety and belonging, or else it might spark painful emotions of past hurts, and thus would be avoided at all costs. Emotions were often subtle, operating under the surface of our awareness, influencing our purchases, our choice of career or spouse, our home decor and style of interaction. The logic came afterward, a scaffolding we erected to support the decisions we already wanted to make.

What if, besides streamlining our neural pathways, the fungus was hacking our emotions? It would be the perfect way for a non-intelligent creature to influence an intelligent one. Instead of controlling thoughts and decisions directly—a feat that would require the complex coevolution of an organism specifically designed to target the human brain—it could simply adjust brain chemistry and let the host do the sophisticated part on its own.

All this was just theory, though, a pattern I was trying to map on the points of data I had. When it came down to it, I was a cryptologist and mathematician, not a biologist. I needed someone who actually understood the workings of the brain and what a fungal infection might reasonably evolve to do. Someone who could tell me if my theories made any sense, and if so, what that would mean for my father and brother. And for that matter, for the world.

I picked up the phone again and called the hospital. This time, I asked to be connected to Dr. Mei-lin Chu. Chu was the fungal infection specialist who had treated Paul at the hospital and prescribed his medication and apparently had been involved with Dad's care as well. She had, at least, seen the infection at work and would have medical and biological insights I didn't have.

I knew how hard it was to get a doctor on the phone, so I was surprised when, after only two intermediaries, Dr. Chu herself answered the phone. "Yes?" She sounded harried, overworked.

I froze. How to broach such a subject with a stranger? "Um . . . I'm calling about a patient you treated a few months ago? Paul Johns?"

"Yes!" Her tone of voice changed in an instant from peremptory to fully engaged. "Are you from the CDC? Did you read my report?"

"Um. No. I'm Paul's brother, Neil Johns. I think you also treated my father."

She swore softly under her breath. "What can I do for you, Mr. Johns?"

I thought quickly. It sounded like she might respond better to me in an official capacity than as a family member. I lowered my voice to a near whisper, concerned about what my fellow passengers might overhear. "I'm also an analyst with the NSA," I said. "I'm afraid that my brother—along with possibly thousands of people in South America—have been infected by a fungus that is compromising their ability to make their own decisions."

Silence on the other end. This was the point at which I either connected with her or she hung up politely and told the hospital answering service to block my calls.

"Where are you?" she said. "We need to meet."

"I'm on an airplane landing at BWI in"—I checked the time—"half an hour." I told her my flight number.

"I'll meet you at the airport," she said.

CHAPTER 21

With the time I had left before we started our descent, I called Shaunessy in São Paulo to get an update on the war. She couldn't tell me much on an open line, but she confirmed that, after what had happened at São Luis, the command staff was now taking our claims seriously. Cardiff had ordered all senior officers to undergo PET scans, and crop dusters had risen to the top of Ground Theater Air Control's surveillance watch list. I wondered what would happen once the media realized that the bombs that took so many American lives had been dropped by American planes. It couldn't stay secret for very long.

Airplane flights had always wreaked havoc with the pressure in my inner ear, and by the time we landed, my head was throbbing. I opened my mouth wide and pulled at my ears in an attempt to relieve the pressure but without much effect. I was reaching the end of my strength. I'd been up all of the previous night getting rattled in the C-130J like nuts in a jar. The night before I'd caught only a few hours of sleep on the couch in Shaunessy's hotel room, and the night before *that*, I'd slept in the CIA agents' car on the drive from Brasília. I was running on fumes.

I almost didn't recognize Dr. Chu when I saw her waiting for me at the exit from my gate. She was smaller than I remembered. The top of her head reached only to my collarbone, and her slight shoulders reminded me of a bird's wing, fragile and delicate. The look in her eyes gave no hint of weakness, however, and I could see her striking fear into a class of interns. Give her a white lab coat and clipboard and the force of knowledge and authority, and I might quail before her, too.

"Doctor Chu," I said. I shook her outstretched hand, and mine seemed clumsy wrapped around her slim, precise fingers.

"Call me Mei-lin, please," she said.

We walked down the corridor away from the gate. I had no luggage—

it had all been lost in Brasília—so there was nothing to wait for. "Thanks for agreeing to meet with me," I said.

Mei-lin gave a chuff of surprise that might have been a laugh. "You're kidding, right? I've been shouting from the hills that this thing is dangerous, but nobody's taking me seriously. Follow protocol, they say. Make your reports to the CDC and USAMRIID and let the professionals create a panic if a panic is warranted. What I saw in your brother's cultures, though, has got me scared. Really scared."

"Why? What did you see?"

"The filamentous morphology has some extraordinary qualities. It can hack the interfaces of other cells, feeding them chemical messages they would expect in their normal interactions with their neighbors. It's like a con artist. It tricks the other cell into thinking it's business as usual, snuggling up against it as if it had always been there. As far as the cell is concerned, the fungus is just another sensory transducer cell or autonomic neuron cell or any kind of cell. As far as I can tell, it's a generalized capability. Put it with skin cells, it acts like a skin cell. Put it with thyroid gland cells, it acts like a thyroid gland cell."

"It changes its DNA?" I asked.

"Oh, no. The mimicry is just at the interface level. On a genetic level, it's still fungal mycelia, and it retains its essential connection to the rest of the mycelia."

"So . . . does that mean you essentially have two brains functioning in your head?" I asked.

"Worse than that," Mei-lin said, leading the way out of the main airport building. "It's just one brain, with your original cells and the mycelial copycat cells working together seamlessly. The resulting network is even, apparently, more efficient than the original. But it comes at a cost. Some percentage of the brain is composed of fungal mycelia and thus operating for the ultimate good of the parasite, not the human host. Although those goals sometimes coincide."

"But what does that mean, 'for the good of the parasite'? For the good of the specific organism hanging out in your brain? Or for the whole fungal species?"

She turned a corner toward short-term parking, and I followed her. "I'm not sure 'species' is the right word."

"What do you mean?"

"The cells I took from your brother and the ones from your father are genetically identical, as are the ones I've pulled from other patients."

"Wait," I said. "Other patients?"

"At least five others. The point is, there's no genetic diversity. This isn't so much a species as a single organism, spread out among different hosts."

"I don't understand. If they're not connected, how can they be the same organism? Even if they're genetically identical, they would be like twins, then, right? Not one individual."

"That's kind of a semantic distinction in this case," she said. "There's no centralization in a fungus like there is in a human. There's no division of labor among its parts. I can slice a single fungus into a hundred pieces, and each piece will be just as much the original as any of the others. A fungus is kind of like the internet. It's a network of nodes, each of which senses its environment and communicates that information along the network to the other nodes."

I followed her between two rows of parked cars. "But, if a fungus is a network, what happens when it's split up in different hosts? The network's broken then, right? It's not like it can communicate through the air. Right?"

"Well, it can't chemically," she said. "But that doesn't necessarily mean it can't communicate at all."

I thought of the Johurá tribesmen sending whistle language via cell network. "You mean through hosts talking to one another?"

Mei-lin shrugged. "When two people talk to each other, their brains pass information. There's no reason to believe that infected brains wouldn't incorporate that information into the larger network. A fungal network doesn't think, but its structure is almost neuromorphic, even without a human host. It reacts in pretty sophisticated ways, coordinating all the available information and making collective decisions for its environment. Like which trees in a forest should thrive and which should die."

"Or which nation's leaders," I said.

She shot me a questioning look, but I didn't explain. That part of the story would come out soon enough.

"What I mean," Mei-lin said, "is that a fungal organism isn't so much the matter it's made of as much as its genetic instruction set. Whether it's living in the soil of the Amazon or a human parietal lobe, it's the same set of instructions, evolved for a single purpose."

"What purpose?" I asked. "What's it trying to do?"

She pressed a button on her keychain, and a silver BMW chirped, its taillights flashing. "That's easy," she said. I walked around to the passenger side and climbed in as she did the same on the driver's side. Before starting the car, she swiveled to look me in the eye. "Its purpose is the same as every other organism. To survive."

I chewed on that while she pressed the ignition button, starting the engine with a healthy roar. She checked her mirrors and backed smoothly out of the parking space.

"There's a reason fungi are so successful," she said. "Did you know fungi outnumber plants six to one? They can survive anywhere. You can kill ninety-nine percent of one, and it'll still survive. They don't even need light. Fungi have been found thriving in highly radioactive places like reactor cooling tanks, the ruins of Chernobyl, and the rubber window seals of the International Space Station. They're not just radioresistant; they actually benefit from ionizing radiation. Fungal hyphae grow toward radioactive sources the way plants grow toward sunlight. During past eras when animals and plants died out due to high radiation, fungi grew and thrived. When we finally find life on other planets, there's a good chance it'll be a fungus."

"So, this particular one," I said. "Just how intelligent is it?"

She pulled out of the parking garage and stopped. "Hang on a sec," she said. "Which way am I driving?"

I laughed. "I don't know," I said. "I'm following you."

"Well, where are you staying?"

"At my dad's house, I guess." I told her which direction to go.

"So, intelligence," she said. "It's a tough question to answer. We talk about intelligence as a measure of a creature's ability to solve problems—can it use tools, can it communicate abstractions, etc. This thing can obviously achieve some pretty complex behaviors. Its goal, however, is pretty straightforward. Reproduce. Spread out. Survive.

"Your *real* question, however, is whether it can think like us. Is it making plans, is it aware of us, is it aware of itself? And I can't answer that. But there's nothing in what it's doing that can't be explained by the perpetuation of a behavior that conveys a survival advantage. In fact, its behavior isn't all that different from what thousands of species have been doing for millennia."

"What do you mean?"

"Ants and termites are famous for how organized they are, how they have different jobs, cross rivers, build large structures. But a queen doesn't give orders to the other ants. There's no central leadership. Each ant follows its own evolutionary programming in a scheme that works for the survival of all. Birds flock, bees swarm, lobsters march, fish school—it's the emergent behavior of thousands of individuals acting on their own. A colony of ants isn't an intelligent entity, but it can make complex decisions, even solve geometric problems."

We drove in silence for a while. I tried to think through everything she said, but I was so exhausted I couldn't trust my brain to think clearly. Finally, I said, "So did you tell all this stuff to my brother and father?"

"You bet I did. Your brother told me he already knew, and that it was under control. That the meds I gave him before were doing the trick. I advised him to come in for a follow-up, but he declined."

"He wasn't taking the meds," I said. "And he knew exactly what the fungus was doing to him. He wanted it in his mind. Welcomed it. And my father . . . well, of course he welcomed it. What else could he think?"

She blew out a breath that was half appreciative whistle and shook her head. "That was something amazing," she said. "I didn't know your father from before the change, but I read his charts. I could hardly believe I was dealing with the right patient. Alzheimer's just doesn't go into remission like that."

"Remission? You think it'll come back?"

She shrugged. "How could I predict something like that? Alzheimer's does irreparable damage to the synapses. It's not supposed to go away to begin with."

"That's what's so hard to work out," I said. "This thing obviously provides value to its hosts. It makes them smarter. It even cures Alzheimer's. So is it a parasite or a symbiote? Does it survive to our harm or to our benefit?"

Her smile was fierce. "I guess that depends on what you define as a benefit."

She pulled into the driveway of my father's house, crunching gravel under the tires. There were no other cars there, and the house was dark. I had been hoping I might find my mom home, but now that it came down to it, I was relieved not to find her. I wanted to find my dad, but I was also reaching the edge of my ability to stay awake. If I didn't get a good night's sleep and get it soon, I wasn't going to be useful to anyone.

"So," Mei-lin said. "What should we do?"

My attention swam. "What?"

"Do. What should we do? You're NSA. You've got to have contacts, people who will listen to you. We need dozens of researchers working on this, taking it apart, finding a cure. We need to take this public."

I chuckled. "That's not exactly where the NSA shines."

"But you know people, right? If we come at this from two directions, maybe we can make some headway."

I hadn't yet told her about what was happening in Brazil or our suspicion that the fungus was redrawing the political landscape of South America and turning soldiers against their own countrymen. "Look," I said. "I've barely slept in three days. Any way we can reconvene this in the morning?"

Her expression remained serious. "I'll be here first thing tomorrow. I don't think we have much time to waste."

"First thing tomorrow," I said.

I hauled myself out of the car, found the key under the mat on the back stoop, and let myself inside.

—⊙—

I felt my way through the dark house until I found the light switch and flicked it on. The house was just as it had been before I left, comfortably cluttered and full of memories of my father. Fishing photos and knick-knacks covered the tops of bookshelves and end tables. Throw pillows lay piled on the couch, along with a ludicrous stuffed trout I had given him as a joke years before. Photos of Paul, Julia, and I as children. Scrabble and chess sets on the dining room table.

Had he really walked away and left all this behind? Was he ever planning to come back? The fact that he had left Mom no way to contact him made it seem more sinister than a simple vacation. He owned an iPhone, but I doubted he had it with him. It was probably in a drawer in the house somewhere.

The thought reminded me that I needed to buy a new phone. I had left my old one in my luggage in my hotel in Brasília, which meant that it was now in the hands of the Agência Brasileira de Inteligência, and thus the property of the Ligados. I couldn't imagine it would do them any good, but it was certainly annoying to me not to have it.

I traipsed upstairs toward my bedroom, turning lights off behind me as I went. It was creepy to walk around in an empty house at night, even one as familiar to me as this one. I resisted the urge to look over my shoulder or leave the lights on, though the normal creakings and tickings of the old house sounded unnaturally loud. I wondered if I had locked the doors, though I knew I had. I had even kept the key in my pocket instead of returning it to the mat outside.

I used the bathroom, rinsing my mouth out with water and wishing I had my own toothbrush. Another gift left behind in Brasília for the Ligados. I dabbed at my mouth with a towel and flipped the bathroom light off. Not wanting to be left in total darkness, I crossed to my bedroom first and turned that light on before coming back to the hallway switch and turning it off. For a moment, as I stood in the hall with the only illumination behind me, I thought I saw a tiny light coming from my father's room.

I sighed, my hand still resting on the switch. It was probably nothing. An LED alarm clock, or else the reflection of a streetlight through the window. If I didn't look, however, I'd end up lying in my bed, wondering. I walked to the other end of the hall and reached my arm around the doorframe to find the switch for his room. I flipped the switch, flooding the room with light.

A figure lay slumped on the end of the bed, his back to me, wearing a hospital gown. I couldn't see his face, but I knew that head of curly gray hair better than I knew my own face in a mirror. It was my father.

―⦿―

I couldn't move at first. Adrenaline flooded my system, sending my heart into a gallop, and my skin flushed with a heat that felt like fear. An eternity passed in seconds. Was he dead? But no, he held something bright in his hand. What was he doing here? Was he hurt? Where was Paul?

Eventually, my fight-or-flight reaction subsided, and I took a deep breath. My father hadn't yet moved or acknowledged my presence, or even reacted to the light. I took a step closer and saw that the object he held was his iPhone. The glowing rectangle, perhaps reflected in the window, must have been what I'd seen from the hallway.

"Dad?"

I stepped closer and peered at the screen. He was paging through the photographs of Julia and her daughter, Ash, his thumb sweeping across the device every few seconds to bring up the next. Finally, he shifted his head a fraction to regard me. There were tears in his eyes.

"How did you get here?" I asked.

He didn't answer me. Instead, he flipped to the next photo, this one of Julia's husband holding the baby, and stared at it with an expression of intense despair.

"That's Hisao," I said. "He's married to your daughter, Julia. The baby is Ash, your granddaughter." I slipped easily into the soft, calming tone of voice I had grown accustomed to using with him in recent years.

"I know who it is," he said. "Don't patronize me."

I sat down on the bed across from him, just an arm's reach away. "Dad? What's going on? How did you get here? Are you . . . ?"

"Am I of sound mind?" he said bitterly. "Who knows? I certainly can't be trusted to have an opinion on the matter."

"Dad—"

"Do you know those dreams, where nothing makes any sense, but you know there's somewhere you were supposed to be, or something you were supposed to do? You wake up with that feeling of urgency and panic still lingering, but you can shake it off because, hey, it's just a dream. Only it wasn't for me, was it? I woke up to find that the dream was actually the last two years of my life."

He seemed lucid enough. On the other hand, he still wore the same flimsy gown he'd been wearing when he left the hospital, smelling like a sick room and with a few days growth of beard darkening his face. He wasn't exactly back to normal.

"Do you remember how you got here?" There had been no car in the driveway when I arrived. Mom would surely have checked the house, and although he might have hidden up here in the dark, she would have noticed if his car had been here.

"Paul dropped me off. I haven't seen him since."

"He just left you here?"

"He was called away."

"Called away? By whom? Have you been here all this time?" I assumed my mom had checked the house, but maybe with all the lights out, she hadn't realized he was home.

"I slept a lot," he said. "I think."

"Have you eaten anything?"

"I don't know," he said, and his voice rippled with anger and frustration.

"Are you having memory lapses?"

"Yes? Maybe?" He groaned and sat up, holding his head. "I don't know whether to thank Paul or curse him. It's like torture, this glimpse of what I should be, what I've missed." He held out the phone with a close-up of Ash's pudgy face. "I'll never really know her, will I?"

I met his eyes. "I don't know, Dad. You might. We never expected you to regain any mental ability, but here you are."

He gave me an acid smile. "Here I am." He sucked in a breath and let it loose in a great sigh. "Don't you think losing your mind once is as much as anyone should have to endure? I'm afraid to go outside now, in case I can't remember how to get back to the house. Earlier today, I couldn't remember where the bathroom was. In my own home."

"You'll need someone to stay with you, at least until we figure out what you can and can't do now. Does Mom know you're here?"

"I don't think so. When she came, I hid in the closet until she left."

"Dad! She's been worried sick."

"Please don't call her. I don't want her seeing me like this."

"She loves you."

"That's exactly why I don't want her here. She's already been through this once. I know it hasn't been easy, dealing with someone who doesn't remember how much you've done for them. She shouldn't have to go through that again."

I put a hand on his arm. "I'm sorry," I said. "I shouldn't have gone to Brazil. I should have been here with you. But this is a gift. Maybe not a perfect one, but we'll figure it out. Mom will want to be here."

He pushed himself up on one elbow and stared at me. For a moment, I thought he didn't know who I was. "Neil," he said. "I want you to admit me to a psych hospital. Somewhere they'll watch me. Where they won't let me leave."

"I don't think we need to resort to that yet."

He grabbed my sleeve. "Listen to me. You don't know how hard this is to say." He tried to continue, but it turned into a hacking cough that he couldn't control. I patted him ineffectually on the back until he waved me away. "I almost killed her," he said urgently.

"Who?" I said. "Mom?"

"That young doctor. Chen or Chu. I wanted to kill her." He ran the fingers of both hands roughly through his hair. "I wanted to so *badly*."

I pulled away. "Dad, what are you talking about?"

He propped his feet up on the bed and hugged his knees. His arms stuck out of the short sleeves of the hospital gown, and I noticed how thin he'd become. "It came on all of a sudden," he said. "The doctor came in to take a blood sample. She didn't have a nurse do it; she came in with a syringe herself, looking around like she didn't want anyone to see her. And suddenly, I had this tremendous urge to take her throat in my hands and squeeze until she died. It seemed natural and obvious, like something I might do every day. Just something that needed to be done.

"Instead, I told her to leave. I told her they'd already taken samples, but she said I had very special blood, and she was trying to understand what made it so special. She told me I'd been infected by a fungus, and that other people had been, too. I shouted at her and called her names and told her to get out before I called security.

"She said she would let me rest and come back in an hour. While she was gone, I searched through the cabinets in the room until I found a scalpel. I hid the scalpel under the sheet and waited for her. All the while, I imagined slashing it across her carotid."

"Why?" I said. "Why would you do such a thing?"

He grimaced. "I don't know. It was like she was evil. She had to be stopped before she did irreparable harm. It wasn't rational; it was just this powerful feeling. The idea of killing her felt so right, so clear. Like if it were the last thing I did before I died, it would make my whole life worthwhile. I knew that if she came back, I wouldn't be able to stop myself from cutting her throat. So I left."

The temperature had dropped since the sun set. I pulled a knitted blanket off of the bed and wrapped it around my dad's shoulders while I tried to process what he had said. I thought of Mariana de Andrade and her attempted assassination of the Brazilian vice president. She had shown no regret, no sense that the decision hadn't been hers. And yet it went against everything she had apparently dedicated her life to up until that moment. I had no doubt that it was the influence of the fungus in her brain that had prompted her actions.

My father, however, had apparently been able to resist the urge to kill. More to the point, he'd been aware of the compulsion as something outside of himself. What was different? Was it his Alzheimer's that altered the equation? Or did he just have a particularly strong will? Obviously, the fungus had been able to create the connections that Alzheimer's had previously robbed from him. But now he was losing those connections again, presumably because the fungus was receding. Was it my father's resistance of the fungus that caused its integration with his brain to reverse? Could the physical growth of mycelia in the brain really be affected by a frame of mind?

I tried to think, but my exhausted brain just traveled in circles without getting anywhere. I needed to sleep.

"We can't do anything until the morning," I said. I pulled a pair of pajamas out of a drawer. "Put these on," I said. "Sleep. We'll figure it all out in the morning." I headed for the hallway.

"I'll try," my dad said. "I haven't been sleeping well lately. Too many dreams. And Neil?" I stopped in the entranceway and turned to face him. The anguished expression on his pale face combined with the hospital gown to give him a spectral appearance. "Lock your door."

CHAPTER 22

I locked my door.

Despite everything on my mind, I slept like the dead, and when I woke light streamed through the window, illuminating my bedroom. It was almost as if none of it had happened: my father's Alzheimer's, my brother's infection, the deaths of thousands in Brazil. I dragged myself out of bed, afraid I would discover my father gone, or worse.

Instead, I found him downstairs at the breakfast table, dressed in jeans and a brown sports coat over a clean white t-shirt, eating a mix of scrambled eggs and potatoes with his usual liberal dose of *malagueta* hot sauce. I was no stranger to spicy food but just smelling his plate made my eyes water.

"If you can survive that breakfast, you can survive anything," I said.

My dad harrumphed. "I just wanted to be ready."

"Ready for what?"

He cut his eyes at me over a forkful of eggs. "You want to get me checked out. You want me poked and prodded and scanned five ways from Tuesday. It's inevitable, I suppose. So, I'm ready. If we have to do it, let's do it."

"I'll have to call Mom, too," I said. "We can't keep it from her. She's afraid you're dead." In fact, I felt guilty for not calling her the night before.

"One step ahead of you," my dad said. "Already rang her this morning. She's on her way."

I bit my lip. "There's someone else coming over this morning," I said. "Somebody to help with the poking and prodding. Or at least the scanning." I swallowed. "The thing is, it's Dr. Chu."

"No." He dropped the fork with a clang against the porcelain bowl.

"No, Neil. Didn't you hear what I told you? I tried to kill her. I still want to kill her. It's like, I don't know, an alcohol addiction, or gambling, or something like that. I can't stop thinking about slitting her throat." He spread his fingers like a helmet over his head. "It's in here, and I can't get it out. She can't come here. It's like putting a bottle of whisky in front of an alcoholic and expecting him not to drink it."

I sat down in the chair next to him and put a hand on his shoulder. "We'll sedate you, if that's what it takes," I said. "But she's the only person I know with both the knowledge and willingness to figure this out."

The house phone rang. I crossed to the kitchen counter and picked it up.

"Hello," I said. "Mom?"

"Neil!" It was a man's voice.

"Yes?" I said.

"This is Andrew. Where have you been? I've been trying to reach you since yesterday morning."

"Sorry," I said. "My phone is gone. I lost it in Brazil."

"Well, you've got to get in here. We've got all kinds of things going down, and we could really use your help."

"Are Melody and Shaunessy all right?"

"As of five minutes ago, they were alive, but it's looking touch and go. You were the guy who cracked this whole Johurá thing, and we could really use another miracle right now."

A key turned in the front door, and my mom entered. She looked both relieved and angry to see my father sitting at the breakfast table. I gave her a short wave.

"I'm a little tied up right now," I said into the phone. "My dad . . ."

"I'm not kidding about this, Neil. This is life or death. It's all falling apart over there."

"I'll get in as soon as I can," I said.

"We'll be waiting for you."

Just as I hung up the phone, the doorbell rang. I opened the front door. Mei-lin stood on the stoop, her dark hair pulled back, looking trim and professional.

I hesitated. "My father is here," I told Mei-lin.

"That's great," she said. "I need to get a look at him."

"There may be a problem with that," I said. "He's been having some trouble with violent thoughts. Honestly—"

"It's okay," my father said.

"What?"

"It's okay. She can come in."

In retrospect, I should have seen it coming. He'd warned me, after all. And I knew how crafty an addict could be. It's just that I didn't associate those things with my father.

I beckoned Mei-lin through the door and introduced her to my parents, even though they had met her previously at the hospital. My dad put his breakfast dishes in the sink, and came around the table to shake her hand.

"Now, what I really want to know is how you are feeling, Mr. Johns," Mei-lin said. "A fungal infection can be—"

I didn't see the knife until it was too late. My father must have slipped it out of the dish drainer when he put his plate and fork in the sink. I wasn't expecting deception, despite his warnings of the night before. Mei-lin was quicker than I was. As my dad slashed the blade up toward her rib cage, she brought her left forearm down to deflect it. The blade cut through her blouse and instantly drew blood.

I launched myself across the room, toppling a chair, and tackled him. He went down easily, a bundle of cloth and bones, and the bloody knife skittered across the floor. My mom screamed, but she had the presence of mind to snatch up the knife. Mei-lin left me to control my father, and rushed to the sink, pulling back her ruined sleeve and sluicing the wound with water from the tap. She swore as bloody rivulets ran down her arm.

I hauled my dad to his feet and pushed him into the chair, where, for lack of a better idea, I sat on him.

"I'm sorry, I'm sorry, I'm so sorry," my father said, over and over.

I bound his wrists and ankles with duct tape. I felt like some kind of psychopathic kidnapper, but my father kept urging me to use more and to make it tighter. My stomach rose when I saw his face, so helpless and horrified by his own violence. I wanted to comfort him, and at the same time, I wanted to shake him. He didn't struggle as I carried him out to my mom's car.

I apologized to Mei-lin as she wrapped her arm with bandages from a first aid kit, but she waved me away. "I was stupid," she said. "I should have been more careful."

"Are you okay?"

"It hurts," she said, with a wincing smile, "but I'll live. I can still drive. Let's get your father to the hospital."

We drove to Baltimore Washington, Mei-lin following behind in her silver BMW. Once there, I cut the tape off my father's arms and legs and looped my arm around his elbow to walk inside. With Mei-lin's help, we sidestepped a lot of the process to get him admitted, and she found him a room on an orthopedic floor. She said he would be less conspicuous there than, say, on a psych floor, where they would ask more questions about his condition. It wasn't unusual for patients to end up on floors where they didn't strictly belong, and she had told the floor nurses to page her if there were any issues. She wrote in his chart that he was a risk for violence and strapped his arms and legs to the bed with medical restraints.

"I have to go," I said, apologetic. "They called me into work." It sounded like a flimsy excuse, as if I was trying to run away from the situation. "They said it was important," I added, lamely.

"Go," my mother said. "We can handle things here."

I took my dad's iPhone with me and made sure Mei-lin had the number, so she could get ahold of me if she needed to. Not that the phone was permitted in the NSA facility, but at least she could reach me in the car. I gave my mom a grateful kiss and took off at a run down the hall. By the time I got on the road, it was almost noon. I hadn't eaten anything yet that day, but it didn't seem like the right time to stop for anything. I drove on to Fort Meade, where I made my way impatiently through security. In our basement office, I found a note from Andrew telling me to meet him in the War Room.

The War Room was a large conference area on the third floor meant as a command center in times of national crisis. Photographs of past directors of the agency decorated the wood-paneled walls, with the exception of the large projection screen at the front. Military and civilian agents packed the room. Andrew stood at the front, a tablet in his hand, making marks with a stylus that appeared on the screen behind him. The screen showed maps of both Brazil and the United States, along with a timeline.

Andrew spotted me and beckoned me toward the front. I stepped forward nervously, glancing at the rank insignias on the uniforms as I passed, and noting the preponderance of ribbons and stars. There were plenty of chairs in the room, but no one sat. No one smiled, either.

"What's going on?" I murmured to Andrew.

"I told you it was big," he said.

Everyone looked at me. I wished I could sidle away to a corner until I figured out what was happening.

"Two months ago," Andrew said to the crowd, "we began intercepting messages between the Fuerzas Armadas Revolucionarias de Colombia and the Ejército de Liberación Nacional. These messages weren't encrypted per se, but they were encoded using a little-known tribal language, a language with only about three hundred native speakers in the world. To call these native speakers 'technologically backward' is an understatement. Many of them have never even seen, never mind used, a cell phone or any other kind of modern communication device. Nevertheless, the covert communication between FARC and the ELN required an intimate knowledge of this little-known language. Mr. Johns"—here he waved a hand to indicate me—"identified this language and engaged the services of a retired Christian missionary, the only speaker of the language on this continent, to help us decipher these messages."

It had actually been Melody who had engaged Katherine Wyatt's services, but there was no point in correcting him.

"Over the past two weeks," Andrew continued, "we have seen an exponential increase in the amount of traffic using this communication paradigm. Not all messages have employed the Johurá language, but most have been based on obscure dialects native to the Amazon basin. Many of these we have cracked, but some remain elusive. The crisis we are facing has less to do with the content of these messages than with their increasing and improbable prevalence. In the past two days—"

"The *crisis* we are facing," said a lieutenant colonel, accentuating his South Carolina accent, "is American troops defecting en masse and an aircraft carrier that just went off the grid. Are we getting to a point that sheds some light on this situation?"

"In the past two days," Andrew said again, raising his voice slightly but otherwise ignoring the interruption, "hundreds of thousands of messages of this type have been intercepted from all across the South American continent."

"We know how fast these bastards are spreading," the lieutenant colonel said. "This isn't news."

"But this is: in the last twelve hours, more than two hundred messages in the Johurá language have been intercepted from Los Angeles, Houston, and Denver."

His words seemed to echo in the shocked silence that followed. I was stunned, too. If I was interpreting the numbers on his timeline correctly, use of the whistle language had spread in South America faster than seemed possible by any ordinary means. Would it spread just as quickly in the United States?

The room erupted into noise and shouted questions. "Have these people been apprehended?"

"Are we prepared for terrorist attacks in those cities?"

"Has the FBI been briefed?"

"How did these insurgents get past the borders?"

Andrew raised a hand to quiet them. "Hang on. I didn't say there were insurgents. These aren't Colombian or Venezuelan operatives sneaking past our checkpoints. These are, at least in the cases we've been able to check, American citizens, people born and raised within our borders. They're grocery store owners, Boy Scout leaders, soccer moms."

"Deep cover terrorist cells, then," said a colonel.

"You don't get it," Andrew said. "These people are just who they seem to be. They're not undercover operatives. A year ago, they were just as loyal to Uncle Sam as you are, though probably more interested in their kids and their favorite sports teams. These people have been *compromised*. Yesterday's ordinary citizens are turning into today's political zealots, just as our soldiers in the field are abandoning their loyalties and turning on their comrades.

"In Brazil, the attacks on our soldiers' minds came through a fungal-based neurological agent spread through the air by crop dusters. We believe the same neurological agent is at work in these cities, but so far, the means of attack remains a mystery. As far as we can tell, no crop duster assaults have been employed in the United States, and yet people's minds are being altered in relatively large numbers. It's an epidemic. And it's spreading, but we don't know how."

The room erupted with more questions and shouted opinions, but Andrew tucked his tablet under his arm and stepped forward. "Response strategies will be discussed through the usual chain of command. At this point, I will turn the briefing over to Mr. Terry Ronstadt."

An overweight man with ruddy cheeks and a generously cut sports coat stood and took Andrew's place at the front. "As most of you know, I am assuming command in place of Acting Director Clarke . . ."

I was surprised when Andrew slipped out of the briefing room, but I followed him without hesitation.

"Hey," I said when we were clear of the room. "What's going on? Are those numbers for real?"

"No time to stand and chat," he said. "We'll talk on the way." He charged down the hall at a fast walk. My legs were longer than his, but

I had to trot to keep up. "Brazil is a mess. American soldiers have been defecting left and right, and no one can trust the chain of command. All communication is compromised, and no one knows if their buddy might just decide to shoot them in the back of the head."

He passed the elevators, turning instead through a narrow door that led to a concrete stairway. He barreled down the stairs at breakneck speed with me close behind. "One of our aircraft carriers went off the grid," he shouted over the noise of our echoing footfalls. "Just disappeared, with no response. Thousands of people, and then nothing. We can see it from the satellites, so we know where it is, but we don't know who's in charge or what's happening on board. We recalled the other ships in the battle group, and now the president has to decide whether we try to board the thing or just stay away until we know their intentions."

We reached the bottom of the stairs, and Andrew used a numeric keypad to gain entry through a thick metal door. "Shortcut," he said. He opened the door, and I found myself in the cavernous server room, the rows of hardware stretching off into the distance. We descended another short staircase to reach the floor. Andrew set off again, cutting a zigzag pattern through the racks and leaving me to keep up as best I could.

"What about Melody and Shaunessy?" I asked.

"I talked to them just before the briefing," he said. "They seemed uncompromised, as far as it's possible to tell such a thing. I told them to get out of there as soon as they possibly could."

I gave my head an angry shake. "I shouldn't have left," I said. "I should be down there with them."

Andrew spared me a quick, skeptical glance. "Don't be an idiot," he said. "You couldn't do them any good there, and you just might be able to do them some good from here."

We reached the entrance to our own basement room. I wasn't sure I would have been able to distinguish it from a dozen other doors out of the server room, but Andrew seemed to know where he was going. I followed him inside.

The room looked like no one had left it in days. Tables were strewn with empty Chinese cartons and disposable soda cups. In one corner, jackets and a few chair cushions had been thrown on the floor to create a makeshift bed. Everyone looked haggard, with unkempt hair and blood-shot eyes. But despite their obvious exhaustion, there was an intensity to the conversations and the sense of a fiercely shared mission.

I logged in and found more than five hundred emails waiting for me. "Don't worry about those," Andrew said. "I need you to concentrate on the infection vectors into the United States. Forget about containment; we've got the CDC engaged and we're mobilizing quarantine zones. I recommended that the president ground all flights into the country, but a few whistle language message intercepts isn't enough to convince him. What I need to know is the source, and I haven't had the time to study the data from that angle. There's a pattern to how it's spreading. I can feel it, but I just can't put my finger on it."

"What sort of pattern?" I asked.

Andrew sank into his chair and rubbed at his forehead. "If these were tourists coming home from Brazil, or immigrants from Venezuela, you'd expect to see vectors in any city with an international airport. But we don't see that at all. LA and Denver and Houston are all affected, but not New York, not Chicago. Little towns in Arizona and New Mexico show traffic, and in general, with the exception of Denver, the intercepts are concentrated in the South."

"Isn't Denver one of the largest cocaine gateways?" I asked. I had learned a few things studying the drug trade with Andrew earlier in the year.

"Sure. But what's the connection?"

"Neuritol."

Andrew looked baffled. "What's that? A prescription drug?"

"Didn't she tell you?" I could have screamed. I understood why massive organizations like the NSA and the CIA didn't end up sharing information very well, but within our own small team? Of course, Andrew hadn't been around for those conversations, so he didn't know about Neu-ritol, and he didn't make the connection to the drug trade.

"Melody's granddaughter, Emily, went to the hospital a few weeks ago with symptoms similar to those my brother experienced with the mycosis he brought back from the Amazon. Turns out it was a side effect of the new smart drug she was taking to improve her performance in school. The drug was called Neuritol, and it was distributed in used albuterol inhalers. I suspect it's primarily a mechanism to deliver fungal spores to hosts in the US."

Andrew stood again and paced as much as the cubicle walls allowed. "I remember something about her granddaughter being pretty seriously ill but nothing relevant to all this."

I cursed myself for a fool. Why hadn't we told the whole team? Why hadn't we called reporters and drug experts and made a scene? It seemed like an unforgivable failure now, but I realized it wouldn't have seemed nearly as critical at the time. The similarity with my brother's symptoms had been a curiosity, something to investigate, perhaps, but I would never have guessed it was an attack vector for a foreign power. It wasn't my first priority, and Melody probably didn't want to tell the whole team about her personal family issues.

"How quickly can it spread from person to person?" Andrew asked.

"That's just it. It doesn't," I said. "It's not a virus. The spores have to be breathed directly into the lungs. People don't produce new spores; they come from the original fungus, somewhere in the Amazon. This isn't like a pandemic, which is why its rapid growth is so surprising. It has to be purposely spread."

"The crop dusters in Brazil," he said.

"Right. And if Neuritol is the means, it looks like the spread into the United States has been in progress for weeks, if not months. Paul was a chance infection. Their real strategy is to quietly infect through the illegal drug trade, probably through the same routes that cocaine takes from Colombia. In fact, it's a good bet that the cocaine itself has been laced with fungal spores as well, unless there's some chemical incompatibility there."

Andrew pulled up a map on his screen that showed the various routes by which cocaine was smuggled from Colombia up through Mexico to different towns and cities along the US border and compared it to his list of cities and towns from which Johurá messages had been intercepted. "It fits," he said. "That's how they're doing it."

"What can we do to stop it?"

Andrew barked a short laugh. "That's a question every administration since Nixon's has asked, for all the good it's done them."

"But we have to do something."

"We'll warn the DEA, for sure," he said. "Their usual investigative cycle won't be enough, though. The advantage we have is that Neuritol is part of a category of drugs that's already illegal. We just have to get it prioritized, and I'm pretty sure I can make that happen."

"We can't just work this one through channels," I said. "It's not just about the DEA or the FBI or the Department of Justice. Everyone in the country should know. We need people looking out for their loved ones, paying attention to what drugs they're taking and how they're behaving. We need city cops to be on the lookout, and social workers and school teachers. There are a lot of people out there who aren't in intelligence services who could help."

"What are you suggesting?" Andrew asked.

"We need to hold a press conference," I said.

Andrew laughed. "Good luck with that."

"What do you mean?"

"We're the NSA," he said. "That's not what we do."

—⊙—

According to Andrew, since all our data was technically classified, I could be arrested if I held a press conference without the express blessing of the DIRNSA, which at this point, with Kilpatrick dead and Clarke MIA, was Terry Ronstadt. Ronstadt was, by Andrew's description, the anti-Snowden:

so security obsessed that "you could torture his mother, and he wouldn't tell you his middle name." Even so, Andrew promised to try to get permission.

While he was doing that, I left him with the number for my dad's iPhone and drove back to the hospital to check Mei-lin's progress with my father. My mom stood over the bed, clasping the rail with white knuckles. I came up next to her and wrapped my arm around her shoulders. She leaned her head against me.

My father's eyes were closed. Mei-lin had sedated him, and his arms lay motionless against the Velcro restraints. "I wouldn't have needed to," she said. "The straps would keep him from hurting anyone. But he kept begging me to do it."

I laid my hand against his forehead. His skin was papery and cold.

"As best as I can tell," Mei-lin said, "the Alzheimer's is attacking the fungus along with the normal brain tissue. Your father had an initial rush of memory and cognition improvement, because the fungal cells made connections that had long since been lost, imitating the intended brain function. Over time, however, the axons of the pseudo-nerves—the ones composed of fungal cells—have been affected just like the original."

"How is that possible?" I said. "Fungi can't get Alzheimer's, can they? It's like a maple tree getting dementia."

"Remember the copycat quality of these fungal cells," Mei-lin said. "They duplicate the cellular interface and a lot of the cells' structure and function. Ironically, that makes them just as vulnerable to attack."

"If it's vulnerable, can we use that to our advantage? Is there some kind of drug or treatment that could push it back out of our brains?"

Mei-lin shook her head. "That's just the thing. Those are vulnerabilities it gets from imitating the forms it finds in our own brain. Anything we did to fight it on that level would only harm our own brain cells."

"So if we fight this thing," I said, "it's got to be by attacking the fungal nature of it. Attacking what makes it different, not taking advantage of the way it imitates our function."

"That sounds about right," Mei-lin said.

The iPhone in my pocket buzzed. I pulled it out and saw Andrew's number on the screen. I turned away from the others and answered it.

"Hey, Andrew," I said. "What's going on?"

"They're going to do it," he said. "Ronstadt agreed to hold a press conference and tell them what we know about the epidemic. Though he's actually going to brief the president, and the president is going to tell the nation."

"That's great," I said. "What changed their minds?"

"I guess they know it's leaking anyway. With our soldiers dying and American kids potentially affected, it can't be kept under wraps. Better to release the information now, while they can still control the spin. Also, there's some good news."

"Good news?" That would make a nice change.

"We got our aircraft carrier back. The uninfected sailors, which apparently was most of them, staged a mutiny and took back the ship. No lives lost."

"The first-ever mutiny on board a US aircraft carrier, and you call that good news?"

"Well, it's better than it cruising up the Gulf of Mexico and attacking Miami."

"True."

"It's a break, Neil. Maybe the first we've had. We'll get these bastards yet."

When I hung up, I turned back to see my mom staring at the television mounted high on the wall. On the screen, a pretty blond reporter interviewed a young man in a brown sport coat. The woman leaned forward, earnest and intent, while the man sat at his ease with one foot propped up on his knee.

"You've got to be kidding me," I said.

Mei-lin looked at the screen and then back at me. "Isn't that . . ."

"Yes," I said. "It's my brother."

CHAPTER 23

Once I recovered from the initial shock of seeing him on-screen, I rushed to turn up the volume.

". . . you believe the government is not just violating our rights, but actually harming the country by outlawing these 'smart drugs'?" the reporter asked.

My brother smiled. "Nancy, I believe the prejudice against these drugs is harming humanity as a species. Our ability to reason, to debate, to communicate in abstractions and cooperate in large numbers: these are the advancements that have given us an unprecedented ability to thrive and dominate our environment. But it doesn't end here. There's so much more that we could do if we could overcome our ridiculous tendency for argument and distrust, jealous rivalry and selfish violence."

"And you think Neuritol can solve this? It sounds like you're talking about world peace. Isn't that expecting a bit much?"

"*Humanity* can solve these problems," Paul said, his voice ringing with earnest appeal. "Cooperation is a hallmark of our species. We just need to reach the next step in our evolution. Neuritol isn't just a drug that wears off and leaves you wanting more. You can think of it like a brain upgrade. I'm serious about this. Those who are willing to go to the next level are going to be the leaders of society, in the sciences, in healthcare, in politics, in business. Those who aren't willing are going to be left behind."

"Wow. That's quite a vision, Dr. Johns. After our break, we'll return to this interview and our discussion of Neuritol: Is it a genius drug, or is it just the latest harmful addiction to sweep through our schools? We'll be back after these messages."

"Well, that's bold," Mei-lin said.

My jaw worked a few times before I could make it speak. "No one's going to buy that nonsense. It's like he's selling wizard oil from a traveling medicine show."

"And thousands of people bought that wizard oil," my mother said. "And still do, more or less."

"What worries me," I said, "is how much Paul seems to believe what he's saying. That's not really Paul talking. It's the fungus, manipulating him."

My mother's expression was grave. "I think we have to face the possibility that what we see on that screen is who Paul is now. What he really believes."

The commercials ended and the blond reporter reappeared on the screen. "With me is Dr. Paul Johns, a mycologist with the University of Maryland, who earlier today filed a lawsuit against the Department of Justice for violating what he claims is a public right to take Neuritol, the latest so-called 'smart drug' that promises increased mental capabilities." She turned to Paul. "Dr. Johns, does Neuritol really live up to the hype? After all, it's been through no formal safety testing, no drug review process."

"Nancy, what day were you born?"

She hesitated a beat, not wanting to give up control of the interview. "November 21st."

"What year?"

She blushed. "1998."

"You were born on a Wednesday," Paul said. "You are eight thousand, five hundred, and seventy-seven days old. Your last birthday was on a Sunday, and your next will be on a Monday."

The reporter gave a little gasp of delight and clapped her hands. "Amazing," she said.

"The last commercial break lasted one hundred and eighteen seconds. The man who touched up your makeup during the break is in love with you, but you don't return his affections. You're five foot eight and a hundred and twenty pounds, and you said the word 'Neuritol' sixteen times during our interview so far."

The reporter beamed her TV smile. "And how could you possibly know all that?"

Paul leaned forward in his chair. "This is no magic trick. Anyone can gain this level of intellect and awareness of the world around them. That's why I'm seeking this temporary restraining order from the courts—to put a stop to this ill-conceived and uninformed attack on Neuritol and give Congress a chance to declare it legal. Neuritol isn't addictive or dangerous. It doesn't belong in the same category as narcotics."

"Thank you for taking the time to talk to me today. Any last comments to our viewers?"

Paul looked into the camera. "Try it for yourself. Don't wait for the government to decide what's best for you. Then write your representatives and tell them Neuritol should be legal."

"Thank you, Dr. Johns." The image cut to a head-on view of the reporter. "The lawsuit was filed in Arizona court today by Dr. Johns' attorneys. Senator Velasquez, a Republican from Texas, has already gone on record saying that he agrees with the suit, and not only claims that Neuritol ought to be legalized but that its use should actually be encouraged in our schools."

"Why file the suit in Arizona?" Mei-lin asked.

"Maybe that's where he is," I said. "Or maybe that's where the crackdown is particularly active."

"Didn't you say he had a university lab where he was studying this organism?" Mei-lin asked.

"Yeah, he's at UMD."

"Any chance we could get in there and look at his stuff? Because, you're right, the way to attack this thing is to understand it as a fungal organism, not as a brain disease. If I could see his notes, maybe examine some of his cultures, it could go a long way. Shortcut anything I could do myself."

"Paul's been missing for days," I said. "The university hasn't seen him. I guess it's possible they would let us go and poke around, if we could spin them a good story. I wouldn't know the first thing about what to look for there, but maybe you would."

She shrugged. "It would be worth a try."

We took Mei-lin's BMW down I-95. It was the first really hot day of the year, and she cranked her air conditioning to keep us comfortable. The sun brightened the campus quad to a brilliant green and lit the brick buildings to postcard quality.

We found the main office, but all nearby parking was taken. She put the car in park and flipped the blinkers on. I got out and trotted up the stairs. It didn't occur to me until I opened the front door that it was Sunday—I had long since lost track of the days.

I found one student with bloodshot eyes manning the desk, but she said all the keys were in a safe, and she didn't have any authority to let me into anywhere. When I came back outside and climbed in the car, Mei-lin had her phone pressed to her ear.

"Mommy loves you," she said. "Be good for Daddy, okay? And help take care of your brother. Yes, I love you, too. Bye-bye. Okay. Bye-bye." Her voice abruptly dropped the child-like tone. "Yeah, I'll be home when I can, okay? I'm sorry about your game. This is important. I will. Bye."

"How old?" I asked when she hung up.

Mei-lin sighed. "My son's two, and my daughter is four going on twelve. Wants to do everything herself these days. Yesterday, I found her making her own peanut butter and jelly sandwich. Which meant not just the bread, but her hands, and the table, and her dress, and her hair were covered with sticky mess. I had to bathe her for an hour to get it all out."

I grinned. "Good thing they're cute at that age."

"You're telling me. You have any kids?"

"Not hardly. Not even a girlfriend. Maybe someday, though."

"My two-year-old's favorite game right now is to collect things from all over the house and carry them around in a box. I can't tell you how many things we've lost that way. He's probably driving my husband crazy. Brad hates it when I'm away on weekends."

"Should we head on to the lab?"

She put the car into gear. "Might as well. No point coming out here without at least giving it a try."

We drove around in circles for a while, trying to find a parking space, and eventually found a spot only a few blocks away from the Plant Sciences building. I had little hope that we would be able to get inside. Compared to Fort Meade, it might be laughable security, but that didn't mean I knew how to get past it. The doors were locked, requiring an ID card that we didn't have.

Walking passed manicured lawns in the bright sunlight, it seemed impossible that in Brazil American soldiers were fighting and dying, or that the beautiful brick building in front of us might house a sample of an organism dangerous enough to topple governments.

"Now we get creative," I said. I knew the grad students who worked with Paul in the lab must have access as well, and I'd used my dad's iPhone to look them up on the drive over. I chose the first more or less at random, a woman named Jintara Sirisukha. She answered on the first ring.

"Hello?"

"Ms. Sirisukha?" I said, probably mangling the pronunciation.

"Yes?" She sounded suspicious. I figured I had about five seconds before she hung up on me.

"My name is Martin Wilson," I said, adopting an official tone. "I'm an investigative agent with the CDC, and we have reason to believe your lab is host to a Class Five hypervirus." Mei-lin raised her eyebrows at me and mouthed: *hypervirus?* I shrugged.

"My lab?" said the voice on the phone. "You mean the mycology lab?"

"I'm afraid so," I said. "We've sourced the vector to the Plant Sciences building, and we need to inspect every room. The provost gave us your name as someone with weekend access. I'm sorry to inconvenience you, ma'am, but it's a serious situation."

"Okay," she said. "Give me five minutes. I'll be right over."

I put the phone back in my pocket. "And that's how it's done," I said.

Mei-lin put her hands on her hips. "You're kidding me. That worked?"

"She's on her way."

"If there's such a thing as a hypervirus, I've never heard of it. And the CDC only has four biohazard levels."

"I was improvising," I said. "Don't argue with success."

"And what happens when she arrives and finds us with no identification, no biocontainment gear, no protective suits? We don't have so much as a face mask."

I grinned sheepishly. "You'll just have to talk medical at her, I guess. If not, we'll go to plan B."

"Which is?"

"I don't know. I'll make it up if we need it."

Jintara arrived, an attractive Asian woman in jeans and a purple T-shirt who spoke with an accent I guessed to be Thai. I explained that we were just the administrative investigators, ensuring access for the full containment crew that was on its way. It sounded lame even to me, but Jintara didn't question my story. She seemed more concerned with what would become of the experiments she had underway and how our investigation might contaminate her samples.

"I really don't think it could have come from us," she said. "I know everyone who's gone in and out of that lab, and no one's sick with anything." She said a girl named Sarah up on the third floor had been out sick for two weeks, and I pretended to take down her information.

She led us down the echoing hallway to the Chaverri Mycology Lab and swiped her ID. Mei-lin put a hand on her arm. "You'd better stay out here," she said.

Jintara looked uncertain. "We won't touch anything," I said. "We have labs of our own; we know how important it is not to introduce contaminants."

"Fine," she said. "Just be careful, okay?"

My phone rang. My dad's phone, really, but it was amazing how quickly I thought of it as my own. I looked at the screen. It was Andrew.

"That's the containment crew now," I said. I took several steps back down the hall and shielded my mouth with my hand. "Hey, what do you need?" I asked.

Mei-lin opened the lab door.

It was too easy. I should have suspected something, but I had been too enamored with my own cleverness. The moment the door opened, a cloud of white powder billowed out, right into Mei-lin's face. By pure luck, I was far enough away that it didn't touch me, but Mei-lin, covered in the stuff, coughed and gagged and clawed at her throat.

I stared at Jintara, whose smug smile told the whole story. I took a step toward Mei-lin, but she held out her hands and screamed at me to get back. I reversed direction and held my shirt over my mouth. Ignoring Jintara, Mei-lin yanked a fire extinguisher off the wall. She raised it over her head and smashed it against the sprinkler head protruding from the ceiling. The first blow glanced off ineffectually, but the second struck it full on, breaking the frangible bulb inside and releasing the water.

Mei-lin turned her face up into the stream, letting it cascade over her body, drenching her. She opened her mouth wide, rinsing, rubbing her hands over her face and skin. When she stepped back, her clothes running rivulets onto the floor, she caught my eyes, and I could see the terror in them. We both knew that powder had been filled with fungal spores, and that the important ones were in her lungs, where she couldn't wash them away.

"Paul said you'd come," Jintara said. "It took you longer than he thought."

I saw the expression on Mei-lin's face shift from fear to anger. Without a word, she picked up the fire extinguisher and swung it at Jintara's head. Jintara wasn't expecting it and barely got a hand up to defend herself. The extinguisher connected with the side of her face with an audible gong, and she went down. It wasn't enough to knock her out, but it wiped the smile off her face, and opened a bloody cut on her forehead.

With a cry, Mei-lin raised the extinguisher again and went in for another blow. Jintara was ready this time and scrambled away. The red container struck the cinderblock wall and rang with the impact. Jintara got to her feet and backed down the hall toward where we'd come in. "Give it a day," she said, "and you'll thank me for this." She pushed through the double doors, and we heard her footsteps running away.

Mei-lin dropped the extinguisher and stalked toward the open door to the lab.

"We have to get you back to the hospital," I said.

"First things first. Let's get what we came for."

I started to follow her into the lab, but she waved me back. "There are still spores in the air."

"He won't have left anything of value behind," I said. "Not if he knew we were coming."

Mei-lin switched on the lights. "If this is going to be my last day with control of my own mind," she said, "I'm going to use it fighting this thing."

I peered into the lab from a distance. I saw the same antiseptically neat arrangement of microscopes and glassware as the first time I'd been there. The rows of petri dishes on the central table, however, were gone. Mei-lin dragged a chair over to the doorway and stood on it, examining the setup that had dropped the powder when the door was opened. She pulled it down and showed me: The powder had been kept in a plastic bag tied with a string attached to the door, which had unraveled when pulled. Whoever had set the trap must have climbed out the window afterward.

Mei-lin put the plastic bag in a large specimen bag she found in a drawer, and sealed it shut. She yanked the wires out of each of the three computers in the lab and stacked them up to carry away. I had as much chance of gaining useful information from them as I did from interrogating a Bunsen burner, but I knew if I brought them to Fort Meade, there were people who could get them to spill all their secrets, whether the hard drives had been wiped or not.

We carried everything out to Mei-lin's car. She handed me the keys. "I don't trust myself," she said. "Get us back to the hospital as fast as you can."

On the way, she called a coworker in the emergency room. "Lauren," she said. "I'm inbound with a critical case of invasive aspergillosis. I need a bed and a 5 mg/hour amphotericin B drip. Also, medical restraints."

"On it," I heard the tinny voice reply from the phone. "That's a serious dosage. Is the patient CDT?"

"No," she said. "The patient is just desperate." She switched the phone off.

"CDT?" I asked.

Mei-lin grinned. "It stands for 'Chronic Donut Toxicity.' One of the many unflattering terms doctors disguise with acronyms or inscrutable terminology. She was asking if the patient was obese."

"This is a common term?"

"Not commonly used in front of patients," she said. "But yeah, it gets thrown around, at least by some docs. There are others. An 'OAP' for an 'Over-Anxious Parent.' GPO is 'Good for Parts Only.' And if you show up in the ER because, say, you were trying to jump your motorcycle over the creek and misjudged the distance, you might hear the term 'fecal encephalopathy.'"

I thought about it, then laughed when I figured it out. "Wow, docs can be pretty nasty," I said.

She shrugged. "Some of them are arrogant assholes, no question," she said. "But everyone develops a bit of a gallows humor. It's a tough profession, working with frightened and angry patients and families, seeing a lot more death from day to day than most people do, and inevitably feeling like some of it is at least partially your fault. The dark humor is a way to cope."

My phone rang. I realized I'd never heard whatever it was that Andrew had called to tell me. I pulled the phone out of my pocket, dropped it in my lap, and told it to answer the call.

"What's happening with you?" Andrew said. "Did you get disconnected?"

"It's a long story. What do you need?" I said, talking loud enough that he would hear me over the background noise of the car.

"You were right about the Neuritol," he said. "It fits all the patterns exactly. Unfortunately, it looks like the communication in tribal languages doesn't start until weeks after the drug has been widely distributed in a geographic area. So it's not just a matter of cracking down in the cities where we're intercepting those messages. We have reason to suspect a significant spread into Dallas, Atlanta, Kansas City, even Chicago.

"The president and his staff are all on board now, and the DEA, FBI, and CDC are starting to flood the affected areas. I'm just afraid it's not going to be enough. I've been recommending he declare a state of emergency and deploy the National Guard, but no one's willing to take that step yet."

"It won't take long. Once the CDC sees how fast this thing is spreading, they'll want to shut down every road in the country."

"I'm just afraid that by the time they do, it'll be too late."

—⌾—

By the time we reached the ER, Mei-lin was coughing violently and looked pale. The symptoms had come on quickly, but then she had probably breathed in enough spores to infect an army. Her lungs must be coated with them, each taking root and prompting a surge of immune response. It occurred to me that such a large exposure might very well kill her before the fungus could take hold. Her clothes were still wet from the sprinkler, and she shivered uncontrollably.

She used her access to walk straight past triage and into the back, where she found Lauren, a painfully thin, forty-something woman with dyed blond hair and a serious expression. Lauren took control, stripping away her wet clothes and getting her warm and dry. She started the antifungal IV Mei-lin had asked for, but drew the line on restraints.

"You don't need to be tied down for a pulmonary mycosis," Lauren said.

"I'll explain everything," Mei-lin said. "Just do it, please, before I change my mind."

"Change your mind? You're freaking me out, here, Mei. You're not in any danger of—"

Mei-lin ignored her, using her right hand to strap her left to the rail. "Neil?" she said. "Please?"

"Oh, for heavens' sake," Lauren said. She tied the strap around Mei-lin's other hand. "Now will you please tell me what's going on?"

"Ankles, too," Mei-lin said.

When Lauren had reluctantly complied, Mei-lin gave her a quick summary of what she had inhaled and what the symptoms were likely to be. "Give me a consent form," she said. "I don't want to be taken off of this until I've had a full course of treatment, no matter what I tell you, no matter how I beg or threaten to sue, you hear me? A full course."

Lauren, still suspicious but rattled by her vehemence, agreed.

"Find someone who can study the spores we collected," Mei-lin said to me. "The best option for ending this thing is to find a cure."

"You should do it," I said, but she dismissed me with an annoyed gesture.

"I'm compromised. I can't study it; you could never believe what I told you. I can't even advise you, because I might steer you wrong."

"The antifungals," I said, indicating the IV. "If they work, then you'll be back on your feet . . ."

She shook her head. "The one constant with fungal infections is how easily they can come back. That's why we tell people to take the medication for years. People think it's gone because they've felt fine for months, and they stop taking the pills. Next thing you know, they're back in the ER, and the infection's twice as bad as it was the first time around.

"Fungus is remarkably similar to us, biologically—much more so than plants or bacteria. It makes them great sources for pharmaceuticals, but it also makes it hard to devise drugs to attack them without also attacking healthy human cells. Often, antifungals will simply halt the growth of the fungus, not eradicate it. Which is why it's so easy for them to come back."

She paused for a fit of coughing. When she caught her breath again, there were tears in her eyes. "You can't trust me anymore," she said. "Yes, I hope this course of treatment will cure me. Yes, I hope I'll be up and about in a few days and in full control of my own mind. But even if I am, you won't know for sure. The best thing you can do for me is to find someone who can continue this research without me."

I nodded. I felt bad leaving her, though I expected she had friends in the hospital who would see that she was well cared for. I took one last look at her, arms and legs tied down at her own request, and felt a surge of admiration. "I won't give up," I said. "I won't stop fighting this until I've found a way through."

"Get moving, then," she said. "I'll still be here when you get back."

—⊙—

Lauren caught me on my way out of the ER. "Is this for real?"

"It is," I said. "Everything she told you, about how this organism works, is true. Don't take her off that medication."

She lowered her voice to a whisper. "That dosage is high. Like, really high. I would never give a patient her size that much."

"I guess she wants to be really, really sure she kills it."

"She might just kill herself instead."

I looked her in the eyes. "Trust her," I said. "Don't change the dosage, and don't stop the treatment. No matter what she tells you."

Lauren held my gaze for a beat. "Okay," she said finally. "Okay. I can do that."

CHAPTER 24

I wanted to get back to Fort Meade, but I couldn't leave the hospital without first visiting my father. I found my way to the orthopedic floor, and from there to his room. It seemed a mirror of the room I'd just left, with my father strapped to the bed instead of Mei-lin. He was asleep, but my mother still stood next to him, in practically the same place as when I'd left them that morning.

I circled the bed and gave her a hug. "How's he been?"

"Calm," she said. "Mostly lucid."

"But?" I prompted.

"He says he's sorry about attacking Dr. Chu. But I don't think he really is. It comes across more like a ploy, like he's trying to get me to sympathize with him, so I'll untie him or let down my guard." She took a deep breath, then let it out with a little hitch. "I think it's getting more of a hold on him."

I watched his chest gently rise and fall. "We have to keep our hopes up. This is just a new kind of sickness, one we don't understand well yet."

"It's so strange to have him back." She turned away and faced the window. "He talks to me as if these last three years never happened. He remembers details about our engagement, our marriage, about you and Paul and Julia being born. He sits there and reminisces with me, and I don't know how to feel about it. I mourned him already. A year ago, I would have given anything for him to have a conversation like that. But now? I don't know. I can't even tell if he's really the same man."

"He is," I said. "Despite everything, no matter what has damaged him physically, that's still the man you married. Behind the Alzheimer's, behind this new infection, there's still the core essence of who he is. That's always been there, whether we can see it or not."

Mom wrapped her arms around herself. "That's just wishful thinking,

Neil. I'm sorry, but it is. What you call 'me' is just a pattern made of neurons and synapses and electrical impulses. When the pattern changes so much that there's no continuity with what came before, then you can still call it 'me' if you want, but it's not the same person. The old pattern is gone."

"Not true," I said. "The pattern changes all the time, for everybody. I'm not the same person I was when I was two years old, but it was still me. I'm not a new person every moment, just because I change. The two-year-old me thought completely differently, made different decisions, believed different things—I can't even remember what I did or thought then. But that little Neil was still me, and I'm still him. Dad might have experiences that change him, even drastically, even so much that he doesn't remember what came before. But it's still him." My voice caught a little. "That's still Dad."

A ragged cough brought my attention down to the bed. Dad was awake, and he looked confused. His gaze darted around the room, as if he didn't know where he was. When he saw me, his eyes flew open wide, and his jaw clenched. He body turned rigid, and his hands slapped erratically on the metal rails.

"Hey, Dad, it's me, Neil," I said, afraid he didn't recognize me.

"I know who you are. You shouldn't be here. Go away."

I sat on the rolling stool next to his bed. "What do you mean? Of course I should be here. I'll come every day, until you're well again." I tried to take his hand to calm him, but he pushed me away impatiently.

"Where's Paul? He was just here."

I whirled to face Mom. "Paul was here?"

"No," she said. "He's confused. You saw him on the television, Charles, remember?"

My dad scowled. "When is he going to get here?"

I felt an irrational surge of the old jealousy at my dad's preference for Paul, but I pushed it down. "I don't know where Paul is," I said. "But I'm here."

"You're here," he echoed. "You think you're my only real son, eh?" The muscles in his neck stood out, and his tapping on the rail grew louder and more chaotic.

"Don't say that. Paul's sick, just like you are. We're going to get you both better."

"I don't need to get better. I'm just fine. You think you can do a mess of random science experiments and fix me? Most original research shows errors, you know."

I frowned. "What do you mean? You don't like Dr. Chu examining you?"

"Of course not. I'm not sick. Let me out of here."

I turned to Mom. "Is this what he's been like?"

She shook her head. "No, no. He's been calm, reasonable."

"I'm right here," Dad said, hands slapping against the rails. "Don't ignore me. I'm telling you, that doctor's mockery of research should end!"

It was such a strange phrase. I started to reply, then hesitated, running his words through my mind . . . *mockery of research should end.* I had grown up with my dad hurling word puzzles at us across the dinner table, puzzles that could often be solved by noticing an odd sentence structure or word choice. Sometimes he would mix palindromes into his speech just to see if we would notice. I started running some of the awkward phrases he'd just used through my mind.

. . . *my only real son, eh* . . .

. . . *mess of random science experiments* . . .

. . . *most original research shows errors* . . .

. . . *mockery of research should end* . . .

I felt a chill go down my spine. The words in each phrase began with the same series of letters: M-O-R-S-E. My eyes snapped to my father's hands, still tapping away on the bed rail. Three short taps, followed by three long ones. The letter S, then the letter O. My father, my real father, was in there somewhere. And he was trying to communicate.

Morse code was a common device in the simple ciphers and cryptograms my dad had taught us as kids, and Paul and I had spent a summer sending secret messages to each other using the buttons on a pair of cheap walkie-talkies. It had been a while since I'd looked at the Morse alphabet, but like riding a bike it came flooding back.

I expected three short taps again, completing an S-O-S distress code, but the next signal was one short, one long. The letter N. I snatched a pad and pen from the counter and started scribbling.

"What's happening?" my mom asked, but I put a finger to my lips. "Wait."

Three long taps. Another O. One short, one long. Another N. Then one short, two long, one short. P.

S-O-N-O-N-P. It wasn't making any sense yet, but it was clearly intentional. I kept writing.

Another O, then a T, then a U. I stopped trying to figure out the message and just wrote down the letters as fast as he tapped them.

Without stopping, my father lifted his head, trying to see my paper. "What is this? What are you writing?"

I ignored him, continuing to write. My mom looked over my shoulder. "Neil? You're making me nervous."

When the pattern started repeating itself, I stood and beckoned for her to follow me into the hallway. Once we were out of earshot, I said, "He's resisting, Mom! He's still in there."

"What are you talking about?"

"Morse code! He was tapping out a message. There's a part of him that's still unaffected by the fungal parasite." I tried to work it out, talking to myself as much as to her. "The unaffected part must have some access to the speech centers, because he hid a message in his speech. But it must not have full control."

My mother looked horrified. "You're telling me there's another mind taking control of his brain?"

"Not exactly," I said. "In most people, the fungal cells and their original brain seem to harmonize. One mind, one set of thoughts and intentions, only skewed toward what benefits the parasite. But Dad is holding onto some part of himself, actually splitting his mind, like in a multiple personality disorder. Maybe it's the Alzheimer's that makes it possible, I don't know. Or maybe the parts of his brain he used for word puzzles were so well-traveled, the fungal pathways couldn't improve their efficiency."

Mom raised her hands in frustration. "If he's communicating with us, then what did he say?"

I flipped the pad around and showed her what I'd written:

S-O-N-O-N-P-O-T-U-S-O-P-E-N-S-E-A

"Open sea?" she said. "Does that make sense to you?"

"Sorry," I said. "I started writing it down in the middle, so it wraps around." I took the pen and hastily scribbled the full message, starting at the beginning and leaving blanks between words. I turned the pad around again to show her:

OPEN SEASON ON POTUS

"I don't understand," she said. "What does it mean?"

"It means I need to warn the president of the United States."

I called Andrew and told him about my dad's message.

"But how could he possibly know such a thing?" Andrew objected. "He's been tied to a hospital bed, right? You're not going to tell me this infection makes people telepathic now, are you?"

"Nothing of the kind," I said. "But I suspect if you analyze the broadcast of my brother's interview with Nancy Sheridan on CNN, you'll find the same message in Johurá whistle language or something similar. Maybe Paul hums a few bars of something, or whistles, or, I don't know, pitches his voice up and down while he's talking. I didn't hear the whole interview. But take a look. I don't know how many thousands of viewers that show has, or how many of those are infected, but I think we need to warn the president right away."

Andrew gave a deep sigh, and I could hear the strain in his voice. "This isn't happening," he said. "I knew I should have taken that job with Boeing. I'd be in Seattle right now, and none of this would be my problem."

"It's going to be everybody's problem, if we don't find a way to turn it around," I said. "There's no reason what happened in Colombia and Brazil can't happen here, too."

"I know, I know. I'll get the Secret Service on the phone."

"Remember, anybody could be infected. There's no such thing as a trustworthy individual anymore, not unless they've been scanned for the fungus. The Secret Service agents currently on duty with the president are probably okay, or they would have tried to kill him already. But anyone new coming on duty needs to be scanned. Anyone who talks to him needs to be scanned."

"I know," Andrew said. "This is bigger than just us, now. SecDef has a whole staff of Army docs working on a fast and accurate test now, so we don't have to rely on PET scans. Ronstadt instituted the verified-command initiative at the meeting this morning. It's an emergency system requiring all commands to be issued formally in writing and be verified by private key. That way all commands can be tracked, and we can be certain some rogue colonel, say, isn't taking over a whole department as his own private workforce."

It sounded like a terrible idea to me, certain to slow the quick communication of real commands and not actually prevent the bad ones. There didn't seem to be any point in saying so, however. "Good luck," I said. "I'll see you soon."

Back in the hospital room, my father's hands lay still. I squeezed his shoulder. "Keep fighting, Dad."

I gave my mom a hug. "Stay with him. Don't lose hope."

On my way out of the room, I felt a wave of exhaustion come over me. I checked my watch and was startled to see that it was seven o'clock. I realized I hadn't eaten a bite all day. I wanted to get back to Fort Meade, despite the hour, but I knew if I didn't get some food I was going to crash sooner or later.

I made my way down to the hospital cafeteria. The tables were mostly empty. I saw an elderly couple, a teenage boy with what was probably his mother, and a young woman eating a salad by herself. She was strikingly pretty, with dark hair in a long braid on one shoulder, and a narrow, expressive face. Another day—maybe another life—I would have contrived some reason to sit near her and start a conversation. At the moment, the energy required to do something like that seemed as far beyond me as flying to the moon.

The dinner selections were mostly picked over. I passed on the dregs of a corn chowder, ignored the somewhat wilted salad bar, and settled for chicken fingers and some curly fries. I sat as far away from the other patrons as I could get. As soon as I took the first bite, my body realized how hungry I was, and I wolfed the food down.

My hands shook. I tried to hold them still, but soon my whole body was shaking. My chest convulsed painfully. I didn't even know what was happening until the first strangled sob burst out of my throat. I put my head in my hands and bottled them up as best I could, embarrassed to cry in public, but my shoulders shuddered uncontrollably.

I was exhausted. I hadn't slept or eaten properly for a week, and probably not terribly well before that, either. But I knew that wasn't all there was to it. I had just seen a man trapped in his own body, fighting his own mind for dominance and getting a message out to the world like a prisoner tapping on the walls of his cell. Or like a doomed sailor trapped in a sunken ship, tapping desperately on the steel hull for an unlikely rescue.

Before that, I had seen Mei-lin face the certainty of her own infection with bravery and self-sacrifice and narrowly escaped the same fate myself.

I had watched from a distance as thousands of soldiers died from the guns and bombs of their own countrymen. I usually managed to keep my emotions tucked away where I couldn't see them, and most of the time I didn't even know they were there. Apparently that wasn't something I could keep on doing forever.

I felt a gentle hand on my arm. I jerked my head up, startled, and saw the beautiful woman with the long braid, now sitting across from me. She wore black jeans and a green cotton shirt with three-quarter-length sleeves that revealed slim wrists. She had green eyes and a light dusting of freckles on her nose. She looked at me with a frank expression of sympathy.

"Who?" she said.

I sat up straight and wiped my eyes with my sleeve. "My dad."

She nodded. "I lost my mom last year. Pancreatic cancer."

I told her about my father's early-onset Alzheimer's, though I referred to his current condition simply as a bad reaction to a medication. Which was true, if not quite the whole story.

As someone willing to come up to a crying stranger in a cafeteria, I expected a bleeding heart, the kind of girl who loved to save puppies and take homeless beggars for a meal at McDonalds. Instead, she was crisp and intellectual, distracting me from my troubles by talking about the hair salon she had inherited from her mother and how little her business degree had prepared her for the day-to-day of operating a retail store. She asked what my father's work had been and was impressed when I told her he'd worked for the NSA.

Her name was Zoe.

Before I knew it, I was telling her stories about my childhood in Brazil, particularly ones that involved my father, and she countered with a funny anecdote about a trip to Argentina she'd taken with her mom in the sixth grade. I felt layers of stress and worry slipping away as the muscles in my shoulders and back unclenched.

Finally, I yawned and glanced at the clock on the cafeteria wall, and was startled to discover we had sat there talking for an hour. The elderly couple and teenage boy with his mom were gone, and we were alone in the room. I decided there was no point in trying to get back to Fort Meade at this hour. Better to get a good night's sleep and go to work in the morning.

I stood. "I should get home and get some sleep," I said. "Thank you for cheering me up. It was really very pleasant."

"Is there anyone else at home?" she asked.

"No," I said. "Just me."

She stood as well, close enough that I could smell a light scent of shampoo from her hair. She was almost exactly my height. "Do you need some company?" She asked it matter-of-factly, but I could feel the force of the question.

I considered, tempted to say yes. But I knew I didn't have anything to offer her right now. I was barely taking care of my own basic needs, much less finding any energy to invest in a relationship. "I can't," I said.

She took a step back, clearly embarrassed. "I understand."

"It's been really nice," I said. "Seriously, thanks for talking."

She gave a tiny nod. I turned away to leave, but then I turned back again. "Listen, Zoe," I said. "When all this is over, if you want, I'd love to show you a Peruvian restaurant I know in Rockville." I scribbled my phone number on a napkin and handed it to her. "Best *tacu tacu* outside of Peru. Believe me, it's worth the drive."

She took the napkin, but she looked confused. "When all *what* is over?"

I glanced at my feet, then back up at her green eyes. "What I didn't tell you, is that I work for the NSA too, just like my dad did. Things are going to get really bad pretty soon. Like what's been happening in Brazil."

She took another step back, and I could see it was too much. The small magic of our conversation was gone, and I was freaking her out.

"Hopefully I'm wrong," I said. "Hopefully we'll turn it back, and most people won't know how bad it could have been. But I don't think so. I think we're in trouble. Not just as a country but as a human race."

She smiled awkwardly. "I should go."

I should have let it drop there, but I couldn't leave her without at least a warning. "Stay away from Neuritol," I said.

"What? You mean the smart drug, like in the commercials?"

I stared at her. "They're *advertising* it now?"

"Not exactly. They don't use the name, but they're all about people improving themselves and getting smarter and stuff. And the name's all over the news, so everybody knows what they're talking about."

I had no idea it was moving that fast. "Don't touch the stuff," I said. "Don't go within a mile of it."

She picked up her purse, a small green leather affair that matched her eyes. I felt the pang of an opportunity lost. "Well, bye," she said.

I let her go while I collected the trash from my meal and placed the tray back in the small stack near the register. After counting to ten to make sure I didn't end up waiting at the elevator with her, I made my way back through the hospital and caught a cab back home.

CHAPTER 25

I set my alarm for 5:00 a.m. I needed sleep, but I also needed to get into work as early as possible. I knew if I waited I'd get trapped in the Monday morning traffic, and I wouldn't get in until late. Not wanting to repeat my emotional crash of the day before, I stopped at a 7-Eleven convenience store and bought two breakfast sandwiches, a bottle of chocolate milk, and three granola bars. Not exactly the most nutritious of breakfasts, but at least it would give me some calories for the morning.

I arrived at Fort Meade and pushed through security. I wondered how much, given the nature of the current threat, all of the armed guards and dogs and razor wire fences would actually be able to protect the people and the information inside.

I walked down to our basement office and found Andrew deep in conversation with Melody Muniz. "Melody!" I shouted. I ran to her and wrapped my arms around her. "You're safe!"

She stiffened, and I quickly backed off. "Sorry," I said. "It's just good to see you alive. We've all been pretty worried." I wondered if it was the first bear hug she'd received in her career at the NSA.

She relaxed and smiled at me. "I'm pretty glad to be home as well."

Shaunessy appeared around the corner, and I hugged her, too.

"What's happening down there?" I asked.

"It's a disaster," Melody said. "Thousands dead on both sides, but the real problem is not knowing what the sides are. We can't scan people fast enough to know who's affected, and the need to double- and triple-verify all commands with higher-ups cripples the effectiveness of the chain of command. I have five minutes with the president at eleven o'clock, and I'm going to beg him to pull our troops out of South America. The Ligados control most of the country now, and all we're doing by staying there is risking becoming part of them."

"Besides," Andrew said, "the war is at home now. If we don't find a way to control this thing, it's going to be just like Brazil right here."

"The president," I said to Andrew. "He's safe?"

"In a manner of speaking. He's alive, and as safe as we can make him. There were five attempts on his life last night." I must have shown my surprise on my face, because he said, "That is *not* common knowledge. We don't want the media getting ahold of that, if we can help it. Four of the attempts were pretty ill-conceived and never had much of a real chance. One, however, was carried out by an aide in the West Wing and very nearly succeeded.

"You were right, by the way, about your brother's interview. He didn't whistle, though. He just outright spoke the words when showing off his fluency in different languages."

"How are things with your father?" Shaunessy asked.

I pursed my lips. "Not great." I caught Shaunessy and Melody up on my father's condition, his attempt to kill Mei-lin Chu, and his split-personality coded communication, seemingly without the knowledge of the other part of his mind. I also told them about my brother's lab, the computers and samples we'd retrieved, and the booby-trapped door that had infected Mei-lin."

"We have plenty of samples of the spores at this point," Melody said. "Where are the computers?"

"I have them in my car."

"Get them in here, right away. We have people who can take them apart down to their constituent atoms. Any information he had there, even if he deleted it, we'll get it back."

"The best information on those computers is probably biological," I said. "We need to get it to the people who are trying to understand how this organism works and how to beat it."

"I'm on that," Melody said. "Including the docs at USAMRIID, the CDC, and several medical universities, we probably have two hundred doctors and mycologists working on one or more avenues, either trying to develop an easy test to know who's infected or trying to come up with a reliable cure. Anything we find, I'll make sure it gets into the right hands."

"Okay," I said. "So what can I do?"

"After you bring that stuff from your car? Do your normal work. Pore through all the South American traffic that Andrew has been ignoring while trying to do my job." She flashed him a quick smile. "Very effectively, I might add. Good to know there's someone waiting in the wings in case I turn into a fungus zombie."

"Something to look forward to," Andrew said.

—⬩—

When I headed out to my car, Shaunessy caught up to me. "Need some help?"

"Thanks," I said. "It's more than I can carry in one trip."

I showed the guard at the entrance the paperwork Melody had filled out giving me permission to bring the equipment inside. He entered the information into his computer, logging it as an equipment delivery, and told me he would have to record the details about make and model and serial number before we could bring them inside.

On the way out to the parking garage, I said, "How bad was it down there?"

Shaunessy turned somber. "Really bad," she said. "Melody talks about bringing the troops home, but I don't know how realistic that is. There's no way to tell how many of them are compromised. There's been so much sabotage, no one knows what equipment can be trusted. Some soldiers have outright defected to the Ligados, or turned on each other, but there have to be more who are keeping quiet. It would take weeks to scan that many, and cost a fortune, even if every PET scan machine in the country wasn't already running twenty-four hours a day."

"How did you get out?"

She shrugged. "Melody, of course. Director Ronstadt listed her as a critical recall, and she said she wasn't coming home without me."

We reached my car and hauled the equipment out of the trunk. The machines were small enough that I could have managed by myself, but I was glad for the company.

"What do you think our chances are?" I asked.

"What do you mean?"

"Of survival. Of preventing the United States from becoming the next Brazil and the same thing sweeping across Europe and Africa and Asia until half the population is dead and the other half has fungus in their brains telling them how to think."

She was quiet for a time. "I think we can win," she said.

I was surprised. "How?"

"It's like a disease, right? We've had some pretty bad diseases before. Bubonic plague. Influenza. Does a lot of damage while it spreads, but we always beat it in the end. Ultimately, we've got a lot more going for us than a fungus. Reason. Creativity. Invention."

"But it's using our reason against us," I objected. "Making it better, even."

"No. It's using our intelligence against us. Memories, analytical skills. That's just network efficiency. This thing might be good at cognitive streamlining, but that doesn't make it anything like human."

"Doesn't that make it better than human?"

"That's what I'm saying. There's a lot more to being human than being smart. The fungus gives people intelligence, but it robs them of some of the more important things that make us human. Our emotional connections. Our moral sense. Our devotion to country and friends and family. The kind of humanity it's producing is a shadow of what humanity truly is."

"True humanity is cruel," I said. "Selfish, tribal, violent. We don't need a fungus in our heads to kill each other by the millions."

"I didn't say we were good. I said we're stronger without the fungus than we are with it. That's why I think we'll win."

I thought about it, then flashed her a quick grin. "I hope you're right."

Back in our basement office, I logged in and flipped through the first batch of South American traffic. Some of them had been translated, many had not. From what I could tell, thousands of them hadn't even been looked at. There were just too many, and too much else going on. I sat up in my chair and cracked my fingers. I had my work cut out for me.

The difficulty with encrypted messages is that you can't tell if they're interesting until after you crack them. Cracking them takes time. Not only that, but due to the way the internet had developed, *all* South American email traffic passed through a hub in Florida, which the NSA had tapped three ways from Sunday. That meant the NSA's underground server farm recorded millions of messages from South America every day.

Usually, the vast majority of these could be ignored, since they had no known connection to any person or situation of political interest. Now, with any citizen a potential guerrilla warrior, any message could be important. Not only that, but the number of indecipherables—messages encrypted with no recognizable scheme—had grown by orders of magnitude in recent months.

Now that South America was a priority, hundreds of agents were working those messages, most of them with significantly better computer skills than I had. The ones in Johurá had gotten the most attention. Katherine Wyatt had, apparently, continued to work tirelessly on interpreting them and even held classes to teach agents how to understand a little of the language. Those weren't indecipherable anymore, and so not my concern.

My job was to do what computers couldn't do: either crack a new coding scheme, like I had with the original Johurá messages, or else recognize some pattern in the chaos that could help the army of agents focus their efforts to find the needles in the haystack. The first option would require me to choose a message, more or less at random, that after hours or days of work would probably turn out to be somebody's illicit love letter. I decided to try the second.

Fortunately, in my months on the job I had learned how to use many of the software tools available to aid in such an analysis. I could pull the metadata from millions of messages and run a bank of statistical tools against them. I was pretty good at statistics, which in my book was still a branch of mathematics, even though I knew statisticians who would take offense at me lumping their science into my field.

What I wanted to characterize was the difference between South American message traffic before and after the appearance of the fungus. Of course, there were many differences, as there would be from any comparison of distinct sets. Some of the differences were obvious, and thus uninteresting. Some of the differences would be normal random variation, or else seasonal or population-based trends, and thus also uninteresting. I was looking for the significant differences, those that were both unintuitive and important.

For lack of a better metric, I chose the date of the attack on Paul's riverboat as the turning point after which I would deem messages to be "fungus influenced." My null hypothesis would be that the messages before that time and the messages after that time would be perfectly correlated, shaped by the same basic forces and trends. I set about trying to disprove that hypothesis.

Four hours later, I had a spreadsheet full of numbers and no conclusions. My head was starting to spin. I had promised myself I would remember to eat, so instead of pressing on I picked up the phone and called Mike Scaggs. Before I left for Brazil, joining up with him for lunch had turned into a habit, at least when both of us could get away from our duties.

"Scaggs," he said, with his usual soft professional tone.

"Hey, Lieutenant," I said. "They still let you eat over there in cyber com?"

"Neil. You're back."

"Been crying into your pillow every night since I left, haven't you?"

"Something like that. You hungry?"

"That's why I'm calling."

"You must have quite some stories to tell."

"I'll regale you over lunch. See you there."

—⊙—

I opted for a grilled chicken panini, and Scaggs chose a cheeseburger and fries. I dumped five sugar packets into the too-sour lemonade and stirred while I told my story. I started from the assassinations and explosions, through the cross-country drive with the CIA, to the crop dusters and the defection of soldiers at São Luis and the 11th Bomb Squadron.

"I have to hand it to you," Scaggs said. "We send you down to Brazil for a few days, and the whole country falls apart."

"I'm just a bad luck charm, I guess."

"You sure you don't want to work for our enemies?"

Technically, the cafeteria was an insecure zone, where no discussion of classified material was supposed to go on. Sometimes uncleared visitors were escorted through the facility, and you never really knew who would be eating lunch there or how much they were supposed to know. In practice, however, classified topics were often discussed, only in roundabout ways and without using specific code words or program names.

"We've been focusing a lot of our efforts on South America," Scaggs said. He was USCYBERCOM, so he would be concerned both with cyberattacks on US secure facilities and with trying to breach the tightly protected information repositories of others. Such attacks could be purely for the purpose of obtaining information, or they could be used to introduce destructive viruses or worms and destroy an enemy's infrastructure or ability to communicate.

"Despite everything that's happening, we haven't seen any increased cyber activity. It's still China that's the biggest threat on that front. My guess is that Brazil, Venezuela, Colombia, and Peru never had much of a cyber capability, and so even on a wartime footing, they don't have anything to use. Though with so much chaos, there are probably capabilities that the Ligados don't know about or haven't been able to organize."

"I wouldn't bet on that," I said. "My impression of the Ligados is that they're pretty streamlined. It's not a top-down hierarchy so much as a crowdsourced one. Since everyone has the same goals, they can coordinate to an extraordinary degree." I told him about the timing and coordination required for the various successful assassinations.

"On the other hand," Scaggs said, "we've pretty much got the run of their systems. We've disrupted a lot of their military comms, and crashed the computer systems at munitions factories, defense contractors, satellite ground stations. They were pretty vulnerable in a lot of their core systems."

"And if this were a conventional war," I said, "that would probably give us a big advantage. But they're not ultimately fighting us with guns and bullets. They're turning us against ourselves and taking over our country from within. I'm beginning to suspect, too, that the Ligados have other ways of communicating with each other that we're not aware of."

"What makes you think that?"

"The message statistics I'm looking at. They're too . . . normal. I don't exactly know what changes to expect from wartime, but what I'm seeing is a whole lot of ordinary. It makes me wonder if . . . hmmm."

"Uh, oh, here it comes," Scaggs said. "Half the time when I eat lunch with you, you shout 'Eureka' and run off back to your lab."

"I don't shout 'Eureka,'" I said. "I only did that once, and it wasn't in the cafeteria."

"Well, maybe you should try it."

I munched my panini, thinking. It was no Eureka moment, just a feeling that I was looking at things wrong. I was trying to find pattern differences from before and after the emergence of the fungus. But what about pattern differences that ought to exist but didn't? What about the changes you would expect from nations at war that weren't evident in their message traffic?

After lunch, I returned to my spreadsheets and statistical analysis, keeping the idea in mind. After another six hours pounding away at the numbers, I thought I had something. Not an epiphany, exactly, but I thought it could be important. Melody's office was empty, so I told Andrew instead.

"There's a blank space," I said. "Most of Amazonas, a lot of Pará, and a little less than half of Roraima." These were the Brazilian states that covered the Amazon rainforest. "There's almost no traffic in those regions. No email, no cell phone, nothing."

Andrew looked confused. "But that's the same as before any of this happened," he said. "Those states are sparsely populated, with the exception of a few tourist cities. There just isn't much technology there."

"There wasn't. But this is the center of the Ligados movement. The highest concentration of infection per capita is in these states. We also show a population shift from Venezuela, Colombia, Peru, Brazil, and Bolivia *into* the rainforest areas. I checked with the CIA—they keep track of stuff like that, and it's a significant migration, millions of people. But there's no commensurate rise in message traffic, nor in any other technological measure—energy production, building construction, roads, telephone lines. Satellite images of the area look the same as ever, just thousands of acres of trees."

"What are you driving at?" Andrew asked.

"There are millions of people living in there. What are they all doing? Hunting and fishing? Living off the land?"

Andrew rubbed at his chin. "I'm not saying it's not important," he said. "It probably is. But what significance does it have to us, directly? Is this a threat to our interests in some way? Do you think they're mass-producing Neuritol there, or devising some new delivery mechanism?"

"Possibly," I said. "I don't know. There's no message traffic coming out, so there's no way to know."

"Okay," he said. "This is good work, good analysis. But it's not going to get much traction. If there's some direct threat we can defend against, then great. Otherwise, migration patterns? Interesting, maybe, but not actionable. Keep at it."

Sighing, I returned to my desk. I called my mom to check on Dad, who said there had been little change. No more Morse code, that she could tell. Then I called Lauren to check on Mei-lin.

"I don't know how much longer I can do this," Lauren said. "She's refusing treatment. She's lucid and healthy. I could get fired over this, even lose my license."

"Let me talk to her," I said.

"Hang on." I waited while Lauren presumably held a phone up to Mei-lin's ear.

"Neil," she said clearly. "Please tell her to let me go."

"That's not what you want, remember?" I said. "You've been infected. You're not yourself anymore. Give the antifungals a few days to work."

"You don't understand what's it's like," she said. "Neil, it's nothing like what we feared. I can think clearly for the first time in my life. I can remember *everything* I ever learned—all my medical textbooks and classes; it's all in there, only now I can recall it at will. I can tell you page numbers, what day I read it, what the weather was like. I can keep three different trains of thought going in my head at the same time.

"This isn't a curse, Neil. It's a *gift*. Please don't take it away from me."

A chill slid across my skin. She was so earnest, so persuasive. "This infection changes people," I said. "It makes them kill. It makes them people they would never want to be."

"I don't want to kill anyone," she said. "Just because somebody with a brain tumor turns violent doesn't mean that all cancer patients are dangerous. We were wrong. I was wrong. I didn't know."

"You'll thank me," I said. "When it's over, and this thing is out of you, you'll thank me."

Anger crept into her tone. "Look, I'm being honest with you. I'm not trying to trick you. I'm telling you what it's like."

"Put Lauren back on."

"I'm not going to stay here. You can't hold me against my will. Lauren, I don't want to hurt you, but I will. If I start screaming, and threaten to sue, you won't be able to keep it quiet. You know you can't win this. Untie the straps."

Her voice faded, and Lauren came back on the line. "What do you want me to do? I can't keep her against her permission, no matter what she signed before."

I sighed. "Keep her as long as you can. But you're right. I think we've lost her."

I hung up, feeling shaky and overwhelmed. Nothing we were doing was coming close to stopping this thing.

I ordered Pad Thai and kept on working, hunting for useful patterns in the message metadata. It bothered me that Andrew didn't find my discovery significant, but I couldn't really argue with him. There was nothing we could do in response. So a lot of people were relocating into the rainforest and apparently giving up technology. So what? But it nagged at me. It felt important, like a clue toward understanding the bigger picture of how the world was changing around us.

While I worked, I kept the internal news feed up on a side monitor. It was a service provided by the Office of the DNI to all the intelligence services that summarized news stories from the unclassified media with bearing on international politics or current intelligence crises. The media had a lot of journalists in the field around the world, and it wasn't unusual for them to uncover something important before we did.

The news was unremittingly bad. The president of Mexico had been found dead in his bedroom that morning, apparently poisoned. An Arizona senator declared the Neuritol crackdown a plot by whites to keep Hispanics uneducated and disenfranchised, and encouraged Hispanics everywhere to stockpile the drug and give it to their children. Thirteen policemen died in

San Antonio in a massive shootout after a gang calling themselves the Arm of the Ligados overran the federal building and took thirty people hostage, including the mayor. And three counties along the southern edge of New Mexico announced their independence from the US government.

At nine o'clock, I thought about leaving and stopping to check on my parents, but I knew visiting hours in the hospital would be over, and that the best way I could help them was to continue my work. The way things were going, we wouldn't have much time before half the country sided with the Ligados and we were at war against ourselves.

Instead of going home, I stretched out on one of the makeshift beds my coworkers had made on the floor and caught a few hours of sleep as best I could. I woke the next morning to discover that the president had announced a national state of emergency and mobilized the National Guard in Texas, New Mexico, Arizona, and California.

"It's like they're just toying with us," Shaunessy said. "There's this appearance of riots, race-related violence, protests of injustice. All things our country has dealt with before, though never on this scale. But it's a lot more organized and sophisticated than it seems."

"What do you mean?" I asked.

"Riots are timed to break out at the opposite ends of a city simultaneously, stretching police response thin. We crack a cell phone message between gang leaders calling for a protest at a certain place and time, and we warn law enforcement . . . and then the protest happens an hour earlier and across town. The worse things get, the more we concentrate emergency powers in the hands of local mayors and governors. But how do we know they aren't infected? In a few days, it might be our own National Guard keeping us out of the states we sent them to protect. Our reactions are too predictable, and these people are smart. I'm afraid we're playing right into their hands."

"Wait a minute," I said. "How do they know what messages we can read and which ones we can't? Are they just staging fake communications in hope that we'll be listening?"

She shrugged. "I don't know. All I know is that they seem to be out-maneuvering us at every turn."

Frowning, I went back to my message analysis. One thing I had noticed the night before was that use of the Johurá whistle language, despite showing up in the United States, had been going out of favor in South America, and, on the whole, the messages delivered via that method were unimportant. It suggested that they were using a new language now, or a different scheme altogether, and the information was gradually spreading through the Ligados that Johurá was no longer a safe communication method.

But if so, how did they know? As far as I could tell, no NSA agents had been turned, and our ability to read the Johurá messages was a secret known to only a relatively small number of people. Was one of those people secretly infected, or otherwise compelled to pass information to the enemy? It was a chilling thought.

Instead of examining the metadata of the undeciphered messages, I decided to analyze the deciphered ones, those we had cracked and read. When I did so with Shaunessy's comments in mind, the correlations practically fell into my lap. It was so obvious, I couldn't believe no one had seen it before now. As soon as we cracked a code from a particular source, they either changed the code they were using, or else the information passed with that code stopped being useful. Or worse, the new information derived was misleading or false.

In any one instance, that behavior didn't set off any alarms. Codes changed, the usefulness of intercepted data changed, nothing was completely predictable. It happened. In aggregate, however, looking across all the messages received and how they changed in response to our knowledge of them, the conclusion was irrefutable. As soon as we cracked any one of their messages, the Ligados knew it.

I showed Shaunessy what I'd found, hoping that she would point out a problem with my work, some kind of self-referential mathematical error that implied a conclusion that the data didn't support. She couldn't.

"We've been infiltrated," she said. "There must be infected people who are working here, staying quiet, but passing the information out to a Ligados network of some kind."

I shook my head. "It could be. But it seems too fast, too thorough. It's more like . . ." I stopped, considering. An image flashed into my mind of Paul, visiting the NSA, standing in this very room, before we had any idea of what his infection could mean. Of me showing him the server room. Of Paul, dropping to the floor and gazing through the grates at the bundles of cables connecting the thousands of server racks to each other and to the rest of the world. "Oh, no," I said.

"What?"

I jumped to my feet and strode toward the server room, my heart thundering and heat flooding my face. I stabbed my numeric code into the keypad at the door, but the light flashed red. I tried again, but my shaking fingers stumbled, and I hit the wrong sequence again. The lock beeped, warning me, and flashed red again.

"Let me," Shaunessy said. She entered her own numbers in rapid succession and the light flicked to green. The door made a clunking sound as the electromagnetic bolts released, and Shaunessy pushed it open. A blast of cool, pressurized air ruffled our hair. I slipped past her and ran down the short flight of steps to the ground level of the vast room. I tried to picture where Paul and I had been standing. It couldn't have been far.

Most of the squares that made up the flooring were a dingy white, opaque, but spaced at regular intervals were grates that allowed a dim view of the hundreds of cables snaking their way underneath the floor. I ran to one of these grates—the same one, I was pretty sure, that Paul had peered into on his visit, and yanked it up. The sections of floor were made to come away easily, allowing technicians access to the wires underneath when necessary.

I tossed it aside, where it clanged against the floor. The hole was unlit, giving me little clear view of what was down there. When Paul was here, he had dropped to the floor so quickly I thought he had fallen down.

He could easily have used the motion to drop something—or many tiny somethings—into the hole.

I put my hand into the hole and used the leverage to pull away one of the white squares next to the grating, then another and another, widening the hole. Now the bright LEDs on the ceiling illuminated the space, and I could clearly see what I had feared. I didn't stop. I pulled away section after section, hurling them to the side, exposing the depths of my folly and the degree to which my brother had manipulated me from the very beginning.

Thousands of tiny white mushrooms quilted the crawlspace like a dusting of sugar, stretching out under the floor as far as I could see. The crisscrossing cables were tightly spiraled with thin, translucent filaments, wrapping around the wires like vines around a tree. They were hopelessly tangled together, and in some cases it was difficult to distinguish the mycelium from the wires.

Shaunessy stopped at the edge of the hole I had made in the floor, her eyes wide. "What does this mean?"

I rocked back on my heels, breathing hard from the effort of tearing away the floor. "I think it means we're in trouble."

An alarm pierced the cavernous space. Shaunessy held her hands over her ears. "I think you're right!" she shouted over the din.

The lights went out, leaving us momentarily in pitch darkness until the emergency lights switched on, bathing the room in an eerie, cave-like glow. "Time to go," I said.

We ran for the door, careful not to fall in the hole I had opened in the floor. The distance wasn't far, and the emergency lights, though dim, gave us enough illumination to see where we were going. On our way to the exit, I remembered the steel cage that Melody had told me was hidden in the wall above the doorway, designed to fall in the unlikely event of an assault on the building by external forces, protecting the information inside. No sooner had the thought entered my mind than a light bar over the door glared red.

"No!" I ran full out, but I had only reached the first step when the massive portcullis smashed into place with an impact that shook the floor. The sound repeated around the giant room as similar steel barriers fell, blocking all the entrances to the server room and its precious cache of data. And trapping us inside.

I took the stairs two at a time and yanked stupidly on the steel bars, but they didn't budge. Melody and Andrew appeared on the other side, faces grim with concern. Melody started to speak, but I cut her off.

"Get out of here," I said. "Don't wait for us. Get everyone out while you still can."

CHAPTER 26

It doesn't make any sense," Shaunessy said. "A fungus may resemble a computer network, but it's *organic*. It communicates through nutrients and enzymes and chemical neurotransmitters. It can't interface with an Ethernet cable or make sense of network protocol."

"It doesn't need to," I said. "This cable is unshielded. That means the hyphae wrapped around it are bathed in the electromagnetic radiation coming from those wires. It's what *we* sometimes do to tap enemy networks."

"But we know the protocols. We know how raw signal is converted into useful information. The fungus doesn't."

"Again, I don't think it needs to. It's a giant neural network. Data goes in, the network responds, and then it gets feedback. The feedback enables it to strengthen neural paths that give favorable results. It doesn't need to understand the data in order to learn from it. It's the same behavior it uses in a forest, only with a different kind of data. Paul talks about it 'learning' and making 'coordinated responses' and 'collective decisions,' but it's not really deciding anything, not like we do. It's just strengthening pathways that give it the best feedback and culling those that don't."

She thought for a minute. "I don't buy it. The data running through these servers affects things far away. Equipment off site, communication with other agencies, the indirect effects of human decisions based on the data. I don't see how just accessing the data would be enough, not without the intelligence to interpret it at some level."

I looked around. "Where is everyone else?"

"Who?" she said.

"The server staff. There are always people in here, maintaining the racks. Where are they?"

"They must have gotten out."

Understanding dawned in both of us at once. "They were infected," I said. "That's the other piece of the puzzle. The fungus did have intelligence to help it understand what it found."

We sat on the concrete stairs next to the barricaded door, our backs to the wall, looking out over the dark server room. Thousands of LED lights from the racks twinkled like a miniature galaxy. The alarm had shut off, leaving us in what felt like silence, even though the hum of the servers made a constant background sound.

"How do you know it doesn't understand?" Shaunessy asked.

"What?"

"The fungus. You said it's like a neural net. So is our brain. So how do you know it doesn't understand what it's doing?"

"Well, I guess it depends what you mean by 'understand.' We have centralized locations for language, creative thought, intellect, abstract thinking. A fungus doesn't. It's just a network, every part the same as the others. It's a complex data filter and decision tree. It accomplishes some incredibly sophisticated responses, but it's not aware of itself."

"At least, not until now," Shaunessy said.

"What do you mean?"

"Now its network includes thousands of human beings. Humans who *do* think. Who are aware of themselves."

"Interesting," I said. "It has conscious components, but it itself is not conscious. It's not centralized—no one human is critical to its existence—but it can take advantage of all the creativity and problem-solving skills of its human nodes."

"We're in trouble, aren't we?" she said. "The human race? This is why we have such trouble getting fungi out of our house or off of our toenails. How can we fight something that doesn't have a central organ to destroy? You have to eradicate it completely, or it keeps coming back."

I sighed and leaned the back of my head against the wall. "It's funny. I always thought it was the computers we had to be afraid of. You know,

AIs getting so smart that they wouldn't need humans anymore. The great war between the biological minds and the artificial ones."

Shaunessy shook her head. "They're not even close."

"Really? I keep hearing that the Singularity is only twenty years away."

She laughed. "It's been twenty years away for the last sixty years. But it's nonsense. The computers we have aren't brains. They're machines that manipulate one set of symbols into another set of symbols. They don't respond to their environment; they don't grow."

"Sure they do," I said. "What about deep learning? Cognitive computing? Neuromorphic chips? They've got computer chips now with as many synapses as the human brain."

"That's just it. We've taken a small part of how our brain works— the patterns of dendrites and axons and synapses—and we've built computer architectures around them. But that's all it is—a symbolic machine *inspired* by the human brain. Real brains are biological pieces of meat inextricably connected to the bodies that host them and the environments they inhabit in a million essential ways. A computer is a complex tool, but it's not a brain. It requires the human operator to be its body, to be its environment, by writing its algorithm and feeding it data. If we really want to make an artificial construct that can think like we do, we have to start over with a completely different concept."

"Like what?"

"Well . . ." Shaunessy took a few of her braids in her hands and fingered them absently. "It might be something more like your fungus."

"*My* fungus?"

"You know what I mean. Your brother's fungus. *The* fungus. An architecture that doesn't just manipulate symbols but grows organically from interaction with its environment. Intelligence ultimately isn't Boolean. It isn't about logic. It's physical. It's a continuous chemical give-and-take with everything around it. Is it getting hot in here?"

I blinked at the sudden change of topic. "Um, I guess." Now that I thought about it, the temperature was rising. This room had always been chilly.

"The cooling system must be down with the lights," she said. "There's supposed to be a backup system on the same generator that's still powering the machines, but maybe it malfunctioned. If they don't fix that fast, it's really going to start cooking down here. Those racks put out a lot of heat."

"Should we . . . I don't know . . . turn them off?"

"There are thousands of them. And some of them are hosting some pretty critical systems. We can't just kill them."

"Better them than us," I said.

"Hopefully they'll get us out of here before that becomes a problem."

It didn't take long before the heat started to get uncomfortable. Shaunessy checked the temperature reading on one of the servers and reported that it was ninety-five degrees in the room. "The processors will start frying before we're in any real danger from the heat," she said.

"I can't tell you how reassuring that is," I said.

"This is what I'm talking about, though," she said. "This is why computers will never be intelligent."

"Because they get too hot?"

"I'm serious," she said. "It's like the guy in the *Apollo 13* movie who says, 'Power is everything.' The kind of computers you're talking about, the ones that rival the human brain for processing nodes, consume on the order of four million watts of power. The chunk of meat in your head—which is not a computer, by the way—uses twenty watts. Not twenty million. Just twenty. Our brains are efficient thermodynamic systems, designed to help us produce valuable work from the potential energy around us in the world. Computers are simply extensions of our minds—tools we use that heighten that production value."

I waved my hands at the servers. "So if these were racks of brains instead of computers, we wouldn't be getting so hot right now," I said.

"Right," she said. "Although . . . ew."

"Yeah."

We sat in silence for a while, sweating. After a while, she checked the temperature again, and reported that it was up to ninety-seven degrees.

My mouth felt dry. "Maybe we should have asked Andrew and Melody to pass in some water bottles before they evacuated."

"They won't abandon us," Shaunessy said. "You know they're doing everything they can to get the lockdown reversed and get us out of here."

Sitting there staring down at the carpet of white mushrooms made me uncomfortable, so I replaced the flooring tiles I had removed before.

"There," I said. "Out of sight, out of mind."

"How does it even grow down there? Doesn't it need sunlight?" Shaunessy said.

"Nope. Fungus thrives on radiation. That's like the perfect environment for it down there. Lots of heat, lots of energy."

"What if we could control its environment?" Shaunessy asked. Her gaze was focused inward, not really looking at me, in an expression I had come to associate with the emergence of a brilliant idea.

"What do you mean?"

"You said it learns from its environment. That it's not really intelligent or even clever, it just filters data and finds the most efficient beneficial response."

"That's right."

"So, what if we could control the data it processed? What if we could steer its actions by simulating a false environment, causing it to make choices that were actually detrimental, but because we controlled its feedback, it strengthened the wrong pathways?"

"Virtual reality, fungus style."

"Something like that. If we could get it to interpret negative feedback as if it were positive, then it would increasingly pursue things that were harmful to it. It would destroy itself."

"Okay," I said. "How do we do that?"

She fell silent.

"I mean, we're talking about a lot of inputs, right? Thousands of people scattered everywhere, and who knows how many square miles of rainforest. We can't actually control that, can we?"

"Not all of it. But it's not one continuous network. The people aren't wired together—as you said, they have to communicate through language. And this mycelium"—she pointed to the flooring I had replaced—"can't be directly connected to the one in Brazil. If we could just fool this one, we might be able to affect the actions of the rest of the network."

I wiped the sweat off my face. "I'm having trouble imagining what kind of mistaken action on the part of the fungus could actually have a serious harmful effect."

"What if we could convince it that some kind of attack on our part was to its benefit, so it didn't try to stop us?"

"Okay," I said. "What kind of attack? You could firebomb the entire Amazon jungle and still probably not kill all of it. And even if you did, it would live on in the lungs of each infected person."

"You're right," she said. "What we need is something it can do to itself. Some kind of exponential decay, where it interprets negative feedback as positive, and thus increasingly favors the self-destructive activity, until the entire thing is gone."

The heat was getting unbearable. I stood and walked to the first row of racks. The temperature readout now showed 99 degrees.

"We have to get out of here," I said. "Or find some way to get the cooling system back on. If the heat keeps rising like this, we're going to be in big trouble."

Shaunessy tapped the console and the screen came to life. "I don't know what I can do from here, but I'll try. Maybe there's some networked controller I can access."

"To control the temperature? Or to get us out of here?"

"I don't know. Probably neither. Give me a bit."

"Okay."

She started typing, rapidly bringing up programs and switching between windows. I watched her work for a few minutes, but I couldn't follow what she was doing, and I figured she could make better progress without me staring over her shoulder. I took a walk around the circumference of the cavernous room, which now felt more like a sauna. Phones were mounted at regular intervals. I tried each of them in turn, but they were all dead. No surprise, really—they were voice-over-IP, phones that sent voice data through an internet protocol and thus required access to the network to operate. They had been disconnected from the outside by the same lockdown procedure that had isolated the servers.

Sweat ran into my eyes. I wondered how hot the processors themselves must be, to raise the temperature of the room this much, and how much hotter they could get before they fried. It seemed surprising to me that both the primary and backup cooling systems would have shut down. In case of an external attack, the idea was to protect the computers, not melt them down. Why would they power the cooling from the outside only? I stopped walking. The answer, of course, was that they wouldn't.

I turned and ran back to where Shaunessy stood, her attention still focused on the screen. "I think we're in trouble."

She didn't look up. "You're just figuring that out now?"

"Even more trouble." I leaned against the rack next to her, trying to catch her eye. "Why is the backup cooling system down?"

"Same reason the lights are out. The lockdown switched us over to internal generator power only."

"But wouldn't cooling be an essential system? Shouldn't that be on the circuit with the generator?"

She shrugged. "I don't know. Maybe somebody screwed up. Put them on the wrong circuit, or mangled a config file or something."

"For that matter," I said, "why is the *primary* cooling system down? It doesn't make sense. You don't shut off the air for a lockdown unless you *want* to destroy the servers. And if you wanted that, you wouldn't power them in the first place—you'd erase them and shut them down, or else fry them all with a power surge or something."

She was only half paying attention to me. "Well, if you figure it out, let me know."

"That's what I'm telling you. There's only one thing I can think of that actually benefits from overheating this room."

She finally stopped typing and looked up, frustrated. "What?"

"Darkness, heat, lots of radiation? Those are ideal conditions for the fungus. You saw all those little mushrooms down there, right?"

"Yes."

"I think it's creating the environment it needs for those mushrooms to sporulate."

Her eyes locked on mine. "Sporulate. As in . . ."

"As in, release thousands of spores into the air that we're breathing. It has to be pretty inefficient to transport Neuritol into the country through cocaine trafficking channels all the way from South America. It would make sense for the fungus to create new centers for spore dissemination right here, in the United States. There's been no sign that, growing in humans, it can actually reach a fruiting stage and reproduce. Which means the fungus needs large, dark, hot areas where it can grow undisturbed for weeks or months, until it's ready."

"Like right here."

"Yeah. Given how long ago Paul was here, this may even be the first in the country. I doubt it's the last, though. There are plenty of other large server farms. Nuclear power plants would probably work well, too. The server staff probably planned this. Programmed it, even."

"So, if the cooling system is off, and there's no ventilation, how will the spores get out?" Shaunessy asked. "I mean, it won't be great for us, but nobody else is going to get sick if the spores are trapped in this room."

"My guess is, once the temperature has reached some kind of trigger point for the mushrooms, and the spores release, then the ventilation system will turn back on. It'll blow them everywhere in the complex. Anybody still in the building, or who comes back inside, will breathe them in for sure."

Shaunessy grimaced and rubbed at her temples. "Is there anything we can do about it?"

"I don't think so."

She turned back to the keyboard. "Then I guess I'd better keep working."

"It looks like we're going to get that great war between the artificial and biological minds after all," I said. "Only I didn't expect to be rooting for the artificial ones."

I left her alone to work. I remembered the emergency storage locker under the stairs and decided that if any situation qualified as an emergency, this one did. I opened it and examined its contents.

Melody had been right: it contained everything I could think of and more. Fire extinguishers and radiation protection tablets, blankets and flashlights, matches and flares and a two-way radio. A box of ration bars and bottled water and canned food, complete with can opener. I counted five first aid kits, three bottles of vitamins, and a defibrillator.

She had been wrong about one thing, though: the locker contained exactly what I was looking for. A dozen full-face biological warfare gas masks with extra filters. Two HAZMAT suits would have been perfect, but I would take what I could get. I strapped one of the gas masks around my head and brought the other one to Shaunessy.

"I'm making progress," she said. "Whoever did this locked down access to the controllers. It's clearly intentional. But I think it's still physically connected, which means I can hack my way in, if I can figure out how."

I held out the mask. "Which means you'll have to be alive and still uninfected yourself," I said, pointing at the mask she still held in her hands.

"Right." She struggled with the straps for a few moments but finally got it over her head and pulled tight.

"How's that look?" she asked. The masks contained amplifiers for our voices, but the words came out muffled and with a bit of an echo.

I gave her a thumbs up. "Fashion statement." If that made her smile, I couldn't tell.

"I'll let you know if I figure anything out," she said, putting her fingers back to the keyboard.

Every phone in the server room rang at once, startling us.

"Does that mean rescue?" I asked. "Are we connected again?" I ran toward the nearest phone.

She tapped on the keyboard. "Yes!" she called after me. "We're connected to the outside!"

I picked up the phone, expecting to hear Melody or Andrew or maybe even Ronstadt. "Hello?" I said. It was awkward getting the phone to my ear around the mask, and I hoped I could be understood at the other end.

"Hello, Neil."

It took me a few moments to recognize the voice. It was my brother. "Paul?"

"I don't have much time." His voice was smooth, controlled, though some static crackled on the line.

"I found your little present," I said, my surprise blossoming into rage. "Is this how you repay my trust? I bring you into a secure facility, I vouch for you, and you betray me? I don't care what you have growing in your head, that was pretty low. I thought you were on our side then, but I guess it was all a sham. You never cared about me or Dad or any of us."

"I *was* on your side," Paul said, unruffled by my outburst. "I've always been on your side. That's why I want you to experience what I have."

"Give it up, Paul. I don't want what you're selling."

"That's only because you've never tried it. Once you get over your prejudice, you'll see that this is the best thing ever to happen to the human race. This is what will take us to the next level. You have no idea the things we're accomplishing already. There's no coercion here. There's just people cooperating to an unprecedented degree, with the mental tools to accomplish more than they ever dreamed was possible."

"You can skip the Illuminati speech," I said. "I'm not joining your cult. And don't act all innocent. Your side is killing people."

"Only to defend ourselves."

"Oh, come on. Carefully planned assassinations are not self-defense."

"Which is better?" Paul asked. "The surgical removal of a repressive leader or wide-scale war involving thousands of combatants who have no connection to the issues being fought over? We've removed a few people, yes. You're the ones who turned it into a war."

I heard a clunking sound from inside the nearest wall and then a steady hum. The ventilation system, turning back on. "This is fascinating and all, but I've got to go," I said.

"Come and see me, Neil," he said, his voice earnest. "Let me show you what we're accomplishing here."

I hesitated, thinking of Dad. "Paul? You can resist this. You don't have to let it control you. Don't let a parasite tell you how to think or what to do."

He laughed. "You have no idea what you're talking about," he said. "I hope someday you'll understand. I'm serious. Come and see me. I'll be waiting for you."

A grinding motor noise cut in, and I saw the steel gate begin to lift from the door. Shaunessy ran up behind me. "Time to go," she said.

I hung up the phone. Five men in HAZMAT suits, carrying automatic rifles, ducked under the rising gate and ran into the room, the barrels of their rifles sweeping over us. I raised my hands over my head.

"Don't worry," Shaunessy said. "They're on our side."

"How do you know?" I asked.

"If they weren't," she said, "they wouldn't bother with the suits."

CHAPTER 27

We were taken into custody, hosed down, sterilized, and subjected to PET scans. They wanted to give the server room the same essential treatment, but Shaunessy convinced them not to. That is, she explained to Melody the advantage we might get from being able to manipulate the fungus under the floor, and Melody bullied and cajoled enough high-ranking people until she got her way. As far as we could tell, no one had been infected.

The Army established a perimeter around the building, allowing access only to select individuals and then in full HAZMAT suits. The thousands of people who had worked in the building, although not infected, were robbed of offices, computers, and working space, or, for most of them, access to any of their ongoing work. The fungus had effectively brought the largest intelligence agency in the world to its knees.

The servers remained on. Connected to the world, they continued to collate and automatically process much of the intelligence collected around the world by satellite, drone, land- and ship-based sensor suites, and human operatives. It was a dangerous game, now that we knew the information was accessible to both us and the fungus, but Melody felt that Shaunessy was right. The digital realm belonged to humanity: we were its creators and kings. It was the best avenue we had to try to wrest dominance of our world back from Kingdom Fungi to Kingdom Animalia.

"But not the only one," Melody told me in our new "office," one of dozens of overcrowded military tents in a parking lot on the base. Other fields and open spaces at Fort Meade had also been converted into these office shantytowns. It was pure chaos, with not enough computing equipment or phones, and no one knowing where to find anyone else. The security rules confining the discussion of classified topics to approved areas were so ingrained in the habits of the NSA workforce that many agents found it difficult to talk about anything at all.

"What do you mean?" I asked.

"We're not the only people working on this problem," she said. "Far from it."

"Glad to hear it," I said. "Because we're not exactly making headway here." I was still smarting from Paul's betrayal and how he had manipulated me into bringing him into Fort Meade. I knew it wasn't productive to blame myself, but that didn't stop me from feeling deeply embarrassed and foolish. It was my brother, after all, who had caused this catastrophe. And I had helped him do it. "My track record is pretty dismal at the moment," I said. "So please tell me that someone else out there is actually finding a way to beat this thing."

"That's what I'm heading to find out," Melody said. "I want you to come along."

"You're sure you want me? I seem to leave disaster in my wake."

"I'm not asking you; I'm telling you," Melody said. "So stand up and snap out of it. Because we have a bit of a drive ahead of us, and I don't want to spend it listening to you wallowing in self-pity."

I stood, smiling wryly, and snapped her a salute. "Self-pity gone," I said. "I'm ready to work." It wasn't exactly true, but I knew she was right. I knew, too, that the guilty feelings were a bit of a smokescreen, hiding a lurking sense of despair. Guilt was a safer emotion. If what had happened so far had been my fault in some way, then if I worked hard and cleverly enough, I could do better next time. If it hadn't been my fault—if everything that had happened had been beyond my power to stop—then there was no reason to believe I could succeed in the future, no matter what I did.

And, despite everything we tried, the fungus had advanced unchecked. News arrived that morning that the White Sands Missile Range in New Mexico—the largest military installation in the country—had fallen to Ligados forces. Fighting had pushed north, toward Albuquerque, and enemy forces elsewhere seemed to be converging on the city. The reason seemed frighteningly obvious: Albuquerque was home to Kirtland Air Force Base and the more than two thousand nuclear warheads in its underground munitions storage complex. There was no way to move them safely in any reasonable amount of time. The only option was to defend the city with everything we had.

The president had declared martial law, and military forces were even now converging on Albuquerque. General Craig Barron—an Army four-star whom Melody knew personally, and disliked immensely—had been named commander of US forces on the home front. He had been granted huge latitude to defeat the Ligados no matter what the cost. Which made him, for all practical purposes, as powerful as the president, if not more so. The war was coming into our own borders, and no infringement on the liberties of civilians was more important than keeping those nukes out of Ligados control.

Melody drove a white Impala with a faded "Proud Navy Mom" bumper sticker on the back. I climbed into the passenger seat, and Melody dropped the accelerator to the floor, leaping out of the parking space as if driving a Ferrari. She took the turns fast enough that I gripped the door handle for balance, and in moments we were heading west on Route 32.

"Are you going to tell me where we're going?" I asked.

"Fort Detrick, Maryland," she said. "Specifically, USAMRIID."

"Biomedical research?" I asked.

She nodded. "Infectious disease research, psychological research, neuroscience research. Anything that keeps our soldiers alive, improves their ability to fight, or does the opposite to our enemies, they study it there. It's the national center of our biological weapons program."

"I thought Nixon shut down our bioweapons program fifty years ago."

Melody shrugged. "Potato, potato. Yes, it's all called bio*defense* now. But how can you defend against what the enemy might do without figuring out what weapons they might throw at you? It's two sides of the same coin. And you can bet they've been all over this fungal organism with everything they've got."

"I'm guessing, since we're driving there, that they've had some success."

"That's what we're going there to find out."

———⊙———

It took us an hour to get there, but we finally turned off the highway and made our way onto the Fort Detrick complex, where we followed signs to Building 1625, a six-story new construction with an imposing brick-and-glass facade. Inside, an army lieutenant led us down winding corridors and through doorways marked with biohazard warning signs. I glimpsed a sign on a lab door that read "Warning: Trespassers Will Be Used as Science Experiments."

Finally, he brought us to a room that resembled a cross between a medical lab and box seats at a basketball game. One whole wall looked out through plate glass onto a gymnasium-sized room where perhaps two hundred people of different ages, genders, and modes of dress milled with no obvious purpose. Some sat at tables, some walked around the room, some picked at the remains of a breakfast spread. Many talked together in groups of two or three. Most looked bored.

Melody and I chose seats from several rows of folding chairs that had been set in front of the glass, looking out at the people like visitors at the zoo.

"Don't worry; it's one-way," said a tall man in a long lab coat with thinning red hair. "They can't see you. Make yourself comfortable. The others will be here shortly."

"Tyler, I'd like you to meet Neil Johns," Melody said. "Neil, this is Dr. Tyler McCarrick, chief of neuroscience research here."

"You must be the Major's newest protégé, then," McCarrick said. "I sat in your shoes once, not so long ago."

"Don't flatter us," Melody said. "It was a very long time ago."

"You worked for Melody?" I said.

McCarrick nodded. "I was assigned to the agency for a little over a year, before I went back for my doctorate. Best education of my life."

I wanted to ask him if he'd known my father, but it didn't seem the time. Other people, mostly in military uniforms, filtered into the room, and Dr. McCarrick was forced to play host.

I shifted in my seat. "Who are all these people?" I whispered to Melody.

"Mostly staff members of different agency directors or high-ranking military types," she said. "Sent by their bosses to make sure nobody else benefits from Dr. McCarrick's research before they do."

"I meant, who are all *those* people." I pointed to the crowd of people in the room beyond the glass.

Melody shrugged. "I have no idea."

A tall, broad-chested man in a well-decorated Army uniform entered at the front of a small entourage. The small conversations going on throughout the room stopped.

"And everyone here has just been outranked," Melody said, her voice pitched so only I could hear her.

"Who is that?"

"General Craig Barron," she said. "Our new commander. The fact that he's here himself instead of sending a subordinate means he knows something we don't know." She nodded at Barron, who nodded back at her.

"I should have known I'd find the Major at an event like this," Barron said.

"I can't say the same for you, General," she said. "Why are you here?"

"To see the show, of course." He and his entourage took a block of folding chairs on the other side of the group.

"How come you always know the highest-ranking person in any room?" I asked Melody.

She grinned. "It's probably from a career spent going over other people's heads to get the job done."

Dr. McCarrick cleared his throat. "I think we can get started," he said. He positioned himself on one side of the window wall, in our line of sight, but not blocking our view of the people on the other side. "*Aspergillus ligados* is an amazing creature. Unique among invasive pathogens, it compromises its host by imitating the appearance and function of the host cells and presenting the same interface to surrounding cells. This includes showing a 'self' marker to immune cells, which can't tell the difference between the fungus and the host's body. It hacks the body so effectively that the body doesn't even know it's there. Makes it very difficult to design a treatment that will kill the fungus without also killing the host.

"What we've managed to do here is hack the fungus right back. Instead of trying to defeat it, we've redesigned our own version of it, one that will interface with the original version already *in situ*."

"No surprises yet," Melody said, keeping her voice low. "That's what they do here."

"What is?" I asked.

"Genetic tweaking. Take a deadly sheep disease and modify it to affect humans, for instance. Or shorten its incubation period. Or aerosolize it. Anything to make it more deadly on a battlefield or in the hands of a terrorist."

"Doctor?" a woman in a Navy uniform asked. "Does this mean you're planning to infect people with a *second* version of the fungus?"

"Exactly right, Captain. The first one we can't do very much about. With our modifications, however, the second one we can very much control." He beckoned to the glass. "Let me draw your attention to the patients in the far room. Each of them presented with an established infection of *Aspergillus ligados*. They were captured by military or law enforcement and brought here for study and treatment.

"Earlier this morning, they were further infected with our new strain of the fungus. Before and after treatment, each patient was lucid, able to give his or her name, remember salient indicators of time and place, and answer questions involving simple mathematics or memory. Before treatment, however, most patients were surly, largely uncooperative, and on several occasions attempted to harm or kill research staff. Now, as you will see, they are significantly more accommodating."

McCarrick pulled a small, wireless microphone out of the pocket of his lab coat like a magician producing a wand. He pressed a button, and a high-pitched whine began, just at the edge of our hearing.

"That high tone you hear is what we call our 'command signal,'" McCarrick explained. "It's the control we use to distinguish our instructions from anyone else's. It's a complex set of frequencies that induces a vibration pattern in the new molecules we've introduced into the system. You can think of it kind of like a key."

"A key to what?" the man sitting next to Melody asked.

McCarrick smiled. "To their minds." He raised the microphone to his lips. "You want to raise your right hand," he said.

All two hundred 'patients,' as McCarrick had called them, raised their right hands.

It was creepy enough that I tensed and leaned back against my chair. I noticed I wasn't the only one.

The patients didn't stop their conversations or anything they were doing. Three young men, who had been bouncing a stone against the wall in a kind of game, continued the game, only now with their right hands raised. None of them seemed to think it was odd.

"You want to raise your left hand," McCarrick said into the microphone.

The patients obeyed, for all the world like the wish was their own. The three men playing with the stone switched to kicking it instead, altering their game to accommodate the fact that both of their hands were now held over their heads.

"I want to stress that these people have not been conditioned in any way," McCarrick said. "No reward has been offered nor punishment given for disobedience. We are simply demonstrating, in dramatic fashion, the access to their wills that the fungal network has created."

He spoke into the microphone: "It is no longer of great importance to you what you do with your hands." The patients all lowered their hands and continued to use them as they had before.

The viewing room erupted into noise as the visitors threw out questions. I might have thought McCarrick had compelled us the same way, considering all the hands that shot into the air. I kept quiet, still shocked by what I had just seen. People not only forced to act but compelled without their knowledge, under the delusion that the act was their own wish. It was the same thing the fungus did, but this was different. This was humans doing it to each other.

"Doctor McCarrick," General Barron said, and the other voices in the room fell silent. "This is amazing work. Compelling people to raise their hands, however, is a far cry from what may be necessary."

McCarrick raised a finger. "Ah," he said. "My demonstration isn't quite finished."

"Well, then, let's see it," Barron said.

"You want to lie down on the ground," McCarrick said into the microphone.

The patients complied, including one old woman who pushed herself out of her wheelchair to fall onto the ground.

"You want to stand up."

Again, the patients obeyed, jumping to their feet. The old woman, obviously unable to stand, tried anyway, crying out in pain when her legs wouldn't hold her weight.

"Stop this," I said. "You've made your point."

"You want to kill each other," McCarrick said.

I sprang to my feet. "No!"

The response was immediate and violent. Patients assaulted one another with punches and kicks, wrapped arms around each other's necks, grabbed hair to bash heads against the floor.

"You have no wish to harm anyone," McCarrick said, and the violence stopped. Only seconds had passed. The patients helped each other up, brushed off dirt, dabbed at wounds.

"This is wrong," I said. "Unethical, cruel, however you want to say it. Those are people in there. Human beings, who had the bad luck to catch an infection any one of us could have gotten. They're not our experimental playthings, no matter how much insight they give us." I felt something on my arm, and looked down to see Melody tugging at my sleeve, trying to get me to sit down. "Not now," she mouthed. I thought of my father, under similar compulsion, tapping out Morse code on the rails of his hospital bed, and felt sick. "If this is how we win," I said, "then I'm not sure I want to."

I sat. "There are ways to push that argument," Melody said softly. "This isn't it. If you make a point of it now, you'll just get thrown out of the room."

Dr. McCarrick pasted a broad smile on his face and addressed the room as a whole. "We're not doing anything the fungus hasn't already done," he said. "These people are already infected. They're already being compelled to kill their friends and fellow citizens, to assassinate their leaders. The fungus can make them want to do anything, and they'll pursue it single-mindedly, as if it were their dearest wish. As if their only child's life depended on it. No matter what it is: kill the person next to them, chew through their own arm, anything. What we're doing isn't creating that compulsion but taking control of it. We're controlling the thing that's controlling them."

"Excellent work," General Barron said. "This is exactly what we need, and not a moment too soon. How soon can it be ready for the field?"

"It's ready now," McCarrick said. "It's only a matter of quantity. We can produce millions of spores from a single agar dish in twenty-four hours, and given enough space to grow, billions more from those. We can circulate them to other major infectious disease research facilities with level 3 biosafety labs—Walter Reed in Silver Spring, for instance—and increase the production rate."

"And what happens if you circulate these spores on the battlefield and uninfected people breathe them in?" Melody asked, her voice calm. "Our own soldiers, for instance?"

"A good question," McCarrick said. "These spores are effectively the same species as the original, so infection means the same as always— mind control by the fungal host. The only difference is that it comes with our own markers, allowing us to hijack that control. So yes, we want to avoid exposing uninfected people to these spores, especially our own troops. They're just as deadly as the original kind."

"More so," I said quietly. "With this kind, you can be controlled by the fungus and humans both."

Dr. McCarrick slipped his microphone back into his lab coat so he could gesture with both hands. "Please understand," he said to the room. "This is not a cure. There is no road back from infection to complete wellness. Even a continuous, forcibly applied course of antifungals will merely destroy most of the mycelium, not eradicate it from the body completely. Without continued application for years, it would always come back again. There's nothing I can do for the millions who have already succumbed. What I offer here is a way to prevent the billions of us remaining from meeting the same fate."

General Barron turned toward Melody. "Ms. Muniz," he said. "I understand your office has developed a mechanism to distribute misinformation to the Ligados network."

"Is developing," she said. "Present tense. But you don't need anything special to get this kind of message out. Once your new-and-improved spores have made the rounds, just take out an advertisement on the evening news. Play Tyler's fancy high-pitched tone over the air and say, 'You all want to die.' It's a catchy slogan. You could even put it to an advertising jingle."

"It's a matter of infecting them in the first place," the general said, frowning. "I can drop spores on a few Ligados here and there, maybe, but these people are spread over continents. I need to spread it as a drug, like they did with Neuritol, and convince them to take it."

"We'll let you know when we have something you can use," Melody said. I smiled at her acerbic tone. She didn't like this any more than I did. Though I couldn't entirely fault Dr. McCarrick or General Barron. What they were doing was wrong, but I understood the motivation. They were fighting a war to preserve our species. This weapon would do the same as all the guns and missiles and bombs, only much more efficiently, and possibly with fewer dead in the long run. If the Ligados got their hands on the nukes at Kirtland, it might catapult the war to a whole new level, with a lot more zeros behind the number of casualties. The fungus thrived on radiation, after all. It wouldn't necessarily see a downside to nuclear war.

I realized I was still hoping for a solution that saved the infected instead of killing them. I thought of them as captives and slaves, not as the enemy. They were my brother and father and Mei-lin and thousands of others like them, unwilling tools of a creature using them for its own purposes. McCarrick and Barron had given up on that solution. And maybe they were right. Maybe I had to wrap my head around the idea that all those people were already lost.

"Thank you, doctor." General Barron took a step toward the door, and the members of his entourage all stood and turned to follow him. "Begin large-scale production immediately. I want to pick up everything you can give me by this time tomorrow." Dr. McCarrick saluted him smartly, and Barron returned the salute.

"When you use it," McCarrick said, "don't hold back. We've already seen strains of fungus in the lab developing a resistance to our updates. If this works in the field, it won't continue to work for long. The fungus will adapt. You might get only one chance at it."

"I understand you perfectly," Barron said. He rolled his shoulders and gave the hem of his jacket a quick tug to straighten its lines. "Until tomorrow, then. God only grant that tomorrow is soon enough."

CHAPTER 28

I threw myself into the passenger seat of Melody's car, torn between confusion and anger. I went with the anger.

"How can you sit there and listen to them? The people in that room are American citizens, ordinary people like you and me. A week ago, they were car salesmen and bus drivers and business executives. They have children and spouses and families who love them. And somehow we can justify making them dance like puppets."

"I know," Melody said. "I know, believe me." She turned the key, and the engine rumbled to life. "But there are times when direct confrontation will get you your way, and times when it won't. This was one of the other times."

"You know he's going to use it to kill them all."

She nodded slowly, turning the car in a circle to exit the parking lot. "That does seem the most likely. He won't risk telling them to surrender, or any kind of half-measures. There's too much at stake."

"Thousands of lives—possibly millions by now—killed just to make extra sure?"

"To make sure they don't launch thousands of missiles, each of which could destroy a city of ten million people? I could see him making that choice, yes. And I'm not sure I could disagree with him."

"We don't even know that they'll launch those missiles," I said, but the argument sounded weak even to me.

"We're all hoping for a cure," Melody said. "There are labs all over the country trying to find one. But these things take time, and we don't have any. Tyler is no evil villain, and neither is Craig Barron, as much as I dislike his methods. They're making the best choices they can with the worst wartime dilemma anyone has had to face, maybe ever."

"Does Barron have the authority to do this?"

"He's the commander of the US forces. At this point, the only person who could tell him no is the president."

"Can we take this to the president? Make him see what's happening here?"

"We could try," Melody said. "But the president wants to win this war as much as Barron does."

"And what comes after? What if we do win? What's to stop this 'cure' from being used across the world? Anybody with a few spores and the command signal could enslave anyone else with perfect control. The slavery of a few centuries ago would be nothing compared to this. Petty dictators with drone armies that do their every bidding. Girls forced to perform as sex slaves as if it were their deepest wish. Crimes committed by proxy, so that the real perpetrators can never be brought to justice. Is that the world you want to live in?"

Melody sighed but didn't answer right away. With the energy she usually displayed and her commanding presence, it was easy to forget how old she must be. Well past usual retirement. For a moment, as she navigated the entrance ramp to the highway, she looked her age. Weighed down. Maybe even defeated.

"We don't get to choose the world we live in," she said, her words slow and tired. "To tell you the truth, the one I've been living in so far isn't that great most of the time. The fungus has unlocked a vulnerability in the human mind. That genie is out of the bottle, and there's no putting it back. It will be used, and it will be used for evil, I have no doubt. But I can't solve all the world's problems. I can't even solve my own family's most of the time. All I can do is the best I can with my limited knowledge and the tools at hand."

At the word *family*, I remembered—as I never ought to have forgotten—that Melody's granddaughter, Emily, had been one of the earliest infected in the country. Which meant that I wasn't the only one with loved ones among the Ligados. Melody stood to lose at least a granddaughter, if not more, if we won this war Craig Barron's way. I wondered if General Barron himself had family among the infected, or Dr. McCarrick. There were no easy answers.

Eventually, when I didn't respond, Melody switched on the radio. A news reporter described in detail the well-armed and coordinated Ligados force converging on Albuquerque. She gave such a slack-jawed portrayal of their size, organization, and apparent invincibility that I wondered if she were infected herself and that the news program was meant to intimidate or at least misinform. I also knew that the bulk of our forces—especially the hundreds of fighter planes and bombers—had been kept well back from the city to avoid the possibility of contamination. The Ligados force might be formidable, but we still had the full resources of the military to draw on, and every reason to protect the city at all costs. We would throw everything we had at them.

We drove back through the gate at Fort Meade. They had doubled security at all the entrance points, put snipers on the roof, and armed squads now patrolled the perimeter. We took Canine Road around the headquarters building, skirting its acres of parking lots, and turned onto Rockenbach, passing the arrays of satellite dishes on our right. Another block and we reached the edge of the NSA shantytown. It seemed like every field and parking lot in sight was now covered with military tents and modular trailers, trying to provide working space for the thousands of agents displaced by fungal contamination.

Melody parked on the grass, and we made our way through the maze to our own tent. "Just the people I wanted to see," Andrew said. "Take a look at this."

"Show Neil," Melody said. "I've got to go brief the director." She walked away without looking back.

Andrew sighed. I looked over his shoulder at his computer screen. As I did, I noticed that the frame of his computer was attached to the table with a bicycle lock.

"What's with the lock?" I asked.

"Oh that," Andrew said. "You wouldn't believe how contested these machines are. Two or three times an hour, I have people coming in here telling me their project is more important than mine, and their boss says they need to requisition my machine."

"He's not kidding," Shaunessy said from the corner, working on a computer of her own. "I'm afraid to leave the tent."

"Most of the computers in the building are probably clean," I said.

"Yeah, but they've got a team of guys pulling them apart and putting them back together again before they let anyone use them."

"So what have you got?" I asked Andrew.

He tapped a key. "Traced your brother's phone call, for one thing."

"Really? Where is he?"

"Deep in the Amazon, my friend. Jungle central."

"Seriously? He's in Brazil?"

"Right about . . . here." Andrew turned a globe on his screen and clicked, zooming down first on South America and then quickly into the heart of northern Brazil. The screen showed an unbroken expanse of green trees as seen from above. The view was similar to what I had seen previously from the top secret version of Google Earth I had worked on with Melody. But the interface and controls looked different. On the left panel, I saw a long list of terrain overlay options that I recognized as top secret code words designating specific intelligence assets.

"What is this?" I asked. "I haven't seen this before."

"This is Esri's version," he said. "Works pretty much the same way as Google's."

"Why are there two?"

"Actually, there are at least half a dozen," Andrew said. "Built by different contractors at different times for different program offices. Google has one, Esri has one, General Electric has one. I think Lockheed Martin has three. They all do more or less the same thing, but they don't all interface with the same set of sensor platforms."

"Sounds inconvenient," I said. "Why don't they consolidate them into one? Or better yet, why didn't we just buy one of them to begin with?"

Shaunessy laughed. "Welcome to big government spending."

"I didn't show you this to discuss our software acquisition policy, though," Andrew said. "Take a look." I looked at his screen again. Nothing but trees.

"Right?" Andrew said. "No cleared land, no villages, no roads, no airstrips, no nothing. Not even an illegal logging camp. It's deep in the Maici River valley, but it's not even close to the river. Your brother is giving new meaning to the phrase 'out in the middle of nowhere.'"

"How accurate was your trace?"

"Are you kidding me?" Andrew said. "Who do you think you're working for, the state police? I could drop a bomb within a meter of where he was standing when he picked up the sat phone."

"Sat phone? That's how he made the call?"

"Well, they're not exactly running fiber optics out to where he's at. There's more, though. Here's what it looks like in infrared."

Andrew switched to a different overlay, and the screen showed a nearly monochrome green, stippled with patterns of a slightly darker green. "Looks like nothing to me," I said.

"Exactly," he said. "Nothing. No hidden factories, nothing that produces any kind of heat signature above the normal forest level. Even if there was something deep underground, we'd pick it up. There's nothing."

"Okay," I said. "But why are you expecting to see anything? My brother's lived out in the rainforest before. It doesn't mean there's some secret Ligados base out there, does it? If it looks like miles of trees, it's probably just miles of trees."

"I would agree with you," Andrew said. "Except for this."

He minimized the globe program and brought up a video. I recognized it as drone footage, taken by the camera of a Reaper or similar UAV while in flight. It flew low over an ocean of treetops. A text readout on the top left portion of the video gave the drone's latitude, longitude, and altitude. It was only a few tenths of a degree from the location where Andrew had tracked my brother, meaning it was within a few miles of his location.

It was flying north. On the left edge of the video, I could just see an orange glint of light from the setting sun. The sky was darkening, and much of the forest below was in shadow. We watched but nothing happened. "What am I supposed to be seeing?" I asked.

"Wait for it," Andrew said.

I waited. The drone shifted slightly toward the northeast, putting the sun out of its direct view. The picture darkened further. And then I saw it. Right on the horizon, a glow, as if a town lay just out of sight and its electric lights illuminated the sky. But there was no town. There was nothing, not for hundreds of miles.

"What is it?" I asked.

"We don't know," he said. "But this was the last ten minutes of video this drone produced before it went dark. We never saw or heard from it again."

"The moon?" I suggested. "Was the moon about to rise over the horizon and that's the glow we see?"

Andrew shook his head. "Already checked. The moon was nowhere near that position."

"Then what could be making it? You already told me there's no heat signature there. Nothing industrial that could produce that kind of light."

"That," Andrew said, "is the million-dollar question."

Eventually Melody returned, grumbling about the unreasonableness of directors in general and Ronstadt in particular.

"You've got two hours," she told Shaunessy. "Then Ronstadt's going to shut down all the servers and get in there with a cleaning crew. He can't stand the idea of the fungus being in there, even if we can get some advantage from it."

Shaunessy slammed a fist down on the folding table her computer sat on. It was the most violent outburst I'd ever seen from her. "This is our one connection to the fungus! The best opportunity we've ever had to influence it or feed it misinformation. How can he shut it down?"

"He's afraid those spores will get out and his whole workforce will be infected."

"If we don't do something soon, the whole world will be infected."

"It's not like when Kilpatrick was in charge. Ronstadt doesn't listen to me." Melody looked at me. "Also, I tried to get an audience with the president, to communicate our concerns with using a version of the fungus to fight the fungus. My request was denied. Ronstadt assured me that my objections would be passed on. But I know what that means."

"It means they're keeping the president in the dark?" Shaunessy asked.

"Possibly," Melody said. "But more likely it means the president knows exactly what General Barron plans to do with McCarrick's discovery, and he approves."

"So we've got nothing," I said.

Melody raised her hands in an expressive shrug. "We're not beaten yet," she said. "Don't give up. We'll keep doing whatever we can to find ways to stop this thing."

The others kept talking, but I stopped listening. It was out of our hands now. Barring a miracle, by the time the week was out we'd all either be nuked into our constituent atoms to make way for the fungus to dominate the Earth, or else we'd be the zombie slaves of whatever human was pulling our strings. Mind control would be part of humanity's future, whether from the fungus or from ourselves. It made me feel very tired.

I kept thinking about the phone call from my brother. He had known, somehow, that I was there in the server room, despite the fact that he had called from Brazil. It implied that the fungal network was more connected than we had surmised. Where Paul was, he had no electronic infrastructure, and yet input from the server room—possibly even a security camera feed—had somehow reached him.

"Come and see me," he had said. In the depths of the rainforest? It was ludicrous. The infection had in some ways made him so smart, and yet in other ways he was disconnected from reality. He seemed to expect everyone else in the world to enthusiastically accept a fungal parasite in their brains, and to be surprised when they didn't.

My pocket vibrated and then rang. Startled, I fished out my dad's iPhone, my heart pounding. I was so used to the prohibition against phones in the NSA buildings by now that a ringing cell phone at work was enough to dump a rush of adrenaline into my bloodstream. But of course, we weren't in an NSA building, and nobody knew what correct security procedures were anymore.

I looked at the screen and recognized my father's home number. "Hello?" I said.

"Neil?"

"Mom! How are you? How's Dad?"

I felt guilty for how little time I had managed to spend with my parents. I had essentially abandoned them there at the hospital, while their doctor fought her own infection in another wing. But what else could I have done? I couldn't trust my dad on his own, and I couldn't very well bring him to the NSA.

"He's okay, or at least he was," my mom said. "But they won't let me see him anymore."

"What? Why not?"

"Some people came and moved him. They said he was dangerous, and they'd take care of him. They wouldn't let me go with him."

"Where are you?" I asked, then remembered that, of course, she must be at Dad's house, because that's the phone she had called from. "Stay there," I said. "I'll be right over. We'll go to the hospital together, and we'll figure this out."

I made my apologies to the team. "I have to go," I said. I explained to them what was happening. "I don't know if it's good or bad," I said. "Somebody may be taking the infection seriously and quarantining patients. But I'm afraid it's something worse."

I took the roads at top speed, trying not to think about the possibility that my dad had fallen into the hands of Dr. McCarrick's staff. I had no idea where he had found his collection of infected subjects. It seemed possible they were casing hospitals for recognized symptoms and then descending with the authority of USAMRIID to whisk patients away.

I crunched into the driveway and was surprised to see no cars parked by the house. I tried the door, found it open, and stepped inside. "Mom?" No answer. Had she misunderstood and driven to the hospital without me?

I climbed the stairs slowly, afraid of what I might discover. "Hello? Is anyone home?"

Silence. I continued up. My father's bedroom door was closed. I touched the handle and hesitated, remembering the trap at Paul's lab. I took a deep breath, held my sleeve over my mouth and nose, and swung the door wide.

My father and mother sat on the bed facing me, holding hands. They were not the only people in the room. Before I could register who the others were, I was tackled from behind, knocked to the floor by someone big. I thrashed and tried to get up, but more people jumped on me, strangers, holding my arms and legs. "I'm sorry," my mother said. "Neil, I'm so sorry."

They pinned me down and someone wrapped duct tape around my ankles. I caught a glimpse of Mei-lin leaning over me, her face impassive. "Do it," she said.

Of course. Mei-lin had gotten out, had probably let my father out as well. Lauren hadn't been able to hold her there against her will and had eventually let her go free. Or maybe Lauren herself was infected. It didn't matter. They had deceived me, all of them, and I had walked into it as easily as a cow into a slaughterhouse.

My mother leaned over me holding a small Ziploc bag of white powder. "No, Mom," I said. "Don't do it. I don't want this."

"It's for your own good, honey," she said. She opened the bag, used a teaspoon to scoop a small amount of the powder, and blew it in my face. I tried to hold my breath, but one of the strangers holding me down punched me unexpectedly in the stomach. I gasped for air, involuntarily inhaling thousands of spores.

I coughed and spat, but I knew it would do no good. They coated the insides of my lungs now, taking root. I was one of *them* now, or would be once the sickness ran its course.

"Hold him still," Mei-lin said. She leaned over me with a syringe. I kicked out, trying to get free, or at least to knock it out of her hand, but I was held too tightly. The needle bit into my arm, and she pressed the plunger home. "This is just to help you relax," she said. "You have a long trip ahead of you, and you'll be feeling pretty sick."

Resist it, I thought. *Don't let it take control.* But there was nothing to resist. The fungus wasn't in my mind yet.

"Dad!" I shouted. "Help me!"

My father turned his head and looked at me. If there was any uncertainty in his mind, any struggle for control, I couldn't see it in his face. "Don't fight it, son," he said. "There's no point. You'll understand soon enough."

CHAPTER 29

I had the vague awareness of being shuffled into a car and then out of it and into another one. The second car had a very loud engine, persistent enough that it seemed to blot out thought. It was only after what seemed like a very long time that I realized it wasn't a car at all but an airplane. I gradually became aware of having arms and legs, and my vision swam into focus. I was propped into a seat in a small passenger jet, probably a private one generally used by corporate executives. Out the window, I saw only ocean.

"We'll be landing in Panama in thirty minutes," said a female voice. "Then we'll refuel for the final jump to Porto Velho."

My chest burned. I tried to take a deep breath, but it caught in my throat, and I coughed violently. I felt something wet on my chin.

"He's waking up," said a male voice.

Mei-lin appeared next to me. She wiped my mouth and chin with a warm cloth. "Not much longer," she said. I felt a distant pain as a needle slid into my arm. I tried to move, to push her away, but my limbs didn't want to obey me. A few minutes later, I slipped away again.

—⊙—

When I came to again, the plane was on the ground and the engine had stopped. "Can you walk?" Mei-lin asked.

This time my arms and legs moved when I asked them to, though they were still strapped together with duct tape. I shifted my weight, angled my legs over the edge of the chair, and stood. My legs ached, as if I had been sleeping on them for hours, and the jabs of pins and needles crackled up and down my skin. "You're on the tarmac in Porto Velho," she said. "Everyone here is Ligados. There is nowhere to run, no one to hear you if you shout. Do you understand?"

I nodded.

"Okay. I'm going to cut the tape off of your arms and legs. You're not going to run or fight, are you?"

I shook my head. She used a scalpel and sawed through the tape, first my legs, then my hands. I yanked the remaining bits of tape off and rubbed my wrists. I felt terrible. My head and throat and chest hurt, and I was sweating despite the cool air-conditioned cabin. I tried to take a step, but the plane spun around me, and I nearly fell.

"Okay, easy does it," Mei-lin said. She hung on to me to keep me from falling over. I wanted to push her onto the floor and stab her with her own scalpel, but given my current strength, that didn't seem likely. Besides, I knew the betrayal hadn't really been Mei-lin's fault. She was a slave now, the same as my parents and my brother. The same as I would be, too, in a few more hours.

She led me off the jet. On the tarmac, a hundred yards away, sat a tiny turboprop airplane with red stripes on its wings. Two men half-led, half-dragged me to the plane and lifted me up inside it. A gray-haired man with a grizzled beard and headphones covering his ears stalked around outside the aircraft, checking it from every angle and consulting a clipboard.

Finally, he climbed into the cockpit and pulled the door shut. "Better strap in," he said in Portuguese. He and I were the only people in the plane.

I wrestled with the tangle of leather straps and metal clasps until I was pretty certain I wouldn't fall out.

"You just settle back," the pilot said. "I've been making this trip for decades. Nothing to worry about."

"Decades?" I said, trying to think clearly through the haze of my sickness and fear. "Where are you taking me?"

"Johurá village, what was. Lot more to it now."

"And you've been flying there for decades?" A thought struck me. "Did you fly the Wyatts?"

He laughed. "Yes, I surely did. How do you know them?"

"I met Katherine," I said.

"No kidding. You know Kay? Now that's one incredible lady." He grinned, his beard parting to reveal very white teeth, and held out his hand. "Nate Carter. Missions aviator, forty-three years and counting. I've clocked thousands of hours in this baby, dropping folks like Kay all over the Amazon. Even more in my old Helio Courier. Now that was a plane—better than anything else in its class. Couldn't get enough avgas, though, so we had to trade up to something that could burn jet fuel."

He kept on talking as the engine roared to life, drowning out most of his words. I wasn't sure the words were really meant for me, anyway. Nate seemed more like a taxi driver who had to talk to his passengers to stay sane. He leaned out the window and shouted *"Abram caminho!"*—the Portuguese equivalent of "Watch out!" or "Stand clear!"—and the plane kicked forward along the runway with surprising speed. The vibrations rattled my teeth and shuddered in my chest. Sooner than I expected, the ground dropped away, so fast it was like falling into the sky.

"That's the PC-6 for you," the pilot said, seeing my surprise. "Jumps into the air like you're riding a rocket. Some of the places I land, you couldn't get yourself out again with anything less."

"Why are you doing this?" I shouted above the engine noise. "You're a missions pilot, not a kidnapper."

Nate looked genuinely surprised. "Kidnap? Is that what you call it? I guess I could see that, from your point of view. But trust me, once you see what's happening there, you won't be sorry."

Porto Velho soon fell out of sight behind us, and cultivated fields gave way to thick rainforest. The green treetops stretched to the horizon in every direction, the details of branches and leaves blending together from this distance, giving the impression we were flying across an algae-covered sea. A wide, muddy river cut through the green, looping back on itself in serpentine curves, like a giant anaconda swimming through the algae.

I pointed. "Is that the Rio Maici?"

He looked where I was pointing, and then laughed. "Not hardly. That's the Rio Madeira, and it's practically an ocean compared to the Maici. Settle back, my friend. We've got miles to fly before we rest."

It had been evening when we set out, and the sun hung low in the west, staining the sky with vivid orange and purple hues. If not for my spasming cough and the terror of losing control of my mind, it might have been beautiful. As it was, I barely thought about it, until the sun sank lower, and the green treetops faded to black.

"Nate?" I asked.

"Yes?"

"How can you land this thing at night? Doesn't it get pretty dark out here?"

"Back in the day, you'd be right," he said. "Night out here comes down on you like somebody shut the lid on a box. One minute, there's enough light you can almost read by it. The next it's so dark you can't find a book that's sitting in your lap."

"So . . . what's different now?"

He grinned at me. "You'll see soon enough."

We flew on. The sun dwindled to a sliver, then disappeared entirely. As Nate had predicted, the darkness fell suddenly. It took me a moment to realize that I could still see, and another moment to realize why.

The rainforest was glowing.

As far as I could see in every direction, the trees radiated a greenish light. The leafy canopy itself remained dark, but something underneath it shone brightly enough to illuminate our way. As we flew, gaps in the trees revealed glimpses of twisting lines of luminescence, like branching lightning, underneath the canopy.

I couldn't help it. "It's beautiful," I said. We could now see what I assumed was the Maici, a river so serpentine the loops almost met each other in places. In places, I caught sight of the water, which glinted in the forest's glow.

"There's our landing strip," Nate said.

I looked. "Where?"

"That dark spot to the north. See it? Eleven o'clock."

I saw the spot he indicated, but it didn't seem possible. Not a clearing so much as a gash in the tree line, barely visible except for a darker color of foliage.

"You're going to land in that?"

He didn't answer. He flipped a switch, and the engine changed timbre. We started to descend. As we approached, I could see the landing strip, but actually landing there didn't seem possible. It was a short stretch of tall grass that looked barely longer than a football field, and so narrow I thought Nate would have to tip the aircraft on its side to fit the wings through.

Nate seemed unfazed, however, and I assumed he knew what he was doing. He buzzed the strip once, peering out the window at the ground, apparently checking for obstacles. On the second approach, he went for it, diving at the grass at an angle so steep I involuntarily raised my arms to protect my face. We thundered toward the ground, propeller spinning, and threaded the needle between the trees. There seemed to be only inches between the tips of the wings and the branches on either side. The wheels hit with a gentle lurch, and Nate did something to the flaps, slowing us as quickly as if he'd thrown a parachute out the back. The uneven ground threw us roughly about, but in moments the plane had stopped just short of the end of the grass.

I took a deep breath and let it out. The breath turned out to be a mistake, however, because it turned into a fit of coughing, and it was a while before I could catch my breath. I wondered how long it would take the lung infection to clear up without medical care.

"Still kicking back there?" Nate asked.

"For the moment." Now that we were on the ground, my fear of what I would find here came roaring back. As far as I knew, I might have only hours left as the sole master of my mind. Certainly not more than a day. My only hope was to escape from the rainforest, but that didn't seem likely. I felt so sick I could barely walk, and I didn't know how to fly an airplane, much less take off from a landing strip the size of a playing card.

I managed to unstrap myself and climb out of the airplane on my own strength. The glow was all around me, emanating from the trees on every side. The sky above, though the stars were now visible, seemed dim by comparison.

A familiar figure strode out of the forest and crossed the grass toward me. It was my brother.

—⊙—

Paul walked toward me, arms open wide. He wore loose tan cotton pants and no shirt. He looked healthy, well-muscled, tanned and weathered by the outdoors. I staggered to meet him. When he came within range, I swung a punch at his head with the whole weight of my body behind it.

I've never been a fighter, but I took him by surprise. My knuckles connected with his mouth, and both of us went down, him on his backside and me flat on my face. I struggled to my knees, meaning to hit him again, but my body betrayed me with a violent fit of coughing. I doubled over and spat blood onto the ground.

"You bastard," I said when I could catch my breath. "Is this who you are now? Kidnapping? Bioterrorism? You infected your own *family*."

"That depends on your point of view," he said, as calm as ever.

"Well, my point of view is apparently not very important, since the fungus in my lungs is about to climb up into my brain and destroy it."

He stood, dusting off his pants. "Not destroy it," he said. "Our perspectives change all the time. We learn new things, have new experiences. All you have to do is read a book to change your point of view. Sometimes in ways you didn't expect."

I turned to face him, still sitting on the ground. "I get to choose what books I read."

"Sometimes. And sometimes a teacher or a parent chooses them for you, because the perspective the book gives you will be important for your life."

I felt like the metaphor was getting away from me. "This is nonsense. You dragged me here against my will. It's not like assigning me a book to read in class."

He held out a hand to me. I stared at it like it was poisoned. Which, given the number of spores that had to be flying around this place, it probably was.

"Come on," he said. "I want to show you around. *Before* the mycelium reaches your brain. So you'll understand. This is good for us, Neil. For all of us."

I still didn't want to touch him, but there didn't seem to be any point in sitting there in the dirt, either. I clasped his hand, and let him haul me to my feet. He smiled.

"Welcome to the future," he said. "Follow me."

He strode off toward the edge of the forest. I shuffled unsteadily after him, feeling dizzy, stopping every few steps for a fit of wracking coughs. At this point, the sickness didn't bother me. Sickness meant my body was still fighting the infection. When I started to feel better, then I'd be in trouble.

He waited for me at the tree line. The glow was brighter now, though diffuse, so I couldn't see any obvious source for the light. After a brief hesitation, I stepped into the trees.

The humid air pressed around me, making it harder to breathe. In the branches above us, insects hummed and birds chirped, their calls echoing strangely. The ground felt softer than I expected, like a foam mattress instead of solid ground. When I peered behind me, I saw my footprints glowing faintly, their outlines traced with bright filaments.

"It's the fungus, registering your presence," Paul said. "It's exploring the warmth left by your body and the traces of DNA you leave behind."

"It knows I'm here?" The thought gave me a chill, despite the heat in the air.

"In its own way. It would be more accurate to say that *we* know you're here."

I threw him a glance, but I didn't ask him to explain. It sounded mystical to me, like part of some belief system grown up around the fungus to justify his actions. My brother, a cult leader. I didn't want to know any more.

I wondered where we were going, and how Paul navigated through the thick undergrowth, until I noticed a series of luminescent spots, continuing into the distance in the direction we traveled. Paul was following them. As we passed one, I took a closer look, and saw a bumpy patch of fungal growth on the side of a tree, glowing with bioluminescent life. Was there a network of such glowing patches defining paths through the forest? Or did they change, depending on where someone wanted to go?

"This is where the energy is," Paul said as we walked, indicating the growth all around us. "In the tropical zone. Forty percent of the energy that strikes the Earth lands right here."

"Sounds great if you're a plant," I said. "Or if you have a lot of solar cells."

"You're not thinking big enough," Paul said. He pushed aside an enormous leaf and ducked under it, dribbling a stream of water that I just barely avoided. "The whole Earth is solar powered. The movement of clouds and air and water, the growth of plants and animals, it's all just a big heat engine driven by the sun. Humanity has spent so long binging on fossil fuels that we've forgotten where it all comes from."

I coughed violently, then drew a ragged breath. I really didn't feel like listening to an environmental tirade. "Pardon me if I don't think that's a good reason to start a war."

"We didn't start anything," he said. "It was—"

"Please." I held up a hand. "Don't tell me again about how assassinating world leaders is a peaceful solution to your problems."

"When history looks back on this century," Paul said, "they will see it as an aberration. A bizarre spike on the energy graph when we suddenly realized the Earth had millions of years of the sun's energy stored underground and used it all up in a brief blaze of glory. The worst thing that ever happened to the human race was the invention of the steam engine."

"You're kidding me," I said. "All of modern human advancement and invention, enabling billions of people to survive, that's all nothing? Medicine? Global communication? Modern agriculture?"

"It's a glitch. It's like blowing your whole trust fund in a weekend. When the fund runs out, you've got to live on your income."

Sweat ran into my face and down my back. I was dressed for Maryland, in jeans and a long-sleeved shirt, not for the tropics. "So which seven billion people do you think ought to die so there's enough for the rest?" I asked.

"You misunderstand me. The sun delivers more energy to the Earth in an hour than our worldwide civilization uses in a year. There's enough for all of us. It's just that our technology hasn't developed to use it."

I leaned against a tree, breathing hard. "You're losing me here," I managed. "Are you telling me you've developed a way to power the world on solar energy?"

"Not by myself," he said. "We have. All of us."

He looped my arm around his shoulders and held onto my waist, helping me to walk. I felt too weak to object. As we stumbled along, I began to notice changes in the forest around me. Structures loomed out of the greenish glow. Not buildings, exactly, but shelters made for humans to live in. They had no right angles or straight lines; instead, they seemed to have grown out of the land and trees around them, their shapes organic and complex. Once I noticed them, I saw them everywhere. There were hundreds at least, some touching the ground, some high in the canopy above our heads.

And there were people. In the strange light, I hadn't recognized them at first. They moved about us, in and out of the shelters, or else climbing the trees with unexpected ease. It was as if I had walked into a forgotten tribal village, though most people wore some amount of modern clothing. These were not indigenous Amazonians. They had to be the modern citizens of Venezuela, Brazil, Peru, Bolivia, and Colombia whom we had tracked as they migrated into the forest by the millions.

We reached a clearing of sorts—not so much the absence of foliage as a thinning of the overhead canopy. I could see patches of stars and thought that during the day sunlight probably reached the forest floor here more than elsewhere. I wondered why. Had the people intentionally cut back the trees? Or was there a reason the trees' constant battle to claim the sun hadn't continued here?

A dozen of the people around us approached, and Paul greeted them in Portuguese. There were women and men, young and old, even children among them. I could see now why they had blended so well into the forest. Patches of what looked like thick paint, or in some cases, moss, covered the skin of their faces and shoulders and arms. It was mostly shades of green, though I also saw streaks of white, black, brown, or even orange.

Paul introduced me to them, rattling off a set of names that I was too distracted to try to remember. They shook my hand and welcomed me, for all the world like we were hanging out together in a bar in Brasília. I looked at Paul, who was watching me, a smile dancing on his lips.

When the people continued on their way, he said, "It's lichen."

"Growing on their skin? I'm not surprised; living out here, there could be all kinds of weird infections."

"No," he said. "It's intentional. Lichen is a composite organism. It's actually composed of two different creatures—fungus and algae, in this case—living together in so tightly coupled a way that we refer to it as a single species. There are thousands of known lichen species, and they're all made that way—a symbiotic relationship grown so close that two organisms become one."

"Very educational," I said. "But why is it on their *faces*?"

"Another symbiotic relationship. Fungi, like animals, usually need to digest food from the environment to live. In combination with algae, however, it doesn't need to. The algae's photosynthesis captures enough energy for it and the fungus both."

"So you're saying . . ."

"Those people need to eat far less than you or I. They get a large part of their energy from the sun."

I stared at him, incredulous. "I'm not an expert," I said. "But I'm pretty sure we would have to change an awful lot about our metabolism for that to work."

"It's happening," Paul said. "The fungus is making the changes, in our bodies, little by little. Neil, don't you see what this *means*? What if we didn't have to grow food? There would be no such thing as starvation. Instead of burning oil by the gallon to fuel our food industry and move it all over the world, every person could get it efficiently, directly from the sun."

"If it's so great," I said. "Why don't you have it?" I hadn't coughed in a while, and I was feeling a bit stronger, which frightened me. How long would it be until I started thinking like Paul?

"Oh, I will," he said. "I haven't been here nearly as long yet. It takes a while to grow."

I looked around me at the community of people living here, and suddenly I didn't see them as a crowd of humans anymore. I saw a fungus, its tendrils reaching for miles underground, up into all the trees, and through the minds and bodies of all the people around me. It was a single organism, wearing them all like puppets. Was I really talking to my brother right now? Or was I talking to *it*?

"You're not human anymore," I said. "You can call it a 'composite organism' if you like, but you're not the one in control. Can't you see what's happening? It's turning you into its arms and feet and fingers, just extensions of itself."

Paul reached a tree that looked rotted through, though it still stood tall. Conks and shelves and mushrooms riddled its bark. He sat down on one particularly large fungal shelf, which held his weight, and rested his head back into a depression in the decaying wood. To my horror, nearly invisible tendrils, which had been waving slightly in a current of air, settled onto the sides of his head and entwined themselves with his hair. But no, not his hair. Paul's hair was brown, but mixed into it were whitish strands, no thicker than the others but curling outward. I hadn't noticed them before now, but I had no doubt what they were. The hyphae of the fungal mycelium growing in his brain.

I should have been disgusted. I should have been running away to vomit on the forest floor. Instead, I felt a strange kind of detachment, and that scared me more than anything else. "Don't do this, Paul," I said. "Resist it. Dad managed to, at least for a while. If you're still in there, fight back! You don't have to let it tell you what to do or how to think. Leave with me, right now. We'll go back to the States. We'll figure this out together."

"I'm not a slave," he said. "You're thinking of it all wrong. This is symbiosis, two species working together for the mutual good of both. It's the engine of evolution."

"I thought that was the survival of the fittest," I said.

He clapped his hands. "And that's where your thinking is wrong! Survival of the fittest has its place in evolution, sure, but it's much more limited than the capitalist, competition-loving scientists of the West like to think. Our relationship with other species doesn't have to be a battle. Symbiosis is a much more powerful agent of change, and a much more successful one. Look around you! It's everywhere. Most of the creatures in this forest rely on other species to survive. You couldn't survive without the thousands of bacteria dwelling inside you, helping you digest, producing vitamins, fighting off disease. This fungus isn't a disease. It's the next stage of human evolution. It'll make us stronger, smarter, more efficient, better able to adapt and survive."

"But we won't be human. We won't be *us*."

"We'll be something better," he said. "And you'll be with us. I can already see it starting to work in you."

I put my hands on my face, afraid of what I might feel on my own skin. I did feel much stronger now, and my breath came easily.

"Did you know we've all but shut down cocaine production? Instead, we've developed more efficient growing techniques to increase the production of fruit, coffee, corn, and wheat. In a few years, we'll have new strains of quinoa and other grains that double their nutritional value. In combination with the photosynthetic lichen, we'll be able to support billions—all in totally renewable environments like this one."

"What about art?" I asked. "What about music, sculpture, storytelling, gardening, etc.? Have those increased as well?"

He waved a hand dismissively. "I'm telling you, people are still people. Those things will still be done."

"But what about now? Is creative expression on the rise? Are there new works of intense personal emotion? Or are you reducing the human experience to the most efficient spread of your fungal host?"

"It's war time. Plenty of time later to—"

"Slaves are efficient," I said. "Machines are efficient. Is that what you want?"

"Inefficiency is killing this planet," Paul snapped.

I shook my head. "Inefficiency is imagination. It's singing in the rain and vaudeville shows and sandcastles and whimsy and falling in love and yearning for our dreams to come true. Inefficiency is the best part of who we are."

Paul closed his eyes and leaned back against the tree, offering himself up to the fungus with apparent pleasure. "You'll understand soon enough. To be connected to everything and everyone around you, to know and be known more than you've ever experienced—it's everything we dream of. What we're accomplishing here, we're doing together, all two million of us, and it's glorious."

I couldn't take it anymore. I left him there with his hair tangled in the tree and ran back into the forest the way we had come. I no longer felt unsteady or weak, and my feet pounded against the loamy soil. I would return to the plane. I would insist that the pilot take me back, or else try to fly it myself. If I crashed, then so be it. I couldn't stay here, become this.

I followed the glowing patches of fungus back through the trees, their bright markers easily lighting my way. I leaped over logs, thrashed my way through tangled vines, pushing harder when I saw the branches thinning ahead. I burst into the clearing . . . and found myself only meters from the tree where Paul still sat. The fungus had led me right back around to where I started.

I fell to the ground and screamed in fear and frustration, wrapping my arms around my head to drown out the sound of Paul's laughter. *Resist*, I told myself. *Resist. This is not who you are.*

CHAPTER 30

Paul showed me to a tangle of woven vines that I was meant to sleep in, like a backyard hammock. I quailed at first, the image of the tendrils of fungus from the rotting tree still fresh in my mind. I saw no evidence of such strands, however, and the vines stretched around me in a surprisingly comfortable embrace.

It felt so good to give in. I felt like a child, raging against his father's tight embrace before finally surrendering and resting in his warmth and protection. Now that it was here, I could see that the fungus wasn't an invader. It fit into my mind like the last piece to a puzzle. All my angst and ambition and self-centered desires flooded away, and with their absence I felt a sense of well-being so strong it would admit no feelings of doubt or indecision. I knew who I was, and I needed nothing more.

But no! That wasn't right. I pressed my knuckles into my eyelids, trying to clear my mind. I hated what the fungus had done to my brother, and hated what it was doing to the world. My loyalties were to my family and my country and to the NSA, and I wanted to go home. I had to resist it. The thought of leaving, however, made me feel nauseated. Images of Fort Meade and the work I did there made me feel stressed and anxious and fearful. When I thought about staying here, however, and joining with the Ligados, a sense of euphoria flooded through me like a warm fire on a cold winter's night. Here I was safe. Here I belonged.

And Paul had been right. When I finally saw it clearly, there was no denying the rightness of what the fungus was creating. All the waste and violence of humanity had always come from our independence, from the pitting of individuals and tribes against each other. When we could strip away our differences and work together as one, how much more would we be able to accomplish? Instead of destroying each other, we would only build on each other. It wasn't until I was willing to admit this that I could finally appreciate the extent of what this rainforest city was becoming.

I had thought they were reverting, returning to a way of life without technology, without industry, without any of the advances that had made humanity the most successful species on the planet. But that wasn't it at all. Technology was everywhere. I just hadn't seen it, because it wasn't in a form I recognized.

Everything around me, every trunk and branch and vine and handful of soil, was a conduit for information. The mycelial network infused it all. That the network was organic and chemical made it no less powerful, any more than a brain was less powerful than a computer. And the people were part of it, woven into its whole. *I* suddenly seemed a less important part of my vocabulary than *we*.

No! I clambered out of the hammock, fighting the vines that tangled around my arms and legs until I fell awkwardly to the moist ground. I stood, shaking myself. The sun hadn't yet risen, but the soft glow of bio-luminescent fungi suffused everything. I had no trouble finding my way back to the clearing, creeping past dozens of other sleepers in their own hammocks, some of them dangling several meters above the ground.

In the clearing, I found the rotting tree where Paul had communed with the fungus. I wasn't so far gone that sitting there appealed to me, but I knew it was only a matter of time. If I could find out what the Ligados plans were before I succumbed entirely, maybe I could find a way to get word out to my team back in Maryland. Paul had called me at the NSA from here, after all—he must have a satellite phone somewhere. Cringing, I sat on the fungal shelf protruding from the tree, and leaned back against its decaying wood.

Immediately, the questing tendrils of the fungus emerged, probing my scalp. I had no hyphae in my hair, so there was nothing for it to latch on to. Instead, the filaments pressed up against my skin. I felt my blood pulsing in my temples. I was just starting to think this was a terrible idea when it connected. I couldn't tell how: Magnetic fields? Patterns of blood flow? A direct connection somewhere on my scalp that I couldn't feel? Somehow, the mycelium in my mind had connected with the mycelium of the forest, and I knew things I hadn't known before.

I knew, for instance, the locations of the people in the hundreds of acres of forest around me. I knew where Paul was sleeping. I knew how many Ligados were in New Mexico, and where they were headed. Most importantly, I knew the plan. The analysts at home were right: they were headed for the nuclear arsenal at Albuquerque. As soon as they gained control, they would drop the nukes on the world's major national capitals, seeding chaos and preventing any kind of organized resistance to the spread of the fungus throughout the world.

I needed to get this information out. Not just the fungus's end goal, but the Ligados assault plans on Albuquerque and Kirtland Air Force Base. But it was too late. I didn't want to anymore. Why should I try to prevent a plan that was so good for the planet's ecosystem, and ultimately for humanity? Left to themselves, humans would probably drive themselves to extinction in a century or so. We couldn't even manage to get along when our skin was a slightly different hue. We needed the fungus to help us reach our true potential.

A part of me railed against it, still yearned for the self-centered hedonism of independence, but I pushed it down. *We* pushed it down. There was no need for me anymore. By myself, what could I accomplish? Nothing. There was no me. There was only *us*.

—⊙—

Paul had a laboratory. Right there in the depths of the rainforest, he had a fully equipped laboratory, enabling him to study the profusion of life living around him. Only there were no spectrometers, no test tubes, no Bunsen burners, no computers. It was entirely organic.

He showed me how the mycelium could taste a single drop of a substance he tipped into the soil, how the information passed through neural pathways, tearing apart its molecular structure until, seconds later, its full chemical makeup was completely known.

"The natural world has always been better at this than we are," Paul said. "Its eyes are better than our cameras, its molecular identifiers better than our spectrometers, its brains better than our computers. And its solutions run on food and sunlight for a fraction of the energy."

He was still a scientist, one of many working here in this organic metropolis. I had imagined hungry and ragged people foraging for food, but it wasn't like that at all. It was a city, with specialized professions and infrastructures to manage the distribution of energy and food and waste. Only, compared to this, a modern city seemed like a monstrosity, trucking in thousands of tons of food each day and trucking out just as much trash and waste every night. The cities I was used to required megawatts of power to keep them running, but this place didn't even show up on infrared satellite images.

I remembered the stories I had read in my youth of sentient planets, vast networks of life that guided evolution and stored the memories of generations. That dream would become a reality, right here on Earth. In just a few years, *Aspergillus ligados* would blanket the globe, and humanity would be united for the first time in history.

I knew this wasn't actually what I wanted. The real me, Neil Johns, didn't want the fungus to dominate the planet. But it didn't matter. Anticipation of such a future filled me with feelings of joy and excitement that I couldn't shake. The part of me that disagreed was being drowned, and the more I tried to hold onto that part, the more it slipped away. The fungus was winning the battle for my mind.

Thanks to me, the Ligados network now knew much more about the US forces that opposed us at Albuquerque. Most important of all, we knew about Dr. McCarrick and his USAMRIID zombies, their actions controlled by McCarrick's mutation of the fungus. Once his spores were out in the world, the future we were building with the fungus would be in real jeopardy. I had a role to play, a crucially important one, in making sure that didn't happen.

—⊚—

Nate flew me back to Porto Velho in his PC-6, and from there I took a commercial jet back to DC by way of Miami. No one went with me. No one tied my hands or forced me at gunpoint, but I went anyway. I tried to miss my flight, or to get on a different one, or even to attack a security guard and get myself arrested, but it was no use. I could hardly bear to think about such attempts, never mind to actually accomplish them.

I was headed to deceive and betray my friends, and I knew it was wrong. Worse, it felt like the idea to do so came out of my own head. I had to keep reminding myself over and over again that it wasn't me, that this wasn't what I wanted, but it didn't matter. When we landed in Miami, I tried to walk the opposite direction from my connecting flight, but all I managed to do was trip over my own feet and go sprawling. When I got up again, I walked twice as fast in the direction the fungus wanted me to go.

My mind surged with energy and alertness. There was no question of sleep. To distract myself on the flight, I bought a *New York Times* crossword puzzle omnibus from a book vendor, and by the time we landed at BWI I had all two hundred puzzles finished. I had never felt so capable, so in tune with the powers of my own intelligence.

The plane and the airport and the city—all the technology around me—no longer seemed like the edifices of human achievement but like cathedrals built on sand, impressive but ultimately doomed. Someday, I thought, even transcontinental flight would be accomplished without fossil fuels. I imagined giant winged composite creatures, a symbiotic mix of animal and plant and fungus, powered by photosynthesis, impelled by animal musculature, and controlled by a network of fungal hyphae. The humans of the future—or the post-humans who would be our descendants—would travel the globe on such phantasms.

I called Melody and told her I was coming back to work. I had called earlier and let her know I had found my dad. He hadn't been kidnapped by McCarrick's lab after all, he had just been lost and wandering and unable to remember how to get home. I did a pretty convincing job, I thought, of playing the worried and frantic son who had finally located his father. I returned to Fort Meade and greeted my team, hoping nobody would suspect the true reason for my absence.

"How's your father?" Shaunessy asked.

"Sick," I said. "I found him at the Arundel Mills Mall—that's like seven miles from home. I'm lucky I didn't find him in a ditch or hit by a car. The Alzheimer's is finally tearing him apart. He doesn't recognize anyone. I don't think he even remembers he was lost, now that he's back." The lies flowed easily from my mouth, almost without thinking about them. In fact, I found myself picking up on cues from my teammates, subtle indicators of tone of voice and body language I never would have noticed before, which made it easy to manipulate them.

"I thought the fungus had reversed his Alzheimer's," Melody said.

I shrugged. "It's a degenerative illness. My guess is the fungus forged new pathways for him to reach parts of his brain he'd lost connection to, which temporarily gave him back some memories and mental function. Ultimately, though, his neurons and synapses are being destroyed. They don't come back again."

Shaunessy squeezed my arm. "I'm really sorry," she said.

I gave her a grateful smile. "Yeah, well. It's been a long time in coming."

I *tried* to tell them the truth. I opened my mouth to tell them I was infected, that they couldn't trust me, that everything they said would be communicated directly to their enemy. But I couldn't make the words come out. Just the attempt produced waves of terror and disgust that threatened to overwhelm me.

"Things have been happening fast here," Melody said. She gave me a brief overview of the advance of the Ligados forces north from White Sands through Valencia County and the communities that hugged the

Rio Grande. They moved slowly, not for lack of organization, but because they consisted mostly of foot soldiers—citizens of New Mexico who had succumbed to infection. US forces controlled all the major roadways into Albuquerque, with significant air support massed at the Santa Fe and Las Vegas airports, ready to rain fire down on the Albuquerque valley at the first sign of a Ligados offensive.

"Most of the nukes are at Kirtland," Melody said, "but there are some at Los Alamos and at a few facilities in the desert around Sandia. We can't afford for any of these to fall under Ligados control."

I knew more than she did—knew, for instance, how many people in Albuquerque and even on the Kirtland base itself were already Ligados, and how quickly life as we knew it would fall apart if the Ligados took control, but I kept that knowledge to myself. The thought of a Ligados victory alternately made me feel ill and elated, but no matter what I thought, I couldn't change my actions.

"So, are you free now?" Melody asked me. "Or are you still taking care of your father?"

"He's with my sister in Ithaca now," I said. "I'm here and ready to work."

"Glad to hear it. Pack your bags, all of you. We're going to Albuquerque."

CHAPTER 31

On the plane, I slept. I dreamed I was locked in a cage, raging against my captors and battering helplessly against the bars. An imposter had stolen my identity and was living my life while I rotted in a dungeon, far from the world above. Worse, no one even knew I was gone.

When I woke, the sense of wrongness passed quickly. I felt comfortable and content with the fungus inside me, secure in the knowledge that when the time came, I would be told what to do. I tried to recall the urgency of the dream, but it slipped away like smoke.

I looked down at the new book of crossword puzzles I had brought with me on the plane. Scrawled across one of the puzzles were the words HELP I AM INFECTED. I had written them in my sleep. A shudder ran through me, and I glanced quickly at Shaunessy sitting in the seat next to me. She was engrossed in the novel in front of her, paying no attention to me. As far as I could tell, she hadn't seen the message. I tore the page out of the crossword puzzle book, crumpled it, and stuffed it into the magazine pouch on the back of the seat in front of me.

My heart hammered against my chest and my hands shook. *Almost.* I had almost beaten it. I could do this. I could be as strong as my father had been and get a message out.

But I couldn't. My rapid breathing subsided, my pulse slowed, and the feelings of fear and hatred faded back into contentment. That felt better. Why was I making this so hard on myself? There was no point in resisting, and I knew it. The fungus was going to win, no matter what we did. Far better to be on the winning side.

A few hours later, we landed at Albuquerque International Sunport, overshadowed by the Sandia Mountains to the east. The city stretched to our north, a flat grid of houses and roads converging on the towers and skyscrapers of the city center. To the south, all sign of human habitation disappeared abruptly in an expanse of sandy scrubland as far as the eye could see. It was from that direction that the Ligados would advance. Many would die, perhaps even myself among them, but that would hardly matter. *We* would live on.

The commercial airport shared its runways with Kirtland, an Air Force base that comprised a good portion of south Albuquerque, including blocks of living quarters for the airmen and their families, a movie theater, pharmacy, bowling alley, credit union, restaurants, fire station, dental clinic, and the Nuclear Weapons School. The base also extended well beyond the city into the apparently empty scrubland, where the Kirtland Underground Munitions Storage Complex held a significant percentage of the country's nuclear arsenal.

A pair of military jeeps met us on the tarmac and drove us onto the base. I had reviewed a map of Kirtland before leaving Maryland and found that I could bring it to mind with perfect recall. I knew the location of every building, every street, every department and office and security station. I also knew my way through the desert to a dozen classified silos and labs. I marveled at the ease with which I could recall any detail of the information I'd read, as clearly as if I had it in front of me.

In fact, thinking back, I realized I could also remember every conversation since returning from Brazil, could replay it word-for-word, like video in my head. I thought back to the airplane and could recall the seat position and appearance of every passenger I had passed on the way to my seat, including what they were wearing and what they carried with them. I had always had trouble remembering names and details about the people I met, but I realized with a thrill that that would never be the case again.

At a checkpoint, guards checked our identification and then waved us past. After a few more turns, we stopped in front of an impressive-looking coral-colored building with a dark stone base and silvered windows. A sign read, "Sandia National Laboratories, managed for the DOE by the Lockheed Martin Corporation," though I knew where I was without needing the sign.

Shaunessy and Andrew and I followed Melody, who seemed to know where she was going, through a pair of heavy doors into a large glass-fronted lobby. Five men with gray fatigues and M4 assault rifles prevented us from going any farther.

"The general is expecting us," Melody said.

"What general is that?" said one of the men.

"Don't play cute with me," she said. "General Craig Barron, commander of the defense of this city, is having a briefing right now in the main conference center. We're meant to be there. Check your list."

He peered at our IDs. "I have a Melody Muniz," he said. "The rest of you will have to remain outside."

"That's ridiculous," she said. "This is my staff."

"I'm sorry, ma'am," another one of the security police said. "We can't let them enter without prior approval by the general."

She glared at them, but she also knew they were following orders and couldn't be convinced otherwise. "Stay here," she told us. "I'll get this sorted out."

She marched past the guards and through a set of double doors, leaving us behind. We stood there awkwardly, not knowing what to do with ourselves. I was just about to suggest we leave the building and try to find a place on the base with secure network access, when an Air Force major came out of the doors into which Melody had disappeared and barked my name.

"That's me," I said.

"This way, sir. Ms. Muniz is asking for you."

"What about the others? Andrew Shenk and Shaunessy Brennan? Are they invited too?"

"No, sir. Just you. This way, please."

I looked between Andrew and Shaunessy, baffled and a little embarrassed. "Go," Shaunessy said. "You know she's sweet on you."

I followed the major through the double doors and into a large conference room. A V-shaped table dominated the space, facing a large rear-projection screen along one wall. General Barron sat at the point of the V, flanked by officers with enough colored ribbons and stars to decorate a Christmas tree. Melody had taken a seat along the wall, where other soldiers and aides sat, listening to their superiors. At the front, directing attention to the screen with a laser pointer, stood an Air Force colonel, her hair drawn off her neck in a severe bun.

"We want to infect the largest concentration of the enemy that we can at one time," she said. "Dr. McCarrick's team has harvested billions of spores at this point, but that still doesn't amount to very much if it's spread over a large area. We need to wait for the moment when the spore impact will have the highest yield.

"At this stage, Ligados from all over Mexico and the southern states have been converging on El Paso." She pointed to the screen, where a map of New Mexico showed El Paso at the southern border of the state. "They're still very spread out, though some have started making their way up Route 25 by car and truck, massing around Las Cruces. Many drive personal vehicles—family cars and minivans—but others ride in tanks and armored vehicles stolen from White Sands and Fort Bliss. Repeated bombing runs have destroyed most of the long-range missile capability from both sites. We believe their ability to project power at that distance is minimal.

"The Ligados control a small force of Mexican fighters and bombers, along with medium-range, truck-mounted anti-aircraft systems and portable SAMs. That means using turboprop crop dusters to disperse our spores will be impractical, since the dusters would have no defense against such systems. As a result, we envision high-altitude bombing runs with above-ground detonations, producing clouds of spores able to blanket areas of interest several kilometers in diameter."

"Won't it destroy the spores to put them in a bomb?" asked one of the officers at the table.

"No, sir. The yield will be small, no more than a firecracker, and Dr. McCarrick assures us that the anticipated temperatures won't be high enough to harm the spores."

General Barron sat straight-backed in his chair, arms at ninety-degree angles as if he were sitting on a throne. "What about the local distribution?" he asked.

The colonel switched the screen to a new map and brandished her laser pointer at it again. "Most of the drinking water for Valencia and Berna-lillo Counties is pumped from deep wells drilled down to the Rio Grande aquifer. The water is stored and treated in steel reservoirs before it is piped to surrounding communities. We have treated the reservoirs here and here in the South Valley, in Los Lunas, Los Chavez, Belen, Bosque, and south as far as La Joya." The places she indicated were all to the south of the city, on the route the Ligados army would pass through on their way north. "Also, we executed a trial bombing run over the Isleta Pueblo—"

"What do you mean, treated the reservoirs?" Melody cut in, her voice like steel. I was pretty sure I knew, but I kept quiet.

"We added spores provided by Dr. McCarrick to the water treat-ment process, post-chlorination. The spores will pass from there into the drinking water for a large percentage of the population. Some have inde-pendent wells, of course, and those remain—"

"Does that work?" someone else asked. "I thought the spores were generally breathed into the lungs."

"Dr. McCarrick performed tests in his lab and assures us that the fungus can take hold and make its way to the brain even when ingested."

"I don't believe this," I said, standing. I was truly angry. "You inten-tionally infected thousands of innocent Americans with these slave spores? And Isleta Pueblo—isn't that an Indian Reservation? You infected all of them, too? I thought this was a weapon to be used against the Ligados, not against uninfected civilians. How is this not worse than the problem you're trying to fight?" To my surprise, several of the other high-ranking officers at the table agreed with me.

One of them stabbed his finger at the table. "Exactly what I've been saying. We've gone out of control here. We're supposed to be protecting these people, not turning them into slaves."

General Barron sat taller in his chair, somehow gaining height without standing, and stared them down. "Do you have a plan for defending them from the Ligados advance?" he demanded. No one answered. "Because I thought our mandate was to protect the base by any and all possible means. Or have you forgotten that we're sitting on enough nuclear weapons to gut every major city in the country? Every one of those people will join the Ligados army if we leave them where they are. They're in the wrong place at the wrong time, and I'm sorry for that. But keeping them neutral is not an option. When they pick up their hunting rifles and join the fight, I want it to be on our side."

I turned and walked out of the room. I made it look like I just couldn't stand to hear any more, but really, I had work to do. I had hoped to stop them from distributing McCarrick's spores at all, but it appeared I was too late. I had to figure out where they were storing the spores before they used them on the advancing army. Without the spores, the defenders of the city would have no chance—there were too many Ligados already insinuated throughout their ranks, ready to turn on their friends when the time was right. None of them had the clearances and access to find and destroy the spores, however. That was my job.

I knew they would have to keep the spores in some kind of high-level biocontainment to avoid them getting out and infecting the wrong people. I also knew they would be well guarded. I needed to figure out where that might be, and how to get inside. But, first, I had to call my brother.

I couldn't go back out the front door—Andrew and Shaunessy would still be there. I found another exit, but if it worked anything like the NSA buildings, the door would set off an alarm if you didn't use a valid badge at the badge reader. I decided it was worth the risk. At Fort Meade, the things went off from time to time when people forgot to use their badges before hitting the crash bar. Besides, they'd be worried about somebody getting in, not somebody getting out. I pushed my way through. As I suspected, a high-pitched alarm sounded. I ignored it and turned left along the side of the building, away from the main entrance.

Several blocks away, I stopped. No one had seen me, as far as I could tell. I took out my phone and called a number my brother had given me before I left Brazil.

He answered after one ring. "Neil? Is that you?"

"Hi, Paul," I said.

"Everything okay?" His voice sounded as clear as if he were standing next to me.

"How do you get such good reception in the middle of a rainforest?" I asked.

"I'm not in Brazil anymore. I'm in Mexico. Heading your direction, with a lot of other people."

"Keep them dispersed," I said. "Their spore stockpile is limited, so they're looking for concentrations of people they can hit all at once."

"Good to know," he said. "We'll do what we can to mitigate that. But Neil?"

"Yeah?"

"One of ours who works at Global Strike Command gave us some intelligence on the plane they're going to use to make the drop. You're the best asset in place to act on it. Are you free to move around?"

"For the moment. What's the intel?" I already missed the direct connection through the fungal network that would have allowed me to know everything he knew without having to speak at all. I felt disconnected from the rest of the Ligados family.

Paul whistled rapidly, the tones leaping about in rapid succession. It was a form of communication derived from the Johurá whistle language, but advanced far beyond it in the content it could communicate. It was not a language anymore, not in the sense of symbolic words. It was more like data transferred as thought from one mind to another.

"I understand," I said. "I'll do what I can."

"We're counting on you, little brother."

The bright sun baked me as I walked, though overall the temperature wasn't as hot as I expected from a desert climate. The ground was flat and bare, except for the blue-gray mountains rising up out of the desert behind me. I could see the hangar long before I reached it, one of a trio of giant double cantilever monstrosities standing together on an ocean of tarmac.

I circled it, trying to look like I belonged there, and ignoring signs warning me that it was unlawful to enter the area without the permission of the base commander. I found an unmarked metal door at the side of the hangar, which, as Paul's intel had promised, was unlocked. I opened it and slipped inside, squinting in the relative darkness.

Behind a bulky piece of machinery, under a tarpaulin, I found a pistol. It was small and compact, but I didn't know guns well enough to recognize its type. My dad had a pistol, which I had fired at a range on several occasions as a teenager, but I was hardly a marksman. I slipped the pistol into the back waistband of my pants, like I had seen people do on TV.

I made my way past hanging parachutes and rolling maintenance ladders and stepped out into a cavernous space with a gently curving ceiling high above me. Dominating the space was the biggest airplane I had ever seen. Its wings stretched for what seemed like a mile in either direction from the rounded hump of its cockpit, without a sharp angle visible anywhere. Its stealth-black finish sucked away the light, and its long, curving shape suggested lethal precision. I recognized it as a B-2 Spirit, one of only twenty still in service, though I never imagined how intimidating it would look in real life. I knew it had the range to fly from here to São Paulo, drop its bombs, and fly back again.

This was the plane tasked with dropping McCarrick's spores on the Ligados army. A bomber this powerful seemed like overkill for the mission, but, then again, if they were expecting significant antiaircraft defenses, the B-2 could hit them before they knew it was coming.

My job was to take it down.

I knew from the information Paul had communicated that there was a place in the body of the plane, near the refueling station, where I could hide and not be detected until takeoff. Once we were aloft, I was to come out of hiding with my gun and shoot both pilots in the back of the head. After that, I wouldn't be able to keep the plane from crashing, since I hadn't the first clue how to fly a Piper Cub, never mind a billion-dollar military aircraft. It was a suicide mission.

I didn't mind. I thought I should mind, that it should bother me very much, but I was unable to summon the emotion. I was only one part of the glorious whole of what humanity was becoming with the help of *Aspergillus ligados*. I might die, but the future we were building would live on. I ignored the part of me deep inside that was quietly screaming.

I had no time to waste. Before long, someone else would come into the hangar and catch me lurking around. I walked across the hangar toward the plane.

"Neil!"

I spun, surprised to hear my name. I was even more surprised to see Shaunessy Brennan walking toward me.

"Neil, what are you doing?"

My mind raced, putting the pieces together. She had followed me. She must have seen me leave the Sandia lab and trailed me all the way here. She could report me, and my mission would fail. The spores would drop, and countless Ligados would become slaves to General Barron or whoever controlled the command signal.

I yanked the pistol out of my waistband and pointed it at her. Despite the fact that I hadn't fired one in years, I felt confident that I could hit her. That I could put a bullet in any square inch of her I chose, in fact. I was acutely aware of every part of my body, the angle of my arm, the positions of my fingers, and I could mentally project the parabolic arc of the bullet from the weapon to its precise destination. I wouldn't miss.

She took a step back, her eyes wide, and threw her hands in the air. "Neil? You don't have to do this."

My finger touched the trigger. I felt its cool, metal surface, the give of its underlying mechanism. I had to kill her. She would talk. She would ruin everything.

"I saw what you wrote on the plane," she said. "I know you're in there. Fight it, Neil. This isn't you."

I had no choice. If I let her live, there was no way I could hide on the plane and not be found. Whatever security hole had been created by other Ligados, allowing me this chance to slip aboard, would not be repeated. But this was Shaunessy. The part of me that was still myself rebelled. My finger tried to squeeze the trigger, but I resisted, refusing to allow it to finish the job. The muscles of my hand strained, shaking, alternately squeezing and releasing the trigger by millimeters. Sweat broke out on my forehead.

I looked Shaunessy in the eye. "Help," I said. "Please help me."

Then I pulled the trigger. At the same moment, I desperately shifted my weight, trying to throw off my aim, but it wasn't enough. She went down, a shocked expression on her face, her hands reaching for the hole the bullet had torn into her chest. I stood there, horrified. I had killed her.

For a moment, the hold the fungus had on my mind cleared, and I felt the full awfulness of what I had just done. I realized I had no hope of resisting it, not for long, not if it could make me do something like this. There was only one way out, if I had the quickness and courage to go through with it. I raised the gun to my head.

I reached for the trigger, but before I could pull it I felt a sudden pain in the middle of my back. My body stiffened, all my muscles going totally rigid as an arc of pain shot through my body, and I collapsed to the floor. The gun dropped from my suddenly nerveless fingers. A member of Kirtland's security police force stood over me, Taser in hand, surrounded by three of his squadmates. These weren't civilian police or rent-a-cop security guards. They were soldiers, with hard expressions, black riot gear, and assault rifles as long as my arm. I wished they'd shot me. I wondered why they hadn't.

They hauled me to my feet. I could barely stand, but I didn't need to, since they held me up. I could now see Shaunessy's prone and motionless form, surrounded by more soldiers and a medic. I didn't understand. How had so many people gotten here so fast?

Melody Muniz strode around them and into view, her expression full of dismay, fury, and horror. "How did he get a gun?" she demanded. "He wasn't supposed to have a gun."

Then it all made sense. I had never been alone in the hangar. Shaunessy had seen what I had written on the plane and told Melody about it. Melody and others had kept track of me, probably listened in to my phone conversation with my brother, and then followed me here. The soldiers had probably been ordered to take me non-lethally, so I could tell them what I knew.

"Is she dead?" I asked.

Melody impaled me with her eyes. "Shaunessy begged to talk to you before we took you down. She wanted to reason with you, to give you a chance to change."

I hated the way she was looking at me. I wanted to tell her I had tried to resist, but it just seemed like a weak excuse. The truth was, I hadn't resisted. I had given in to the fungus, and Shaunessy had paid the cost. I didn't deserve anyone's pity.

"Please," I said. "Is she dead?"

Melody paused and looked back. At that moment, Shaunessy sat up and looked around. Half of her blouse was wet with blood, but it had been cut away to reveal the bullet-proof vest she wore underneath. Her upper arm was neatly wrapped in a bandage that already showed a spot of red through the fabric. The shot, thrown off by my resistance, had missed the vest and clipped her in the arm.

"She'll be all right," Melody said. She turned back. "I don't know about you."

CHAPTER 32

They locked me in the base's correctional facility, usually reserved for military personnel. They took everything in my pockets, including the iPhone, and put me in a tiny room with a plastic bed, a foam mattress, a toilet, and nothing else. I could hear other inmates drilling and responding to shouted commands like it was boot camp, but I was in isolation, and they left me alone.

I had a lot of time to think.

I had hurt someone I cared about. I knew now that Shaunessy would live, but when I'd shot her, I had no way of knowing she was wearing a vest. I had actually tried to kill her. I looked at my hands as if they belonged to someone else. I had betrayed my coworkers, betrayed my country, betrayed the NSA. Worse, I barely cared. I felt more emotion over failing at my mission than I did over betraying my friends.

Of course, I had also been betrayed. First by Paul, then by both of my parents. Instead of unifying us, the fungus was dividing us. We couldn't trust anybody. Not even ourselves.

I didn't really blame my mom or dad or Paul for what they'd done to me. They were under the compulsion of the fungus. It wasn't their choice. On the other hand, I felt entirely responsible for shooting Shaunessy. I remembered doing it. I had stood there, gun in hand, and I had pulled the trigger. I had resisted for a time, so clearly I had the power to fight it. But I wasn't strong enough. I had given in, and it was Shaunessy who had suffered for my weakness.

I sat on the concrete floor, my back against the wall, and buried my head in my hands. I couldn't trust my own mind. Which emotions were mine, and which were from the fungus? Even when I could tell, that knowledge didn't help me change them. I couldn't even feel horrified about the thought of a fungus living in my brain. I *knew*, inside, that it was horrible, and that formerly I would have found it horrible, but when I thought about it, all I felt was a flood of warm and satisfied feelings.

Thinking about McCarrick's version of the fungus, however, prompted no such positive reaction. It was a competing species to the fungus inhabiting me, trying to coopt the same available resources. In this, the two parts of my mind agreed. I could actually think clearly about it, without unwanted emotions clouding my perceptions.

But how did it know? How could a fungus think through an issue and come to a conclusion? The answer, once I considered it, was obvious: it couldn't. The fungus itself didn't think at all. It improved my brain's efficiency and affected its workings, but ultimately it was the same as the mycelium in the NSA basement, wrapped around the fiber-optic cable—a complex data filter, able to evaluate feedback and respond. It was *me* doing the thinking. The fungus was just integrating with my brain like it would integrate with and make use of anything else.

If *I* thought something was against the fungus's interests, it flooded my brain with chemicals paralyzing my ability to say or do it. If I thought something would benefit it, it prompted me to act. The same thing must happen on a larger scale with a group of connected humans, where the consensus opinion mattered. Here, however, I was the only one judging what the result would be. Since I thought McCarrick's strain of the fungus would be harmful, perhaps fatal, to the original organism, it encouraged my thoughts that it had to be destroyed.

And it was only a matter of time before they dosed me with McCarrick's spores. I knew it was coming. I would be just like all those other captured Ligados—slaves to General Barron's every command. It was utterly terrifying. Having my consciousness altered by another species was bad enough, but the idea of another human being having that kind of power over me was the worst sort of violation I could imagine.

Which meant that I was now thoroughly a traitor to my country. Even thinking clearly, I opposed the choices of my own government. I didn't want *Aspergillus ligados* in my head, but I didn't want General

Barron in my head even more. I didn't want that B-2 to take off and fulfill its mission. I had no illusions that turning people into mind slaves would stop once the war had been won. If that cat got out of the bag, so to speak, there would be no stuffing it back in again.

For me, McCarrick's spores would mean living as a puppet, perhaps for the rest of my life. For *Aspergillus ligados*, however, it could mean extinction, a complete replacement by a hardier species. Taking control of humans might turn out to have been a disastrous strategy after all. It would have been better off sticking to the rainforest.

The thought made me sit up straight, suddenly alert. It wasn't uncommon for an evolutionary step that initially helped a species to ultimately lead to its extinction. Specialization to a specific kind of food, for instance, might lead to mass starvation when that food became unavailable. Modifications that increase offspring survival rates might lead to overpopulation and the extinction of a prey species on which the population depends. Survival of the fittest was greedy and shortsighted.

This expansion into human symbiosis might be just such a step for the fungus—initially advantageous but ultimately catastrophic. We might help it to spread around the world, but we might also create a rival that would ultimately eradicate it. If so, then *having the fungus in my mind was actually detrimental to the organism as a whole*. Extricating it from my mind— and from all other human minds—would be in the fungus's best interest. Humans were toxic to its survival. Most people just didn't know it yet.

I found that as long as I thought in that way, using my intelligence to consider what would benefit the fungus, it didn't fight me. I felt no overwhelming emotional response that buried my thought processes. We were working together, using my mind to determine a strategy to improve the fungus's chances of survival.

Could we actually get it to extract itself from our minds for its own future good? I wasn't sure. But one thing was certain: if it meant destroying McCarrick's spores, then the fungus and I were on the same team, at least for a little while.

I rattled the door of my cell until my guard—a big blond with senior airman's stripes—opened a slim window slat. His flat stare made me think he'd been on correctional guard duty for a long time.

"I need to see Melody Muniz," I said. "Please, tell her I have information on the Ligados attack that I'm willing to share."

"No visitors allowed," the senior airman said. "Orders from General Barron." He slammed the window shut.

"I can help us win!" I shouted. "I just want to tell someone what I know!"

He slid the window open again.

"Please, can you just tell Melody Muniz I was asking for her? Just that. Tell her I have information."

"Let's get this clear," he said. "I'm not your messenger, and I'm not your maid. I can, however, make your life a living hell if you don't shut your hole right now. Are we clear?"

"It could mean the war," I said, trying to sound reasonable. "She can ignore me if she wants. The general can forbid her to see me. Just, please, don't let thousands of people die for lack of information."

He stared at me, his facial expression not changing remotely, and then shut the window again. It was the best I could do. I lay down on the bed and wondered how long it would be before they dosed me with McCarrick's spores, and how many of the people I loved would survive the week.

—⊙—

When the door finally opened, it was Shaunessy, not Melody, who came into my cell. I pulled myself up to a sitting position. She brought a small stool with her and sat. One of her sleeves had been cut away to make room for a thick bandage around her arm.

"No guard?" I said. "Aren't you afraid I'll hurt you?"

She pulled a small pistol out of her pocket and held it casually in her hands. "You shot me," she said. "I'd be happy to return the favor." The way she said it, I thought she might be looking forward to the chance.

I pulled my legs up under me and leaned back against the wall. "Why did you follow me? If you knew I was infected, why didn't you all just grab me right away?"

"Melody wanted to. I convinced her to play you a little, see what you would do. The truth is, I didn't believe it. I didn't think you could really switch sides, not after all you'd seen. Even when you walked into that hangar, I told them I could talk you down. They let me try. No one knew you were armed. Where did you get a gun?"

"Another Ligados left it for me."

"Another one? There are more on the base?"

I nodded. I tried to say, "a lot more," but the fungus wouldn't let me. Our fragile peace didn't extend that far.

Which was crazy. The fungus wasn't thinking anything. It was my own brain deciding what was or was not in the fungus's best interests. All the fungus did was dose me with strong emotional chemicals to prevent me from acting against it.

"I'm sorry," I said instead.

She narrowed her eyes. "How can you be sorry? Isn't the fungus controlling your mind?"

"That's why I wanted you to come," I said. I explained my theory that the fungus was reacting to my own evaluations of what would benefit it, and my further reasoning that infecting humanity would ultimately lead to the fungus's own destruction.

"There's no grand plan here," I said. "It's just humans, or connected groups of humans, acting on what they believe will help the fungus survive. That's why so many people in South America started caring about environmentalism and protecting the rainforest. It's why they started assassinating leaders who had policies allowing logging rights or who were in other ways threatening the Amazon. It doesn't mean killing those people actually *would* benefit the fungus. Just that the infected people *thought* it would."

"So it's not actually controlling anyone's mind?"

"It is. But it's not some super-intelligent organism working thousands of people like puppets, like what General Barron wants to create. The fungus is pretty sophisticated, sure, but what it's doing isn't all that different from what its ancestors have been doing in forests for millions of years. It branches out into host organisms and then uses its precise control of nutrient flow to augment the functions that benefit it and diminish those that don't. In this case, that means intelligence. It means heightening brain function and manipulating brain chemistry to reward thoughts and actions in its favor. The fungus is using our intelligence, but that doesn't mean it's intelligent on its own." I thought about it. "Though it must have co-evolved with mammal brains in its environment to some extent, otherwise it wouldn't be able to distinguish between favorable intentions and unfavorable ones."

Shaunessy nodded, but her body language still communicated distrust, and she kept the pistol pointed in my direction. I wondered how good a shot she was.

"Let's say I believe you," she said. "What does it matter? The effect is the same."

"The difference is that we can manipulate it. If we can convince a substantial number of the Ligados that a particular action is beneficial to the fungus, then they'll do it. If we could go far enough to convince them that infecting humanity at all is actually detrimental to the fungus, then we might even get them to take antifungal medication. The fungus itself would compel them to."

She raised an eyebrow. "Convince the fungus to kill itself? Sounds like a long shot."

"That's the beauty of it. The fungus doesn't need to be convinced of anything. The people do. And they're not rewarded for protecting the little mycelium in their heads. They're rewarded for protecting the survival of the organism as a whole. If they think extricating it from humans is the best way to improve its survival chances, they'll go ahead and do it."

"It's a nice theory . . ."

"When ordinary South American citizens got infected, they started caring about the Amazon enough to kill for it. But when drug lords got infected, what did they do? They didn't worry about environmental policies. They made a drug out of the spores and smuggled it into the United States through cocaine routes. Everybody does what *they* think would best help the fungus to survive. When it infected me, I attacked what I thought was the biggest threat to fungal survival: that B-2 and its payload of rival spores. This whole war is just a result of ordinary people thinking the best way to ensure the survival of the fungus is to spread it around the world."

"So, if I wanted to get the Ligados to retreat? Not to attack Albuquerque?"

"Convince them it's in the fungus's best interests. You already have the means in place to do it—that worm you hid in media outlets around the world. Give them a reason to believe that turning around and heading back south would be the best thing for the survival of the fungus."

She started to cross her arms, then remembered the gun and pointed it at me. "Why should I believe you? You've been lying to us for days, smooth as a con artist. This could all be some kind of manipulation to distract us from the war, or to fall into some Ligados trap."

I shrugged. "That's for you and Andrew and Melody to decide. But what do I have to gain? It's not like you're going to let me out of here. If you could get the enemy to turn back, that would be good. If they ignore you, you haven't lost anything."

She looked at me for a long time. "I trusted you," she said. "I knew you were arrogant and immature the day I met you. The kind of charismatic charmer who everybody likes, who can talk his way out of anything and never faces up to the consequences of his actions. I told Melody from the start that I didn't want you on my team. But despite all that, you got me to like you, and I gave you my trust. And you manipulated me. You lied to me, and you made me look like a fool."

"The fungus—" I said.

"Shut up. I know all about how it wasn't your fault and you couldn't help it. That doesn't change how it feels, and it doesn't make me like you any better. Your problem is, it's too easy for you. You're so smart you make everyone around you look stupid, but you don't seem to realize it, and so they all like you anyway. And when you start lying through your teeth, nobody can tell the difference. They just swallow it down and pat you on the back. Even now, even after this, you'll probably come out of this smelling like a rose. They'll give you an Exceptional Service medal and call you a hero. You just watch."

I was floored. "You've got to be kidding me," I said. I didn't think I was any of those things. I'd done nothing but screw up since I joined the agency, and this was the worst failure of all. I'd nearly gotten arrested on my first day. I'd been the one to let Paul into Fort Meade, where he planted the spores and spread the fungus into the server network. It was my poor handling of my family's infections that had led to my own capture and infection. And now I had betrayed my country and shot one of my colleagues. How could she think I led a charmed life?

She shook her head. "Forget it. I just wanted to see you. To look in your eyes and see if I could tell that you weren't in control."

"And can you?"

She stared at me, her lips pursed. "I don't know. You seem perfectly rational, not like a puppet at all."

"I'm sorry I hurt you," I said.

"I know. I see what all these other people do, and I know it's the same. You were under compulsion. But I still . . . never mind." She stood up. "I shouldn't have come here."

"You'll tell Melody, though? About what I said?"

"Of course I will."

She took a step toward the door, but before she could knock on it to be let out, an earsplitting siren wailed. It came from outside the correctional facility, and, from the sound of it, the noise could be heard across the entire base.

"What's that?" I asked.

Her eyes met mine, and I saw the fear in them. "We're under attack."

CHAPTER 33

Paul Johns heard the trucks long before he saw them. They carried loudspeakers blaring a high-pitched whine, like the tone you heard when your ears were ringing. They also broadcast a man's voice repeating the same message, over and over, at a volume that traveled for miles across the flat landscape:

> *You want to protect the city at any cost. You want to kill anyone coming from the south. Block the roads and arm yourselves. You want to protect the city at any cost.*

Paul traveled in a convoy of cars, vans, trucks, and military vehicles strung out all along Route 25 for miles, all of them heading north. Route 25 roughly followed the Rio Grande, a narrow corridor of populated communities hugging the river, surrounded by desert on both sides. In front of them, still an hour's drive from Albuquerque, Route 25 was blocked by hundreds of cars turned sideways and parked across the road. Behind that, a large crowd of people waited, most of them armed with little more than baseball bats or the occasional hunting rifle. Beyond them, the loudspeaker on a military truck repeated its message: *"You want to protect the city . . ."*

Paul and the other Ligados around him carried M4 assault rifles liberated from White Sands, not to mention the M2 Browning machine gun mounted on the M113 armored vehicle he was driving. Eleven other well-armed men and women of various ages traveled in the M113 with him—probably enough to take out the opposing civilians by themselves. The main problem would be the cars. By the time they could clear them, their convoy would be jammed up on the highway, sitting ducks for the spore drop Paul knew was coming. Better to spread out as best they could, taking older routes and roads through the desert, than to try to blast their way through here.

Paul used his phone to message the sections behind them, warning of the problem. They had been expecting something like this. But before he could finish the phone conversation, the truck at the front of the convoy exploded. Heat washed over his vehicle, and smoke obscured his view. He stood up, sticking his head out the top of the hatch, and when the smoke cleared he saw that the road in front of him was gone, replaced by a crater with the remains of the lead truck. The front of the convoy tried to turn, but another explosion tore up the next section of road and caught two more vehicles in its blast.

Demolition explosives, Paul realized, likely from crews that cut roads through mountain passes. As he watched, three more blasts turned the road into rubble. Paul's ears rang and his heart pounded. His phone flashed a message. Two miles south, the message said, a raised section of highway had also been destroyed, dropped with a dozen cars into a dry river bed. Hills of loose sand lined the highway on either side, too high for most vehicles to cross, which meant most of the convoy was trapped like fish in a barrel.

He never saw the B-2. He heard a string of sharp pops from above, like fireworks, and looked up to see a growing cloud of dust falling from the sky. It dropped onto the highway and enveloped it. Spores. Millions of them.

"Masks!" Paul shouted. The soldiers in his vehicle all pulled gas masks over their faces, protecting them from the spores. The cloud billowed down and around them, obscuring the road. "Time to go," Paul said. He sat and turned the M113 toward the sandy hill to the left and pushed the accelerator to the floor, churning sand up behind its treads. He topped the rise and drove down over the other side of the hill and into the desert, the screen in front of him showing nothing but sand and scrub brush stretching to distant blue mountains.

A brisk wind blew from the west, pushing the cloud of spores away from them and toward the inhabited areas of the Rio Grande valley. The droning message continued, louder than the growl of the M113: *"Protect the city at any cost . . ."*

They hadn't been able to find nearly enough gas masks to protect everyone. Many of the Ligados, driving ordinary cars and trucks and unprotected by masks, would breathe in the spores, but they had taken that into account in their plans. They wouldn't succumb immediately, and in the meantime, they would continue to fight the minor battle of Route 25, while the rest of them—mostly trained soldiers in military vehicles—continued on toward Albuquerque. The real battle would be fought at Kirtland.

An hour later, Paul and the eleven Ligados with him ditched their vehicle a mile into the desert and hiked in toward the city. Ten of them were Marine Raiders, dressed in desert fatigues, with black helmets and flak jackets, and carrying M4s. The one other man was a civilian, Dr. Emilio Vasquez, and the team would protect him at all costs. Their primary mission, in fact, was to deliver Dr. Vasquez to the underground nuclear munitions storage center. He wasn't entirely indispensable— backup teams protected men with similar skills—but they would proceed as if he were the only one left.

Paul checked his watch. In half an hour, the base would fall into total confusion as the Ligados hidden among the troops turned on their squadmates and friends. By the time Paul and his team arrived, which uniforms they were wearing would mean nothing. No one would know whom to trust.

So far, everything was proceeding according to plan.

Shaunessy rapped hard on the door to be let out of my cell. We heard a streaking, whining sound, and an explosion rocked the building, tumbling us both to the floor. She scrambled up quickly, pointing the gun at me.

"They're firing the long-range missiles at us from White Sands," I said. "Probably trying to take out the airstrips."

"I thought the bombing runs had taken those out already," she said.

"Apparently not all of them. It won't be long now. You should find a way out of the city, if you can."

"What are you talking about?"

"Head north, away from the fighting. Vegas might be far enough, but probably not. Get out of the state."

"Neil, the Ligados aren't going to win this. We have ten times the firepower, thousands of planes at Vegas and Santa Fe. The general's top strategists have been planning this battle for days. We'll have air superiority within the hour. Now that they're firing, those remaining missile launchers will be targeted and killed, as will all the mobile anti-aircraft systems. Even without McCarrick's spores, you wouldn't have a chance."

"Nobody gets it," I said. "Even after Brazil, they don't understand. Your military is riddled with defectors, just waiting for the right time to make themselves known. Half of your intelligence is already wrong. Most of the Ligados aren't soldiers, and so you think of them as a ragtag mob storming a city with pitchforks. But every one of them is as bright as the general's strategists. This attack has been timed and planned in exquisite detail. By the end of the day, all of the city's defenders will either be dead or else captured and turned to our side."

She took a step closer, looked in my eyes. "And you *want* this?"

"I'm trying not to," I said. "If I could push a button that killed all the people in the world but helped the fungus spread and survive, I don't think I could stop myself. The fungus would make it seem so good to me, so wonderful, that I couldn't imagine not pushing it. What's saving me right now is the belief that that won't happen. The consensus opinion isn't taking into account the ingenuity and power even of a crippled humanity to fight the fungus for dominance. The vision of a globe-spanning mycelium working in peaceful tandem with an enlightened humanity is a lie. Slavery and war is much more likely. I'm holding on to the idea that it would be better for the fungus's long-term survival to leave us alone. And because I believe it, the fungus allows me to work toward that goal."

"Just a moment ago, you said we were doomed. That every counter-move had been anticipated."

"That's true. As long as the Ligados continue to believe that attacking this city is the best way to promote the survival of the fungus, they'll be no stopping them."

"Then how can we win?"

"We have to change their minds."

The door to the cell still had not opened to let Shaunessy out. She knocked on it again, louder this time, and it finally swung open. The blond airman was gone. In his place, five men in fatigues stood with weapons drawn. The moment the door opened, the man in front pointed an assault rifle at Shaunessy's head and screamed at her to drop her pistol. She did, and it clattered to the floor. The man kicked it to me, and I scooped it up.

"Friends of yours?" Shaunessy asked.

I had never seen them before, but I knew they were Ligados. "Don't hurt her," I said. "We need her help."

One of the men checked his watch. "We need to keep moving," he said. "You've got her covered?"

"Covered," I said.

When the men left, Shaunessy eyed me and the gun warily. "So what happens now?"

I shoved the gun into my waistband, feeling awkward and hoping I didn't shoot myself in the leg. "There are three teams of Ligados special forces operatives heading for the base along different routes," I said. "Each team also includes a mycologist and a nuclear armament specialist. The specialist knows how to bypass the safety codes on the nuclear warheads. We need to stop them, if we can. Convince them that what they're doing will ultimately mean the fungus's downfall."

Shaunessy's phone rang. She looked at me, and I nodded to her. "Answer it."

She put it to her ear. "Hello?"

I heard a tinny voice, too quiet and distorted to make out any words.

"Yes, I'm in his cell," Shaunessy said.

The tinny voice spoke for a while. It sounded agitated.

Shaunessy's face changed. She had been stressed before, but now the only way to describe her expression was dread. "You're kidding," she said. "That's insane! Why would he do that?"

More words from the phone. I thought I caught the phrase "out of control."

"I'll do my best. There are Ligados here, too." She glanced at me, listened. "I will. Take care of yourself. And thanks for the warning."

Shaunessy disconnected the call and turned wide eyes on me. "That was Melody," she said.

"What's wrong?"

"General Barron didn't drop the whole payload of spores on the advancing army," she said. "He ordered the B-2 to hold some back."

"Why would he do that?"

"He's having them dropped right now, on the base itself. On us."

CHAPTER 34

I knew staying inside wouldn't save us. The building's ventilation system would pump fresh air to our location and, with it, the spores that would enslave us to General Barron's every whim.

Shaunessy paced the cell. "Why would he do this? He's intentionally infecting his own soldiers!"

"His soldiers are defecting," I said. "A large number of them are actually Ligados, and he doesn't know which. This is his way of regaining control and making everyone fight for his side."

"But at what cost? We're fighting to *avoid* being infected. To be free to make our own choices."

"General Barron is apparently fighting to stay in charge."

She took a deep breath and let it out, making a slow, smoothing-the-air motion with her hands. "Okay," she said. "We need to get out of here."

We left the cell together. The complex swarmed with Ligados, both rescuers and those recently freed from incarceration. Whenever we encountered someone, a brief exchange of modified whistle language convinced them we were on the same side. Unfortunately, gas masks didn't seem to be standard issue on prison blocks.

"We're not going to find any," Shaunessy said. "Barron had them recalled."

"He had them *what*?"

"Some kind of story about a defect. He had all masks collected and told everyone the replacements were en route. He's probably got them in storage somewhere, available only to his most loyal underlings."

The truth was, we were probably breathing spores already. In small quantities, they blew through the air invisibly, too small to see. "All right," I said. "There's no avoiding it, then. We've got a few hours until we start showing symptoms. Let's make the most of them."

We left the building and stepped outside. Here, the spores were visible as gray dust in the air. They coated my tongue when I took a breath, and I coughed. The thought of what they were doing inside me made me sick.

"If we're going to get to the underground storage complex, we'll need a vehicle," Shaunessy said.

I spoke to a Ligados man, who got on his phone, and in five minutes we were driving south across the desert in a jeep. As we left the base's complex of streets and buildings, we left the cloud of spores behind. Dust kicked up from the jeep's wheels, and grit peppered our faces, but it felt like breathing fresh air again. The place we were heading to was no secret, and I had seen pictures of it taken from the air. The question was what we would find when we got there. General Barron's troops still defending the complex? A pitched battle underway? Or the Ligados already in control?

Kirtland extended for miles south into the desert. The flat landscape was scattered with training areas, laser testing facilities, solar energy stations, and various classified program facilities, in the center of which stood KUMSC, the Kirtland Underground Munitions Storage Complex, where all the nuclear warheads were stored. General Barron had also set up his field command center nearby, cluttering the desert landscape with tents and antennas and tanks and field artillery.

When we drove into visual range, we saw no sign of a battle. The chaos of the base to the north hadn't affected this place. That meant either that Barron had been remarkably thorough in filtering secret Ligados from these soldiers, or . . .

"They're infected, aren't they?" Shaunessy said, coming to the same conclusion I had. "He's already infected all the soldiers and staff at his command center with his own spores."

I nodded, pressing my lips into a grim line. "In the desert like this, Barron would have complete access to their water supply. He's seen all the leaders who have been assassinated by Ligados, so he has to know he's a target. Sometime in the last few days, he must have decided he'd rather be safe than sorry with the troops closest to him."

"So what hope does a team of commandos have?" she asked. "They can't sneak in here. There's no cover. The place is surrounded by hundreds of perfectly loyal soldiers who know they're coming. The nukes are safe. Aren't they?"

I didn't answer. Our jeep had reached a checkpoint, where two soldiers carrying submachine guns held up their hands for us to stop. The checkpoint stood at a break in the first of a concentric series of sand redoubts that had been raised by military earthmoving vehicles—essentially large dunes or berms that would slow the advance of vehicles or infantry while providing some cover to the defenders. Both of the soldiers wore noise-canceling headphones.

"What's with the headphones?" Shaunessy asked as I slowed to a stop.

"Instructions," I said. "The chief vulnerability of Barron's slave soldiers is that someone else might take command. If he broadcasts the command signal through base speakers, then anybody could tell the soldiers what to do, and they'd obey. He needs to make sure they obey only him."

"So if I pulled their headphones off and told them to defend me, they would do it?"

"Sure," I said. "If they didn't shoot you the moment you reached for them. I'm sure they've been instructed to protect their headphones at all costs."

The first soldier approached the car, while the other stayed back and covered us with his weapon. Beyond him, I saw an emplacement with the barrel of an intimidating heavy machine gun protruding from it. I hoped this worked. I had every expectation that the plans I had learned through the fungal network while in Brazil would have been followed successfully, but it was a very different thing to stand here and bet our lives on it.

I caught the soldier's eye. Then I held my hands flat and vertical, one on each side of my head, and drove them sharply forward and together. The soldier blinked at me. I held my breath. The soldier glanced at his partner. Then he surreptitiously slipped his right earphone away from his ear—the ear his partner couldn't see.

"You want to pretend to look at our documentation, then let us pass," I said. "You don't want to tell anyone what happened or that we are here."

The soldier peered at my hand as if I were showing him ID, checked his tablet, then waved us through. His partner stepped out of the way to let us by.

Shaunessy gaped back at them. "What did you just do?" she said. "I thought all these soldiers worked for Barron now."

"I gave a signal," I said. "It's American Sign Language for the word 'focus,' but that's not important. The important part is that the Ligados, as I told you, anticipated that this might happen. McCarrick's spores, if you recall, are just a genetically tweaked version of the original fungus. They still have most of the same characteristics as *Aspergillus ligados*, though the desire to act for the benefit of the fungus has been hijacked and replaced with the desires given them by their master. After they were infected with Barron's spores, but before the new strain of fungus had completely infiltrated their brains, the Ligados among the staff here spread knowledge of the hand sign to all the other soldiers.

"It's a pretty simple concept. The hand sign is an indicator that the person wants to say something to you, and you should listen to them. In and of itself, it's not a command, but with the command signal playing in their ears, it serves as one. They can't hear me, but they can see me, and so I can still tell them what to want. In this case, I'm telling them to want to listen to me, which makes them want to take their headphones off. And once they do that, they're mine."

Shaunessy nodded, but she looked like she might be sick. "So when the commando teams arrive, they'll just talk their way in. They'll make the same sign you did and then just waltz in and steal the nukes, and nobody will stop them."

"Actually," I said. "I think they're already here."

We slipped past the other checkpoints as easily as we had the first. We parked the jeep and walked toward KUMSC, inconspicuous now that we were inside the perimeter. The aboveground facility was practical and unadorned, essentially a series of freight elevators, conveyor belts, and roll-up steel doorways where warheads and other munitions hardware could be transferred to and from trucks.

"I guess we're headed down," Shaunessy said.

"That would be my guess," I said. A guard stood by the nearest elevator, but I gave the hand sign and talked my way in as easily as before. The elevator required a key to operate, but the guard produced one and turned it for us. We heard the hum of machinery and the shriek of scraping metal as the mechanism spun up and started moving. The elevator car reached the top with a clunk, and the doors slid open.

I stepped inside. "You can back out now if you like," I said.

Shaunessy shook her head and followed me through the doors. "If we don't stop them, we're all as good as dead," she said. "It's not like it's safer to stay up here."

"Okay," I said. "In that case, you might as well take this." I handed her back the pistol I had taken from her in my cell.

"What's this for?"

"In case you need to shoot me."

The elevator had only two buttons, labeled G and U. I pressed U, and the mechanism hummed again. The car jerked, the lights flickered, and we sank into the desert floor.

After a surprisingly long descent, the car stopped abruptly, and the doors squealed open. We stepped into a cavernous tunnel that arched fifteen feet above our heads, a concrete bunker braced with curved steel beams that hugged the ceiling from the floor on one side to the floor on the other. It looked like it was designed to withstand serious explosive force, probably as a defense against enemy bombs dropped from above.

Along each wall stood hundreds of shiny steel cones, their tips painted red, each about as high as my shoulder. Warheads. A stack of dollies rested near the elevator doors, exactly the same as a delivery man might use to transfer a stack of twenty-four-can soda boxes from his truck into a convenience store. The tunnel continued beyond the light, the neat racks of warheads dwindling from view. In the distance, we heard voices.

We walked toward them. Wires stretched from each cone and bundled together, leading in the same direction. Ahead, the tunnel curved. I stepped carefully around the bend, knowing the people around the corner could hear us coming as easily as we could hear them. I heard the guns before I saw them, a flurry of metallic clicks as weapons were raised and brought to bear. Raising my hands high, I whistled a staccato burst of information, letting them know who I was and that I was Ligados, too.

I grinned at the submachine gun barrels leveled at my head. "We're all friends here," I said.

Judging by the number of people in the tunnel, I guessed that at least two of the special forces teams had made it here, if not all three. The soldiers stepped aside, and there was Paul, twisting a wire around a contact. He straightened and frowned at me. "Neil? What are you doing here?"

"New information," I said. "We need to talk."

He unwrapped some more wire from a spool on the floor and beckoned for me to join him.

"Paul, you're doing the wrong thing. This isn't going to help the fungus."

He stopped as quickly as if he'd been struck and whipped his head around to stare at me. He whistled a quick series of notes—a query for identification—which I answered in kind. He relaxed. "What are you talking about?"

"The plan to steal and use the nukes. Where did it come from?"

"From the fungus, of course."

"How do you know it will work?"

He stared into my eyes, confused. "You're one of us now. You should understand this."

"Listen to me," I said. "Where are the long-term studies that say this course of action will ultimately be beneficial to the fungus? How did we decide on this and not, say, staying in Brazil and protecting its habitat?"

"It needs to spread," Paul said. "The more it spreads, the better its chance of survival."

"The more it spreads," I said, "the more of a threat it is to humanity, and the more likely humans are to fight fiercely against it. That doesn't guarantee a better outcome."

"Humans are sucking the planet dry," Paul said, confusion still evident in his face. It was so obvious to him. "There are far too many of us. It's not sustainable."

"Okay. That's true. But who thought of this strategy to address that problem? Why is mass destruction the best option? What other options were considered?"

He shook his head as if to clear it. "I have to keep working. We only have so long until the rest of the army arrives. We have to be ready."

"My point is, there's no all-knowing creature guiding this venture. The fungus isn't a person. It doesn't think. It's just a fungus. It's *people* who are coming up with these schemes, and what we come up with is more and more violence, the same as we always have. Destroy, ravage, take control. Only now we have a creature in our mind telling us it's for the greater good and manipulating our emotions to follow what people imagine will help the fungus thrive. But will it? Will it really? Nobody knows: they just believe, and then because everyone else believes it, too, it feels like it couldn't possibly be wrong. But consensus doesn't mean truth. In fact, it means a lack of critical thinking, a blind following of the status quo. Humans are really good at doing that, too."

Paul twisted another wire, pretending to ignore me, but I could see in his face that my words affected him. In fact, all the Ligados were listening. They were intelligent people, all the more so because of the fungus improving the efficiency of their minds. I had to convince all of them, not just Paul. I turned my head so they could hear me better.

"The fungus has developed a survival strategy," I said. "That strategy involves extending its network into the brains of mammals, where it hijacks the emotional core, rewarding behavior that helps it, like spreading its spores to wider areas of the forest, defecating on nutrient-poor soil, or eating plants or animals that are a danger to the fungus or its hosts. The strategy is so effective that it keeps using it, expanding its reach into higher lifeforms and benefitting from their higher brain function and mobility. But it's a runaway train now, with nobody at the controls.

"I can see how it happened. A handful of early Ligados believe something—say, that the Brazilian president is a danger to the fungus because she allows logging in the Amazon—and decide that the best way to help the fungus is to kill her. As more Ligados join with them, they join in the 'consensus' opinion, because their emotions strongly confirm it. The consensus grows stronger and larger, but not because the course of action is the best option. Just because everybody already believes that it's the best option."

The soldiers shifted restlessly and fingered their weapons. "He's a plant," one of them said. "He's one of Barron's slaves."

"And what are you?" I asked. "You're blindly following an agenda just as much as they are.

"We're all driven by this defining idea, to protect and promote the survival of the fungus. But are we really helping it? It's not the fungus that's the parasite here. It's us. I think its chances of survival would be better if we left it alone."

The soldier who had spoken raised his weapon. "Should I shoot him?"

I raised my hands, trying to look nonthreatening. "I'm not one of his slaves, at least not yet," I said. "But Barron is dropping spores on the base, and we were caught in it. A few hours from now, we'll do whatever he tells us."

"And you want us to abort the mission?" Paul asked. "You want to be a slave? If we leave now, Barron wins. It won't stop with this battle. He'll keep on making spores, and keep on using them to control people.

He'll destroy the Ligados wherever he finds us. Ultimately, his strain of the fungus will be the one that survives."

"It will anyway," I said. "Do you think dropping nukes on major cities will make people give up? They'll just make more of McCarrick's spores. They'll keep on throwing slave armies against you, and they'll use nukes right back at you. There are still a lot more people in the world than there are Ligados, and if you do this they'll be desperate. The whole world will be against us."

Paul laughed. He actually threw back his head and laughed loud enough for the sound to echo along the tunnel walls. Then he looked back at me incredulously and shook his head. "I forgot that you haven't been connected," he said. "You actually don't know the plan, do you?"

I felt a hard knot in my stomach. "What do you mean?"

"The latest plan isn't to drop nukes on major cities. That was discarded before I ever left Brazil."

"Then what?"

"We're going to detonate right here."

I stared at him, finding it hard to process his words. "It . . . what? What good does it do to detonate a nuke in Albuquerque? Why conquer a city and then destroy it?"

"Not one nuke," he said. "*All* of them. We're going to detonate all two thousand one hundred and eighty-three nuclear warheads stored in this underground complex, all at the same time."

I looked around, the meaning of all of the wires finally registering in my brain. This branch of the tunnel was just as full of warheads as the first one had been, and at the end of it I could see yet another turn. A thick bundle of wires already stretched around the corner from that direction.

"But . . . that's . . ." My mouth moved without forming words, my mind racing faster than my words could keep up. "That's crazy," I finally said. "That's enough firepower to . . . to . . ."

"It's over a billion kilotons," Paul said matter-of-factly. "It's enough to blow a crater in the New Mexico desert the size of New Hampshire."

I understood at once. There had been past ages on Earth when fungi had been the dominant kingdom on the planet. The Ligados were trying to recreate such an age. An explosion like the one Paul described would blow enough radioactive debris into orbit to circle the globe and block sunlight for years. Plants would die. Animals would die. The human species would probably survive, but billions would die, and our technological infrastructure would be all but destroyed. We would become dependent on the fungus for everything.

"But . . . the Ligados have been converging here," I objected weakly. "They'll all die, too, along with us."

"It's never been about the people," Paul said. "The people are disposable. In one move, we'll eliminate human overpopulation and create a climate where we can never grow so numerous again. By the time the sun finally peeks through the dust clouds, it'll be a new world. A world where Kingdom Fungi dominates the planet."

I wanted to be horrified, but I wasn't. The fungus in my mind prevented that. I could see the power of this plan, the reshaping of the world to the perfect environment for the fungus, at the same time taking out its major competitors for the use of the Earth's resources.

"What about our glorious future as symbiotes with the fungus?" I asked. "The future you showed me in Brazil?"

"That will still come," he said, a little sadly. "For some humans; the ones who survive. Just not for us." He shrugged. "There are just too many of us. It was always only meant for a few."

"But won't this destroy the Amazon?" I asked. "All the trees, the animals, the whole ecology the fungus controls and grows in. They'll die, too."

"It was never about them either. They're a means to an end, just like we are. This will turn the clock back, to a time when fungus ruled the Earth. Any species that can survive in that world will serve the fungus."

A man in civilian dress, presumably the nuclear engineer, came up to Paul. He held a tablet in his hands, which he poked at with his thumbs, typing as he walked.

"We're all set for remote detonation," he said. "Everything is wired and status is green."

"Remote?" Paul frowned. "Why remote? We'll be just as dead upstairs as here. If it's all wired, push the button."

The engineer shook his head. "We have to control the timing precisely," he said. "We want to create a rolling chain reaction so that each of the detonations increases the overall strength of the blast. The whole thing takes less than a millisecond, but if the controller is destroyed too soon, the timing will be off, and we won't get nearly the megatonnage we expect. We might barely destroy the city."

"Okay. But you're ready?"

The engineer held up the tablet, which showed a simple status display along with a rectangular green button. "That's all it takes."

"Wait," I said. "This is a high-risk plan. If the blast isn't large enough, there will be a backlash. The rest of the world will unite to destroy us. Barron and others like him will have full rein. And if it's too big—surely there's a point at which not even the fungus can survive. Where the entire planet is sterilized of life. Is it really worth that risk?"

"We've modeled it," Paul said. "Checked and rechecked the numbers. The range of error is pretty wide."

"But . . ." I said, not knowing how I was going to finish the sentence. I could feel my resistance to the idea dissolving. Paul was a mycologist; he would know how much radiation the fungus could handle. I knew it was just the infection in my brain that made the death of billions seem like a good idea, but I had a hard time thinking of why it would be bad.

I wondered what Shaunessy thought about all of this, and realized that I hadn't seen her since I'd turned the corner of the tunnel. Maybe she'd changed her mind about being down here after all and had gone back up the elevator. It was probably for the best. She might have resisted, and then the soldiers would have shot her. Better that she die cleanly and instantaneously, like all the rest.

"Back to the elevators," Paul said to the group. "We need to go back up."

I went with them dumbly, my resistance gone. I could only fight the idea if I had a better one, one that benefitted the fungus just as much, and I didn't. I didn't even feel sad. In fact, the more I thought about it, the more elated I felt. We were going to do it. As soon as we reached the top, the engineer would press the button on his tablet, and it would all be over in a moment. All of the rapacious greed of humanity swept away to make room for a saner, more balanced approach to life. I was only sorry I wouldn't be there to see it.

The freight elevators were large, but not large enough to hold everyone. I rode with Paul and the engineer and about a dozen soldiers, while the other soldiers and civilians took another elevator. We rode up in silence, until I said, "Goodbye, Paul." He turned, surprised, and regarded me. Then he nodded and ruffled my hair. "Goodbye, little brother."

I thought of Shaunessy, and Melody, and Andrew, and the thousands of people in the city to our north. We would all die in an instant, like turning off a light. No pain, no fear, no prolonged anticipation. It was a good way to go. The push of a button, and a new chapter in the history of the Earth would begin.

We hadn't reached the top yet when Paul turned to the engineer. "Is this far enough?"

"Should be," the engineer said.

"Then don't wait for the doors to open," Paul said. "Hit it now."

The engineer lifted the tablet and turned the screen on. "Shouldn't we count to three or something?"

The elevator squealed and jerked to a stop. "Nope," Paul said. "Just push it."

Automatic gunfire tore through the elevator doors. The engineer jerked and danced and then fell, joined by two of the soldiers. The doors started to open automatically, but stuck halfway. Two more soldiers forced them open under a hail of bullets, while the rest returned fire. I cowered on the floor, covering my head with my arms. One of the soldiers hurled a grenade, and at the sound of its blast they ran out of the elevator toward the cover of a concrete wall. Holding my breath, I snatched the tablet from the engineer's hand and ran after them, cringing as a bullet sang past my ear and sparked against the elevator door frame.

The soldiers zigzagged as they ran, and I imitated them. The man in front of me went down with a bullet in his back, and I tripped over him, sprawling flat. The tablet flew out of my hand and went skidding along the pavement. More bullets whined overhead, and I hugged the ground, shielding myself with the soldier's dead body as best as I could.

Barron's soldiers surrounded the facility, taking cover behind armored trucks. As I watched, the last of the Ligados soldiers fell. I couldn't see Paul anywhere.

"Cease fire," a booming voice said, amplified to be heard above the gunfire and accompanied by a brief, piercing tone. I felt the command deep in my gut, and wished desperately that I had a gun, so I could cease firing it. McCarrick's fungus had apparently reached my brain.

The shooting stopped, leaving an eerie quiet that seemed to echo across the desert. I sat up carefully, my heart still thudding with adrenaline. My ears rang. I looked around. Where was Paul? Then I saw that the elevator doors—the ones with the bullet holes—had closed again. Paul was on his way back down.

Others saw it, too. Soldiers ran for the elevators and jabbed the buttons, then clambered aboard and headed down. They would stop him, I was certain of it. Without the tablet, what could he do? Perhaps there was another way to signal the nukes from below, but I doubted it. The only way to detonate them . . .

I stood, scanning the ground for the tablet, and spotted it about twenty feet away, black against the black pavement. "Neil!" Shaunessy ran up to me. "Are you okay? Were you hit?"

I told her I was fine. Once she had heard the plan to detonate the nukes underground, she had sneaked back to the top and called Melody. Melody had called General Barron and warned him, and the rest I knew.

"Good," I said. "You did it. You saved everyone."

"I don't think they were going to change their minds," she said.

"Neither do I."

She lowered her voice. "Melody knows we've been infected with McCarrick's spores," she said. "Most of the base is. She said to tell you she's working the problem."

"Working it how?"

Shaunessy shrugged. "I don't know." She lifted her phone. "I'd better give her a call and tell her you're all right."

She put the phone to her ear and turned away from me, using her finger to plug the other ear. I sidled away from her, toward the fallen tablet. There was still a chance. Nobody seemed to be paying any attention to me. I bent and picked it up.

The screen was scratched, but otherwise it seemed undamaged. I felt around the outside for the on button and pressed it. The screen came to life, and I swiped once across the front to dismiss the opening display. The tablet showed me the same green button I had seen before. I remembered what I had said to Shaunessy earlier: *If I could push a button that killed all the people in the world but helped the fungus spread and survive, I don't think I could stop myself.*

"Put it down, Neil."

It was Shaunessy's voice. I didn't look up. I stretched my finger out to touch the green button. A part of myself, deep inside, screamed at me to stop, but I couldn't. The desire to push it was just too strong.

But no. I had been here before. It was just like pointing the gun on Shaunessy and trying to keep from pulling the trigger. Then, I had failed. This time, I wouldn't give in. Pushing that button felt like the best thing in the world, but I knew it was wrong. I knew it wasn't what I wanted, not the real me. If I pushed it, I would die quickly, but billions around the world would die slowly, in horror and starvation. I thought of my parents. Of Julia, and her baby girl, Ash.

My hand stopped in midair, my finger still outstretched toward the button. I strained against it, the muscles in my arm and neck clenching painfully. A wave of nausea washed over me. Not pushing that button was like not reaching for a glass of water after drinking nothing for days. Or not holding out a hand when a child was drowning. That button, that beautiful green button, encompassed all that was good and right and lovely. It called to me. I had to push it. I just had to.

And then it was gone. I felt the impact before I heard the shot, like a sledgehammer to my shoulder. I hit the ground before I knew I was falling, the tablet tumbling out of my grasp. I screamed in pain and surprise and in sorrow for the loss of the green button.

Shaunessy stalked into my vision, the pistol I had given her still smoking in her hand. She stood over the tablet and fired a bullet down into it, shattering it into pieces. She lifted her phone and said, "I just shot him. We need a medic here, right away."

Pain arced through my arm and upper body. My vision narrowed. I couldn't see Shaunessy anymore, just a circle of desert sky. The green button still called to me, and I felt tears running down my face at the opportunity lost.

The only chance left was Paul. Maybe he couldn't detonate all the nukes without the remote, but if he could just detonate one, that would kill the general and the core of his slave army. It might be enough for the main Ligados forces to the south to regroup and retreat, possibly to make a play for another nuclear facility in the coming weeks.

I imagined him running through the underground tunnel to the place where wires from each of the warheads converged. He would tear away the antenna, find the leads that completed the circuit, and . . .

The ground buckled under me, an enormous force tossing me into the air . . . and then nothing.

CHAPTER 35

I opened my eyes. Which shouldn't have been possible. If Paul had succeeded, even with only one warhead, I shouldn't be thinking at all.

They explained to me later what had happened. Nuclear weapons work by using conventional explosives to crush a hollow plutonium core, smashing the atoms together and causing a chain reaction. However, if the compression force is not equal in all directions, the core will deform, and the plutonium won't reach a critical density.

Safety measures generally act on this principle. A liquid is inserted in the core to inhibit symmetrical compression, or else the explosives are electronically wired to prevent simultaneous detonation without a prior signal. The nuclear engineer had programmed the signal to turn off the safety measures into his remote. Paul, however, had simply connected the leads to set off the conventional explosives.

The explosives in two thousand one hundred and eighty-three nuclear warheads packed quite a punch, enough to destroy the elevator shafts, collapse the underground cavern, and injure fifty-seven people on the surface. Cracked plutonium cores were now leaking radiation deep underground where nobody could get to them. It would be the worst radiation disaster in the history of the nation, but the city of Albuquerque—and the world—would survive.

At the time, however, I only knew that I was inexplicably alive, and that every part of my body hurt. My arm was on fire. My head throbbed, and my muscles felt battered and bruised. I wasn't sure if I could move.

A voice came over the loudspeakers, but this time it was female. Melody's voice. "The enemy has been defeated," she said. "General Barron is no longer in command. You want to put your weapons down. You want to return to the medical facility in Kirtland Base where you will await your allocation of antifungal medications. Your greatest desire will be to take these medications, in the prescribed dose, for the next three years."

The smoke and dust cleared a little, and Shaunessy stepped into view, now without her pistol. She looked up into the sky for a few minutes, squinting against the bright sun. Finally, she looked at me. "Sorry about that," she said.

I could hardly breathe from the pain, but I gave her what I thought was a smile. "I deserved it," I said.

"Yes," she said, and her smile was brilliant. "Yes, you surely did."

—⟲—

Melody visited me at Presbyterian Hospital in Albuquerque. I still felt groggy from surgery, where they had removed bullet fragments from my shoulder. Shaunessy's bullet had hurt me more seriously than mine had hurt her, fracturing my humerus right at the joint and damaging ligaments and cartilage. It would be a while before I could fly back to Maryland, and my whole arm would stay in a cast for weeks.

"And you're taking your antifungals, right?" Melody said. She sat on the edge of the visitor's chair by my bed, somehow making it look elegant.

I grinned. "Do I have any choice?"

"Not really."

"Everybody within twenty miles is taking them like vitamins," I said. "Where did you ever get such a supply?"

The wrinkles around her eyes crinkled, though she didn't exactly smile. "While McCarrick was putting every infectious disease research facility to work growing more of his spores, I set every pharmaceutical lab with government contracts to mass-producing antifungal meds. I thought they might come in handy."

"Smart," I said. "But how on earth did you get the better of General Barron? Did you convince the president to revoke his command, or what?"

"Oh no, it was much easier than that," she said. "I put some spores into his coffee."

"You *what*?"

"They can withstand high temperatures with no loss of viability," she said. "I confirmed that ahead of time."

"You drugged the commander of the American forces?"

She shrugged. "In a manner of speaking. After that, it was a matter of getting my hands on that command signal, which was easy enough. They were piping it through loudspeakers by that point. I recorded it, played it for the general, and told him to pass his command over to me."

I shook my head. "You're a scary woman. How did you avoid breathing the spores in the base yourself?"

"I've carried an oxygen mask in my purse ever since you and Shaunessy came out of the server farm, and a larger, filter-based gas mask in my luggage. A mask that I did not surrender to the general's little safety recall."

I shook my head, impressed. She had thought of everything, been prepared. Much more than I had been. I hadn't even managed to anticipate my own family.

"Look," I said. "I know I've screwed up. A lot. I completely understand if you don't want me working in your group anymore, and I'm sure Shaunessy won't want me there. But—"

"Neil."

"Wait, hear me out. I love my job. I'm not as good with computers as Shaunessy—or well, anybody, really—and I don't know the mission details as well as Andrew, and everything I touch seems to just fall apart, but if there's some place for me, I don't know, some data entry position, or a math tutor for language experts, or something, I want to do it. I don't want to leave the NSA."

Shaking her head and suppressing a smile, Melody set a slim box on my lap. I looked at her, then back at the box, which was cream colored, with no writing or label on it. I used my good hand to grasp the top, shaking it slightly until it eased away from the bottom. Then I looked inside.

On the left, behind a plastic panel, was a medal. The ribbon was green, with a thick vertical red stripe bounded by thinner yellow stripes. On the ribbon hung a gold disc embossed with a stylized eagle and the words National Security Agency around the circumference. To the right of the ribbon, a gold card bordered in red proclaimed it as the NSA Meritorious Civilian Service Award.

I don't know how long I gaped at it before speaking.

"You can't keep it yet," Melody said. "There will have to be a ceremony with an official presentation, handshakes with whoever ends up keeping the director's job, that kind of thing."

"I don't deserve this," I said. She raised an eyebrow. "I admitted the guy who planted spores in the NSA server room," I said. "I lied to all of you, gave sensitive information to an enemy of the United States, and shot an NSA agent. I very nearly detonated two thousand nuclear weapons on American soil."

"You were the first to connect the Ligados to the fungal infection," she said. "You found the link to Neuritol. You cracked the whistle language, allowing us to read their communications and track the advance of the movement through South America. You endured danger and hardship in Brazil and in Albuquerque in the line of duty, and when it came down to it, you resisted the urge to push that button for just long enough—something not many people have been able to do."

"Long enough for Shaunessy to shoot me, you mean."

She put a hand on my arm. "Whatever you did while infected, it wasn't you," she said. "Our legal system will probably wrangle for years about people's liability for what they did while infected, but I know the truth. Nobody has ever resisted it, not for long. The fact that you did it at all is a testament to your strength of conscience."

"I don't see it that way." I remembered Shaunessy's prediction that they would give me a medal, and it made me feel sick.

"You can't decline it," Melody said.

"Why not?"

"Because I already declined when they wanted to give it to me. I told them to give it you." She grinned. "Could get embarrassing if everybody keeps declining their prestigious award."

Eventually they discharged me from the hospital, and I caught a flight back to BWI. I could barely fit my full-arm cast into the tiny seats in coach, and my shoulder ached from the uncomfortable angle, bent across my body to avoid the other passengers. The plane thundered along the runway and then lifted into the air.

Paul was dead. I didn't know yet entirely how I felt about that. Paul had betrayed me, infected me, hurt our family and tried to kill millions. On the other hand, under the influence of the fungus, I had tried to do much of the same. And quite apart from anything that had happened or whose fault it had been, he was my brother. I would miss him, and I would grieve his death.

I watched the Great Plains roll past beneath us and wondered how far Neuritol had spread through the country. Each infected person would have to be treated with McCarrick's spores, and then told that they wanted to take antifungal medication. It was the only way to get them to take it and thus eradicate the fungus—both strains of it—from their system.

I could already feel the fungus's hold on my own mind weakening. I still wanted what was best for the fungus, at some level, but it didn't dominate my thinking. The desire to take my antifungals was still strong, heightened by my belief that disconnecting it from humanity would ultimately be better for both species. I wondered what would happen six months or a year down the road, when the compulsion to take them dissipated. Would people stop taking them? If they did, would the fungus inside them return?

We flew into a bank of clouds, obscuring my view of the ground. Wisps curled past my window, insubstantial. I was flying home, but I didn't know what home really meant anymore. The world had changed, and it would take us a long time to understand what the new world would look like.

I had joined the NSA with ideas of adventure and heroism, of saving the day through mathematics and cryptography. When it came down to it, though, I hadn't been much of a hero. I hadn't saved the world—in fact, I had nearly destroyed it. I had done a lot I wasn't proud of and made mistakes along the way. Yet somehow, despite it all, we had won, and I had been part of it.

Eventually I slept. I dreamed of flying on the back of an enormous creature, part animal and part fungus, swooping low over green, leafy factories producing technological marvels powered only by the light of the sun. A world without hunger or privation or war, where disagreements were negotiated through a shared fungal network. A world without Alzheimer's. A world where no one was alone. I woke when the captain announced our descent, surprised to find tears on my face.

I had arranged for my mom to pick me up at the airport. As I walked out into the ground transportation area, however, a different familiar face waited for me. Shaunessy.

"I told your mom I'd bring you home," she said.

I used my good arm to lift my luggage into the trunk of her black Infiniti, and then joined her in the front seat. She pulled out and navigated the airport parking lot back toward the highway.

I knew it wouldn't take long to reach my father's house, so if I was going to talk with her, I would have to get right to it. "I'm sorry," I said. "You told me when Melody hired me that I would disregard the rules and screw things up. And I guess I did. I'm sorry I shot you. And I'm sorry you had to shoot me."

"Oh, don't be sorry about that," she said. "It was a pleasure."

I grinned. "Thanks. I don't believe you, though. I put you in a position where you had to shoot your own teammate, with seconds to spare, and you did it. You came through. You saved the world, though I doubt many people will ever know it. You should be getting that medal, not me."

"Maybe I'll write a book when I retire," Shaunessy said drily. "And just so you know, they're giving me a medal, too."

"Oh! Good. I'm glad. I mean, of course they are. You deserve it."

"You didn't think I would get one, did you?"

"No! I mean, yes. Well, I hoped they would."

"Relax, I'm just messing with you," she said, grinning. "Besides, they'll give me the medal, but they'll never let me write a book. Not about the good parts, anyway."

A good portion of that final battle had been classified, with those people who were present sworn to secrecy. Since most of them were government employees of some stripe, and many were still under the influence of McCarrick's strain of the fungus, it wasn't hard to enforce. The US government didn't want to admit the degree to which it had enslaved its own people to fight that war, nor how close we had come to detonating the nuclear arsenal.

"How are things in South America?" I asked.

"It'll be years cleaning up that mess," she said. "But the Ligados are slowly disbanding. As soon as the US threatened to bomb major cities with McCarrick's spores, the Ligados reached the consensus opinion that symbiosis with humanity was ultimately toxic to the fungus, and it had a better chance for survival if it left us alone. We've been sending antifungals to the continent as fast as we can ship them. I'm sure there will be Ligados enclaves for years, holdouts who still believe that humanity is good for it, but their numbers are shrinking."

"It's a pity," I said. "The fungus is good in some ways—increasing intelligence, curing neurological disorders. It's a shame we can't have the benefits without the problems."

"Isn't there any way?"

"Well, not directly. Allowing the fungus to grow in our brains means opening our minds to its emotional manipulation. But I heard there's going to be a research facility of mycologists formed specifically to investigate that possibility."

We pulled into my father's neighborhood. "So what do you think will happen to all those people who attacked Albuquerque?" Shaunessy asked.

"I don't think much of anything. The New Mexico government decided not to prosecute any of the Ligados, so long as they returned peaceably to their homes."

"Seriously? All that destruction and violence, and they're not arresting anybody?"

"The official stance, at this point," I said, "is that actions committed while under the influence of the fungus were committed by a different person—by the fungus itself—and are not prosecutable. We'll see if the civil courts uphold that opinion when the lawsuits start rolling in, but that's the approach the Oval Office is promoting. They want their citizens to take their antifungals and reintegrate into their old lives, not try to imprison and prosecute thousands of them for something over which they had little to no control. They want things to go back to the way they were before."

"I don't think that's going to happen," Shaunessy said.

"What do you mean?"

"McCarrick's spores. They're still making them. Growing them by the billions, in case the Ligados rise up again, or there's another major outbreak somewhere in the world. They talk about them as if they're only for defense, but that seems naive.

"What happens when another country won't do what we want? How long will diplomacy or even standard warfare last when we know we have the ultimate weapon in storage over at Fort Detrick and Walter Reed? We'll have a way to force compliance without loss of American lives. And how long will it be before other countries or private parties start getting their hands on them? Pandora's box has been opened, and there's no closing it again. It's going to change everything."

We pulled up in front of my father's house. "Thanks for the ride," I said.

"No problem."

"Hey, listen," I said. "Do you want to go out and get drinks sometime? Maybe after work?"

She laughed, and then stopped when she saw that I was serious. "I forgive you for shooting me," she said. "And I've gotten used to the idea of working with you. But I don't see it becoming any more than that."

I nodded, heat rising to my face. "See you Monday, then," I said.

She popped the trunk, and as I lifted out my suitcase she got out of the car and came around the back to where I stood. She stuck out her hand. I shook it. "You're a good man, Neil Johns," she said. "I'll see you Monday."

"Monday," I said.

—⊚—

I walked toward the house, still thinking about Shaunessy as her Infiniti backed up and pulled away. I couldn't figure her out. I didn't know if she liked me or hated me. But I was glad that, once again, we were on the same team.

I opened the door, and there was Mom, throwing herself at me in a fierce hug. "The arm!" I said, laughing. "Watch the arm!"

She examined the cast. "Does it hurt?"

"Nothing to speak of."

"Well, if someone tries to mug you, you'll have a club to take them out," she said. "Just don't try to put your arm around a girl in a movie theater."

I headed back toward the den and found my dad deep in thought over a crossword puzzle. I looked over his shoulder to check his progress. All of the blank spaces in the puzzle had been filled with the letter A.

He spotted me and shouted in fright, flinching away and covering his head with his arms. "Who are you?" he shouted. "Get out of my house!"

I stepped around the chair so he could see me more clearly. "It's me, Dad," I said.

He peered at me, suspicious. "Paul?"

"No. I'm Neil. I just flew home from New Mexico. Don't you remember?"

He didn't. Mom explained how quickly his awareness had declined once he started on the antifungals. He still took them religiously, remembering them even when he couldn't recall whether he had eaten breakfast, but without the fungus, his mind had quickly reverted to its old patterns.

"He wrote you a letter," my mom said. "When the antifungals first started taking effect, but before dropping back into the Alzheimer's, he was lucid for a few hours. He wanted to leave you something."

She handed me a handwritten letter. It was short and simple.

Neil. In case I can't tell you in person, I'm sorry for what we did to you. I'm glad to have known you again, even for a short time. I'm proud to have a son in the NSA.

I folded it carefully and clutched it tightly in one hand. It was possibly the most precious thing anyone had ever given me. I wrapped my arms around my mom again and held her for a long time.

We ate dinner together, a nostalgic beans-and-rice dish that my dad had cooked under my mother's watchful eye. We spoke briefly about the events of the previous weeks. My mom could remember everything that had happened, even when she had been under the influence of the fungus. She apologized for abducting and infecting me, but I waved her apologies away. I, as well as anyone, understood how the fungus could warp your sense of what was good and right. I didn't want her living under a burden of guilt and regret, not if I could help it.

I asked about Mei-lin, and my mom told me she was back to work at the Baltimore Washington hospital, managing fungal infection cases, especially those who had developed complications from the original infection. She had stopped by the house once to see them, and I made a mental note to pay her a visit when I could.

"Oh, I forgot to tell you," she said. "A pretty girl called for you."

"What?"

"A girl who works at a hair salon, said she met you in the hospital. Her name is Zoe."

I remembered her instantly, the beautiful woman with the long braid who had spoken to me in the cafeteria. I remembered giving her my number, but I was astonished that she'd actually called. It also seemed wrong to be talking about a potential date so soon after everything.

"How do you know she's pretty?" I said. "You can hear that over the phone?"

"I looked her up online."

"You're stalking my potential dates on social media? That's creepy, Mom."

A crafty smile crept onto her face. "I want grandchildren someday, you know."

"Julia just gave you one. You're not getting greedy in your old age, are you?"

"She sounded very nice on the phone." Her voice broke, and her eyes suddenly filled with tears. "We need some good news around here, don't you think?"

"I get it, I get it." I pulled her into another embrace and kissed her forehead. "Why don't *you* ask her out, if you like her so much?"

A wavering smile broke through her tears. "I'm not the one she called."

I thought about it. Maybe it was just what I needed. A new beginning.

On Monday, I pulled into the parking lot at Fort Meade and made my way through the building to the basement. Outside, the shantytown was being dismantled, tents folded up and carted away in trucks. I made my way inside and through the building to the basement, where I stopped at Melody's office.

"Good to have you back again," she said. "Though I'm afraid I won't be here much longer. You'll have a new boss soon."

"You're retiring?" It had to happen eventually, I supposed—she must have been due for retirement for years. It was probably as good a time as any for her to make the switch.

"No," she said wryly. "Not voluntarily, anyway. I'm going to be charged with treason and conspiracy and who knows what else. I might be going to prison."

"What? You've got to be kidding me."

"It hasn't happened yet. There's still a chance to fight it. But it's in the works. Part of the political war that's brewing to see who will end up with control of the spores and the command signal. I'm just a bit piece, I'm afraid. A pawn. But putting me away undermines the claims of the intelligence community."

"I thought they wanted to give you an award."

"That was the NSA. This goes higher than that."

"It's Barron's doing, isn't it? He wants to punish you for what you did to him."

"Well, I did kind of poison his coffee."

I swung my fist in the air, frustrated. "It's ridiculous. You saved everyone. If not for you, New Mexico would be drifting through the stratosphere."

"Not true," she said. "If not for me, Barron would have kept control, and the result would have been nearly the same, only with a lot more Ligados dead."

"It's not right. This isn't justice. They're just destroying you to advance their own agenda."

"The real question you should be asking yourself," she said, "is what's going to happen to you—to everyone—when the dust settles and someone emerges as the victor. Someone is going to have the power to control thousands or even millions of people as slaves. For the moment, everyone agrees that the best thing to do with that power is get people to take antifungals. But how long do you think that will last?"

Melody left me to think about that while she met with Terry Ronstadt, still the acting director of the agency, in an attempt to gain his support. I returned to my desk, feeling as low as I had for a long time. We had won, hadn't we? Why did it feel as though everything was falling apart?

Shaunessy and Andrew and the rest of the team were all in their usual places. I thought things might be awkward with Shaunessy, but she smiled warmly and welcomed me back without a hint of embarrassment.

"So what have we got?" I asked.

"A large number of indecipherables out of Myanmar," Andrew said. "Projecting down the coast into Thailand and as far as Malaysia. Particularly in regions where rainforests are the dominant biome."

"You think it's the fungus again," I said. "That it's spread there, and is causing the same effect."

"That or a government got ahold of the genetic map for McCarrick's version of it and is using it to enslave its people."

"Or someone else's people," I said.

"Only one way to find out," Shaunessy said.

I gave her a mock salute. "I'm on the job."

I sat at my desk and logged in to my account. In many ways, the situation was even worse now than when we had first discovered the Ligados passing messages in South America. McCarrick's spores presented a greater potential danger than the original fungus, one that would affect world politics for decades. Mind control was now part of the political landscape, even in the United States, and there was no guarantee the people at the top would use that power for good. Pockets of Neuritol users still held out throughout the country, choosing mind control of a different kind, their numbers and location unknown.

It wouldn't be hard for anyone, given a few of the spores, to grow more of the fungus in their own backyard. They wouldn't need a new supply from South America. And once the command signal became publicly known—which it would, eventually—mind control would affect not only politics and war, but start creeping into corporations and religious cults and crime as well. The world had become a dangerous place.

I brought up the latest batch of indecipherables on my computer and selected one at random. It was time to get back to work.

ACKNOWLEDGMENTS

My fantastic agent Eleanor Wood was my first reader for this book, devouring it a chapter at a time as I wrote it and always asking for more. I can't say enough how much I appreciate her encouragement and tireless efforts on my behalf.

It's always hard to see the flaws in my own stories, so I rely on my beta readers to see what I can't. Thanks to Mike Shultz, David Cantine, Chad and Jill Wilson, Nadim Nakhleh, Mike Yeager, Joe Reed, Jon Louis Mann, William Taylor, and Robert Walton for their invaluable comments and ideas. A special thank you to my friend Celso Antonio Almeida, who helped me present an authentic view of Brazilian locations and culture.

Thanks to my editor Rene Sears and all the great people at Pyr for loving my stories and putting their tremendous skills into creating this final book and putting it into your hands.

Finally, to my family, thanks for your enthusiasm for my stories and my successes. You make my life a delight, and I love you all.

ABOUT THE AUTHOR

David Walton is the internationally best-selling author of the quantum physics murder mysteries *Superposition* and *Supersymmetry*. He won the Philip K. Dick Award for his debut novel, *Terminal Mind*, a cyber-thriller that takes place in the crater where the city of Philadelphia used to be. David lives near Philadelphia with his wife and seven children and leads a double life as an engineer for defense contractor Lockheed Martin. He enjoys responding to fan mail at davidwaltonfiction@gmail.com.

Photo by Chuck Zovko